MW00442887

DEAD *Tired*

Also by Kat Ailes

The Expectant Detectives

DEAD *Tired*

A MYSTERY

KAT AILES

MINOTAUR BOOKS
NEW YORK

This is a work of fiction. All of the characters, organizations, and events portrayed in this novel are either products of the author's imagination or are used fictitiously.

First published in the United States by Minotaur Books, an imprint of St. Martin's Publishing Group

Printed in the United States of America. For information, address St. Martin's Publishing Group, 120 Broadway, New York, NY 10271.

www.minotaurbooks.com

Design by Meryl Sussman Levavi

Library of Congress Cataloging-in-Publication Data

Names: Ailes, Kat, author.
Title: Dead tired : a mystery / Kat Ailes.
Description: First U.S. edition. | New York : Minotaur Books, 2024. | Series: Expectant detectives mystery | First published in the United Kingdom by Zaffre, an imprint of Bonnier Books UK, 2024.
Identifiers: LCCN 2024003549 | ISBN 9781250322739 (hardcover) | ISBN 9781250322746 (ebook)
Subjects: LCSH: New mothers—Fiction. | LCGFT: Detective and mystery fiction. | Novels.
Classification: LCC PR6051.I355 D43 2024 | DDC 823/.92—dc23/eng/20240129
LC record available at https://lccn.loc.gov/2024003549

Our books may be purchased in bulk for promotional, educational, or business use. Please contact your local bookseller or the Macmillan Corporate and Premium Sales Department at 1-800-221-7945, extension 5442, or by email at MacmillanSpecialMarkets@macmillan.com.

First published in the United Kingdom by Zaffre, an imprint of Bonnier Books UK: 2024

First U.S. Edition: 2024

1 3 5 7 9 10 8 6 4 2

For Mum, Dad, and Colin, with love and gratitude for the many, many stories shared over the years

DEAD *Tired*

CHAPTER 1

THERE USED TO be an advert for Boursin herby cheese that showed a couple enjoying a picture-perfect picnic in a meadow—only to zoom out and reveal a combine harvester heading straight for them. Picnicking with babies—and my dog—is very much the scene of devastation *after* the combine harvester has passed through.

We'd gone for a picnic because it seemed like a "new mum" thing to do. I wasn't sure if calling us new mums when the babies were now one, and therefore possibly no longer babies, was stretching it a bit, but I definitely still felt new to the job—that morning I'd managed to put Jack's diaper on back to front and had been forced to use some of my moderately expensive face cream on him because we'd run out of baby lotion.

But picnics are what you do on maternity leave—I've seen the pictures on people's social media. You and your new-parent friends sit around drinking rosé, smiling and laughing and swapping comical stories about how little sleep you're getting and how many bodily fluids you've dealt with in the last twenty-four hours. All while gazing adoringly at your gurgling, content offspring, who smile adorably for the camera. You imagine a sun-soaked meadow, maybe one of those wicker hampers with actual genuine crockery in it, and probably a fancy French cheese wrapped in cloth. You lounge gracefully on your tartan rug, laughing elegantly as the summer breeze gently ruffles your hair.

Yes, picnics are one of those charming fantasies/lies. The reality is an hour-long search to find a large enough cowpat-free area, grass that is weirdly spiky and gives you a disconcerting rash, and an ensuing war of attrition to keep the dog from gnawing through your Tupperware and eating Babybels with the wax still on. And that's before you add children into the mix.

I had to admit though, the general setting for this one was pretty decent at least. It was unseasonably warm for May and the sun had that early summer glow—before the burn really sets in. We were in an honest-to-goodness meadow, the grass still lush and long from spring. It looked like the whole blimmin' scene had an Instagram filter on it (if you didn't look too closely, that is).

The new-parent friends were all right too: Hen, Ailsa, and Poppy, whom I had met the previous year at prenatal class and gone on to solve two murders with (or possibly three, depending on your take), one of which had actually taken place at our prenatal class. There had been, let's say, unforeseen consequences for several of us, following our sleuthing debut, but we were moving past that. I think. We were joined by our five babies and three dogs. This did a lot to undermine the perfection of the scene. While Poppy's greyhound Sultan was posing exquisitely at a slight distance, casting us the occasional look of mild disdain, her other dog Ronnie was alternating between pinching sausage rolls and mounting my dog, Helen. And as for the babies . . .

"I still can't believe you didn't tell us you were having twins." I shook my head at Ailsa, watching her twins, Ivy and Robin, rolling back and forth, rubbing jam in each other's hair.

Ailsa shrugged. "I'm sure I mentioned it."

"I think we'd have remembered."

"I knew," interjected Hen. Ah yes, well, the Hen–Ailsa relationship defied explanation; I had never met two more opposite people. In looks alone they were chalk and cheese, Ailsa's ruddy dreadlocks and patched dungarees in stark contrast to Hen's sharp black bob and actual branded maternity wear. Then there was Ailsa's commitment to all things natural, organic, and preferably made from hemp, set against Hen's apparently pathological need to douse every surface, including her daughter, in industrial-grade cleaning products. Ailsa performed sun salutations and was on first-name terms with the moon goddess; Hen worshipped at the altar of Baby Boden and Petit Bateau. But they'd gone for that whole opposites attract thing and were alternately best friends and archnemeses. It seemed to be working for them.

Hen smoothed imaginary wrinkles from her daughter's white frock and adjusted the parasol over her. Arora, just over a year old, was eating strawberries with impeccable daintiness. Next to her, my own son, Jack, was solemnly posting hummus down his diaper. Other than the diaper, he was entirely naked, because babies.

My dog, Helen, escaped Ronnie's clutches and came trotting over, one ear inside out and a crazed look in her eye. She gave Arora's face a hearty licking. For some reason, best known to her, she adored Hen's baby. She was broadly indifferent to Jack, whom she lived with and, I hoped, regarded as part of the family.

"Has she eaten any cowpats?" asked Hen sharply.

I shrugged helplessly.

"It's Helen," said Poppy, who was lying on her back, eyes closed, face to the sun. "If it's just cowpats you'll be lucky." I felt this was a tad unfair, as Ronnie posed almost as much of a hygiene risk as Helen. I didn't say anything though—Poppy had seemed . . . subdued of late.

Out of the corner of my eye I saw Hen sanitize Arora's face.

"Weaning's going well then." Ailsa nodded toward where Jack was now stuffing a fistful of grass in his mouth. I sighed and removed it from him. He gave me a deeply hurt look.

"It's good for his gut bacteria," I replied. Behind me, Poppy snorted. Her own son, Noah, was curled up next to her. He had inherited Poppy's afro, but whereas hers was small and neat, Noah's was wild and filled with grass seeds—probably courtesy of my own son, it has to be admitted. Mother and son were snoozing idyllically in the shade of an enormous gold umbrella. I watched them covertly. Poppy had always had a driving force behind her, a dynamism that I quite frankly envied. But over the last few months it seemed to have drained out of her. Of course, she was tired—we all were. Noah and Jack had just turned one, meaning it was one whole year since either of us had slept properly. I just hoped that was all there was to it; it felt as though a distance had opened up, not just between Poppy and myself, but between Poppy and the world. She had barely spoken during the picnic, rousing herself only infrequently to liberally suncream

Noah. Then again, it was hot—like is-this-really-England hot—too hot for conversation, really. The day had that peaceful heaviness that covers you like a warm blanket of sunshine and invites one of those half waking, half sleeping naps. I wondered whether Jack and Helen would manage not to destroy the picnic/meadow/themselves for a full five minutes if I closed my eyes.

In a swift response to this thought, Helen flopped down heavily in the middle of the picnic, flattening several unfortunate sausage rolls and spraying Arora with guacamole.

Hen squealed, immediately produced an enormous pack of wet wipes and began dabbing at her daughter, who now looked like she was splattered in avocado boogers. Arora simply giggled and shared a conspiratorial look with Helen.

Luckily, I was saved from Hen's wrath by Poppy, who had half opened one eye at the commotion.

"Oh look, people," she said drowsily.

I squinted through the sun to where two figures had emerged from the cluster of ancient trees that grew in the center of the meadow. I couldn't see so well because I had lost my sunglasses—by which I mean I was pretty sure either Helen or Jack had buried them—but even blurred . . .

"Are they naked?"

At this Poppy rolled over to get a better look. It was the first time she'd moved in an hour.

"Ooh, I think they are you know."

"Nothing wrong with that." Ailsa sniffed.

"I didn't say there was," I pointed out. After just over a year of life in Penton, a town on the further end of the hippy spectrum, I liked to think it would take more than a couple of nudists to faze me. My first year living here had introduced me to such Pentonic delights as gong bathing, ritual aura cleansing and a plethora of herbal, crystal, and chakra-based remedies. While I seldom dipped more than a toe in the more alternative side of Penton life, I enjoyed watching it from a distance with mild amusement and cynicism.

"No wait, I think they're wearing *something* . . ." Poppy narrowed her eyes. "Or maybe it's paint?"

“I think they’re coming over,” I said. “What should we do?”

“Take our clothes off,” suggested Ailsa. I wasn’t sure if she was joking. In many ways, Ailsa remained as much a mystery to me as she had before a year of enforced mat-leave friendship. Which, by the way, I had greatly enjoyed, although I sensed Ailsa was still on the fence about me.

The two figures were close enough now that even my sun-dazzled eyes could tell that yes, they were naked, and yes, they had words painted across their torsos.

“Save our . . . corpse?” read Poppy hesitantly.

“Copse,” corrected Hen automatically, although she hadn’t appeared to even glance at the figures. “Means a small group of trees.”

“I know what it means.” Poppy sniffed. “It’s my eyes that don’t work, not my brain.”

I kept quiet—it was entirely possible I’d never heard this word before.

The figures waved as they approached. At which point Helen erupted from the picnic blanket, catapulting crisps and chocolates over the assembled babies, and greeted the newcomers in her own special way—a maelstrom of tail wagging, high-pitched chicken squeals and, in this case possibly inappropriate, licking.

“Sorry! Sorry!” I scrambled to my feet, accidentally sending Jack flying into the hummus, and fumbled to get Helen under control before she washed off all their body paint.

The newcomers were a man and a woman—very definitely so—and both, I couldn’t help noticing (I mean, I really couldn’t), impeccable physical specimens. They looked like those Roman statues you see in museums, all toned abs and chiseled jaws—although with more limbs than your average ancient statue. The man had a mane of glossy black hair with an oil-slick feather braided into one side. The girl had close-cropped hair, also black but with a blue sheen that suggested either a dye job or a hint of petrol in her genetics.

“Hi!” they chorused as I finally managed to restrain Helen.

“Lovely day for a picnic,” said the man, looking disproportionately serious about the fact.

“Beautiful,” I agreed, making aggressive eye contact to avoid my gaze falling anywhere else. I sought for a suitable conversational gambit—they’d already commented on the weather, which left me fresh out of ideas for polite conversation.

"Er, would you like some sunscreen?" I asked, noticing a pink tint already burnishing the man's milk-white body. Not that I was looking. Just—there are some places you really don't want to burn. "It's kids' sunscreen," I rambled on, as is my incredibly socially engaging way. "But, I mean, what difference can that really make? Other than adding an extra four quid on the price. It might blur your body paint though, that could be a problem."

"Lovely day for a naked stroll," interrupted Ailsa, which was probably for the best. "Soaking up some sun?"

"Do you normally slogan yourselves before nude sunbathing?" I added, before I could help myself.

"Oh, we're not nudists," laughed the woman, slightly derisively. Well, you could've fooled me.

"No?" Hen raised a skeptical eyebrow.

"This is just for the protest," said the woman, gesturing to her slightly Helen-smeared body paint. "We're protesting against the desecration of this ancient meadow and copse by the building of a wind farm."

I glanced around, unsure exactly who they were protesting to. Far off on the horizon, a handful of cows seemed unmoved by their searing political statement.

"This is just a preliminary photo shoot," explained the man. "My brother's a photographer. He's coming up to photograph us for the protest website."

Ailsa had propped herself up on an elbow looking interested. "What's this about a wind farm?"

Hen, I noticed, had flushed slightly and was fiddling with the straps on Arora's pinafore dress.

"It's a local green energy company, you might have heard of them," said the woman. "Aether? They're based just over the hill in Bishop's Ruin."

"So-called green energy," broke in the man. "If you can call the complete desecration of a thriving, delicately balanced ecosystem 'green.' Just to serve our endless greed for more energy, more power."

Ah. Aether. No wonder Hen was looking so awkward. This was going to be interesting.

"Anyway," continued the woman, "they've somehow managed to buy the lease on this meadow and are intending to build a wind farm here—including cutting down the sweet chestnuts that have been here for over five hundred years." She gestured toward the copse of ancient and gnarly trees that hunkered in the center of the meadow and which I knew well, having sheltered there during many a rainy dog walk. I felt a twinge of sadness that after so many centuries, and having sheltered many thousands of dog walkers, the trees were fated to be cut down.

"How have they got permission?" asked Ailsa, now fully sitting up. "I did some fieldwork here a few years ago—it's Jurassic limestone, there are all sorts of rare flowers up here. There was Cotswold Pennycress growing last I looked. That's incredibly rare, and it's a declining species—they can't just destroy an endangered habitat like this!"

"Cotswold Pennycress?" The man looked interested. "A rare species?" He turned to the woman. "We should make a note of that."

She nodded and her hand moved involuntarily toward a pocket—and presumably phone—that wasn't there. She looked around vaguely as if a notebook or scrap of paper might appear. I was going to suggest she use some body paint to make a note on a blank stretch of thigh, but the man was talking again.

"Companies like Aether have no time for the environment—oh, I know they say they're a green energy company," he cut across himself as Hen opened her mouth to speak, "but it's a classic case of greenwashing. Would a company that really cared about the environment be prepared to bulldoze a meadow and tear down an ancient copse of trees?"

"All they really care about is the bottom line," chipped in the woman. "Raking in the profits while presenting a respectable environmentally friendly face to the world."

They both had the slightly over-bright eyes of the true zealot.

"It's a fair point," said Ailsa. Hen shot her a look.

"I'm sure that's true of a lot of companies," said Poppy soothingly, before Ailsa could say any more or Hen could throw a cake at her. "But what makes you so sure that's the case with Aether?"

The man and woman exchanged a dark glance. "We have evidence," said the woman shortly.

"So what are you planning to do about it?" I asked. "Naked photoshoot aside?"

"The photos are just a small part of it, we're a whole movement," said the man earnestly, his eyes practically glowing now. "We're part of the Earth Force protest group. We've been trying to expose Aether's greenwashing for the last year. I'm surprised you haven't heard about us—it's been in the news quite a lot."

I had last read the news about twelve months ago, before parenthood had reduced my available mental capacity to approximately that of Helen. Ailsa, however, was nodding. "I think I've heard about it. Didn't some of you naked gatecrash an Aether press conference the other day?"

Oh good, more nudity.

The not-nudists nodded enthusiastically.

"Yes, that was Raven and couple of others from the group," said the woman earnestly.

"And you would be . . . Raven?" I asked the man.

He nodded. "And this is Leila." He gestured to the woman. It had been a good ten years since I only found out someone's name *after* I'd seen them naked. I noticed Hen start slightly, shooting Leila a sharp look, almost . . . accusatory?

"It's nice to meet you," I mumbled. I was about to announce my own disappointingly ordinary name, Alice, but Ailsa cut across.

"So what's your plan to halt the wind farm?" she asked, sounding genuinely interested. This kind of thing was right up her street. Since meeting Ailsa she had introduced me to such eco-friendly delights as reusable diapers (yep, it's a thing) and reusable wipes, and treated me to several lectures on the perils of junk food (my main food category) and in fact eating anything that wasn't organic, local, and sustainably sourced. For my birthday she signed me up to Greenpeace.

"We're on our final chance," said Raven somberly. "Aether has construction vehicles coming in on Thursday to take down the trees."

"And lay concrete foundations in place," cut in Leila angrily. I had to admit—it did seem a shame.

"So it's time to take more forceful action. We'll be staging a sit-in protest on Wednesday night," continued Raven. "Chaining ourselves to the trees."

"If they want to take the trees out, they'll have to take us out with them," declared Leila defiantly.

"I thought protestors mainly glued themselves to things these days," I said absent-mindedly.

"We did think about that," said Raven earnestly. "And we had a lot of success gluing ourselves to the Aether company headquarters a few months ago. But we were worried the glue would harm the trees, so we're going old-school and using chains."

Idly, I wondered how they'd eventually unglued themselves, because I'd recently glued one of Jack's toy trucks to my hand while trying to fix it, and it turns out the slogan "The bond that never breaks" is terrifyingly accurate. I'd had to soak my new Transformer-hand in a weird hand-bath for nearly an hour.

"We're having a meeting on Monday evening to plan the sit-in," said Leila. "You should come along, find out a bit more about the proposed development and the untold harm it will cause. And how we're going to stop it."

"Um—" I began.

"Sure," broke in Ailsa. "We'd love to."

"Would we?" I asked blankly. She ignored me.

"Eight o'clock, Monday," said Leila. "At the school hall in Bishop's Ruin."

"Sorry, where?" I asked.

"It's a village in the next valley," said Ailsa.

Of course it was. I'd never get used to the bizarre names they had for villages in these parts—personal favorites being Petty France and the unforgettable Upper and Lower Slaughter. With my track record for finding bodies in the Cotswolds, I was steering well clear of the latter.

"I think that's Sam," said Raven, shading his eyes with his hand and peering at a figure (possibly clothed, possibly not) that had appeared on the horizon. "My brother," he added to us.

"How come your brother is called Sam, and you're called Raven?" I asked. "I don't mean to be rude, I'm just saying, there's a bit of a disconnect."

"Raven is my chosen name."

I didn't have much of an answer for that.

"Well, we should get on with the photos," said Leila, sounding slightly less enthusiastic all of a sudden. "I think your dog might be trying to get involved."

I yelped and looked round; Helen was indeed making a determined beeline for the distant newcomer, presumably in the hope that his pockets were inexplicably full of cheese and sausage. This rarely happens, but she never gives up hope.

"Helen!" I shouted, without much conviction. "Helen?"

"Your dog's called Helen?" Raven asked curiously.

"Yes, why?"

He shrugged. "That's an unusual name for a dog, that's all."

I stared at him—was he serious?

"It's her chosen name," I said flatly.

CHAPTER 2

THERE WAS A slightly awkward silence after Raven and Leila left. I wondered who was going to be the first to bring up the elephant at the picnic.

"Did you hear what he said to her as they left?" asked Poppy. Ah good, we were avoiding the subject.

"Yeah, he said, 'Play nice with Sam now,' or something like that," Ailsa replied.

"Neither of them look the playful sort, if you ask me," I said. I've always struggled with earnest people; as someone of few moral convictions and the ethical depth of a spoon, I tend to have very little in common with them. This was one of my many moral failings that Ailsa was working hard to correct.

Hen still hadn't said anything. She was avoiding meeting any of our eyes.

Eventually, Ailsa went there—she was usually the bravest.

"So, did you know about the wind farm?" she asked Hen. I felt myself tense involuntarily. Ever since Hen had started her job as personal assistant to the CEO of Aether, she and Ailsa had been clashing more than ever. The two of them had been almost inseparable since Hen's husband had . . . left. Like Hen, Ailsa was also going it alone—with the added challenge of twins which, let me tell you, is *more* than twice the work. Or perhaps that was just Ailsa's particular brand of twin. I knew Ailsa stayed over at Hen's several nights a week, pooling resources, as it were. But they also bickered worse than an old married couple over everything from whether to give the twins jam to the environmental costs of certain types of green energy. When Hen's new status as a single parent had forced her to find a job after just six months of maternity leave, Ailsa had initially been enthusiastic and entirely supportive of Hen's new job at Aether. But there had been growing whispers in the community of late that Aether was not quite the wonder-solution people had initially hoped, and Ailsa had fast turned skeptical. This latest news promised to deliver a real doozy of a row between the two of them.

Hen met Ailsa's eye defiantly. "Of course I did, they've hardly talked about anything else at work all month. It's going to be a major project."

"You never mentioned it," objected Ailsa.

"It never came up. I didn't know you'd be interested."

"You thought I wouldn't approve," needled Ailsa.

"That's not true," said Hen hotly. "If anything I thought you *would* approve. It's renewable energy! You'd rather we burned fossil fuels? Or chucked particles at a nuclear reactor and flooded the area with radiation? You'd rather have fracking until the whole valley caves in?"

"I'd rather," said Ailsa, a slight chill in her voice, "not flatten an ancient copse and destroy a thriving and biodiverse ecosystem. Do you know how fast meadows are vanishing across the UK? I can't believe this isn't a protected site! Especially with the Cotswold Pennycress, and the ancient chestnut grove."

Hen threw her hands in the air in exasperation. "There's no perfect solution, Ailsa! Aether has done their due diligence—the environmental impact of building here will be minimal. All the reports said so. When it comes to balancing the impact of one relatively small area of grassland against the ongoing *catastrophic* impact of fossil fuel energy—"

Ailsa snorted derisively. "Come on, Hen, the habitat degradation alone . . ."

"Did you recognize Leila?" I broke in to ask Hen, hoping to head things off before they went nuclear.

"No, why?" she said curtly.

"I don't know, you just looked at her a bit weirdly, that's all."

"Your imagination is running away with you, Alice."

I have to admit, I do have a pretty active imagination, though in this case, I wasn't so sure. But when Hen clammed up you'd have more luck persuading an oyster to spit out its pearl, to mix my sea metaphors. The argument mutated into an impassioned debate as to whether Cotswold Pennycress could still be found in the meadow, and this time I left them to it, turning my attention to Jack and Noah, who were peacefully smearing mayo on Sultan's nose, as the regal greyhound lay motionless, possibly content, possibly utterly defeated.

HEN AND Ailsa eventually returned from a fruitless search to see if they could spot any Cotswold Pennycress. They appeared to have made up—I saw Ailsa hip-bump Hen affectionately as they made their way back up the slope. Poppy and I sat up and made some effort to look like we had been actually minding the babies, as requested. I smeared some suncream on one of the twins—probably Robin?—where it mingled with his jam body paint to create quite an appealing abstract art effect.

"Find anything?" asked Poppy, draping a wet muslin over Noah's head. I had done the same thing to Helen—partly to cool her down, partly because a blanket over her head appeared to switch her off, which was to everyone's benefit.

"Too hot to look properly," huffed Ailsa, after chugging from her water bottle. "It must be six thousand degrees out there."

"Ailsa's dedication to the cause couldn't take the heat," teased Hen. They clearly *had* made up, because Ailsa's only response was to flick water at Hen, who turned her face to the spray with an expression of bliss.

I rolled onto my stomach and rummaged through the detritus of the picnic, looking for any remnant that wasn't melted, squashed, or covered in dog hair. It was slim pickings.

"Can you not?" I said to Ailsa through a mouthful of reconstituted meat and egg, without needing to look round.

"What?"

"I'm trying to enjoy my Scotch egg and I can feel you glaring at me."

"It's disgusting, that's all," she said matter-of-factly. "When are you going to go veggie, Alice?"

"I have low iron," I retorted.

"So eat some spinach."

I ignored her and continued trying to enjoy my Scotch egg of doom.

Around me, Hen had started bustling, tidying away rubbish and putting the remains of food into Tupperware and beeswax wraps, muttering about the sun getting too hot for the babies—which was probably true; it was definitely getting too hot for me. With a sigh, I sat up and began wiping Jack down—a thankless and ultimately pointless task. Helen lent a hand, or rather a tongue, with considerably more enthusiasm and, it has to be said, more efficiency than me.

The walk back to the cars, laden with now very hot and grumpy babies, and almost certainly inedible picnic remnants which, as always, seemed to have exponentially expanded from the amount of food we'd actually brought, seemed much longer than the walk out. The meadow still looked idyllic—grasses shifting ever so slightly in a barely there breeze, the occasional flash of color from a wildflower—but seemed to have stretched into a savannah.

In the distance, we could hear faint voices floating across the still air from the copse, and I could make out the pale, naked forms of Raven and Leila draped across various trees, as a third figure ducked and weaved around them.

"Are you still staying over tonight?" I heard Hen ask Ailsa in an unusually small voice.

With an exasperated sigh, Ailsa put her arm around Hen—which seemed a sticky move in this heat, in my opinion. "Of course I am, you idiot. I'll cook. We can watch a movie and not think about—y'know. Him."

This, of course, was why we'd been picnicking today. Not that we'd mentioned it. It was one year since the door had closed, finally and dramatically, on Hen's marriage. We didn't talk about it much, but it had felt important to all be together today. I was glad Ailsa would be with Hen tonight—it wasn't a night to spend alone.

"D'you think Hen will be OK tonight?" I asked Poppy, as we loaded the children and dogs into her car to be ferried home.

"Hmm?" Poppy sounded distracted—which seemed to be the case more and more these days, as though she wasn't fully there.

"Hen," I repeated, wondering anxiously whether Hen wasn't the only one I needed to be worried about. "Do you think she'll be all right?"

"Oh, right. Yeah, of course she will," said Poppy vaguely. "She's got Ailsa to look after her."

I wasn't sure whether this was a positive or a negative; being looked after by Ailsa sounded a bit like how I viewed exercise—dubious bordering on painful at the time, but ultimately extremely beneficial.

"Makes you grateful for Joe and Lin, huh," I prodded Poppy gently, as I buckled Jack into his car seat and drew the straps so tight he squawked—I wasn't taking any risks. Joe was my scatterbrained, haphazard, and deeply irritating partner whom I was nonetheless extremely fond of. Lin was Poppy's capable, efficient, and all-round lovely wife.

"Hmm, yeah," said Poppy, her mind still clearly elsewhere.

I eyed her worriedly as she drove us back toward town. I made a few attempts at conversation around our nude picnic-crashers—surely a rich topic—but Poppy remained withdrawn, an unusual state for her, although I reflected that it was becoming increasingly common of late. I lapsed into silence, an unusual state for me. Of course, I could always make up for this when I got home and filled Joe in on every minute detail of my day.

CHAPTER 3

"AND THEN HELEN mugged the photographer because it turns out he *did* have cheese in his pocket. Well, a cheese sandwich anyway," I concluded to Joe, who was looking slightly glazed, possibly from the onslaught of my picnic tales, possibly just from lack of sleep.

We were bathing Jack, something we still often did together, mainly because we were both terrified of doing it alone. Babies are extremely slippery when wet.

"So hang on, rewind. Is the wind farm a good thing or a bad thing?" asked Joe, looking confused.

"Er, so I think it turns out it's actually a bad thing," I said, admittedly with very little confidence. "According to Ailsa."

"I thought wind farms were good—renewable energy and all that?" Joe's forehead wrinkled, either in confusion or concentration as he meticulously washed between each of Jack's ludicrously tiny toes. Jack chuckled and squirmed.

"It's . . . complicated," was the best I could manage.

"Everything is these days," sighed Joe, sounding about 105 years old. Jack cackled some more, and Joe fixed him with a stern look. "I don't know what you're laughing at, Jacky Boy, this is your future we're trying to save."

Jack looked contrite and ate some bath foam.

"Something to do with damaging the ecosystem." I shrugged. "I guess I could tag along to this Earth Force meeting. I'm sure they'd be happy to fill me in."

Joe frowned. "You're not actually going to go to the meeting, though, are you?"

"You're the one who said I should get out more," I pointed out.

"I meant to like a mum and baby group," he retorted. "Like that baby sensory thing you went to with Poppy. Why did you stop going to that?"

"It was weird," I said defensively. "They kept turning the lights out and waving torches and scarves around. And we had to sing nursery rhymes like every week. I hate nursery rhymes."

"So nursery rhymes are weird, but chaining yourself naked to a tree isn't?"

"I'm not chaining myself to a tree!" I protested. "I'm just *considering* going to a meeting! Fully dressed!"

"That's how it always begins," said Joe mournfully. I felt this was a little unfair—while circumstances have been known to, at times, get a tad out of my control, I was yet to chain or glue myself, naked or otherwise, to anything. Apart from Jack's toy truck, which was unintentional and had very few ramifications on a national level.

At this point Helen sidled into the bathroom and began covertly lapping at the bathwater. She loves the taste of Jack's baby oil and despite our best attempts has consumed a disgraceful amount of it. She must have the most lubricated digestive tract known to man or dog.

I was about to shoo her away when my phone pinged. I fumbled at it, narrowly avoiding dropping it in the bath. It was Ailsa, on the group chat.

Ailsa: Are we going to the meeting or not?

Dunno, will I have to take my clothes off?

Ailsa: 🙄

Poppy: I thought it sounded interesting

Ailsa: @Hen, you in?

Hen: No way. I need this job. And to be honest I'd rather you guys didn't end up getting me fired.

Poppy: We won't get you fired, Hen. We're just going along to find out a bit more

I promise we'll be discreet

Hen: Yeah, you're good at that.

Was that sarcasm? I was pretty sure that was sarcasm.

Ailsa: Great, @Poppy @Alice I'll see you there

Hmm, I wasn't quite sure how my lukewarm "dunno" had translated into an "I'll see you there." But that was Ailsa for you. I put my phone away.

"Ailsa wants us to go," I announced to Joe, as if that decided the matter. Which, in many ways, it did.

AS I pottered about the kitchen warming Jack's evening milk bottle (babies are all little princes and cannot abide their milk fridge temperature), the radio twittering away in the background, the name "Aether" caught my ear.

". . . in the early hours of this morning. The unknown assailant threw an inflammatory device into the home of Owen Myers, the owner and co-founder of local energy company, Aether. Myers was entertaining a female guest at the time, neither were harmed in the attack."

Inflammatory device? That didn't sound great.

"The police have refused to comment on whether they have any suspects. The attack has shocked residents of Bishop's Ruin, where Myers lives, and where he is celebrated as a local wunderkind. His green energy company Aether has revolutionized how we power our homes and was at the forefront of energy companies taking the leap into providing fully renewable energy at affordable prices. The Aether headquarters, based in

Bishop's Ruin, have provided a stable source of local jobs and Myers has always employed local people on a matter of principle.

"The current heatwave looks set to continue into next week. Local farmer Joan Selwyn said that . . ."

I dabbed some of Jack's milk on my wrist, as per the YouTube tutorial. Interesting that the news presenter hadn't—*OW FUCK*, I'd absolutely nuked his milk. I ran my wrist under cold water and mulled over the news. Clearly the news presenter had been firmly Team Owen. Earth Force, on the other hand, viewed Owen Myers as no different from the other corporate fat cats and felt all his eco-friendly posturing was no more than greenwashing. The impression I'd picked up of him from Hen was somewhere in between. He seemed to be a decent boss, but a shrewd one. And from what Hen had insinuated he could be pretty ruthless when it came to his staff. He may employ local people on principle, but he had no hesitation about firing them either, as Hen had hinted darkly. Could the attacker have been a disgruntled employee? Or, the thought crossed my mind, could it have been Earth Force? Raven had been quite vocal in his preference for, how did he put it, "more forceful action."

As I swirled the milk bottle under the cold tap I allowed myself to acknowledge that the Earth Force meeting next week could be quite interesting after all. It would be good to do something that wasn't entirely parenting-related for a change. And, well, it sounded like things might be heating up around this new development, and I do enjoy a bit of controversy. Why not find out what all the fuss was about? What was the worst that could happen?

CHAPTER 4

I DON'T KNOW what I'd expected from my first protest meeting. Possibly more placards and shouting? Maybe some light supergluing to the furniture. I hadn't expected juice and cookies. But the woman handing round a Tupperware of almond cookies wouldn't have looked out of place at a PTA meeting; she had the perpetually harassed but essentially kind look of a mother of five children. And the jugs on the sideboard held a very acceptable fruit juice.

As I helped myself liberally to refreshments, I eyed up the protest group. They were a motley crew. Raven was there, of course, and looking exactly as I expected a protestor to; tatty patchwork waistcoat over a faded black T-shirt, and jeans that had gone way past distressed and looked frankly distraught. His raven feather was still in place, now accessorized with multiple bead necklaces and bracelets and a healthy smear of eye makeup. Leila looked stunning in some sort of woven Tinkerbell dress, which suited her elfin face and pixie crop. It was strange to see them with clothes on—and even stranger to find that strange, if that makes sense.

Raven appeared to be very popular within the group. Among the crowd surrounding him I spotted several hopefuls sporting a very Raven-esque look; one had gone so far as to copy the feather, which I felt was a step too far—play it a *bit* cool. Leila, although never far from Raven's side, seemed to be slightly more on the periphery. I wondered if they were a couple. Normally, I wouldn't have to ask this after seeing two people naked together, but normal rules didn't seem to apply here.

Ages ranged from, well, the twins, I supposed, whom Ailsa had brought along as Hen flatly refused to babysit, up to an elderly gentleman in the corner who had possibly simply fallen asleep in the preceding meeting (on brass rubbings in local churches, according to the noticeboard) and decided to stay on because he had the comfiest chair in the room.

The meeting was called to order by a woman who looked to be in her fifties, with a mass of gray curls and a broad, friendly face that looked like it spent a lot of time in the sun. She wore sensible linen overalls and Doc Martens that looked like you could drive a tank over them.

"Right then, chaps!" She clapped her hands together in a businesslike way and gradually the room stuttered into silence. "We've got some new faces joining us tonight"—she beamed over to where we were huddled in a corner—"so I thought a quick round of introductions before we get stuck into business. I'm Maryam, I've been a member of Earth Force for, oh, longer than I care to remember!"

"She's pretty much in charge," whispered a low voice next to me. At some point Raven had appeared at my elbow. "We wouldn't get anything done without Yam. She's the *soul* of the group."

I could see that—she was rattling through introductions with great speed and efficiency. In rapid succession we were introduced to Frank, Cecily, Norah (the lady with the cookies), Thomas, Julia, Enderby—although I might have misheard this last—after which I lost track, some twenty members in all.

"And, ah lovely, another newcomer?" She paused at a man, probably in his mid-forties, who was sitting quietly and unobtrusively at the back of the hall.

He inclined his head in a rather old-fashioned gesture and raised a hand. "I'm Richard. Hi. I'm just here to hear what you have to say." He gave a small polite smile and faded back into irrelevance. He appeared to have perfected the art of cultivated insignificance, from his forgettable haircut to his exceptionally nondescript jeans and jumper combo. Maryam gave him a slightly bemused smile and turned her attention to us.

"So who do we have here? Friends of Raven and Leila's, I believe?"

I felt this was stretching it a bit. Although it's true we'd got to know them on a relatively intimate footing pretty early on.

Ailsa introduced us, because she's good at these things. We were met with a combination of enthusiastic smiles, curious looks, and a few slightly uncertain ones. I couldn't help but notice that Leila, however, had barely spared us a glance. Her eyes were still fixed on mild-mannered Richard, with a carefully blank expression on her face.

"On to the matter in hand," boomed Maryam, jerking my attention from Leila. "*Wednesday*."

There was a chorus of cheers and boos. The energy in the room ratcheted up a notch. I noticed Anonymous Richard at the back of the room shift ever so slightly in his seat.

"This is our last chance to snatch victory from the jaws of defeat," cried Maryam. Another round of cheers. "And we *cannot be defeated*. Half a millennium of ancient woodland depends on us. We will not be moved!"

At this last there was a rousing cheer.

"In terms of practicalities, we will begin the sit-in before sundown, giving us plenty of time to get ourselves sorted before we lose daylight. We'll assemble at the Hawkbit Meadow car park at 7 P.M. and make our way to the copse. Raven and I will bring the necessary equipment—you just need to bring yourselves and any supplies you will want for the duration. Of course we'll have Norah on standby, bringing us meals and hot drinks. Thank you, Norah. Any questions?"

"Should it be a nude sit-in?" This, I was unsurprised to see, came from Raven.

"I don't think so, not this time," said Maryam robustly. "If nothing else, temperatures are still dropping to twelve degrees at night. We don't want any cases of hypothermia. Which reminds me—everyone needs to remember to wrap up warm—that means thermals, fleeces, hats, decent socks and boots. And don't forget your sit pads. I know, I know, it's a heatwave, but those clear skies mean cold nights. You have been warned. Now, moving on to what we need to achieve this evening—"

"Are we going to talk about what happened at the weekend?" called a voice from the middle of the room. "Are we going to talk about the unplanned and unsanctioned attack on Myers's *private home*?"

There was an outburst of muttering. Several eyes swiveled toward Raven.

"I know what you've been whispering, Enderby," said Raven hotly. "But I don't know anything about the attack."

"It's exactly your style, Raven," taunted Enderby. "Weren't you saying just last week that we hadn't pushed hard enough? That we needed more, what were your words, 'shock tactics'?"

"And I stand by that!" said Raven, his voice rising. "We're *not* pushing hard enough. That's why I called for the sit-in on Wednesday night. We have to take frontline action, we have to—"

"But you couldn't wait until Wednesday, could you," cut in Enderby. "You had to take matters into your own hands."

"I have told you, I did *not*—"

"We're supposed to operate as a group," continued Enderby, raising his voice over Raven's. "We're supposed to only act on decisions that have been ratified by the group. If we have lone rangers firing off left, right, and center, particularly in savage and unprovoked attacks like this one on Myers, we lose credibility as a group. We lose the goodwill of the nation!"

I wasn't entirely sure how avidly the nation was watching as events unfolded in this sleepy Cotswold village, but nonetheless I felt Enderby had a point. Ailsa appeared to agree.

"He's not wrong," she said in a low voice. "People don't react well to attacks on individuals. It's one thing to target the company, but to go after Owen Myers himself . . ." She shook her head. "Bad move." She was watching Raven critically, and she wasn't the only one. Perhaps featherboy wasn't quite as popular as I'd first thought. Leila, however, stepped closer to Raven and twined her fingers through his.

Maryam stepped in, once more clapping her hands for silence.

"Thank you for raising this, Enderby," but there was a slight frostiness to her voice. "Yes, we operate as a group. We also operate on *trust*. Which means that as Raven assures us he had nothing to do with the attack, we take him at his word. Does anyone have a problem with that? No? Good. Onward. I've organized you all into three task forces this evening . . ."

"Of course she'd defend Raven," I heard Enderby mutter to the girl beside him. "He's practically her son."

"Perhaps she thinks he's got the right idea," she whispered back, and the pair exchanged a dark look.

There wasn't much time for any further dissent in the ranks—Maryam soon put an end to that. I suppose I had thought that protests just sort of happened—but there was a hell of a lot more to it than that. We were split into three groups: logistics (sourcing chains, blankets, Thermoses, and informing the police of the peaceful protest), media (contacting local—and national—press, updating the group's socials), and placard painting. In all the bustle, I saw Anonymous Richard slip out of the door. I thought I was the only one who had, what with all the frenetic energy in the room, until I saw Leila's eyes on the door as it swung quietly closed. Norah, the friendly lady with the cookies, was also staring at the door with an unreadable expression on her face.

I was put on placard painting duty, which felt a little bit like being sent to the children's table, but I wasn't going to argue, I know my limitations. Ailsa thrust a twin at me as I departed to collect my poster paint.

"Take a baby, will you?"

Leila had also been assigned to placards, and was making it clear she wasn't happy about it.

"I'd have thought that with my background I'd be far more useful on the logistics team—or media comms," she was complaining, but Maryam was bustling around directing the setting up of trestle tables and barely seemed to notice Leila trailing behind her. I wondered what Leila's background was, which made placard painting so beneath her talents.

It turned out that my talents certainly did not include placard painting. I spent a good ten minutes staring at my empty placard, while around me people began sketching out slogans ranging from the almost poetic, if a tad clichéd, WE SHALL NOT BE MOVED to the more forthright FUCK OFF GREENWASHING BASTARDS.

Next to me, Ivy, aged not quite one, was doing a considerably better job of her placard, which she'd smeared with green and red paint. It looked quite modern. She'd also painted quite a lot of herself, but I figured if Ailsa hadn't wanted that she should have given Ivy to Poppy, who was on logistics and who was also a more competent baby-supervisor.

"How did the photo shoot go?" I asked Leila conversationally as we painted.

"What? Oh, yes, really well," she said. "The pictures are up on the website now, you should take a look, they're good! Sam does know his stuff." Her praise of Sam's work sounded slightly grudging.

"You don't mind having your photo on the internet—you know—in the nude?" I asked curiously, reaching out to stop Ivy poking a paintbrush in her eye.

Leila shrugged. "It's for a good cause," she said. "And I asked Sam to make sure my face wasn't visible in any of them. And made sure he stuck to that," she added.

"Where is Sam?" I asked, glancing round.

"He rushed off back to London," she said dismissively. "His commitment to the cause is weak, if you ask me. He considers himself an artist, and the art comes first. Or so he says."

Her voice was hard. There was clearly no doubting her own commitment to the cause. I hoped Leila wasn't going to question *my* commitment to the cause, because in all honesty I wasn't sure where I stood. I was, obviously, fully in favor of green energy—I want there to still be a world for Jack to grow up in, after all. And part of me wondered if Hen had a point—that there were no perfect solutions and sometimes we have to choose the least destructive option. But I also appreciated Ailsa's arguments that greenwashing and irresponsible behavior on the part of green companies was deeply damaging and essentially an extension of the capitalist leanings that had led us to this point of collapse in the first place (her words not mine, but I often borrowed her words for these matters). It just felt as though sometimes, in trying to improve matters, we accidentally made things worse. By "we" I meant humanity, not specifically myself. Although also myself.

I sighed and began painting a wonky tree on my placard. The modern world was far too complicated, but a tree was a tree. Except when drawn by me. Ivy leaned over and smeared a hand across my artwork, actually somewhat improving the overall effect.

Ailsa, who had been on the media task force, came over and looked at my placard, then at me.

"Isn't your job literally coming up with slogans?"

"I'm an advertising copywriter," I said with dignity.

"LEAVE THE TREES ALONE," she read slowly. "Wow, your company is lucky to have you."

"I was put on the spot," I said defensively, privately wondering whether my brain would ever function to the same standard it had pre-baby.

"Anyway, it's satire," I argued. "Like . . . Leave Britney Alone?"

I wasn't entirely sure "satire" was the right word. And even less sure, judging by Ailsa's face, that my cultural reference would land with this crowd.

"WELL, DO let us know if we can expect to see you at the protest on Wednesday night," Maryam said as we left, beaming and waving cheerfully as if she'd just invited us to a coffee morning.

Ailsa looked at Poppy and me expectantly.

"No," I said firmly—and I meant it. "Out of the question. Absolutely no way am I doing that."

CHAPTER 5

"I CAN'T BELIEVE I'm doing this," I moaned.

It was a beautiful early summer's evening, the low sun painting the long grass of the meadow gold and illuminating the outlines of the ancient sweet chestnut trees. The perfect evening for some light protesting. Or some intense chaining-yourself-to-a-tree protesting—either was good.

"Yes, I can't believe you're helping save a small piece of our dying ecosystem, how shocking," said Ailsa dryly.

"I'm missing *Love Island*," I grumbled, although I knew this would cut as much ice as a blunt spoon with Ailsa, who didn't even own a TV and would probably eat her own toes rather than watch *Love Island*.

"It's on like every night," said Poppy bracingly. "Why don't you come over to mine on Friday and we can binge-watch this week's while Lin and Joe are at the pub."

"We'll probably still be chained to trees on Friday," I said mournfully, determined not to be cheered up. But Poppy just laughed.

"I'm kind of excited," she admitted. "I've never done a proper protest before."

Love Island aside, I had to agree, and it felt like we were going big with our first. Chaining yourself to a tree had to be about as classic as it comes, right? Besides, it was good to hear Poppy sound genuinely enthused for the first time in months—although I did wish she could get her kicks from something a little more sedate like, I don't know, fancy cookies or 3-for-2 wine deals.

"Tourists," muttered Ailsa, shaking her head, but there was a hint of a smile on her face, and I got the feeling she was pleased we'd come along.

"How did you convince Hen to babysit tonight?" asked Poppy curiously. Hen had declared us all traitors for attending the protest and announced that she was muting our group chat until we stopped "trying to sabotage her job."

"I didn't," said Ailsa, a little uncomfortably. "Jane's doing it."

This was only marginally less surprising. Ailsa had a complicated relationship with her sister, the esteemed and humorless Detective Inspector Jane Harris, potentially stemming from the time Jane had arrested her. That tended to put a dent in any sisterly affection. But I had to hand it to her, since the arrival of the twins, Harris had been, well, not *supportive* exactly, but definitely helpful. This wasn't the first time she'd babysat the twins, she sometimes shopped and cooked for Ailsa, she'd even bought the twins tiny police outfit onesies that Ailsa hated. The sisters were, to everyone's surprise, not least theirs, currently living together in Harris's cottage in town. Of course, they still clashed constantly, but it was starting to feel more like sibling angst and less like actual hatred.

"Your sister is babysitting—so you can attend a protest?" I asked disbelievingly. Inspector Harris was *not* a fan of anything even mildly disruptive. I had some hazy idea that Ailsa's controversial arrest at her sister's hands had been something to do with a protest.

Ailsa snorted. "Of course not. I told her I was going to a charity auction for homeless dogs and it would be late so I'd stay over at Alice's afterward."

I squawked in protest. "Why me? Did you have to drag me into your web of lies?"

"What, it's not like she's ever going to find out," said Ailsa dismissively. "Come on, let's find ourselves a tree."

WE ENTERED the copse, which was a hive of activity. Maryam, of course, was in the center of it all, directing people toward trees, laying out lengths of chain which were, to my relief, not dissimilar to the chain of a bike lock—I had been picturing full-on heavy-duty medieval chains, the clanking sort favored by ghosts and S & M fans.

Norah, in her apparently permanent role of Earth Force's unofficial mum, offered me a bamboo Tupperware. "Chia seed energy ball?"

"I'll pass, thanks," I mumbled, clutching my rucksack slightly tighter in case an incriminating cookie fell out.

Everyone seemed very busy and purposeful but strangely unbothered, as if they did this every weekend, like popping to Aldi.

"What should we do?" I asked Ailsa, slightly nervously.

"Stake out our places, I guess," she said unconcernedly.

"Is there a hierarchy or anything?" I asked. "Like, as the newbies should we take an edge tree or something?"

Ailsa shrugged. "I doubt it. This looks like a good one."

It looked exactly like all the other ones to my inexperienced eye. We slung our bags among its roots, which were as thick as a person. Ailsa took my placard from my hand and gave it a slightly despairing look before leaning it, face down, against the tree.

"I'm so pleased you're joining us." It was the earnest voice of Raven. "Taking a stand for this planet is the most important thing we can be doing. If everyone realized what's at stake . . ." He shook his head sadly. "I can't believe the whole village hasn't turned out to be honest. It's a great disappointment. But it's good to have you on board." I wished he would blink a bit more often.

"Couldn't stand by and let them plow up the meadow," said Ailsa matter-of-factly. "Let's hope they see sense."

Raven gave us a sincere nod. He went to walk away but seemed to remember something and turned to me instead, rummaging in his bag.

"Oh, and I brought you this—I thought as it was your first sit-in you might not have brought one." Raven proffered me something—on taking it, I realized it was a diaper, albeit a surprisingly large one.

"Oh, it's OK, thanks," I said, trying to hand it back. "I left Jack at home with his dad." Which I thought should have been quite obvious due to the lack of baby attached to my person.

"It's not for your baby," he said, looking at me as if I were mad (which seemed a tad unfair). "It's for you. We'll be chained to these trees for hours. Possibly even days."

This last statement alarmed me; I'd told Joe I'd be home in time for lunch tomorrow. Raven, on the other hand, looked delighted at the prospect of diapering up and sitting under a tree for three days. It takes all sorts to make a world.

"Yeah, no thanks," I said weakly. "I think I'll just . . ." I gestured vaguely to the surrounding area. I wasn't a huge fan of wild pees, but a lackluster approach to my pelvic floor exercises, combined with a dog that demanded a minimum hour's walk per day, meant I had pretty much perfected my technique.

Raven frowned. "You can't just unchain yourself every time you need to go to the bathroom."

Correction: I could and would be unchaining myself every time I needed to go to the bathroom.

"Really, I'm OK," I insisted.

Raven gave me a disappointed look before disappearing into the trees, presumably to diaper up.

"Wow, he makes you look tame," I said in an undertone to Ailsa. She scowled.

At that point, Maryam strode into the center of the copse, clapping her hands to get our attention. It made me feel oddly as though I were on a bizarre school trip.

"Time to get going, folks," she called briskly. "Take your positions and Norah and I will be coming round to chain you up."

I felt a shiver of dread at this slightly foreboding pronouncement, but it was too late to back out now. Well, technically it wasn't, but it would be too embarrassing to.

"Where's Leila?" I heard Maryam ask Raven, sounding uncharacteristically snappish.

"I don't know." Raven shrugged. "But she'll be here. She wouldn't miss it."

"Is she with Sam? He's late too."

"Well, that's not particularly surprising, is it?" There was a slight edge to Raven's voice. "And no, I highly doubt Leila is with Sam. They can hardly stand to be in the same room as each other these days."

Maryam harrumphed and came marching toward the three of us with alarming purposefulness.

"Come along, ladies," she said as she chivvied us toward a tree like a primary school teacher marshalling errant children. Although I believe chaining them up is not approved teacher practice. The three of us shuffled into position around the tree and waited for Maryam to loop a length of chain around us. I was slightly disconcerted to discover just how firmly I was to be attached to this tree. This wasn't a symbolic once-looped around the trunk job that I could wriggle out of if needed. I was secured snugly across the chest (beneath the armpits, allowing me the use of my arms), and several times around the waist, tighter than I had anticipated. Finally, Maryam clicked a solid looking padlock in place. I wasn't going anywhere.

I was starting to think the adult diaper might not have been such a bad idea.

"The keys will be with Norah," said Maryam, gesturing to where Norah was setting up a small tent just outside the copse, her headquarters for dispensing tea and cookies throughout the sit-in. I watched jealously as she pulled an inflatable mattress out of her pack.

"If you need anything," continued Maryam, "just give Norah a call and she'll be with you right away. She's also a qualified first aider and in charge of the medikit."

I had a strong suspicion Norah's medikit would consist of some bamboo plasters and willow bark tea, but it did feel reassuring that there would be one person not chained to a tree—just in case the developers decided to go nuclear and just flatten us all.

At this point Leila made her entrance. She dashed into the copse, her anorak slipping off her shoulder and her bag (probably filled with adult diapers like a pro) trailing behind her.

"Sorry I'm late." She breezed past Maryam, who was scowling, and planted a kiss on Raven's mouth—aha, they *were* a couple then. Probably. Maybe.

"Where have you been?" asked Maryam grumpily. "We said to meet at six thirty."

"I got caught up," said Leila, not sounding remotely apologetic. "Did you pick us a tree, Ray? This one? Perfect."

I twisted round trying to see where Raven and Leila were planting themselves, but it seemed to be on the other side of the tree to me.

"Where were you though?" I heard Raven ask in a mutinous undertone.

"Does it matter?" was her breezy response.

I turned back to face my immediate neighbor, chained to the tree next to ours—realizing that I was going to be staring at this man, at a distance of about five feet, for the next twelve hours, minimum. Awkward. I tried giving him a comradely smile. He inclined his head ever so slightly, not smiling. Wait—I recognized him. It was Enderby, Raven's nemesis. Oh good, I would spend the next twelve hours staring at the only man in the group who had even less of a sense of humor than Raven.

MY LEFT butt cheek had gone entirely numb. Why only one side, I couldn't say.

"How long have we been here?" I hissed.

"Nearly twenty whole minutes," replied Ailsa dryly. "Do you think you'll survive?"

There was a brief silence.

"I think I'm sitting on a pinecone." There was definitely something pointy getting more intimate with me than I cared for.

"It's a chestnut tree," came Ailsa's voice, ever sympathetic.

There was a slightly longer silence.

"I'm bored," I announced. Enderby scowled over at me.

Ailsa gave an exasperated sigh. "Didn't you bring anything to read? What's in that massive bag?"

"Er, snacks." Stupid question.

"Haven't you got anything?" Ailsa asked. "A sudoku? Spot the difference?"

I ignored this last slur on my intelligence. "I've read all of Twitter and my phone's low on battery."

There was a thud, and a battered paperback landed in the dirt next to me. I picked it up: *Anna Karenina* by Leo Tolstoy. It sounded Russian and was about five thousand pages long.

I groaned and opened the first page: *Happy families are all alike; every unhappy family is unhappy in its own way.*

OK, well this was acceptably cynical.

Twenty pages later I was hooked. It was great!

I only gave up on Anna when it grew too dark to read. I supposed that meant it was time to sleep, although that seemed foolishly optimistic.

What with the still relatively new baby who insisted on feeding every couple of hours throughout the night (to be fair, he took after me in that respect), I was at least practiced in extreme sleep deprivation. But when most new parents get a night away from their babies they tend to opt for spa days, hotel breaks, boozy nights out with pals. Not me, apparently. I don't know if you've ever slept chained to a tree but news flash: *it's not comfortable*.

I wanted to listen to a podcast, or music, anything really to take my mind off my physical discomfort, but my phone battery was already critically low. The faint sound of crackly speech started up on the other side of the copse. Some more experienced person had bought a portable radio with them. Unfortunately, it was too far away for me to make out anything other than the odd word.

". . . now to the news at ten . . . body washed up . . . young man in his . . . near Wapping . . . paint . . ."

Eventually, I gave up trying to listen in and instead decided to focus on the incredible levels of discomfort I had reached. Despite the numb and possibly terminally frozen bum, despite the inconveniently placed branch stub attempting to impale my back, I eventually managed to drop off.

I dozed sporadically, woken what felt like every five minutes by suspicious noises from the surrounding nature. It was extremely dark—which feels like a foolish thing to say; I know it was nighttime, in the depths of the countryside, but I mean, where was the silvery moonlight? The twinkling stars? And what the hell was making that noise in the undergrowth?

At one point I was woken by a faint crunching noise, like footsteps over dry bracken. I wondered if someone was making a break for it under cover of darkness, perhaps forsaking the adult diaper for a covert bush-pee. My bladder gave a sympathetic twinge. I wriggled against my bonds, but there was no way I was getting out without dislocating every joint in my body—how had they managed it? I strained my eyes through the darkness but couldn't make out anything beyond the vague looming columns of the trees.

"Poppy?" I hissed into the darkness. There was no response. "Ailsa?"

Nothing. For God's sake, were they actually managing to sleep? Some people have all the luck.

I WOULDN'T call it sleep—sleep, to my knowledge, doesn't normally leave you feeling like you've been mugged by a forest—but I guess I must have drifted off again, because some time later I was awoken, partly by the rising sun but mainly by my bladder. God, I needed to pee. I tried to distract myself by rummaging through my snack bag, severely decimated by several late-night raids. All the high caliber snacks were long gone. I tried to open a Mini Roll as quietly as possible; the crackling of the wrapper seemed indecently loud in the silent early-morning air. As I savored the chocolate and fake-cream-foam goodness, I gazed around. It really was a beautiful scene; the sun was just rising, and early morning rays lanced through the canopy, throwing soft, dappled light across the fern-speckled copse floor. The trunks of the huge chestnuts were like cathedral pillars. And slumped at the foot of each was a peacefully sleeping protestor. Across from me, Enderby was spark out, head back, the gentlest of snores vibrating from his throat and, to my delight, a half-eaten Twix clutched in one hand. No chia seed power balls for Enderby apparently. I allowed myself to drift in a Mini-Roll-and-nature-induced state of dreamy half-awakeness.

Then I was fully awoken by Poppy's scream. There is nothing more terrifying than hearing a friend scream while you are chained to the far side of the same tree, unable to get to them or even see them. I'm sure you know the feeling.

"Poppy?" I yelled. Her only response was another scream.

I tried to wrestle myself free of the chains but Maryam had done a worryingly professional job on them. If anything, the chains tightened around me, as Ailsa also struggled to free herself. I could hear her yelling to Norah to come and free us, but by now the whole encampment was carnage. Unsurprisingly, Poppy's screams had woken everyone—rather abruptly. There was much panicking, jangling of chains and irate swearing. I may have also done a small amount of screaming myself. Enderby jolted awake and attempted to jump to his feet before realizing he was chained to a tree, essentially performing the Heimlich maneuver on himself.

Norah came tumbling out of her tent and hurried over, fumbling with a bunch of keys. But when she reached our tree she stopped dead, staring past me at something I couldn't see. The keys dropped from her fingers and her hands sprung to her face.

"Oh God . . ." she whispered. She took a tentative step forward, completely ignoring both mine and Ailsa's repeated pleas for her to unlock us.

I couldn't bear it.

"What the hell is going on?!" I bawled at the top of my voice. This seemed to snap Norah out of her trance. She knelt, scrabbled shakily for the keys in the dirt and, on the fourth attempt, inserted the correct key into our padlock.

It sprang open and there were several more minutes of confusion as Ailsa and I accidentally throttled each other in our haste to scramble free. Then we threw ourselves round the trunk to where Poppy sat, pale and trembling but no longer screaming, staring straight ahead of her.

"Are you OK? What's wrong? Are you hurt?" I was frantically patting Poppy all over as if searching for some kind of mortal wound. Quite gently, Ailsa took both my hands in her own, and nodded to something behind me. I turned around to look where both Poppy and Ailsa were staring.

Leila sat facing us, her back against the tree, her hands upturned in her lap as if meditating. But she had achieved a stillness that even the most elevated inner peace can't bring.

"Is she . . . dead?" I hated to ask the obvious question, but I also wanted to be sure. The waxen pallor of her face, the deep red welt around her neck, and the way her tongue protruded from her blue lips were all dead giveaways (apologies, that was an awful choice of words). But it's extremely important to be very sure of these things before jumping to conclusions.

"I think so," said Ailsa softly. She turned her back on the awful scene and began helping Poppy to her feet. I hastened to help her. Poppy looked like she might be going into shock. I suppose waking up, chained to a tree, faced with a corpse, will do that for you.

CHAPTER 6

"YOU HAVE GOT to be kidding me."

Inspector Jane Harris had arrived. And, unfortunately, we were old friends. Old friends with a habit of bumping into each other over dead bodies. Inspector Harris had been in charge of the investigations the previous summer and had, inexplicably, resented our help, which she appeared to have misconstrued as "meddling." The fact that we had then solved the case before her had been the final nail in the coffin.

"If it isn't my darling big sister," said Ailsa, who, despite her bold tone, looked a tad apprehensive.

Inspector Harris glared down at us. We were sitting wrapped in foil blankets in the meadow just beyond the boundary of the copse, which had been taken over by the police and entirely encircled in blue and white police tape like the world's worst present.

"Charity auction for dogs? You've got a bloody nerve, Ailsa."

"Where are Ivy and Robin?" asked Ailsa, looking around as if she expected Harris to have brought them along for the ride.

"With Nana Maud," said Harris dismissively, not to be derailed. "I swear, Ailsa, if you turn up at one more crime scene—"

"You'll what, arrest me?" interrupted Ailsa. "Been there, done that."

Inspector Harris glared at her sister—and then at the rest of us, which seemed a little unfair. She looked ready to chain us all back to the trees and throw away the key.

"Care to tell me what you're all doing here? At the scene of *another* murder?" She was actually tapping her foot. I couldn't help being slightly entertained by Detective Inspector Jane Harris, her exasperation was so endearingly caricatured.

Ailsa was still trying to keep up her rather shaky show of bravado. "Isn't it obvious? We were protesting, same as everyone else here."

Well, not quite everyone else, I thought. Someone had evidently decided to indulge in a spot of light strangling alongside their protesting. Unless, of course, it was someone from outside the protest . . . That was possible—in fact, maybe even probable. Everyone in the protest group had been chained to trees after all, and I knew firsthand that extricating yourself from one of those binds, silently and without alerting anyone else, would have required ninja-like stealth. Not to mention that all the keys had been held by Norah. Did that make Norah the prime suspect? Surely that was far too obvious, you'd have to be mad to commit murder when you were the only one holding the keys. Plus Norah was, well, so very *Norah* . . .

I realized I was doing it again. Trying to think like a detective—when in fact I was a sleep-deprived mother of one with chronic mastitis and a dog with behavioral issues. I was not qualified to stick my nose in, I told myself firmly.

"How did they do it?" murmured Poppy in my ear. Damn, she was thinking along the same lines. And if Poppy decided to get involved, I knew from dire previous experience that I was powerless against her superior willpower and determination.

I gave a shrug, designed to indicate that I wasn't that interested, although I think it looked more like a nervous twitch.

"Although, of course, it wasn't necessarily someone from the protest . . ." mused Poppy. Goddammit! Although I was pleased to notice that she looked somewhat more herself, a little color returning to her cheeks.

"What was that?" interrupted Inspector Harris sharply.

"Nothing!" said Poppy hastily, the picture of innocence. Harris shifted her accusatory gaze to me; I did my best outraged expression. I had *not* been encouraging Poppy!

With a final suspicious glare, Inspector Harris stalked off to harass some other innocent protestors. Probably innocent. Except perhaps one of them . . . No. I wasn't going down that route.

I texted Joe, giving him the bare bones of the situation (sorry—another poor word choice) and asking him to come get me asap. I should have phoned him, I knew that, but I had learned from experience that telling Joe about murder was best done with a suitable buffer zone—not something I had ever expected to know about my boyfriend, but there you go. Hopefully this way he would do most of the freaking out before he actually arrived.

Don't bring Helen.

I sent the swift follow-up message in alarm. I'd had to restrain Helen at a crime scene before and no one needed the additional stress right now.

Then, as in all times of crisis, I turned to my best friend Maya, currently over a hundred miles away in London where she lived a blissfully crime-free existence, unlike my murder-ridden country idyll.

You're not going to believe this.

Omg! He said his first word!

Was it "Maya"?

Maya is more obsessed with Jack than I am.

What?

No!

I've just witnessed a murder

Well I missed the actual murder itself

But I was THERE

Hang on. I'm getting déjà vu

I know . . .

Please tell me it wasn't at a baby class or something because that is dark AF

No no, at the protest I told you about

Oh yeah, the nude one?

FFS it wasn't nude

We were interrupted at this point by an official-looking person in one of those hazmat/intense DIY paper suits, who took down our details and then asked us to follow him to have our fingerprints taken.

"Mine are already on file," I said breezily, thankful that I wouldn't need to go through that rigmarole again.

The officer immediately shot me a deeply suspicious look.

"Oh, I'm not a criminal," I explained hastily. "I just contaminated some evidence in a previous case."

He didn't look overly impressed by this.

"I did *find* the evidence in the first place," I said a little defensively. "Well, my dog did. She's an excellent sniffer dog."

Poppy gave a derisive snort at this.

At this point Ailsa decided to step in. "Mine and Alice's fingerprints are on file from previous cases, entirely unrelated to this mess. You can ask Inspector Harris about it if you need to."

"She's Ailsa's sister," I put in helpfully.

Ailsa gave an Inspector-Harris-worthy eye roll. "Poppy, can you take Alice somewhere and, I don't know, shove her in a tree or something?"

The officer left. I couldn't blame him.

NORAH APPEARED beside us, holding out a Thermos of tea.

"Hot drink?" she asked rather shakily.

"Please." I dug around in my backpack for my camping cup and held it out. Norah tried to pour, her hand shaking so much most of it splashed over my shoes.

"Sorry," she muttered. "I'll find a cloth or something." She looked around vaguely.

"Norah." I put a hand on her arm. "It's fine, don't worry about it."

She gave me a weak smile. "It's just awful," she whispered. "Who would do such a thing?"

I opened my mouth, not sure what I was going to say; I'd been asking myself the same question all morning. A voice behind us cut in.

"Oh, I don't know—maybe Aether?" It was Enderby. Like everyone else, he was white as a sheet, but he also looked as though he was simmering with rage. "It's one way to discredit the movement—kill off the protestors."

Norah fumbled her Thermos and it fell to the ground, but she didn't seem to notice.

"How can you say such a thing!" she gasped at Enderby. "Of course it wasn't—he wouldn't—it wasn't Aether!"

Enderby's face twisted. "I wouldn't be so sure." He stooped, picked up the Thermos, held it out to Norah, and left without another word.

I glanced at Poppy and Ailsa—that brief exchange had felt more loaded than an entire demolition crew.

Before any of us could speak, a bloodcurdling shriek split the air—again. The four of us jumped out of our skins. I actually grabbed hold of Ailsa, who was nearest—a risky move at the best of times.

"Sam!" The solid figure of Maryam burst out of a nearby cluster of protestors and hurled herself across the meadow to where a figure was shambling across the grass.

"Oh phew, I thought for a minute it was another body," said Poppy weakly.

"I think it's Raven's brother, the photographer," said Ailsa. "He was meant to be documenting the protest wasn't he—and will you get off me, Alice? You're cutting off the blood supply to my arm."

I let go sheepishly, but also a bit reluctantly. For all her spikiness, Ailsa was a very reassuring presence.

Without discussing it, we found ourselves edging closer to where Maryam was clinging to the late arrival, part hugging him, part berating him. She seemed quite hysterical—which on the one hand was completely understandable, a member of her protest group had been rather brutally murdered after all, but on the other hand . . . she didn't even like Leila, that much had been plain.

"Where *were* you, Sam? You were supposed to be here last night! I was so worried! I thought—"

Sam attempted to disentangle himself gently. "I'm so sorry, Yam. I got held up at work."

I stifled an incredulous noise. I'm no expert on these things (well, not anymore—but I used to be) but he had the sweaty sheen and sunken eyes of the almost terminally hungover. And, yep, there it was—a distinctive whiff of booze drifted past.

"What's going on?" Sam looked around at the police tape, the foil-wrapped protestors in sad little huddles, interspersed with the black uniformed officers. "They called the police in? It's a peaceful protest!"

Ah. Who wanted to explain the whole peaceful-protest-turned-murder-scene situation?

"It's Leila . . ." Maryam managed, before drying up.

"What's she done?" asked Sam sharply.

Interesting.

"No, no," said Maryam, shaking her head as though trying to dislodge the most recent image of Leila. "It's not . . . she hasn't . . . she's dead, Sam."

There was absolutely no reaction from Sam. He stared at Maryam unblinking. There was a timeless pause. Eventually, he seemed rouse himself.

"Where's Raven?"

We all looked around. Raven sat cross-legged, cocooned in silver foil like a giant Hershey's Kiss. Occasionally a tremor ran through his body, making the foil whisper.

Sam strode over to his brother, knelt beside him and grabbed both his shoulders. Raven stared up at him blankly, then the two brothers were hugging hard, the foil crunching and crackling between them.

I WAS shocked by Leila's death—and particularly the manner of it. Of course I was. And I was upset. Leila had seemed a nice girl, if a little earnest. But a small part of me was also interested, in a detached sort of way, at how everyone else was reacting. I hope that doesn't make me a psychopath or anything. It's just, those few unfiltered moments after it's happened tell you so much, before people have had time to assemble the "correct" response. We're all pretty adept at instantly, subconsciously, curating our responses to the minutiae of everyday life—well, I fear I am slightly below par at this—but when something unexpected happens, like a murder for instance, your brain scrambles to find an appropriate response. There are no presets to select from.

Maryam now seemed to be closing in on herself, her brief hysterics when Sam appeared having abated, and she stood watching Raven and Sam until Inspector Harris touched her arm and asked if she could ask her a few questions. Maryam looked at Harris without appearing to really see her, before her gaze slid back to Raven and Sam. Harris wasn't to be put off, however.

"I understand you're in charge of the group?"

"I suppose so," Maryam replied distantly. "We don't really have a leader as such. We're a community of equals."

"Of course," said Inspector Harris. "But if you wouldn't mind . . ."

Maryam inclined her head slightly, and Harris produced her notebook from her pocket. I shuffled a tad closer. My phone was buzzing in my pocket but it would have to wait.

"Had you known Leila long?"

"Hmm? Oh, about six months, I think. Yes, she joined Earth Force just before Christmas."

"And was she known to you or the group before she joined?"

Maryam shook her head slightly. "I didn't know her, no. She just . . . arrived one day. Or wait, I think maybe Raven and Sam had met her before at some protest. I can't remember."

Inspector Harris made a note. "I understand she lived locally, in Bishop's Ruin, do you know if she'd been living there for long?"

"I don't know. I don't think so?" Maryam shrugged slightly, her gaze drifting back to Raven.

"Do you have an address for her?" pressed Harris.

Maryam shook her head again, looking slightly frustrated. "No, I mean, I don't know—you'd have to ask Raven. Or Norah, she looks after the group admin."

Another note.

"And do you know of any next of kin we should inform?"

Maryam shook her head slightly. "No . . . No, I don't think so. Raven might know, but . . ."

"Raven was close to Leila?"

Maryam gave a strange half-shrug, almost a twitch.

"Were they romantically involved?" pressed Harris.

"I suppose so."

Inspector Harris closed her notebook. "And which one is Raven? I'd like to have a word with him."

At this Maryam roused herself slightly. "Can't it wait? The poor boy's in shock. He's just lost his . . . Can't it wait until tomorrow?"

"I just need to take some very basic details, it will barely take a minute of his time."

"Really, Inspector, I don't think that's very sensitive . . ."

I almost huffed at this—Inspector Harris wasn't known for her "sensitive" questioning. Last summer she had questioned Hen within twenty-four hours of giving birth. Sure enough, Harris was already steering toward Raven. As they moved out of earshot, my phone buzzed angrily again.

When I finally checked my phone, to the tune of four missed calls from Maya and a further six from Joe, Maya was ready to commit murder herself. But my mind was more focused on the conversation I'd just overheard.

Come on, Al! You can't drop a bombshell like that then go dark on me

Helloooo

Al??

Shit, you haven't been murdered too have you?

Al?? Speak to me!

Sorry!

Nope!

Not murdered

(Yet)

All fine—I'll call you later

I hate you

CHAPTER 7

JOE CAME MARCHING across the meadow, Jack strapped securely to his front. As he drew closer, I could see the emotions storming across his face like a battling weather front. Concern, exasperation, relief, fury . . .

"I let you out of my sight for one night . . ." he began, then pulled me into a crushing hug. Jack squawked his protest at being sandwiched inside such an intense embrace.

"Are you OK?" whispered Joe into my hair.

"Can I get back to you on that?" I replied into his armpit. He gave a shaky laugh.

"Come on, let's get you home." He wrapped an arm around me. There was nothing I wanted more—well, actually maybe one thing, but I'd broach that in the car. But first . . .

"Is Lin coming to get you?" I asked Poppy.

"On her way," said Poppy, looking relieved at the prospect.

I turned to Ailsa; I couldn't leave before I knew someone was coming for her.

"Can Hen . . . ?"

"She's at work," said Ailsa abruptly. "Look, I'll be fine."

"No way. Come back to mine," I said. "You don't want to be on your own."

"I'll be fine," insisted Ailsa again, but I could see a slight fracture behind her determined expression.

"I'm insisting," I said firmly. "Go get your stuff and—"

"Ailsa?"

Oh good, Inspector Harris. She gave Poppy and me the briefest of glances. "I'll need to speak to you two later," she said shortly. "But first I need to get this one home to the twins."

"Ivy and Robin," corrected Ailsa automatically—she hated us referring to her babies as a single unit.

"Nana Maud can look after you till I get off shift—which is going to be about midnight at this rate."

"I don't need looking after," protested Ailsa, but there were times when Inspector Harris's force of will could rival even her sister's.

"Selby," Harris called to a nearby officer. "You're in charge here till I get back. I won't be an hour. Once you've got names and details for everyone you can let them go home. We'll draw up a list for questioning back at the station."

She turned back to Ailsa. "I've got your bag, come on, let's go."

Ailsa gave us a defeated shrug and followed her sister toward the car park.

"Think she'll be OK?" I asked Poppy, slightly nervously. I just couldn't get my head around Inspector Jane Harris in "big-sister" role.

"She'll be fine, Harris will look after her, I guess," said Poppy, looking over my shoulder. "Oh thank God, Lin's here." Sure enough, a determined blond-haired figure was half running across the grass, clutching a baby. Poppy dashed toward her.

I felt an arm slip round my waist and allowed myself to be shepherded away by Joe.

"Home," he said firmly.

"Yes," I agreed. "But first, do you think we could . . ."

McDONALD'S IS my happy place. So sue me. When I've had a shock—like, for example, discovering a dead body—I need a McDonald's. There's something about that soothing blend of fat, salt, and sugar that is balm to my soul. Joe gets this and doesn't judge me for it, which is one of the many reasons I love him.

We sat in a booth at McDonald's and spread our feast before us. We used to be very much a drive-thru couple, but now that we had Jack we tended to eat in—it felt more like taking our child out for a meal and less like bad parenting.

"Isn't it a bit contradictory?" asked Joe, unwrapping his McCrispy burger. "Protesting against a green energy company because they fall slightly below the high standards set for the emerging green industry, but then going to McDonald's, who are pretty much single-handedly destroying the Amazon?"

"Yes," I replied shortly. I did not appreciate having to think about this just as I was about to bite into my Big Mac. And I did not appreciate Joe sounding like Ailsa—I already had one Ailsa in my life and she was filling the role admirably.

"Sorry," said Joe guiltily. "Poor timing."

I took a huge bite. Fuck, it was delicious—even with the slightly sour undertone of guilt.

"I'm trying," I said through my full mouth. "*We're* trying. We do the reusable diapers and wipes, and all Jack's stuff is secondhand, and we hardly ever cook meat at home now. But it's so hard to live up to your own standards."

"Let alone Ailsa's," commented Joe dryly.

"Exactly," I agreed. Ailsa was my moral compass, and I definitely wouldn't be mentioning this little trip to her. It's good to have a friend who is morally superior to you in almost every respect—it gives you someone to look up to, someone to hold you accountable, someone to lie to on a regular basis.

I pried the lid off Joe's milkshake and dipped a couple of chips in. I knew this would shift the conversation away from uncomfortable moral dilemmas.

"You always say you don't want a milkshake, and then you always dip your chips in mine," complained Joe reliably. "And make it taste all salty and weird."

"Sweet and salty is the food combination of the gods," I retorted, going in for another dip.

"So," said Joe, and he was using his serious voice now. "What the hell happened up there?"

I shrugged helplessly. "I wish I knew. Everything was going as it was supposed to—at least I think it was—and then morning came and . . ."

"Dead body," supplied Joe.

"Dead body."

"Who was it?"

"A girl called Leila, I told you about her—the naked one we met up at Hawkbit Meadow the other day. The one who persuaded us to join the protest."

Joe cast a glance at Jack in his high chair, who was merrily banging his cup against the tray, oblivious to us. Nonetheless, he covered Jack's ears with his hands just in case.

"And what happened to her?"

"Strangled." There was no delicate way to put it. "I'm pretty sure." An image of Leila's face swam across my vision and I shuddered, putting down my Big Mac. Joe let go of Jack's ears and reached across to grab my hands.

"You're OK," he said reassuringly. "And that's the main thing. Just—don't get involved in this one, yeah?"

I nodded uncomfortably. "I'm afraid I might already be involved though," I admitted. "What with being there and everything. Again."

Joe looked frustrated. "Just, try and take a back seat? Please?"

"Of course," I said, feeling slightly like I was lying, although I wasn't yet sure if I was or not.

While we had been talking, Jack had been inching his hands toward Joe's milkshake, which he now managed to knock over with a howl of delight. Most of it went into Joe's lap. He leaped backward, spraying vanilla milkshake everywhere. Jack chuckled delightedly.

"If you hadn't taken the lid off . . ." growled Joe, dabbing at himself with a napkin while I tried not to laugh.

"If you'd been keeping an eye on your drink . . ." I countered, knowing it was a weak comeback.

After a year of parenting, we still hadn't got our heads around the fact that anything that could possibly be grabbed, spilled, or broken, would be. To be honest, after over two years of Helen we really ought to have been on top of this a long time ago. Our house was a Jackson Pollock of assorted stains bearing testimony to this.

"Seriously though," said Joe, gesturing to the chaos of our table. "I think we've got enough on our plate right now without you getting mixed up in some sort of murder investigation, *again*."

"Yes, yes, you're right," I said soothingly, chucking him another bundle of napkins. "I think Hen would disown us if we got involved anyway."

"How very sensible of her. Why?"

"Well, the company we were protesting against, Aether, is where she works," I explained. "She thinks we'll get her fired. She's going to do her nut when she finds out there was a murder." I felt a guilty twinge; I really ought to text Hen and let her know. Although she was going to find out sooner or later, so did it really have to be me who told her? Also . . .

"There is something else," I said hesitantly. "I think Hen knew Leila." I hadn't mentioned this to Poppy or Ailsa, because that felt disloyal somehow. It was different saying it to Joe, who probably wasn't paying attention anyway.

"Oh, why's that? Did she recognize her at the picnic the other day?"

I hesitated. "No, I don't think she did. And I don't think Leila recognized her. But . . ." I tried to clarify what I meant. "I think she recognized Leila's name when she introduced herself."

"Have you asked her?"

"Yeah, she said I was imagining things."

"Well, it wouldn't be the first time," said Joe, rather uncharitably I thought.

"I don't think so," I said slowly. "She's definitely being off about something. More than usual, I mean."

"Hen's weird," said Joe, as if this settled the matter.

"You think all my friends are weird."

"Well, they are."

"Lin's not."

Joe had to concede this. Poppy's wife, Lin, was gloriously normal.

"Anyway, you just said Hen was sensible," I pointed out.

"Yes, well, it suited me to agree with her at that point," he replied. Well, I couldn't fault his honesty.

I noticed that Jack, having successfully dealt with the milkshake, was now making eyes at my chips, pudgy little hands stretching toward them.

I pushed them out of his reach and handed him a carrot stick. He gave me an understandably aggrieved look.

"Can't he have a chip?" Joe asked.

"No salt," I reminded him.

Joe sighed. "I feel bad, bringing him here and making him sit and watch us eat chips and a milkshake while he has carrot sticks . . ."

"We're bringing him up to be a better person than either of us," I reminded Joe.

Joe looked pensively at Jack, who gave him his best soulful expression. Joe sucked a chip for a minute or so until it was, to his mind, thoroughly desalted, then held out the soggy stick to Jack, who took it in delight.

"Problem solved."

I put the carrot sticks back in my bag. Truly this was parenting at its finest.

Talking of which . . . Joe and I exchanged glances.

"Diaper situation," said Joe in a serious voice. There was a tense silence where we wouldn't meet each other's eye.

"I've been on full-time childcare for the last twenty-four hours," said Joe.

"I've been at a murder scene," I pointed out.

It was pretty much a stalemate.

CHAPTER 8

THAT NIGHT I had mastitis.

I don't know what I'd expected, after chaining myself to a tree for twelve hours during which I neither breastfed nor pumped milk.

The human body is a finely honed machine. The act of procreating and raising the ensuing offspring utterly and irreparably destroys that machine. Right now, my left boob was a mass of red-hot needles of pain. OK, so it probably wasn't full-on mastitis—which comes with a side order of raging fever and the full gamut of flu symptoms—but it was one hell of a blocked duct. This is one of the many beautiful aspects of motherhood that inexplicably doesn't get so much airtime.

I sent out a cry for help to the usual suspects. Responses ranged from "gross" (Maya) to "try feeding two then you'll know pain" (Ailsa).

Poppy of course helpfully sent me a video of how to use an electric toothbrush on your boob to help loosen the blocked duct. Being an old-school manual brusher I don't own an electric toothbrush, and it felt inappropriate to use Joe's, so, after a brief and unsuccessful dalliance with a milk frother, I ventured into the dark crawlspace of the eaves and unearthed my long derelict vibrator. It didn't have any batteries—they'd probably been taken to power the Wii console or one of Jack's demonic toys. I felt this state of affairs said a lot about my life. But you know what, once I'd dusted it down and cannibalized some batteries from a toy piano, it did the trick.

I sat in the dark and mused as my left breast vibrated painfully. There were so many unanswered questions swimming through my head. Leila had been late to the protest—where had she been? Sam hadn't shown up at all, not until the following morning. Unless, of course, he *had* been there that night, unseen . . . The footsteps I'd heard in the dark . . .

And Leila herself was one big unanswered question. We'd barely got to know her. I'd got the impression she was pretty deep into the whole earth activism—but it was just that, an impression. I didn't know anything about her as a person. I pulled out my phone to Google stalk her, then paused. Leila . . . Leila what? I didn't even know her full name.

Change of plan. I texted "Earth Force (Aether sucks)," the group chat Ailsa had created with me and Poppy so that we didn't constantly annoy Hen with Earth Force messages. I suspected Hen also resented us having a group chat without her, but it was something of a lose-lose situation. Fortunately for me, both Ailsa and Poppy were awake—this was something of a given with Ailsa, who after all had two babies to feed throughout the night and no one to take shifts. It didn't bear thinking about. I wasn't sure she had slept in a year (this is not a welcome development in a friend who leans toward tetchy at the best of times).

What was Leila's surname?

Poppy: Oh! I don't know?

Ailsa: Hang on let me look in Jane's office.

Ailsa could always be relied upon to break into her sister's home office and go through her confidential police documents. It was a real blessing that her moral scruples didn't extend to petty crimes like this.

Ailsa: Hmm

Ailsa: Leila "Smith"

Oh good

Either the most common name there is, or the most unimaginative fake name

Poppy: I'm thinking the latter

Why?

Poppy: Not sure, getting a weird feeling about Leila

Over the year I'd known her, I'd come to respect Poppy's hunches. And I had to agree. If you have no suspects—or all your suspects were chained to trees at the time of the murder—then you focus on the victim, it makes sense. And we knew very little about our victim.

I tried googling Leila Smith and was hit with pages and pages of results. I skimmed through the first few. A hairdresser in Bolton. A professor of applied mathematics in Sheffield. A reiki master in Carlisle. None of them seemed to fit the profile—too old, too young, or a photo showing someone that was definitely not Leila.

Eventually, I gave up and turned on the telly, which was where Joe found me half an hour later.

"What are you doing?" He stood sleepily at the bottom of the stairs and looked at me in confusion. I sat, mini Magnum in one hand, vibrator in the other, jammed into my left breast, watching decade-old reruns of *Don't Tell the Bride*.

"Boob stuff," I said vaguely.

He nodded with the care and compassion of a man practically sleepwalking and returned to bed. I watched him go and marveled at the speed with which our relationship had catapulted through heady new romance and into surprise pregnancy, through an urban-to-rural relocation that had unexpectedly involved several murders and a hell of a lot of family drama. And now parenthood. Which was the hardest challenge yet, by a long shot.

Neither of us had found the newborn thing easy. When I first had Jack, of course I loved him. I loved him because he was my baby, because he needed me, and because it was exciting, kind of like having a new pet. Did I experience the overwhelming rush of maternal love people talk about?

Nope. Did I feel like that made me a bad mum—or actually just an overall terrible person? Yep. It had been the same for Joe. The first few months of parenthood had been a soupy miasma of fear and exhaustion with no end in sight. I hadn't been prepared for a brain-suffocating sleep deprivation that took me to hallucinatory levels. Joe hadn't been prepared for the way Jack's crying would drive a chalk-tipped drill down the blackboard of his spine. Neither of us had been prepared for the way we would suddenly cease to find each other remotely amusing and instead be wildly irritated by those endearing personality quirks that had initially attracted us to each other.

But like all the best relationships in my life—Joe, Maya, my new Penton friends, even Helen—Jack had been a grower. One year in, and both Joe and I were pretty obsessed. And definitely less irritated with each other. In fact, it was fair to say that without Joe I'd be a twitching wreck on the floor. More so than was currently the case, anyway.

Of course, a lot had changed in our relationship, undeniably. I shifted the vibrator slightly and fetched another mini Magnum.

Once I felt the burning pain in my boob begin to subside, I took the batteries back out of the vibrator and returned it to its cave in the roof to wait out another mastitis attack.

CHAPTER 9

IT HAD NOT been a good night. Well, even with the mastitis I suppose it had been a considerable improvement on the previous night—a bed rather than a tree, unlimited access to a functioning bathroom, no dead bodies. But Jack had woken up to feed approximately every five minutes, which had felt particularly unfair as I'd run out of mini Magnums early on. He currently sat beaming, well rested and fed and generally delighted with the world, while I stumbled blearily around the kitchen and accidentally trod on Helen's tail, which she had left inconveniently in the way. Any minute now—There was a knocking on the door. Shit. Hen was here already. And by "already" I meant she was on time, as she was every week. Why couldn't people have the decency to be late?

On Fridays, Poppy, Ailsa and I looked after Arora while Hen was at work. Since Antoni's departure, Hen's circumstances had changed somewhat. When I first met her, she had been a housewife, fully occupied in maintaining their immaculate and very swanky mansionette. OK, so it probably hadn't been a mansion *technically*, but it had been one of the largest houses I'd ever been inside without paying. She was now a single parent, trying to work and raise Arora in a one-bedroom apartment—all to her impeccably high standards—so we pitched in where we could to help.

Needless to say, despite having two of us to hand, Joe and I fell far below Hen's minimum standards. Possibly in life as well as childcare. I stood in the doorway trying to block as much of the view behind me as possible—a scene of devastation where Helen and Jack vied to eat Play-Doh, and the remains of breakfast were scattered across the table and floor. Fortunately, Hen showed no signs of wanting to come in.

"Diaper bag, snack box, bunny, child," she said briskly, thrusting each item at me in turn.

"Nice to see you too," I remarked, trying to tuck Arora under one arm along with the snack box. "Hen, did Ailsa tell you—"

"I'm in a bit of a rush, Alice, can it wait?"

"I guess, I just thought you might want to know that—"

"Owen phoned while I was on my way over. Apparently there's some crisis, he needs me in asap." She cut me off, stooping to kiss Arora's forehead.

"About that—"

"I'll see you at half five!" She was already halfway down the garden path. Oh well, she'd find out about the murder soon enough. And probably blame us for not telling her.

FRIDAYS MEANT forest school. This is a thing. It did not feature either in my thoroughly urban upbringing, or even more urban working life in London. But out here, it was the thing to do. So once a week we took the children to Feathernacke Forest where they spent three hours playing with mud, painting with mud, making mud pies and, frequently, eating mud.

As soon as we arrived, I stripped off Arora's dainty pale pink frock and re-dressed her in some of Jack's more hard-worn outfits—leggings with holes in the knees, a T-shirt with vampiric spaghetti stains down the front, and some wellies that Helen had mangled. Hen never failed to comment, always in a tone of surprise, on how pristine we managed to keep Arora. This was because Arora's outfits spent the entirety of Fridays in a sealed sandwich bag in the glove box of my car.

My phone pinged. It was Hen.

> YOU DIDN'T THINK TO TELL ME ABOUT THE MURDER?

I sighed and set the children and dog loose. Arora toddled off with dainty steps. Jack took one step, face-planted, then began to drag himself determinedly toward Noah, who was already here, sitting in a pile of leaves and looking extremely pleased about it.

Forest school was held in a wide clearing, scattered with tree stumps for seats (extremely uncomfortable) and an assortment of nature-based activities. A handful of wholesome-looking parents milled around while their offspring communed with nature, often by eating it.

I joined Poppy and Ailsa, who were supervising Noah, Robin, and Ivy as they diligently built up Noah's leaf nest.

"You brought Helen again," commented Ailsa dryly. Helen had disgraced herself the previous week by eating all the children's mud pies. I personally felt that the outrage had been a little overdone, given that this was broadly what the children also did.

"Sultan is here," I pointed out, well aware that this was no comparison. Sultan, a regal greyhound with all the poise and elegance his name suggested, sat primly beside Poppy, looking thoughtfully into the distance. Helen licked his nose a few times but, receiving no response, gamboled away to annoy someone else.

"Yes, but you'll notice I haven't brought Ronnie," countered Poppy. Ronnie was, unbelievably, worse behaved than Helen, albeit considerably more intelligent.

I wanted to stick up for Helen, I really did, but the evidence was all against me. I shrugged. We'd just have to see what happened and deal with the consequences.

"Have either of you heard from our beloved Inspector Harris yet?" I asked, settling myself on a particularly uncomfortable tree stump.

"Nope," said Poppy.

"We're pretty far down Jane's suspect list this time round," said Ailsa. "She's focusing on the Earth Force members first."

"We're on her suspect list?" I yelped, alarmed.

Ailsa shrugged. "We were there when Leila was murdered. I don't see how we're any less suspects than the rest of the protestors."

I sensed that, if anything, Ailsa was a little annoyed at being further down the suspect list than the other protestors. I, on the other hand, was just fine with being bottom of that particular pile.

I groaned. "I'd like to get through a year of my life without being suspected of murder, thank you."

"I guess we'll just have to clear our names," suggested Poppy, with a familiar and dangerous gleam in her eye.

"No," I said firmly, and quite reasonably, I thought. "That's a job for the police. Not us. We're parents now, responsible people."

"The police didn't get anywhere last year," said Poppy. "No offense to your sister, Ailsa."

"Offend away." As mentioned, Ailsa and her sister didn't exactly see eye to eye, despite Harris's newfound attempts to make an effort at auntiehood, in her own joyless and begrudging way. This despite the fact that the twins were clearly on a path to be up in front of the police before the age of five—damage to public property, damage to private property, disruption to public order, harassment in search of snacks . . .

"We were the ones who solved it last year," continued Poppy.

"At considerable personal cost," I put in, thinking back to the horrific weeks following the "successful" resolution of our investigations last year. There had been more than a few ramifications, many of which we were still dealing with a year on.

"It had to be done," said Poppy quietly but firmly. "And I'd do it again, if it meant that the right person was caught."

I groaned. I knew we were going to do it, I just wanted to feel that I'd put up a decent resistance. I also had to admit it was good to see Poppy looking so energized. Even her hair seemed to have perked up at the mere thought of an investigation. But even so . . .

"Hen won't like it." I played my trump card. But Ailsa merely shrugged. "Hen doesn't have to get involved if she doesn't want to."

This was a little cool from Ailsa. I wondered if the two of them had had one of their frequent fallings-out.

"How come you hadn't told her about the murder?" I asked.

"I tried calling her last night but Robin got stuck in the bin just as she picked up and I had to go sort it. I tried to call back but she didn't answer. It didn't seem right to tell her in a text."

I couldn't tell if there was an undertone to this. As two single parents, one to twins, there was a lot of "you didn't answer my call" between Hen and Ailsa. Poppy and I were slightly more accessible, having an extra pair of hands at home, but much as we tried, neither of us could provide for Hen and Ailsa in the way it seemed they provided for each other.

I was distracted from my thoughts by Ailsa poking me with a stick. "Can you stop Helen from peeing on my child's artwork."

I looked over to where Helen had cocked a leg over a jumbled pile of pinecones and twigs.

"Artwork?"

"Ivy spent ages arranging those."

I hauled Helen away before she could desecrate any further masterpieces.

As I tried vainly to interest Helen in an alternative stick on the far side of the clearing, Ailsa appeared beside me.

"I know you don't want to get involved in investigating Leila's death," she said abruptly.

"Nope," I agreed. "It's not our business. And we have babies to look after. It's irresponsible." I threw the stick for Helen. It landed about two meters away. She looked at me in disdain.

"No one is suggesting we get the babies involved," replied Ailsa. "And look, can't you see the difference it's making to Poppy, even just thinking about it?"

I stiffened. We hadn't discussed Poppy before and the fact that she may or may not be struggling. I'd been increasingly worried about her over the last few months, but had only confided my concerns in Joe.

"What do you mean?" I hedged, retrieving the stick and waving it vaguely at Helen.

"We've all noticed," said Ailsa flatly. "Well, Hen and I have—and I know you have, you're her best friend. She's not been herself for ages. She needs something to spark her up again. And discussing this investigation is the liveliest I've seen her in months."

I briefly wondered how I'd ended up with a best friend who got "sparked up," to borrow Ailsa's phrase, by investigating a murder. But Ailsa was right—Poppy needed something to lift her out of herself, and maybe, just maybe, this was it.

I nodded curtly and launched my stick again. Helen rocked back on her haunches to scratch an ear and fell over.

"I know," I said. "I just . . . the babies . . ."

"We'll be cautious. We'll be responsible," said Ailsa, in what she probably thought was a comforting tone. "We'll keep the babies well out of this."

I suppressed a sarcastic laugh. Investigating a murder was, to my mind, the definition of incautious and irresponsible. But when had that stopped us before?

"Let's just . . . We'll keep it light," I bargained. "Just to help Poppy get back on her feet, OK?"

Ailsa nodded approvingly and turned to head back. I scanned the ground for where my stick had fallen.

"Give up, Alice," she called over her shoulder. "She doesn't want the damn stick."

POPPY WAS gently separating Noah and Jack, who appeared to have fallen out over the possession of a particularly prized leaf, when I returned with Helen and without the disappointing stick. Helen immediately resolved the argument by pinching the leaf in question and eating it.

"So just supposing we *were* asking questions about the murder," I said carefully, picking up Jack and consoling him over the loss of his leaf. "I'd be wondering who stood to gain by Leila's death."

Poppy immediately put down the pie tin she was filling with mud. "Enderby was throwing Aether out there pretty early on," she recalled. "But, I don't know, I can't see it. Is there any advantage to them? Surely it's bad publicity and I doubt it's going to get the construction of the site going any quicker, now that it's a crime scene."

"If anything it would delay it," I agreed, getting drawn in despite myself.

"Plus if it was anything to do with Aether," countered Ailsa, "then why Leila? Why not Maryam, or Raven? They're far more influential in the group."

It was a good point.

"I don't think we can necessarily rule Aether out," said Poppy thoughtfully. "But it does seem unlikely. I think we need to look elsewhere."

"Unless," said Ailsa slowly, "unless it was retaliation . . ."

"What do you mean?" I asked.

"For the attack on Owen Myers's house."

"You think Leila might have been behind that?"

Ailsa shrugged. "Enderby certainly thought Raven was behind it; it could have been the two of them—Leila and Raven."

I reached over to where Jack was trying to spoon-feed his mud pie to Noah.

"Not for eating," I said absently. "Just for pretending, OK?"

Jack gave me a solemn look and posted the contents of the spoon down his diaper instead. I sighed and unpacked my voluminous diaper-changing kit. Thanks to Ailsa and our reluctant conversion to reusable diapers, this was a complex and multi-stage process requiring more paraphernalia than an overnight camping trip. (In all honesty, it actually wasn't as bad as I'd feared, but I would never admit this to her.)

As I peeled the soggy and mud-stained layers of bamboo booster and fleece liner away, my mind was (thankfully) more on the murder than on the task in hand.

"Putting Aether aside for one moment," I said thoughtfully, "I've got a more pressing question. Where was Sam on Wednesday night?"

"Ooh yes!" said Poppy, her eyes lighting up. "He was supposed to be at the protest to photograph it for the press."

"But he didn't show up until the next morning, looking considerably worse for wear," I concluded.

"And we know him and Leila didn't get along," said Poppy eagerly. "There was some serious tension there by all accounts."

"Not getting along is one thing, killing someone is a whole other level," pointed out Ailsa.

"True, but I at least want to know why he bailed on the protest, and if he's got an alibi," I said firmly.

"And I want to know a bit more about Leila," added Poppy. "Like, whether 'Smith' is her real surname, 'cause I've got some major doubts there."

"About that," said Ailsa. "I heard Jane on the phone this morning—they're having difficulty tracking down Leila's family. Seems pretty likely she's no Smith."

"In which case, who is she . . . ?" I mused. I was still sure Hen had recognized Leila's name, and was now even more determined to confront her about it. Then I remembered that Hen was mad at me for not mentioning the murder this morning—despite my best efforts.

"I forgot the start of a case is like this," said Poppy, her eyes gleaming. "So many unanswered questions!"

I was pleased to see a hint of Poppy's old enthusiasm, of course I was, but did it have to be kindled by the prospect of what I knew would involve situations of mild peril, awkward social encounters in the guise of "questioning suspects," and heavy disapproval at my involvement from Joe? Even Helen had been dragged in last time and Lord knows no one wanted that. And yet . . . Poppy's enthusiasm was a little contagious. I *did* want to know more about the mysterious Leila. Where—or more precisely who—had she been before she turned up at Earth Force six months ago? Who might have killed her and why?

"There's an Earth Force meeting at Maryam's tomorrow," said Ailsa. "We should go. I expect Raven and Sam will both be there, maybe we can get a few answers from them. Sensitively," she added hurriedly, seeing Poppy open her mouth.

"We said we'd go to soft play with Hen," I reminded her.

"The meeting's in the morning, we can meet Hen after," said Ailsa. "I mean, how long do you actually want to spend at soft play? After an hour I want to claw my eyes out."

"Agreed," said Poppy. "Come on, Alice. Let's just have a little poke around. This is what we do best!"

I wanted to argue that what we were *supposed* to be doing best was parenting. But it did feel like we'd done a *lot* of parenting of late. Maybe there was room for a . . . hobby? We were pretty much nailing the parenting already, right?

At this point Helen emerged from the undergrowth dripping with water and pondweed like some kind of swamp beast, terrifying the assembled toddlers out of five years of growth. It was probably time to go home.

IT WAS always a nervous ten minutes after I'd returned Arora to her pristine outfit in advance of Hen arriving to pick her up. Today, I'd opted for draping her with multiple tea towels while bribing her and Jack to sit still on the sofa with snacks—a cookie for Jack and a sugar-free pumpkin muffin for Arora (Hen provided Arora's snacks for the day as she, quite rightly, didn't trust me with this task).

As soon as I heard Hen's car outside, I whisked the tea towels and snacks away, grabbed the nearest book and planted it in Arora's hands.

"I've got time for one cup of tea while you explain this murder and how exactly you're involved this time." Hen swept past me into the house. She brushed some crumbs off a chair, inspected it, then laid a muslin over it before sitting down.

I didn't recall offering a cup of tea, and had really hoped that the job of "explaining this murder" would fall to Ailsa. Hen had made it abundantly clear in the past that my explanations of anything tended to lack detail, coherence, and basic sense.

"You know, I *did* try and tell you this morning." I thought I'd get in early with my defense. Hen gave me an arch look.

"It's been carnage at work today," she said, as if this were my fault. "The developers have had to be put on hold, PR are trying to keep the media at bay, the police aren't telling us *anything*."

"No, well, what do you expect from Inspector Harris," I said sympathetically, searching fruitlessly through the cupboard for an unstained mug.

"All we've been told is that one of the protestors, Leila, was murdered—strangled? And that no one has been arrested yet."

Was it just my imagination, or did Hen's voice falter over Leila's name?

"Well, that's pretty much it in a nutshell." I shrugged. "Everyone was chained to trees, apart from Norah, who had the keys. And I really can't see her strangling anyone. Poisoning some cookies, maybe, but nothing violent. It's all a bit of a mystery, really."

"And where were you in all this?"

It was as bad as being interrogated by Inspector Harris.

"Chained to a tree, same as everyone else." Not a sentence I'd ever expected to say.

Hen picked at her fingernails.

"So we're not involved this time," she said, not quite meeting my eye. "And I'd quite like to keep it that way. I can't afford to lose this job because my friends have gotten mixed up in something unsavory."

"That's one way to put it. Look, Hen, I don't know. Harris is going to want to talk to us, we won't be able to avoid that."

"Yes, but beyond that, there's no reason for any of you to get involved, right?"

She gave me a pleading look, which was so unusual for Hen I felt moved to try and reassure her.

"It's got nothing to do with your job. I expect it's got nothing to do with Aether—I mean, how could it? If companies went around murdering everyone who protested against them it'd be a bloodbath. It'll be something else—a lover's tiff, or money, or something like that."

Hen looked unconvinced.

"You didn't know Leila at all, did you?" I couldn't help asking as I placed Hen's tea in front of her.

"What? No!"

"It's just . . . you looked a bit surprised when she introduced herself the other day."

"Never met her in my life." Hen rubbed absently at a stain on the table.

"It won't come out," I offered. "It's beetroot."

"I didn't know you ate vegetables."

"Ha, ha. It wasn't me anyway, it was Jack. Or possibly Helen. And don't change the subject. What's the deal with Leila?"

Hen gave a sigh, but she knew I wasn't going to let this one drop.

"I don't know if it's the same Leila," she began. "And if it is . . . well, she must have had quite a change of heart."

I sipped eagerly on my tea and burned my mouth.

"Pah! Sorry. How so?"

"She used to do my job. She was Owen's PA at Aether."

I sat down abruptly.

"What now?" It looked like Aether had just re-entered the picture.

Hen fiddled with her teacup. "Have you tried white vinegar? Or salt and lemon?"

"What?"

"For the beetroot stain."

"We're not talking about the damn beetroot. Leila used to be Owen's PA? For how long? When did she leave? Why?"

Hen shrugged. "I don't know. I guess she must have left about six months ago, seeing as that's when I started? But there wasn't any handover, she'd already gone when I joined. I got the impression she left quite . . . abruptly. To be honest I think that's how I got the job so easily—I was available to start straightaway and they desperately needed to fill the role."

I should probably have said something reassuring at this point about Hen getting the job because she was the best candidate, but I was still processing this development.

"Was she fired?" I asked.

"I don't *think* so; I think she left of her own accord. But I assume she didn't work her notice, or they'd have had time to hire a replacement before she left. I don't know, it's all a bit murky."

At this point we were interrupted by Arora climbing onto her mum's lap and waving her book in Hen's face, trying to get her attention.

Hen lifted the booklet out of her daughter's hands and raised an eyebrow.

"*Ferret Housing and Husbandry: Captive Breeding of the Common Ferret*? Do I want to know why you even have this in the house?"

"It's educational?" I tried.

"Please, Alice, and I mean this sincerely," Hen sounded genuinely concerned, "do not get a ferret. You already have a Helen. I don't think any of us could take it."

"We are not getting a ferret," I said with dignity, taking the pamphlet back from her. "Joe picked it up at the farmer's market, I think he was just too polite to say no to the man handing them out. But we're getting off the subject—again." This happens a lot with babies in the mix—the ability to hold a conversation to the end is a little known and tragically uncelebrated art that you only appreciate when it has gone.

But Hen shook her head and stood up. "I'm sorry, Alice, I better get going. I want to make bean casserole for dinner, there's laundry needs doing, and it's bath night for Arora."

Of course children also provide an excellent alibi when you want to get out of an awkward conversation.

Hen scooped up Arora and marched out of the cottage to tackle an evening of parenting and chores with terrifying efficiency.

CHAPTER 10

"DO YOU ALWAYS drive like this?"

I was already regretting offering Ailsa a lift to the Earth Force meeting.

"Like what?"

"Like a granny who's forgotten her glasses."

"Would you rather walk?"

"It would probably be quicker."

It was possible she had a point. But the roads leading to Maryam's house had grown progressively narrower and twistier, the road appearing to sink as the banks rose on either side until the trees nearly met overhead. It gave the impression that we were driving into a fairy tale—one of the proper old fairy tales that is, before they were Disneyfied, all sinister forests and crones and some sort of twisted moral.

"I think it might have been the turning back there," offered Poppy from the back seat. "Sorry, my phone must've lost signal and Google Maps wasn't updating."

I huffed in frustration. "Well there's nowhere to turn around."

"Can't you just reverse?" This was Ailsa, whose back seat driving really was exceptional.

"The turning's only like two minutes back," said Poppy helpfully.

Slightly over half an hour later we backed slowly and stressfully into Maryam's drive, past a wonky sign declaring it "Fox Hollow," with a few new scratches and a nice big dent in my car.

"Nice house," commented Poppy, as I mournfully inspected my car's paintwork. I looked around.

It was nice, I suppose. In a higgledy-piggledy kind of way. We were in the yard of an old farmhouse. The main house occupied one side, and enclosing the yard on either side were what looked like an old converted stable block and a barn that wouldn't stand up to a stiff breeze. I noticed curiously that the glass of the final set of windows in the stable block had been painted black. Various rusting bits of farm machinery poking out of the barn suggested that this had once been a working farm, many eons ago. I guess it had a certain rustic charm, but mainly it made me wonder if I was up to date with my tetanus jab.

"Quaint," I offered weakly.

The door to the farmhouse was open—another countryside thing. Perhaps people felt that if a burglar had made the effort to navigate the treacherous lanes and lack of Google Maps, they at least deserved to be let in for a nice cup of tea. We let ourselves in.

The various members of Earth Force were gathered around the kitchen table and perched on various stools and mismatched chairs. Raven was holding forth. He looked like an Old Testament prophet, his hair wild, his eyes even wilder. His grief appeared to be channeled into ever greater heights of fanaticism.

"It's what Leila would have wanted," he was insisting. "She wouldn't want us to give up! She died for this cause! We have to honor that!"

There was some uncomfortable shuffling and clearing of throats.

"Do we actually know that?" one slightly braver soul piped up. I wasn't surprised to see it was Enderby. "I mean, we don't really know why she died, do we?"

"It was Aether!" thundered Raven. "It was those lying, greenwashing, murderous bastards!"

"I'm not saying it wasn't," replied Enderby calmly. "And when it comes to what Aether are capable of, very little would surprise me." For some reason, his eyes flickered over to where Norah stood by the sink. Or at least, I thought they did. Then he continued addressing Raven; perhaps I had just imagined it. "I'm just saying, how much did we really know about Leila?"

Raven appeared to choke on his own outrage. But I felt Enderby had a point. Of course, it could well be something to do with Aether—my rather awkward and confusing conversation with Hen had certainly raised some questions there. But it was quite a jump from some light greenwashing to murder. And I'd already seen enough of the Earth Force group to know there were plenty of tensions closer to home. There was Raven himself—it was *always* the boyfriend, and he did seem rather keen to point the finger at Aether. In fact, I recalled Enderby making the very same swift judgment call on Aether just hours after Leila was killed, yet now he seemed to be casting the net wider, which was interesting. Maryam had no great love for Leila; nor did Sam. Or then again it could be some hitherto unknown party with an as-yet unmentioned motive. In his haste to take action against Aether, Raven was jumping to conclusions faster than Inspector Harris. Not to mention that "dying for the cause" had a martyrish air that made me feel uncomfortable.

"It doesn't feel right," said a quiet voice. Several heads turned in surprise, looking for the speaker. It was Norah. She kept her head down, apparently addressing the kettle she was filling, but she had her say, nonetheless. "Using Leila's death as a . . . a . . . a weapon against Aether?" she continued. "It's indecent. She's barely been dead three days and you want to politicize her death?"

"And how many other deaths will there be if companies like Aether continue down these paths?" shot back Raven, his eyes practically glowing. "If we use it to take down those bastards then Leila's death will mean something."

"I agree," said Maryam quietly. "We can't let Leila's death have been in vain. Otherwise, what a waste . . . What a tragic waste . . ."

She broke off, a hand to her mouth. I was a little surprised by the display of emotion; she seemed a lot fonder of Leila in death than she had in life. But perhaps I was being uncharitable. Either way, Maryam's opinion seemed to settle the matter for the group, and they fell to discussing how best to publicize Leila's untimely demise.

I felt slightly nauseous. I had to agree with Norah on this matter. It felt . . . wrong, to capitalize on Leila's death like this. But then, I'd never had a "cause." I'd never felt so strongly about something that I might be tempted to fall into "end justifies the means" thinking. All I had was a firmly held conviction that most problems could be fixed with a snack, and a sneaking suspicion that dogs might be better than people. It wasn't exactly an ethos to live, or possibly die, by.

I shared an uneasy glance with Poppy and Ailsa, who appeared to be thinking along the same lines—well, maybe not the bit about snacks and dogs. Even Ailsa, who *did* have a social conscience, seemed to think this was a bit much. We hovered awkwardly on the edge of the group, trying not to get drawn into the discussion.

Unfortunately, we weren't allowed to get off quite so lightly. As the group discussed the legal ramifications of spray-painting MURDERERS across the gates of Aether headquarters—strongly endorsed by Raven; mildly disputed by Norah—Enderby turned to face us.

"And what do the newcomers think?"

Part of me felt nettled at being labeled the "newcomers"—OK fine, we'd been involved less than a week, but that week had involved chaining ourselves to trees, a murder, and very nearly adult diapers. Hadn't we earned even a smidgeon of kudos? Although it had to be said that in this instance I had very little to offer when it came to the finer points of UK libel law.

As ever, Ailsa stepped up. "Personally, I think it's too much." She shrugged. "And, like Norah said, I think you open yourselves up to all sorts of legal trouble. I think the focus should be on the criminal action we *know* Aether were taking in the destruction of the meadow—not speculation on something they may have had nothing to do with."

There were a few nods at Ailsa's words and the discussion broke down into warring factions: Raven and his coterie pressing for harder, more aggressive action, and Norah, Enderby, and a few others insisting he was going too far.

Eventually the group dispersed, with no particular consensus reached, but no one seemed to be making any moves to actually leave. A few people sauntered outside to enjoy the early summer sunshine, a few people disappeared into the depths of the house. Raven had slumped down on a chair by the empty hearth, his head in his hands, apparently now spent. Norah, unsurprisingly, was making yet more cups of tea. We wandered out into the yard and milled about uncertainly, unsure if it was OK to leave now. Seeing us dithering, Maryam came over, beaming, but in a slightly unfocused way. She looked a little frayed around the edges, her hair was disheveled and her overalls buttoned up wrong, although she did have a rather snazzy pair of gold laces in her ancient Doc Martens.

"Is the meeting over?" I asked uncertainly.

"I think so, for now," she said. "We might pick up again in a bit if people feel there's more to say. We're a very informal group," she added, seeing my confusion. "Feel free to stick around, have a cup of tea, chat to the rest of the group. Most people do."

She wandered off toward Raven and his coterie, throwing back over her shoulder, "Make yourselves at home. *Mi casa es su casa*."

"My house is your house," translated Ailsa helpfully.

"My parents do live in Spain," I replied, a little irritated. "And that's exactly the sort of shit they have on tea towels."

"How come they moved to Spain?" asked Poppy curiously. "Isn't your brother there, too?"

"Er, yeah, he is. It's a long story." I edged away from the question. "And I don't think I know all of it myself."

"We've got time," said Ailsa, settling herself comfortably on a piece of decomposing farm equipment.

"I'm not sure we have," corrected Poppy, nodding toward the door of the farmhouse. A girl with a cheerful expression, wearing denim shorts and a Greenpeace T-shirt, was coming over.

"Hi, I'm Sian," she said brightly. "Maryam said you were new to the group, so I thought I'd come say hi. Sorry I missed you all last week, I was away. I missed the protest and . . . well . . . everything."

Her sunny smile faltered at this, as we all contemplated the "everything" she had missed.

"You missed quite a week," observed Ailsa dryly.

"Tell me about it." She raised her eyebrows. "I still can't believe it . . ." She shook her head, looking troubled.

"Were you close to Leila?" asked Poppy gently.

Sian looked thoughtful. "Not really, to be honest. Her and Raven have their own following in the group, and I tend to keep out of that. I'm just here to do my bit, speak out against things that shouldn't be done. Speak up for things that should."

Ailsa nodded approvingly. "Same here."

"And Earth Force has done a huge amount of good," said Sian, slightly defiantly, as if we'd said something to the contrary. "Last year we persuaded the local council to fund solar installation for the primary school and library. It might be small, but these things make a difference."

"Massively," agreed Ailsa. "If more local groups were influencing decisions like that, the cumulative impact would be huge."

"That's exactly what I think," said Sian. "Local action has its role to play, for sure. There are so many issues that are best tackled on a local level. And that's what Earth Force is all about. Even if it's been a bit . . . single-minded of late."

"You don't agree with the focus on Aether?" I asked.

Sian shrugged. "I don't think the meadow should be destroyed. It seems completely unnecessary—surely there are other, less critical sites the wind farm could be built on. So yes, I think we should be protesting against it. But recently, some of the action we've been taking . . ." She broke off and looked back at the farmhouse. "That was all a bit intense in there, wasn't it?"

"Do you think they'll really use Leila's death to attack Aether?" I was still a bit shaken by the whole meeting.

Sian looked uneasy. "I don't know. I hope not. But the group's changed recently. It didn't used to be like this. It didn't used to be so . . . angry."

"What changed?" asked Poppy curiously.

Sian gave us a frank look. "In all honesty? Leila. Since she joined about six months ago, we started focusing more and more on Aether. Her and Raven, well, they're so determined to bring Aether down. It's like it's become a personal vendetta, when it's supposed to be about protecting the meadow."

"Looks like the meadow might be safe for now, at least," I said. "I'm assuming Aether won't be plowing in there any time soon, not while the investigation's still ongoing."

"Yeah," she said, nodding. "Fingers crossed. If I'm honest with you, I don't think the wind farm would be the end of the world. I mean I'd definitely prefer it not to be built on the meadow! But, I don't know, I'm just not sure it's the battle we should be fighting right now."

This was practically rebel talk in Earth Force territory. I opened my mouth to make a probably ill-advised joke about this, but Sian glanced over my shoulder and cut in. “I should head off. I’ll see you guys around. Thanks for joining up!” She gave a slightly forced smile and hurried away. I looked round to see what had caused her abrupt departure.

Raven was making his way toward us with his usual intense expression.

CHAPTER 11

RAVEN LOOKED LIKE he hadn't slept since Wednesday. Or, quite possibly, showered. His eyes were sunken, with a worrying gleam in their depths.

"I, *we're*, so sorry about Leila," I faltered. It felt so inadequate.

"They won't get away with it," was his slightly alarming response.

"You mean Aether?" I asked.

"Of course. Who else?"

"Er . . ." *You? Your brother?* It didn't seem a tactful thing to say.

"Did you know she used to work for Aether?" That probably wasn't tactful either but it was Ailsa asking, and she usually got away with these things.

"Of course," said Raven, looking rather taken aback by the question. "That's why she joined us—she grew disillusioned with the company, with Myers, so she quit and found us."

Poppy shot Ailsa a disapproving glare.

"Are you OK?" she asked. "Do you have someone staying with you? Your brother?"

"Ha!" Raven gave a humorless laugh. "Sam disappeared back to London yesterday. He's got a big art show next week." He scowled. I was surprised—when Sam had arrived on the scene on Thursday, Raven had seemed to be his first priority. But this chimed with what Leila had said to me about Sam at the protest meeting the previous week—maybe even his brother had to take a back seat to his art.

"You shouldn't be on your own," said Poppy, sounding concerned.

"Oh, I'm not," said Raven. "Yam's always here, and there are normally a few people from Earth Force knocking around. Believe me, it's hard to be on your own here."

"You live here?" I asked, surprised.

"On and off, yes," said Raven. "Yam is my aunt. But when I say aunt . . . she more or less brought Sam and me up after our mother died."

"I'm so sorry to hear that," said Poppy.

Raven nodded gravely. "Thank you. I have to be honest, I barely remember her. I was only five when she passed away. It was worse for Sam, he was eight at the time."

I suppressed a shudder. I couldn't bear the thought that if, God forbid, something were to happen to me or Joe, now or even in the next few years, Jack would barely remember us. It seemed inconceivable; we were his whole world, and he ours.

"What about your dad?" asked Ailsa.

"He passed away a couple of years ago. But, to be honest, we didn't see so much of him growing up. He fell apart a bit after Mum died, and that was when Yam stepped in. She's his sister. So yeah, I live here most of the time, and Sam is in and out. He's mainly up in London these days—reckons his photography career's about to kick off and, well, it's probably not going to kick off down here . . ."

"I don't know," objected Ailsa. "The Cotswolds have produced a fair few artists."

Raven nodded vehemently. "That's what I told him! But he's very invested in the London scene."

"Is that where he was on Wednesday night?" I asked cautiously, not wanting to sound like I was probing.

"He said he had a meeting with a potential agent, to represent his photography, and it turned into an all-night session."

"So he just bailed on the protest?" This seemed a bit of a poor show to me, but Raven just shrugged.

"Sam's very ambitious. He's desperate to secure an agent to land him the bigger commissions. He'll get there, I'm sure—have you seen his work? He's incredibly talented. But he's not particularly patient, he wants it all to happen now."

"Still . . ."

But Raven just shrugged. "What's going to get him noticed—a few photos on a protest website? Or a London agent? And when it comes down to it, he wants the same things as us. He's part of an artists' collective in London, all geared toward environmental activism. He's fighting the same fight as us, he's just taking a different route."

Sam sounded like an interesting character. I'd barely met him—once when Helen was harassing him for a cheese sandwich and once when he'd just found out his brother's girlfriend had been murdered. It's not really enough to form an opinion on a guy.

"So you live here on the farm?" Ailsa was asking with interest.

"In the stable block," said Raven, nodding toward the converted outbuilding. With a lick of paint, maybe some potted plants, and a crane to remove all the rusting farm machinery, it would have looked just like the quaint Airbnbs that the Cotswolds have in such abundance. As it was, it looked just about habitable.

"What's with the blackout?" I asked, nodding toward the painted windows at the end of the block.

Raven looked over. "Oh, that's Sam's darkroom." He caught my blank expression. "For photography."

"Oh." I was surprised. "Isn't photography all digital these days?"

Raven scoffed slightly. "Proper photographers still work with film and develop in their own darkrooms. It's an art."

I didn't disagree, although I reckoned there were a fair few "proper" digital photographers out there who would have done.

"Wow, a darkroom!" said Poppy enthusiastically. "I've always wanted to see one!"

I shot her a skeptical look. Had she, really? I could read her overly innocent face like a book and knew what was coming next.

"I don't suppose we could have the teeniest look inside?" she asked beseechingly. "I'd love to see how it's done—*properly*, you know."

Raven looked uncertain. "Sam's not here . . ." he began.

"Just the smallest peek?" Poppy persisted. "I saw his photos on the protest website and they were amazing. I'd love to see the process behind it." She looked so very earnest. She was good at that.

Raven wavered—and gave in.

"OK, a super quick look. The main door is locked and Sam has the key, but there's a door from my room."

We followed him into the stable block, which turned out to be a large single room that formed a sort of studio apartment, with a small kitchenette at one end.

"'Scuse the mess," he said curtly.

It was pretty bad—and as a high-level mess-maker I felt extremely qualified to judge. The place looked like Helen and Jack had been through it, and I do not say that lightly. The bed was not made (which I fully accept as standard practice), clothes and general detritus were strewn across all possible surfaces—and when I say general detritus, it's because I don't really know how to classify it. There were feathers stuffed in jam jars, an old ice-cream tub filled with what could have been moss, and what looked like a fox's skull, alongside the more usual stacks of books and sketch pads, a couple of placards leaning against the wall and, unexpectedly, a full-size, golden shop mannequin, wearing a tattered sequined waistcoat and a dusty fez. It was the kind of room you want to explore but in great trepidation of what you might actually find.

Raven ushered us through quickly, as if in the hope that, seen at a blur, the room might look more acceptable. He pulled open another door at the far end of the room, kicking aside a taxidermy badger that had taken up residence as a doorkeeper, and stepped back.

"There's not much space," Raven said, hovering in the doorway. "I'll just be—" He gestured to the landslide behind him.

We could hear Raven in the room next door, shoving clothes in drawers, piling crockery and straightening bedsheets. Then we turned to view the space we had just entered.

The darkroom was . . . dark. I know, Captain Obvious here. But I mean, creepily so. A lamp in the corner, the bulb painted over in red, saturated the room in a blood-tinted hue. The benches around the walls were covered in bottles of chemicals and trays, and littered with developed or semi-developed images that looked ghost-like in the strange light. There were two large, stained farmhouse sinks that looked more sinister than sinks should. More photos hung on strings across the room like mad bunting, so we had to duck to get inside. In the corner sat a weird machine like a giant mounted egg; I'd love to be more specific but I had literally no idea what it was.

"So this is a darkroom . . ." said Poppy.

Ailsa flicked a print with her finger, setting the whole string of images dancing disconcertingly. "Yep. You always wanted to see one, so now you know . . ."

"You know why I said that," said Poppy in an undertone. "Quick, have a poke around. Quietly."

"What for?" I hissed under my breath.

"Anything interesting," was her suitably vague reply. Great.

I ducked under another string of photos and turned to view them. The naked bodies of Leila and Raven swung inches from my face.

"I don't think we should be doing this," I said awkwardly. "It's like naked photos and stuff."

"Oh that's just the photos he took for the protest site," said Ailsa glancing over. "Come on, Alice, don't be a prude."

"Yours and my ideas of 'prude' are very different," I said archly, moving away from the swinging photos and over to the corkboard on the wall opposite, which looked like it contained more receipts and fewer nudes. Then I paused.

"Guys," I said. "Look at this."

I reached out and unpinned a folded over piece of paper paper-clipped to a strip of photo negatives—something I hadn't seen since I was about ten years old. But, more importantly, on the paper was scribbled "For Leila."

Poppy and Ailsa popped up, like the devil and angel on each of my shoulders (hard to say who was which).

"Read it then," urged Poppy.

I unfolded the paper. There were only a few lines scribbled on it.

> They're yours. Take them, burn them, whatever—I don't care.
> I haven't made copies. Now leave me alone. And if you could
> leave my brother alone too that would be a bonus.
>
> S.

"Take what? Burn what?" I flipped the paper over but there was nothing more written there.

"The negatives, dummy," said Ailsa, grabbing the strip of celluloid. "What's on them . . ." She held the strip up to the red light, but its glow was so dim and the pictures were so tiny there was no making anything out. Ailsa swore in frustration.

"Here." Poppy whipped out her phone and flicked the torch on, trying to angle it so we could get a glimpse of the tiny windows. But just then the door behind us scraped open. Ailsa flung the note and negatives onto the desk behind us—there was no time to re-pin them.

"Seen everything you want to see?" Raven peered round the door, blinking in the gloom.

"Yes, yes. He's taken some lovely pictures of you and Leila," I gabbled, gesturing at the prints, before remembering that they were nudes and that this could be perceived as a slightly weird comment. But Raven gave me a look of solemn gratitude.

"He really captured what we were trying to achieve." He pulled down one of the photos, of Leila hip-deep in meadow grass, hands on waist, staring straight into the camera in a defiant, powerful gesture. It was actually a pretty striking photo. Raven evidently thought so too. He pressed it to his forehead in a gesture I would usually have dismissed as melodramatic, but which was clearly heartfelt, then slipped it into his pocket.

"You must miss her a lot," said Poppy gently.

Raven looked almost surprised at the comment. "Miss her?" he said, as if trying to understand Poppy's words. "No," he said shaking his head slightly. "No, I don't miss her. Not yet. It doesn't feel as if she's gone. I just assume she'll appear at the door any minute now, or text me with a new idea for the campaign." He looked down at the silent phone in his hand. "Any minute now . . ."

Poppy tentatively laid a hand on his arm.

"I'm so so sorry," she said gently.

Raven turned to look at her. "Yeah. Me too," he said gruffly. Then he stepped to the side, one hand extended toward the open door—a clear invitation for us to leave. I cast a half glance at the negatives lying on the table behind us—so close! But Raven was watching, waiting for us to vacate the darkroom, and I couldn't think of a single good excuse for pocketing them. Reluctantly, I turned and left.

"Did Leila stay here much?" I couldn't help asking as we made our way back through the pit of Raven's room.

"No," he replied. "We tended to stay at her place." He paused and seemed to wilt slightly. "I'll need to go over and collect my stuff. The police said they're finished at her apartment. I just can't—" He broke off.

"I'm so sorry," I stumbled. "I didn't mean to—"

"I can't imagine how hard that will be," Poppy said quietly. "Is there someone who can go with you? Sam or Maryam?"

Raven shook his head. "Sam won't be able to spare the time, not with his exhibition next week." There was an edge of bitterness to his voice that I fully understood. It seemed a little selfish of Sam to be putting his exhibition ahead of supporting his grieving brother. The tiny cynical voice that lives inside my head but is definitely not me piped up, *Unless Sam's got something to hide, unless he's got another reason for staying away . . .*

"Maryam?" asked Poppy.

Raven gave a short, humorless laugh. "She and Leila didn't exactly see eye to eye."

My ears pricked up. I'd gathered as much from the way the two of them had interacted at the first meeting we'd attended, but hearing Raven say it out loud was another matter.

"Oh? Why not?" I asked, super casually (I hoped).

Raven sighed. "They were just very different people."

"I know we've only just met you," said Poppy softly, "but would you like us to come along and help you?"

My eyebrows shot up at that. Raven seemed equally perplexed.

"Er, no, it's OK," he mumbled. "That's kind of you, but . . ."

"You shouldn't be doing it by yourself," Poppy insisted. "Facing that alone, without support."

"Really it's . . . that's very kind of you, but . . ."

"We'll just be there if you need us, otherwise we'll keep out of your way," she persisted. When Poppy was on a roll it was like being bulldozed by a fluffy cloud.

"I suppose so," said Raven uncertainly. "I was going to go tomorrow, so it's a bit short notice . . ."

"We can meet you there tomorrow morning, really it's no problem."

I watched Raven scribble down an address for Poppy, looking slightly bewildered, as if unsure why he'd agreed to this. I could sympathize entirely.

I fought the urge to put my face in my hands. Good God. Here we go again.

CHAPTER 12

SOFT PLAY IS where you go when you need to low-level parent for a couple of hours. The clue's in the name—everything is soft and therefore safe. Baby-proof. Although not quite adult-proof; I had once received a friction burn going down one of the slides, and Joe had twisted his ankle quite badly in the ball pit. But broadly speaking you could insert the babies into the under-twos play area—fully netted on all sides, padded floor, assorted soft and non-hazardous toys scattered around—get a cup of coffee and sit in a near-catatonic state in the café, which was right next to the play area should your child attempt to do themselves some damage with a giant foam banana.

"What's in that?" asked Hen, looking at the mound of whipped cream and golden sprinkles on my coffee when we met her there that afternoon.

"Extra shot of espresso for the caffeine, vanilla syrup for the sugar, cream for the calories," I explained.

"What are the sprinkles?"

"I think they're just pure sugar?"

Caffeine and sugar had become the columns holding up my shaky sanity. The first coffee I'd had, after nine months of caffeine deprivation, had hit me like a ton of cocaine. But I'd been intrigued and then saddened to see how quickly my caffeine resistance had built up again, battling as it was against the chronic sleep deprivation of parenthood.

Hen peered anxiously through the netting to where Arora was patiently building a tower of (soft) blocks, which Ivy and Robin were then knocking down. Arora seemed quite happy with the arrangement so we left them to it. Jack and Noah were in a corner giggling over a not particularly funny ball.

"So," said Hen, settling back and looking at us. "How was the meeting this morning?"

"Tense," said Poppy.

"Unsurprisingly," said Hen dryly. "Given that one of their members was just murdered."

"Yeah, that came up a fair bit," I agreed.

"What did they have to say about it?" asked Hen. "I don't suppose any of them confessed to it?"

This was awkward. "Well, no, not exactly. I suppose they're more of the opinion that . . . Aether did it?"

"Oh for God's sake," exploded Hen. "What on earth would Aether have to gain by killing one of the protestors?"

"That's what we thought," said Poppy soothingly. "Look, I think they're all just upset, and on edge. I'm sure no one *really* thinks Aether are behind it."

I wasn't so sure about that, but tried to smile reassuringly nonetheless.

"Who do you think did it?" asked Hen bluntly.

I pondered this briefly.

"Well. The boyfriend is the usual suspect, which would mean Raven," I said. "Although that would mean he'd somehow unchained himself in the middle of the night, slipped round the tree and killed Leila, and then chained himself back up."

"Not impossible," pointed out Ailsa.

"No, not impossible," I agreed, "but pretty damn close. And quite risky. Also, do we have a motive for him?"

"No motive yet," said Poppy. "When it comes to that, the only vague suggestion of a motive we have is Sam."

"Who didn't like Leila and had had some kind of falling-out with her," I filled in. "Plus he didn't show up that night."

"We need to speak to this agent he was supposedly with," said Poppy. "Establish his alibi."

I fidgeted with my elaborate coffee. "Need is a strong word," I mumbled. "I mean, we don't *need* to talk to them. We could leave it to the police."

"Very true," said Hen. "That's very mature of you, Alice." She gave me an approving nod. It felt slightly patronizing and if anything made the weather vane of my emotions swing back toward the idea of investigating.

Poppy was looking stricken. "Come on, Alice," she pleaded. "You can't be serious. You want to spend the last few weeks of mat leave on *this*?" She gestured dismissively at the mayhem of toddlers, assorted garish plastic food items, and giant squashy emojis surrounding us.

Ailsa gave me a pointed look, and I knew she was thinking about our brief conversation at forest school the other day. The prospect of an investigation seemed to have brought Poppy out of whatever pit she'd been descending into. Was I really going to turn my back on that? And, I supposed, what harm could a few questions do? There was no law against asking questions. Was there? If there was, Harris would have us for breakfast. Gah, what was the *right* thing to do?

I realized the others were watching me, as if I held the final vote over our fledgling investigation. This seemed far too much responsibility for the likes of me—they'd be better off asking Helen.

"We don't even know the name of the agent," I demurred.

"We could find out." Poppy shrugged.

I sighed, and folded like a wet tissue. "We could find out," I agreed. "Raven or Maryam will probably know."

Poppy's face broke into a delighted smile. And seeing that was—probably—worth the upcoming tribulations of a seriously sleep-deprived and incredibly amateurish investigation. I took a fortifying mouthful of intensely sweet coffee and prepared to engage.

"What I want to know, is what was on those negatives in Sam's darkroom," I mused. "Obviously something Leila didn't want Sam to have, even though they were photos he'd taken. Was that what they fell out over?"

"We should've nicked them," said Ailsa. "Got them developed ourselves."

"I know, I thought about it at the time," Poppy said, frustratedly. "But Raven was watching us like a hawk."

I snorted. Poppy looked at me questioningly.

"Sorry," I said. "But Raven—hawk. Mixing your birds there."

I was trying to line up a joke about "Hen," but the caffeine was warring against the sleep deprivation in my brain and giving me nothing. Besides, I suspected Hen would beat me to death with a foam sausage.

"So," I coughed. "The photos could have been . . . incriminating somehow?"

"More nudes?" suggested Poppy.

"I don't see why that would be a problem," I pointed out. "She'd voluntarily posed for a load of nude shots with him."

"There's nudes and there's *nudes*," said Ailsa darkly.

"What are you talking about?" burst out Hen. "Honestly, it's bad enough you've all joined this group without me, and against my express wishes I might add, but if you're going to talk in code like this the whole time I'm going to have find myself some new friends to hang out with!"

I started guiltily; we hadn't meant to make Hen feel left out, but it was inevitable in some ways. It had begun back when Hen had had to take a job while the rest of us still had six months of maternity leave to spend in each other's company—our new involvement in Earth Force was only making matters worse.

We all began talking over each other, trying to fill Hen in, when Ailsa nodded toward the play pit.

"I think Jack's escaped by the way."

What the . . . The little Houdini had somehow wriggled underneath the floor-to-ceiling netting and made his way determinedly into the two-plus arena, which contained such deadly hazards as slides, tunnels, and nets and was only to be attempted with the supervision of a competent adult—or failing that, an incompetent one.

I don't know why soft plays weren't built on an adult scale, because there are always a minimum of ten adults in there, trying to coax nervous toddlers along wobbly walks, or rescuing over-adventurous children hanging upside down by their ankles in the climbing nets.

Jack was disappearing into a tunnel that I could probably squirm along on my stomach. I snagged him by one ankle and hauled him back out as he shrieked with delight. I had to admire his adventurous spirit. I wasn't quite sure where he got it from, possibly Helen.

"So I was just saying, Jane managed to contact Leila's family at last," Ailsa said conversationally when I rejoined the group, having deposited Jack safely in the ball pit with Arora, whom I felt could be trusted to put a stop to any further escape plans.

"Oh yes?"

"Yeah, she wouldn't say much about them, which was annoying, but you know—Jane. Anyway, she did let slip that none of the family came down for the formal identification yesterday."

I immediately lost interest in my cold and sugary coffee and turned to stare at Ailsa.

"They didn't even come to identify her body?" I asked, shocked. I wasn't exactly close with my family, and they did live in another country, but I hoped one of them would at least manage a Ryanair flight to identify my body. "Isn't that like a legal obligation or something?"

Ailsa shrugged. "Dunno. Anyway someone did come to identify her but he was a business manager or something, no relation at all."

"A business manager? What does that even mean?" I wondered aloud.

"Someone who manages business?" offered Poppy.

"Thanks, genius." I flicked a glob of whipped cream at her. "It's a bit weird though, isn't it? I mean, either she was super close to this manager, or that's super cold of her family . . ."

"Some families are like that," said Hen. "Look at Antoni's family." This was true, after a family tragedy over a decade ago, Hen's husband Antoni had barely spoken to his family; Hen had only ever met her in-laws twice.

"True, but there's normally a reason behind it," I pointed out. "And it's definitely starting to feel like there's something a bit off about Leila's background."

"Did you find out her real surname?" Poppy asked, but Ailsa shook her head.

"Jane didn't say, and she took all the papers with her when she went out. I checked her office."

"Unbelievable." We really relied on Ailsa's access to her sister's office at home, although Jane Harris was such a neat freak she often left us frustrated.

"What name did she use at Aether?" I asked Hen.

"Leila Smith." Hen shrugged. "I guess they didn't look too closely into hiring her."

This seemed a little slapdash to me—not that I'm known for my professional rigor—but I wondered under what circumstances Leila had joined the company.

"Maybe we'll find something at her apartment tomorrow," said Poppy hopefully.

I hoped so. The beginning of a mystery felt so laden with unanswered questions it was hard to know where to begin. But I was finding myself more and more intrigued by the enigmatic Leila. Who *was* she?

Ailsa jerked her head toward the playpen. "Jack's gone again."

I sighed and braced myself for another entry into the toddler pit of doom.

CHAPTER 13

WE MET RAVEN at Leila's apartment early the next morning. First impressions: it was a hell of a lot nicer than I'd expected. Between Raven's single-room pit and Leila's position as an as-far-as-we-knew unemployed ex-PA, I'd been expecting something pretty modest. But no, Leila had occupied the penthouse apartment in one of the fancy converted warehouses down by the canal. One of the apartments had been up for rent when Joe and I first moved to the area. We hadn't even bothered viewing it—ostensibly because Helen wasn't suited to apartment living, but in reality because until one of us inherited a small fortune from a long-lost aunt the monthly rent would have crippled us.

How had Leila ended up with the closest thing Bishop's Ruin offered to *Selling Sunset*? Oh, she'd tried to play down its more luxe aspects—she'd hung batik throws and shabby slogan posters on the walls, shoved candles in empty wine and gin bottles, she'd even spray-painted a huge melting earth across one wall of the sitting room. It was like a carefully designed set for a film: "Set 14: Activist B's home." But with a few overlooked errors. When I tweaked aside one multicolored throw on the wall it revealed an enormous TV. The appliances in the kitchen were all so fancy I didn't even recognize the brands (I am very much in the "Kenwood is aspirational" social class): one of those juicers with the oranges rolling down a chute that you only see in cafés; a coffee machine more hi-tech than my laptop; a glass-fronted fridge. Ooh, actually that last one was less pleasant—you should only have one of these if you literally live in a home decor magazine and subsist on bottled mineral water and lemons. And no one had thought to empty Leila's after it became evident she wouldn't be needing the contents anymore. I suppose it didn't really fall into the police's remit. Who empties the fridges of the deceased?

Raven was standing helplessly in the middle of the sitting room.

"Do you want a hand getting your stuff together, or would you rather we gave you some space?" asked Poppy gently.

Raven shook his head slightly. "It's OK, I can do it. I'll, er, I'll just . . . I guess I'll start in the bedroom."

He drifted through a bead curtain (which looked very out of place) into what was presumably the bedroom. We sprang into action as the beads rattled behind him—well, Poppy and Ailsa did. Poppy disappeared into the bathroom and Ailsa began opening kitchen cupboards. I hung around uncertainly on the rug until Ailsa hissed at me to "get looking," then I sidled toward the bookcase and began half-heartedly pawing at books. I found this aspect of detecting (or whatever the hell we were doing—poking our noses in mainly) intensely awkward. I would never get used to the feeling of invading someone's private life when they weren't there to protect it. I shook myself—I didn't *need* to get used to it. We weren't private detectives, or any sort of detectives! I shoved Leila's battered paperback of *How to Be a Woman* back onto the shelf and turned determinedly, about to tell Poppy and Ailsa, in no uncertain terms, that what we were doing was wrong and we had to stop. However, at this moment, Poppy poked her head out of the bathroom.

"Have a look at this," she said.

Morals be damned, the familiar adrenaline rush swept through me and I hurried over.

"Have you found a clue?" I asked eagerly.

Ailsa rolled her eyes. "For God's sake Alice, clues only exist in those awful ITV crime dramas you watch."

I ignored her.

"Well?"

Poppy was gesturing to the open vanity cabinet in the bathroom. It looked pretty similar to every vanity cabinet I'd ever seen: a jumble of half-used products along with the unopened bath bombs and rose-scented hand creams that your mother gives you for Christmas every year. (Except my mother. Last year she had sent me a Botox voucher accompanied by a Christmas card "to a loving son.")

"What exactly are we looking at?" I asked, feeling slightly disappointed. "It's just face cream and stuff, isn't it?"

"Yes," agreed Poppy. "But it's not just any face cream. I reckon the contents of this cabinet cost as much as your car." She paused, no doubt recollecting the bone-rattling journey to Maryam's in my car. "Make that *more* than your car."

She started sifting through. "La Prairie, Guerlain, Barbara Sturm, La Mer, Chanel—"

"Oh Chanel I know!" I interrupted, delighted to have recognized *one* brand. "Never heard of any of the others."

"Good," said Ailsa tersely. "They're morally corrupt corporations and most of them have a horrible impact on the environment."

"Which begs the question," said Poppy slowly, "what are they doing in the bathroom of an ardent climate activist?"

I picked up a minuscule tub of face lotion and had a little dab. It felt rich and oily and expensive.

"Don't do that," hissed Ailsa.

I didn't see why not, but put it back anyway, knocking over several other bottles as I did so. Ailsa rolled her eyes and left the bathroom. I set the various bottles and tubs upright again, having the odd sniff or dab of them as I went, now that Ailsa had left. They were all heavy, ceramic or glass, unlike my own battered plastic bottle of Simple face moisturizer that was my sole concession to a skincare regime these days.

"I'm guessing this is the one she carried around with her though," I said, holding up a battered old Green & Free moisturizer bottle that proclaimed itself "cruelty-free and vegan." "Fits with the whole eco warrior persona a bit better."

"Probably decanted one of her fancy lotions into it," said Poppy cynically.

I had a little sniff and wrinkled my nose; it smelt sour and unappealing. "Don't think so," I said, pulling a face. "This is the real cheap deal."

We returned to the main room in a thoughtful silence and recommenced our search with slightly more purpose. Looking, I suppose, for more anomalies. I had barely pulled open a drawer, however, when the bead curtain clattered and we all jumped guiltily into the center of the room, hands shoved in our pockets. Raven emerged from the bedroom clutching a duffel bag and looking slightly red-eyed.

"I'm going to have a cigarette." He gestured to some French windows behind gauzy curtains which I presumed, given we were on the third floor, led to a balcony. He stepped through.

"Go with him," I hissed, pushing Ailsa toward the curtains.

"What! Why? I hate smoking. And he looks like he might cry!" The redoubtable Ailsa looked positively terrified at this last prospect.

"Keep him occupied while we—" I nodded toward Leila's bedroom door.

"Can't you—"

"Nope. Talk to him about activist stuff. You know, the ozone layer and"—I waved my hands vaguely—"stuff like that."

Ailsa just had time to roll her eyes at me before I virtually pushed her through the curtains.

Poppy and I made a dash for the bedroom.

It was the same story in here. On the surface, it was the bedroom of someone who cared deeply about the environment. Above the bed was a huge Just Stop Oil sign. On her bedside table was a well-thumbed copy of *This Is Not a Drill*, the Extinction Rebellion handbook (Ailsa had given me a copy, but I confess I was yet to read it because I was scared). But when I opened the wardrobe and began leafing through, in among the obvious charity shop finds was the odd item that I didn't even need Poppy to tell me were very expensive indeed.

"Some pretty nice designer bits in here," I called from the depths of the wardrobe.

"And look at these." Poppy shuffled out from under the bed clutching a pair of white slip-on slippers.

"They don't look very fancy to me," I objected. They looked like the free ones you get at . . . ohhh, at the spa.

"Gilpin Spa," I read on them. "I'm guessing that's a pretty fancy spa . . ."

Poppy tapped on her phone then held it up, showing the Gilpin Spa web page.

"From £485 per room per night . . ." I read aloud. "Yeah that's no Travelodge."

From outside we heard Ailsa saying, too loudly, "Well, we should probably make a move then," and dived out of the bedroom just as Ailsa and Raven re-entered the sitting room. Raven's eyes slid to the swaying, clattering bead curtain. *Damn*. Who has bead curtains in this day and age?

"Do you think you have all your stuff?" Poppy asked into the awkward silence.

Raven hefted his duffel bag. "I guess," he said uncertainly. He looked unwilling to leave, however.

"Do you want to take a minute?" asked Poppy gently.

Raven shrugged helplessly. "It's just . . . weird. I guess I won't be coming back here."

We all made vague, sympathetic noises.

"Had she lived here long?" asked Poppy, still in the softened voice that people adopt when speaking to the recently bereaved.

"About a year," said Rowan, running a hand along the back of the sofa.

"Where did she live before?" Ailsa asked.

"She moved around a lot," he replied, shrugging slightly. "I don't know, she said she'd never really settled anywhere. But she . . . she liked it here. She was going to stay." There was a slight catch in his voice.

We all nodded sympathetically, tamping down any private skepticism.

"It's a really nice apartment," I said carefully.

Raven looked around as if he'd only just noticed. "I suppose it is."

"Did Leila own it, or rent?" I asked, eyeing up the spray-painted wall.

Again, Raven shrugged. "I don't know. We never really discussed it." He seemed to wake up slightly, and looked at me with a little more focus. "Why do you ask?"

"Just interested." I tried to sound casual—and almost certainly failed. "We moved here a year ago too, and we're still renting, I guess I was just wondering what the property market's like here. Oh God, I'm not saying we'd buy her place, that's too creepy. Not creepy, I mean, I just don't want to sound as though I'm . . . Anyway we have a dog so apartments are pretty much out."

I could see Ailsa and Poppy staring at me in horror as I rambled incoherently about the local property market.

"Shall we go for coffee?" I asked brightly.

We left in the kind of awkward silence only my inappropriate commentary could have brought on. But even so, as Raven locked up behind us, I couldn't help myself: "Someone really should empty that fridge."

CHAPTER 14

RAVEN HAD DECLINED to go for a coffee; I suspected he wanted rid of us—I would've done the same if I were him. He had thanked us politely for accompanying him to Leila's apartment, and told us the funeral was due to take place on Wednesday, up in London. We weren't sure if this constituted an invitation, or if he was just telling us the facts.

We'd collected Hen for a dog walk in the woods. We had extended the invite to Lin and Joe, but after a morning of baby-watching they'd opted to wait for us at the Cross Keys with a pint, while we relieved them of baby duty for an hour.

As I pulled up at the woods, Poppy was already waiting with Noah strapped to her front and Ronnie thrashing about on the end of his lead like a dying fish.

"No Sultan?" I asked as Helen caught sight of Ronnie and plastered herself against the rear windscreen.

"He's at the pub with Lin; two dogs and a baby is too much, especially when one of them is Ronnie."

This was extremely wise. I found one dog and one baby quite enough to cope with. I released Helen from the trunk and made no attempt to restrain her as she threw herself on Ronnie. When Ailsa and Hen drew up minutes later, Ronnie was enthusiastically humping Helen, while Poppy and I covered the babies' eyes.

"Do they have to do that?" protested Hen as she climbed out of the car.

"Yes, yes I think they do," I replied. "Nature and all that. Look it only lasts a few seconds anyway."

This was true; the dogs were already done and hastening into the woods to find something gross to roll in. The romantic life of dogs is truly a thing of wonder. We followed them at a more sedate pace, barely encumbered by the babies strapped to our fronts. I enjoyed walking with Jack in his baby carrier, even though he now weighed nearly as much as me, according to my aching back. It felt almost like we were one person again, which now seemed six thousand years in the past (and in all honesty was not a phase of my life I'd particularly like to return to). But I loved the physical closeness with Jack and the sense of wholeness that it brought with it.

The woods were also blissfully cool, and it was a relief not to have to re-suncream the babies every thirty seconds. Everyone seemed affected by the stillness and tranquility, as though the cloud of harassedness that perpetually followed us had been left back at the cars. Even the babies were quiet, with the exception of the odd bird-like chirrup that Jack made when he was content.

"How was it at Leila's apartment this morning?" Hen asked. She sounded both slightly grudging, and at the same time genuinely curious—like she couldn't help asking for updates despite disapproving of our involvement in the case.

"Weird," I replied. We filled Hen in on Leila's mysteriously swanky pad.

"So Leila was rich." Hen shrugged. "Is that a big deal?"

"Not exactly," Poppy admitted. "It just doesn't quite fit with what we know about her. And she'd made these sort of half-hearted attempts to hide the fact that she had money."

"Loads of people do that," argued Hen.

"That's true," I agreed. "But I do think there's a bit of a question mark over where the money was coming from. It wasn't from work—she didn't get another job after she left Aether, according to Raven. So did it come from someplace it shouldn't . . . ?"

"Or from her family," countered Hen.

"But if it was just from her family, why be so secretive about it?" Poppy asked.

"People from rich families are always trying to hide their wealth," supplied Ailsa. "They're embarrassed because they didn't do anything to earn it."

"Yeah, so maybe there's nothing unusual about that," I conceded. "Although there is something weird going on with Leila's family. Like, why did she use a fake surname? And how come none of them even showed up to identify her body? I want to know who they are."

"Like, they might be famous?" offered Hen.

"Mafia?" chipped in Ailsa.

"Royalty?" I suggested.

Hen snorted with laughter, although I'd only been half joking. It was good to see her joining in with the conversation though—she seemed a lot happier to discuss the case now that attention seemed to be shifting away from Aether and toward Leila herself.

At this point the conversation was truly derailed by the return of Helen and Ronnie—and a small fluffy white dog that they appeared to have stolen. The dog kept trying to turn back but Helen and Ronnie were always there, urging it forward.

"Your dogs are bullies," observed Hen.

"I think bullies is a bit harsh, they're just bad influences," I defended them.

The owner of the fluffy white dog appeared through the undergrowth. "Fenella! Fenella! Come!"

This man was bucking every dog-looks-like-its-owner trend. He was well over six foot and powerfully built, wearing hard-worn overalls splattered with oil, and looked like he should own a wolfhound.

"Sorry, I think our dogs dognapped yours," I apologized, hastening to put Helen on a lead—or trying at least. She danced backward, staying always just an arm's length away. Jack found this hilarious.

The man merely grunted, scooping Fenella up in a single bear-paw hand and hurrying away from the terrible influence of our dogs, picking bits of fern out of Fenella's fluffy white tail as he went. Helen and Ronnie stared soulfully down the path after their lost playmate.

"Cheerful guy," remarked Poppy.

"Your dogs did steal his dog," pointed out Hen.

I looked at Helen in despair. "What am I going to do when I actually have to parent?" I wondered aloud. "I can't even keep a dog under control. What if Jack starts stealing children from the playground?"

"You might have been OK with a normal dog," commented Ailsa, which felt like both a compliment and an insult simultaneously.

"And what do you mean, when you have to parent?" demanded Hen. "What are you doing at the moment?"

"You know, when they're older," I tried to explain. "At this age it's more just sort of keeping them alive, fed, and clean-ish. Making sure they have enough spoons to entertain them. That sort of thing."

Hen snorted derisively but Ailsa nodded. "And when there's two, clean-ish and entertained is optional," she added.

I looked at Ailsa, with the twins in their double carrier (yes, this is a thing), and marveled again at how parenting can uncover hidden depths in a person. Ailsa was not, perhaps, the most maternal person I'd ever met, but watching her with the twins (two! I cannot state it enough. There are TWO of them!) she parented as if born to it. Then again, I hadn't exactly been a contender for maternal candidate of the year, so who was I to judge. And I liked to think I was pretty good with Jack. I certainly enjoyed it more than I'd expected, and found myself surprisingly unselfconscious about the whole thing—which as someone who will analyze their interaction with a Costa drive-thru attendant for an hour after it took place, is quite something.

"I disagree." Hen was pushing back on my not-yet-parenting claim. "This is a hugely important developmental period for them! Their social and emotional development alone is crucial at this age. Then there's language and communication, and their physical development. I worry Arora isn't spending enough time developing her gross motor coordination."

"You need to lower your standards," advised Ailsa, and Poppy and I agreed wholeheartedly.

"I mean, yeah, obviously they're developing loads at the moment, but we don't have to do like *discipline*, or teaching them stuff yet," I clarified. Again, my attempts at this thus far had produced a dog that stole other dogs and didn't know her own name.

And just like that the conversation had turned relentlessly to parenting, as it was wont to do these days. Even when we had a murder to discuss. You can fight against it, but you're going to end up having at least one conversation about Sudocrem/sleep cycles/baby-led weaning per hour.

I zoned out of the conversation—on the benefits of free-play—and checked the time on my phone.

"Can we pick up the pace a bit?"

The others looked at me in surprise: I wasn't usually the pacesetter of the group.

"They always run out of the lamb roasts at the Keys by two and I've been thinking about that roast all day."

THEY HADN'T run out of the lamb roasts, thank God, although I did think the Yorkshire puddings were a bit subpar this week. Joe and Lin had even managed to snag us one of the prime tables in the pub garden with an actual functioning sunshade, right next to the sandpit in which we could conveniently deposit the babies.

It turned out Lin and I were the only ones having a roast, the others, even Joe, declaring that it was too hot for one. This was not an excuse that sat well with me. I frowned over at where Hen and Ailsa were sharing a summer salad (whatever that was) and chips. Who shares a salad? Then it occurred to me that this was probably stretching the household finances for both of them. It was stretching it for me and Joe come to think of it, especially as the bounty that had been statutory maternity pay had now run its course.

Halfway through lunch, Rowan turned up. Rowan is Joe's half brother, who lives up at the hippy commune in Stricker's Wood, run by their dad. Joe's parentage is a long and complicated story involving the Second Summer of Love, a *Mamma Mia*-esque trio of dads and, inevitably I suppose, my mother-in-law. I prefer to leave the details hazy.

Rowan took the seat farthest away from Ailsa—now there's another long story, involving another summer of sort-of love. Ailsa and Rowan had been friends at school, and then slightly more than friends. Their romance had come to a rather sticky end when Rowan had cheated on Ailsa (there was a lot more to this story, which included a brief and thankfully mistaken period when we thought he'd cheated on her with his own sister—*this was not the case*), but there was definitely still something unresolved between them. For a while I'd strongly suspected he was the father of the twins but Ailsa had refuted this, while declining to offer up any other candidates—that particular mystery remained unsolved. Today, however, Rowan had other issues on his mind, and launched immediately into the murder.

"It's all anyone's talking about at the office." Rowan was a journalist for the *Penton Bugle*, the local rag that provided all the town's news since the town crier was retired a few years ago (true fact). "Joe tells me you guys were actually at the protest where she was murdered. I don't suppose you want to go on record for the paper?"

"Are you allowed to print anything yet?" asked Ailsa with a frown. "I thought Jane was suppressing it for now?"

"She can't suppress it," pointed out Rowan. "But she's been withholding any police information—until today. But now that the family has been notified we've been given the basics and we're moving ahead with the story—*with* Jane's blessing."

"So what've you been told?" I asked eagerly.

"Precious little, to be honest," admitted Rowan. "Dead at scene, cause of death strangulation, family notified, police pursuing several leads. Nothing on what those leads might be, of course. But"—he leaned forward conspiratorially—"there's a lot of talk at the office about Leila and Owen Myers, you know, the guy who founded Aether, the green electricity company."

We all glanced at Hen, who was staring fixedly at her half of the summer salad.

"No one really knows much about him," continued Rowan, oblivious. "I mean the guy's clearly a genius. He revolutionized green energy with this new type of solar-powered wind turbine—he developed some kind of hybrid charge controller—anyway that's not relevant right now. Might put it in the story but I don't know how much traction that'll get . . . Anyway, basically, he patented this new turbine like fifteen years ago, and since then he's developed it into a massive energy corporation. But here's the thing, he's basically a recluse—no one ever sees him. And no one knows anything about his private life. He never married, never had kids, people say he's married to his work—I know, clichéd. Except, rumor has it, Leila managed to break through."

"You mean she had a relationship with him?" Poppy asked.

Rowan shrugged and sat back. "She had *something* with him, or that's the rumor anyway. Apparently, she used to be his PA."

Again, all eyes slid to Hen.

"Anything you want to say?" she asked icily.

"Hen is Owen Myers's new PA," I not-very-subtly whispered to Rowan.

Rowan turned an almost predatory look on Hen. "Oh *really*."

"Yes, and I quite like my job and would like to keep it please, so before you ask, *no*, I am not commenting for your rag of a newspaper."

I could see Rowan itching to get his notepad out.

"Do *you* ever see Myers?" Ailsa asked Hen.

"Of course I do," she snapped. "I'm his PA, what do you expect?"

"Just wondering," said Ailsa calmly. "If he's as reclusive as people say. Like, does he come into the office much?"

"Yes, he does," said Hen waspishly. "Of course he's always very busy and he has to attend a lot of out-of-house meetings, but he's in the office all the time. He's in tomorrow as a matter of fact, for our company quarterly review. Not that it's any of your business!"

Ailsa's eyes gleamed, and I feared she was concocting A Plan.

"I think he's amazing," chipped in Lin, successfully diverting an immediate Hen explosion, but potentially guiding us into equally treacherous waters. "Businessmen like him are going to be the future of the planet. If we can't rely on governments to take the climate crisis seriously, it's going to be entrepreneurs like Myers that provide the solutions."

"I agree in principle," said Ailsa cautiously. "But it's still got to be done right, you know. And corporations . . . I just struggle to trust anybody where the ultimate goal is to make money."

"I think you might have to get over that, I'm afraid," said Joe, rather bluntly.

Ailsa fired up immediately, as Joe had known she would, and began lecturing him—and by extension all of us—on the evils of late-stage capitalism. Despite the fact that she had converted, or at least browbeaten, most of us to her way of thinking by now. I happened to know that even

Joe broadly agreed with her anti-capitalist agenda, he just enjoyed riling her up.

The rest of the afternoon passed in an enjoyable haze of Yorkshire puddings, vaguely political wrangling that struggled to take hold in the summer heat, and the frequent suncreaming of babies. Eventually, we felt that the babies had eaten their fill of sand, and it was time to head home.

"Alice, give me a hand with Robin and Ivy will you?"

I paused, surprised. It was unlike Ailsa to ask for help, let alone from me. I scooped up a twin—probably Ivy—and was about to head toward the car park when Ailsa laid a hand on my arm.

"We should go to Aether tomorrow."

"What?"

"Hen said Myers is going to be there tomorrow."

"So?" I hissed. "What you gonna do? Doorstep him?"

"You heard what Rowan said, there was something going on between Myers and Leila. We need to talk to him."

"We can't turn up at his work, or more specifically we can't turn up at *Hen's* work, and interrogate him about some fling he may or may not have had half a year ago!"

"No, we'll just pop by to visit Hen and, if he happens to be there, we might casually mention that we knew his old PA, get him talking . . ."

"That is the worst plan you've ever come up with. Including that time you made me try combat juggling," I retorted.

Hen was waiting at Ailsa's car and we fell silent. "What are you two whispering about?" she asked suspiciously.

"Alice was just saying how much she enjoyed the juggling," said Ailsa breezily. "See you tomorrow, Alice!"

"Wait, we're not doing anything tomorrow," I protested, but Ailsa had already turned away.

THAT NIGHT I sat up in bed, Jack plugged in to a boob, while I was plugged in to my laptop. I could find surprisingly little about Owen Myers online. He had a Wikipedia page, of course, which listed his various academic achievements, which actually seemed pretty modest up until the point at which he had invented the wind-solar hybrid charge controller for his wind turbines. Under "Personal Life" the website simply stated that "Owen Myers grew up in the Cotswold village of Bishop's Ruin where he attended the local secondary school. He continues to live there and his company, Aether, is also based in the village." Which told me literally nothing about the man himself.

Online articles about him were similarly bald, stating the facts with very little embellishment. There were plenty of them, pages and pages of Google hits, but the contents were disappointingly business-like, focusing on Myers's contributions to green energy technology and inexplicably leaving out any mention of his private life whatsoever. They were almost always accompanied by the official company portrait of Myers that appeared on the Aether website in which he looked . . . very normal. A man in his early forties, moderately attractive but really quite nondescript—brown hair, a slightly recessed chin and the small tight smile of someone who would prefer not to be photographed. Other than that, I turned up a couple of blurry photos of him at some corporate gala (what even is a gala?) and an impeccably staged but lifeless photoshoot for *Time* magazine. He had no social media accounts, and I could find just a single YouTube video of an interview he'd given over a decade earlier, but when I clicked on the link the video had been taken down.

Was this suspicious? Or was this quite simply a man who, despite enjoying substantial business success, had no desire to participate in the celebrity culture that comes with this, and instead protected his privacy?

I sighed and closed my laptop. Leila "Smith" and Owen Myers definitely seemed to be an enigmatic couple. If, of course, they'd ever been a couple. I was intrigued; I wasn't used to the internet letting me down like this. But intrigued or not, I wouldn't be joining Ailsa on some mad Myers hunt the next day. No way.

CHAPTER 15

"HEN IS NOT going to like this. She is not going to like this at all." I kept up a constant litany en route to Aether the next morning, just so that I could say "I told you so" to Poppy and Ailsa when Hen turned out not to like this.

I knew from my extensive googling that Aether cultivated an approachable and friendly appearance. Aether was the company of the people, here for you, me, and the cat next door. It was a local, homegrown business that had, somehow, expanded into a nationwide corporation but retained its cozy attitude of being one big family of happy local employees. Or so Owen Myers would have you believe.

The three sets of security gates we had to pass through to enter the compound somewhat belied this cozy fiction. Although to be fair I could still see the half-scrubbed-off spray paint on the outer wall, DESTROYERS, courtesy, perhaps, of Raven and his pals. So maybe fair enough.

We parked up, loaded ourselves up with babies, and entered the reception, which had definitely been taking notes from Facebook and Google. The entrance lobby looked like a soft play had crashed into a frat house. It was a huge open-plan space, featuring table tennis and foosball, a small but well-stocked bar with fashionable and uncomfortable-looking seats, and an elaborate fruit display. Several pod-shaped chairs hung on long chains from the ceiling, swiveling slightly in the draft from our entrance. There was an honest to goodness ball pit in the corner. I don't know why Hen didn't just sack off the childcare entirely and bring Arora into work with her.

There was a central command pod that was way too fancy to be described as a "desk." An exceptionally chic-looking woman was tapping away at a computer, wearing a Bluetooth earpiece; I couldn't decide whether this was incredibly state of the art or hopelessly nineties (much like the phrase "state of the art"). She gave us that "I'm sure you're really important and I'll be with you just as soon as I've placed this Net-a-Porter order" smile that receptionists are so good at.

With a final elaborate tap, she turned to us. "How can I help you, ladies?"

"Er, we're here to see Hen, I mean Henrietta Parks. She's PA to Owen Myers."

"Hen? Do you have an appointment?"

Damn, the receptionist brought up what was presumably Hen's work calendar.

"Er, no, not exactly." I looked desperately at Ailsa and Poppy for help.

"We're looking after her daughter this afternoon and Hen forgot to drop off Arora's medicine, you know, for her ear infection. So we're just swinging by to pick it up," lied Poppy smoothly.

The receptionist looked dubious; anyone who'd worked with Hen for six months would be aware that the likelihood of Hen forgetting something like this was slightly less than zero. But at the same time, we were three women of Hen's age, all clutching babies. We weren't exactly espionage from Big Oil. I could see the decision cross her face that we simply weren't worth the hassle.

"She's up on the second floor, follow the corridor past the juice bar and swing a right at the Thought Pod. You'll see her desk straight ahead of you."

The Thought Pod?

After watching our futile search for a lift or, failing that, some good old-fashioned stairs, the woman directed us to a paternoster in the center of the reception space which I had assumed was some kind of installation artwork. Of course, I did not know the word paternoster—why would I? Later, after the trauma of using one, Ailsa explained both the name and the concept to me, so that I can avoid them for the rest of my life.

A paternoster, for the uninitiated, is a lift of death. It has no doors, just a series of perpetually rising and falling boxes that you have to jump—yes, *jump*—into as they scroll past. And then jump out again at your floor of choice. Or, in my case, fail to jump out because you're terrified and have no desire to plunge you and your baby to certain doom.

So while Ailsa and Poppy hopped out on the second floor. I rose ever higher until finally pitching myself and Jack out on floor five, driven by the fear that the box would presumably flip over at the top and send us, screaming and upside down, back down to the ground floor.

The fifth floor seemed to be a largely deserted web of corridors stretching in every direction. I felt like a lab rat in a maze.

"Where are all the people?" I muttered to Jack. He gave the contented gurgle of a baby who doesn't give a shit, after all this is a grown-up's problem to solve. I wondered what age he'd be before he worked out that the grown-ups in charge of him had less clue what was going on than the dog.

"Hello," said a friendly voice behind me. "Can I help you?"

I turned round and found myself face-to-face with the man from my first Earth Force meeting. At least, I was pretty sure it was him . . .

"Anonymous Richard?" I couldn't help blurting out.

He looked amused. "Most people just call me Richard. And who do I have the pleasure of speaking to?"

"Sorry! I'm Alice. Sorry. I just couldn't get off the lift in time, I'm supposed to be on floor two but it was all going so fast . . ."

Behind me the paternoster creaked on, slightly pacier than your average snail.

"Ah yes, you're three floors too high here." He took in my panicked expression. "Would you like to use the stairs?"

"There are stairs?" My relief was pathetic.

"Only for those in the know." He winked—which I dislike on principle. Who actually does that? But he seemed inoffensive so I trotted meekly after him down a maze of corridors until he opened a door onto a blissfully utilitarian-looking set of stairs.

"Three flights down, it's signposted," he said in a carefully non-condescending tone.

"Thanks," I said. "Glad I bumped into you. I guess you work here?"

"Not exactly."

And with that enigmatic statement, he let the door close behind him and disappeared back into the maze of floor five.

HEN WAS not pleased to see us. Surprise! At least my little detour via floor five meant that by the time I arrived she had already vented most of her spleen on Poppy and Ailsa.

"Completely unacceptable," she was still muttering under her breath.

"Come on, Hen," said Poppy easily. "We were in the area and we just wanted to pop by and say hi."

"Don't try that on me," snapped Hen. "I know exactly why you're here."

"We were just exploring Bishop's Ruin and, well, this place is kinda hard to miss," said Ailsa in her most innocent tone. This is not one of her key skills.

"We brought you snacks," I tried, fishing in my bag in the certain knowledge there would be at least three types of chocolate in there. I produced a Twix and one finger of slightly melted Kinder Bueno, which looked a little disturbing.

"Leave the Twix in my in-tray," she sniffed, looking very slightly mollified. "I don't know what that other thing is but I don't want it."

I obediently placed my sacrificial offering in the in-tray, and covertly unwrapped the Kinder Bueno myself.

"I should never have mentioned the quarterly gather, should I?" said Hen, shaking her head at us in disappointment. "Well, you've had a wasted journey. Owen won't be in until the afternoon. And if he was here now, I certainly wouldn't be letting you in to speak to him. What are you playing at? Are you actively *trying* to get me fired?"

"Of course not," said Ailsa, affronted. "We're just trying to find out why a girl was murdered last week!"

"Keep your voice down!" hissed Hen. "Oh for God's sake, we're not having this conversation here. Come with me."

She hustled us down a corridor and into a glass-fronted meeting room. As seemed to be Aether's way, it looked like a standard office had been hijacked by Teletubbies. There were no uncomfortable modernist office chairs around the central table, instead there were squashy beanbags scattered haphazardly, and a few rogue yoga balls rolling about. There was a huge interactive screen mounted on one wall, but the opposite wall featured a huge primary-colored mural of a rolling hillside dotted with white windmills, and running along the other wall was a long wooden sideboard loaded with glass jars of sweets.

"Ooh, jelly beans!" I couldn't help myself.

"Don't touch those," snapped Hen as I reached out.

"What, has Owen counted how many beans are in each jar?"

"They're for staff and clients—of which you are neither."

Fair point.

"Look, just pull up a chair and let's at least *look* as if we're having a civilized conversation, in case anyone walks past," said Hen.

"What chairs?" asked Ailsa dryly, earning herself a Look from Hen.

Once we were all beanbagged and balled, Hen took her position at the top of the table. I bounced over on a yoga ball. "Ooh, it's like being back at prenatal class, isn't it?"

Hen gave a tight little smile and I felt a bit guilty for bringing it up. Our brief foray into prenatal, where we had all met, had involved Hen giving birth rather dramatically and extremely unexpectedly above a hippy crystal-and-dream-catcher shop, and also our first murder. It had been an unusual start to any friendship.

"I just meant—I'm sorry—I'll shut up now."

"Actually, I'd like all of you to shut up for a moment," said Hen, looking serious. "Look, this absolutely isn't on. I know you're playing detectives again. I've already asked you not to, which you all comprehensively ignored. Fine. It doesn't make me feel great, but fine. But when it comes to actively jeopardizing my job—*which you are doing don't interrupt me, Ailsa*—that's too far. You know how much I need this job. I really appreciate all the help you guys have given me over the last year—really, I do. It's been the only thing keeping me going. But this? Turning up at my work and hoping to sideswipe my boss? Totally out of order."

We all stayed silent, chastened. Hen was completely right, we had *way* overstepped the mark.

"Hen, we're so sorry," said Poppy eventually.

"Sorry, Hen," muttered Ailsa and I, like naughty children confronted by an angry teacher.

Hen sighed. "I don't want to fall out over this. I need you guys. And I don't mean just practically speaking. But please don't make me choose between my job and my friends. Because my job is how I support myself and my daughter, and I need that too. OK?"

"Hen, we're so so sorry," I said. "We didn't mean to make you feel like that. We're horrible people."

"Don't be silly," said Hen briskly. "You're good people, you just get carried away. You do realize you talked about pretty much nothing else yesterday? I mean, I wish I could join in. But I can't. So it gets a little tedious."

"But, Hen, I'm just saying, what if Aether *is* involved somehow? Wouldn't you want to know?" This was Ailsa. Who was looking Hen straight in the eye.

Hen stared back at her—initially defiant. Then suddenly she sagged.

"I just want to not be involved for once," she said quietly. "The murders last year . . . Becoming a single mum. Now this? It's been . . . a bit much. I just want to be left alone to bring up Arora. Without any of this drama."

"Shouldn't have moved to Penton then," I tried to lighten the mood. "This place is worse than Midsomer."

Hen gave a small smile.

"We really are sorry," I said, and I hoped she could hear how much I meant it. "Look, let us do something nice for you, to make up for ambushing you here. Why don't you come over after work and we'll get takeout pizza? My treat." I guiltily wondered what Joe would make of this offer, but I felt Hen's needs were greater.

"Or you could cook for us?" suggested Ailsa, wrinkling her nose at the thought of *fast food* and all the toxins and planetary hazards that came with it.

"You don't want that," I assured her.

"No, I don't think I do," agreed Hen. "Takeout pizza sounds . . . nice. I'll bring wine."

As we left, Hen slipped something into my pocket. I put my hand in and felt the cold, hard chink of a handful of jelly beans.

CHAPTER 16

"WELL, THAT WAS a waste of time," grumbled Ailsa as we made our way out. "All we achieved was pissing off Hen."

I didn't say "I told you so" but I hoped my face was saying it for me.

"You're just as guilty as the rest of us," Poppy said, elbowing me.

"At least I gave her a Twix," I countered. "And you'll never guess who I bumped into."

"Owen Myers?" asked Poppy eagerly.

"Er, no," I admitted. "No, I bumped into that guy from the Earth Force meeting. Richard. You know, the boring-looking one."

Ailsa and Poppy were both looking at me blankly.

"Who?" asked Ailsa, disinterestedly.

"Anonymous Richard?" I tried. I turned to Poppy. "You remember him, right?"

But Poppy had already turned away and was gazing off at the extensive grounds that stretched in every direction beyond the Aether complex.

"I suppose, seeing as we're here, there's no harm having a little wander round the grounds," she said thoughtfully.

"What? Yes! There's a lot of harm in that!" I protested, alarmed. "It's called trespassing and I'm pretty sure it's a criminal offense!"

"We wouldn't be trespassing," said Ailsa, who'd brightened up at this suggestion. "We were buzzed in, all legit."

"On false pretenses!" I argued, but Poppy and Ailsa had both already veered away and were heading for a footpath that snaked around the side of the Aether main building.

"What could you possibly expect to find in the grounds," I tried again. "An incriminating bench? A suspect tree?"

"Well, that's what detectoring is all about," called Poppy over her shoulder. "You just sort of wander around until you stumble across something."

I wasn't sure that was what detectoring was all about, but it was, admittedly, how we did it. And it had worked for us before. With a sigh, I hurried after them. Sweat began to pool on my chest, in the dips of my collarbone and between my boobs; carrying Jack in the sling was like having a hot-water bottle strapped to me in stifling heat.

The path skirted round the building, then struck off across a grassy expanse that was neither lawn nor field but somewhere between the two. I kept glancing nervously at the building behind us.

"Hen's desk was in the center of the building," said Ailsa. "There weren't any windows."

I'd often thought that Ailsa could read my mind, an alarming prospect at the best of times. But I did breathe easier as the path suddenly descended steeply, and the building was cut off from view. It wound its way through what I would vaguely term "shrubbery" before coming out on the side of a small lake, or possibly merely an aspirational pond. A couple of ducks floated serenely in the center.

"Ooh, look, a grotto," said Poppy, pointing to a weird cave-like rocky structure protruding from the shore just along the waterline from us.

"Like, Santa?" I asked uncertainly.

"Like an artificial cave," said Ailsa, rolling her eyes.

"Let's take a look," said Poppy enthusiastically, setting off around the lake edge.

The grotto was actually rather pleasant. It was quite spacious inside, and provided some welcome shade from the heat of the day. The lake lapped up against the cave mouth making a soothing, cooling sound, and throwing watery lines of light reflecting across the craggy ceiling. A handful of artfully scattered rocks offered rudimentary seating. I tried perching on one and immediately decided I would be more comfortable on the ground.

Without saying anything, we all whacked out a boob—me and Poppy left, Ailsa right—and attached a child.

"What do you think—" began Poppy, but I interrupted.

"Shh! Voices."

Despite Poppy and Ailsa's assertion that we weren't trespassing, they both shut up immediately. On encountering a trio of breastfeeding women in a cave, most people's first reactions won't be to call the police, but it might provoke awkward questions.

The voices swam into focus right above our heads; whoever it was, they must have been standing on the bank where it overhung the grotto.

". . . never would have expected this of you," a man's voice was saying. "How did you even get in here?"

"Oh come on, Owen," replied a woman's voice. We all exchanged glances—could it be the reclusive Owen Myers above our heads? "It's not exactly Fort Knox," the woman continued. Was her voice faintly familiar? It put me in mind of . . . juice and cookies?

"Well, you shouldn't be here!" Owen spluttered. "This has got to stop. I don't want to go to the police over this, you know I don't, but if you force my hand then I'll have no option. Turning up at my work, at my house, what are you *thinking*, Norah?"

Norah? Of course, it was Norah's voice. Lovely Norah from Earth Force, with her fruit juice and chia seed energy balls.

"Don't be cruel, Owen." There was a slightly panicked note in Norah's voice. "If you would just *talk* to me I wouldn't have to—"

"There's nothing to talk about," he interrupted brutally.

At this point Robin poked his sister in the eye and she let out an enraged squawk. Ailsa hastily freed another boob and clamped Ivy onto it, but the damage was done. The voices above had stopped abruptly.

"What was that?" asked Owen sharply.

"Probably a duck," said Norah. "Look, I just want to talk to you. You can't freeze me out like this Owen, not after everything we—"

"I'm not freezing you out, Norah. I'm not talking about this. You can see yourself out or I can have security escort you out, the choice is yours."

Heavy footsteps stamped away. There was a moment's silence, then the patter of lighter footsteps also faded into the distance. We waited in silence for a few moments longer. I was sure I'd been holding my breath the whole time.

Eventually, Poppy broke the silence. "I told you detectoring was about wandering round till you stumble on a clue."

"Was that a clue?" I asked.

"I'm not sure what that was," mused Ailsa.

"Owen and *Norah*? From Earth Force?" I couldn't quite get my head around it.

"Having what sounded like a lovers' tiff," added Poppy.

"Or an ex-lovers' tiff more like," I agreed. "Talk about sleeping with the enemy though!"

"There seems to have been a lot of it about." Ailsa shrugged.

"None of it proven though," I cautioned. "All purely speculation so far."

We began packing up in silence, boobs back in, babies re-slinged, mulling over what we'd just heard. Jack began to drowse off against my chest, full of milk and sunshine.

"Do you remember that attack on Owen's house? The firebomb?" I asked as we made our way slowly back toward the cars.

"Oh, yes!" said Poppy. "I'd completely forgotten about that."

"I hadn't," I said. "I heard about it on the radio, and they said Owen had been entertaining a female guest at the time of the attack. I'd been wondering if it might have been Leila. But now I'm wondering . . . could it have been Norah?"

"But she seems so . . ." Poppy gestured vaguely with her hands.

"Juice and cookies?" I supplied. "I know. But you never can tell, and we don't really know her at all."

By now we were back at the cars. A small red car was disappearing out of the gates. The person driving was just a silhouette, but could conceivably have been Norah. Then again, it could conceivably have been just about any adult human.

I was just edging my own car out of the gate when something caught my eye. I nudged Poppy and pointed. A man had emerged from the phone booth opposite. He gazed after the red car as it disappeared down the lane, then swung his leg over a bicycle propped against the booth, and pedaled off with angry vigor.

It was Enderby.

CHAPTER 17

BY THE TIME I got home, sweaty and exhausted—because going anywhere with a small child is quite exhausting—I was seriously regretting my impulse invite to the others to come round for pizza that evening. I stood in the middle of our small sitting room and surveyed the carnage around me. Jack's toys were scattered everywhere in various states of disembowelment courtesy of Helen. Dishes were stacked precariously in the sink and the kitchen surfaces glistened with some sort of mystery liquid. There was some several-day-old oatmeal crusted to the baseboard that I'd been really hoping Helen would deal with, but she had, once again, let me down.

Jack crawled off, making determinedly for the dog bed, where he curled up and promptly fell asleep. This was not as unhygienic as it sounds, as Helen *never* slept in the dog bed, disdaining its polyester meanness in favor of the human sofa and velvet cushions. Making our sofa far more of a flea pit than the dog bed.

I looked at the clock. I had two hours to make the place Hen-acceptable. I was broadly unbothered by Poppy and Ailsa's opinions. Joe would be home in an hour, but there was a distinct possibility he would make the situation worse, not better. Also the problem was, with Jack already asleep, I just knew I was going to take a nap . . .

I WOKE up with twenty minutes until Hen, inevitably, would arrive on time. Unfortunately, Jack also woke up wanting to be fed. Have you ever tried to breastfeed while tidying the house? It cannot be done.

And yet somehow, twenty minutes later, the worst of the mess was tidied away (shoved in cupboards or upstairs), and after de-dog-hairing the sofa had proved impossible, I improvised by throwing a duvet cover over it that could potentially pass as a throw. The doorbell rang just as I shoved the washing-up bowl—still full of dirty dishes—into the cupboard under the sink.

We stowed the sleeping twins and Arora in their pram bassinets up in Jack's room—which, given that Jack slept in little more than a cupboard, was like a particularly tricky game of Tetris. Jack, having napped until half an hour ago, was wide awake and would probably remain that way until 10 P.M. I was awaiting the inevitable lecture on the importance of regular sleep schedules from Hen. We knew we were on limited time, being able to bring the babies along to evening social events, letting them sleep in prams and bassinets—soon we would be limited to 7 P.M. bedtimes and quality adult time would be relegated to quarterly evenings in the pub which we would spend discussing how very tired we were.

With the babies settled, except for Jack who was lurking in our bedroom with Joe, I settled the adults on my duvet-throw sofa. I saw Hen's eyes stray to the oatmeal on the baseboard. I had tried, I really had. But that stuff is worse than cement. Once it's dried, you might as well just paint over it.

At least there was wine, courtesy of Hen and Poppy. And pizza, blessed pizza, was on its way.

"You didn't have to do this," said Hen eventually.

"We wanted to," Ailsa said bluntly.

"We're sorry," said Poppy. "We shouldn't have turned up at your work like that."

"And I know it's all a bit . . . messy," I put in. "This whole murder thing. What with Leila having worked at Aether and everything."

"It's not that I don't want you investigating on principle," Hen said. "It's just that I can't lose this job, I really can't. I *need* this job. With Antoni . . . you know . . . I'm on my own. I have to bring up Arora, I have to feed her and clothe her. We already lost the house, I can't lose any more."

We'd all tried to offer Hen financial help. In my case, Hen had looked absolutely appalled and had told me that if I had money to spare I should be spending it on dog obedience classes. So we helped how we could, non-financially, but it was a struggle for Hen. Every day.

Ailsa shuffled over and wrapped an arm protectively around Hen. "You're not on your own. You know that."

Hen leaned in to her. "I know. I just . . . didn't want this."

What to say to that. We'd all found parenting to be unexpected in our own ways—Jack had been unplanned, I'd fallen pregnant less than a year into my relationship with Joe, which certainly brings its own challenges; Ailsa had been similarly caught unawares, with the added bonus of twins and the ongoing mystery of their paternity; and while Poppy and Lin arguably had their shit together more than most, it seemed increasingly clear that Poppy was struggling with elements of parenthood, even if she didn't want to talk about it yet. As for Hen, in the year since her daughter arrived she'd lost her husband, her home, found herself a job and now her predecessor in the role had been murdered. It was a lot to take in.

"Anyway." Hen sniffed, visibly pulling herself together. "I knew you wouldn't be able to get to the bottom of it without my help, so I did a little digging. But this is the *last of my involvement*, OK? I mean that."

We all nodded, wide-eyed and eager, like Helen confronted with a sausage. Hen pulled a sheet of paper from her bag.

"I went into Leila's old email account," she began.

"You can do that?" I asked, slightly appalled. "Could people get into my email account at my old work? Theoretically?" I mean, mainly they'd find extensive email chains with Joe discussing what dog breed we were going to get (hellhound, as it turns out), and even more extensive email chains with Maya complaining about our hangovers and debating where we were going to go the next night. But still—boundaries!

"I got IT to give me access," Hen said. "I told them she hadn't left a full account of correspondence with the construction firm for the new site—which was pretty much true. Anyway. I think she was probably pretty good at deleting anything not work-related, but I did find one interesting item in her Sent box. From just before she left."

She slid the piece of paper toward us.

from: Leila Smith
to: Owen Myers

12 November 19:47

Owen, you're overreacting. I'm not resigning, there's no need.
The deal's still on. Usual place tomorrow?
L x

That was it.

We all sat back.

"But what does it mean?" I asked eventually.

"Well, for a start, it definitely sounds like Leila didn't leave of her own accord, or at least not exactly," Ailsa said slowly. "I wonder why he asked her to resign?"

"Whatever it was, she pushed back!" I said, feeling slightly impressed at Leila's balls. "I didn't know you could do that."

"I'm starting to get the impression Leila didn't really care what you're supposed to do or not," said Poppy thoughtfully.

"When I started the job, Owen made it sound as though Leila had to leave quite suddenly for personal reasons," said Hen. "But there was definitely something quite odd about her leaving—no handover, no trace of her in the office, and Owen has hardly ever mentioned her since I started."

"Isn't it obvious? He asked her to resign because they were having an affair," said Poppy. "'Usual place tomorrow.' That's definitely an affair."

"I don't know," I objected. "What about 'The deal's still on.' That's hardly how you'd talk about an affair! Unless you're really weird. Who refers to their relationship as 'the deal'?"

We threw ideas back and forth—Ailsa and I favored blackmail, Poppy an affair.

"It's not exactly romantic," argued Ailsa. "'The deal's still on'!"

"Who signs off a blackmail note with a kiss?" countered Poppy.

"But blackmail could explain where she was getting the money to buy all those fancy things," I chipped in.

"Or they could have been presents from Owen, if they were having an affair," replied Poppy.

"That's a lot of really nice presents," I pointed out. "Like, *a lot*."

I tried to remember what Joe had gotten me for my last birthday. Was it . . . hair rollers? Because he'd seen something on Twitter saying that they were back in? Mind you, I think I'd bought him a woolly hat for his last birthday, which I'd then basically stolen after Helen ate mine . . . Perhaps Joe and I weren't the gold standard for gift giving.

"He is a millionaire," said Poppy. "A weekend at a luxury spa is probably a millionaire's equivalent of giving, I don't know, a toothbrush for most of us."

Interesting. Maybe Poppy and Lin were even worse at gifting than us.

"What do you think?" Ailsa turned to Hen. "Do you think he might have had an affair with Leila?"

But Hen was staying resolutely out of the conversation.

"I've done my bit," she declared. "The rest is up to you crack detectives."

"We'd be lost without you," I said earnestly.

"I know," said Hen with a small smile. "In repayment, one of you has to come to the Aether summer garden party with me next Wednesday, and one of you has to babysit."

She looked pointedly at Ailsa, who sighed.

"Garden parties are not my thing."

"You'll love it, you can look down on all the people trapped in the corporate rat race," said Hen briskly. "Including myself."

"That's not fair," countered Ailsa.

"And you can lecture them about green energy," offered Hen.

"Hmmm." Ailsa was clearly weakening.

"But you're not allowed to mention the wind farm or Earth Force—no excuses."

Ailsa scowled. "Boring."

"For me?" pleaded Hen.

Ailsa crumbled. "Fine. So long as Jane can have the twins."

Hen leaned over and kissed her on the cheek—which was more affection than I'd ever seen her show anyone, except perhaps Arora. Ailsa blushed and pushed her away.

"I'll babysit Arora," offered Poppy, and Hen gave her a smile.

"I'll just be on standby, shall I?" I volunteered.

Hen didn't respond immediately; she shifted uncomfortably in her seat. "Alice, have you put a duvet cover over the sofa? It's got buttons!"

I was saved from answering this question by the doorbell.

"THIS IS going to blow your mind," I told Ailsa dramatically, taking the stack of pizza boxes from the delivery man.

"I can't believe you've never had Domino's." Poppy shook her head.

"I have a healthy respect for my digestive system," said Ailsa, wrinkling her nose. "And the planet."

"We got you a Vegan Vegi Supreme!" I flipped the lid and displayed it to her. "Entirely plant-based!"

"I refuse to believe those plants lived a full and happy life," said Ailsa, picking at a limp mushroom. "What is this? A slug?"

"I don't think that would count as vegan," I said distractedly, checking through the boxes. "Unbelievable. Who forgot to order stuffed crust?"

"Well, you did the ordering," pointed out Poppy. Dammit. My standards were clearly slipping.

Joe stuck his head into the room, immediately followed by Helen, both of them sniffing the air.

"Do I smell pizza?"

"I got you the Meatfielder because I liked the pun," I said, handing over his box.

"Sounds about right."

"Are you joining us?" asked Poppy, attempting to make room on the sofa, which involved her more or less sitting on Ailsa's lap.

"Nah, you're all right," said Joe. "I imagine you'll want to talk about babies and murders and stuff."

This seemed pretty accurate, so nobody quibbled.

"Plus there's a snooker match on," I said under my breath, as Joe tucked a bottle of milk for Jack under one arm, balancing the pizza box with another and trying to fend Helen off with his knee.

Once we were all established with our pizza—Ailsa had moved to the other end of the sofa to be as far away as possible from my Mighty Meaty—talk returned to the murder.

"We can't discount Raven," I said through a mouthful of cheese and pepperoni.

"I don't know, isn't that a bit clichéd?" said Hen. "The boyfriend? What's his motive supposed to be?"

"You just don't think Raven did it because you think he's hot," I pointed out—rather shrewdly I thought.

Hen flushed. Ailsa goggled.

"Wait—you think *Raven* is hot?"

"You mean you don't?" put in Poppy reasonably. She had a point. I mean, sure, he needed a haircut—and preferably a shampoo while they were at it—but the guy was legit smoking.

"Well, yeah, but I didn't think Hen would," said Ailsa. "He's so not her type!"

"What do you mean by that?" fired up Hen.

"I just mean, you married a suit in pharmaceuticals . . ."

"Yeah, and look how that turned out. So let's hope for everyone's sake I don't have a 'type.'"

Ouch. Cue awkward silence.

"Anyway, if Raven found out Leila was having an affair with her old boss—there's your motive right there," I said, more to break the tension than anything else.

"Firstly, we don't know it was an affair," said Hen, picking this up gratefully. "And secondly, even if it was, there's nothing to suggest it went on after she left Aether. Which is when she met Raven. So in all likelihood there was no overlap."

This was true. Although we also had no evidence that it *hadn't* overlapped.

We'd got through two bottles of wine by this point and I felt it might be acceptable to return to the subject of Owen Myers.

"What's Owen like to work for?" I asked cautiously, not wanting to cross any boundaries.

Hen shrugged. "He's OK. Bit full of himself." She paused and considered. "Very full of himself actually. I suppose it's justified to an extent, I mean look at what he's achieved, and he's got to be less than ten years older than us."

This was a depressing thought.

"I guess he's like any other big corporate boss"—Hen was picking her way through her thoughts carefully—"but he thinks he's different because his company is 'good,' you know? But whether or not that's the case, and I'm not going into that now"—she held up a warning hand to stave Ailsa off—"he can still act like a bit of a prick quite a lot of the time."

"How so?" I asked curiously.

"He's got this whole misunderstood genius thing going on. Which personally I think is a bit overrated. I mean nowadays he's got whole teams of techs and engineers who come up with all the ideas for him. And Simon from Accounts was saying the other day that it wasn't even Owen who came up with the original patent for the Aether wind turbine, it was his business partner. So I'm not sure Owen's got so much to be all high and mighty about."

"Simon from Accounts, eh," said Ailsa in a disapproving tone—although I wasn't sure if she was disapproving of the office gossip, Simon, or accountants generally.

I was interested though.

"It's not his patent?" I asked. "Who's his business partner?" In all my googling of Aether there had been no mention of a business partner, and everything had suggested that Owen Myers had built up Aether single-handed.

"Oh, some brainiac," said Hen dismissively. "I'm not sure they even have a stake in Aether anymore; I've got a feeling the partnership dissolved a while back. They're not on the board or anything—I take the minutes and I've never seen them."

I resolved to do a bit more internet digging. I had great faith in the internet and suspected that 90 percent of detecting could probably be done from the comfort of my own sofa courtesy of my Wi-Fi.

Unfortunately, it didn't look like I was going to get away with this particular sofa-bound form of detecting for long.

"We should go up to London for Leila's funeral," Ailsa was saying.

"When is it?" asked Poppy.

"Wednesday. Day after tomorrow. In Kensington, I think."

"I don't know, isn't that a bit weird?" I demurred. "We barely knew her."

"Quite a few of the Earth Force lot are going," replied Ailsa.

"Yes, her friends and co-protestors of a good six months' standing."

"It'll be fine. It's a funeral, it's not invite only."

"How do you even know Earth Force people are going?" I asked Ailsa.

"Don't you *ever* check the Earth Force group chat?" she asked exasperatedly. I remained guiltily quiet; I had muted the group chat almost immediately.

"Why don't we head up, and if it looks like it's a really small affair, like family and close friends, we'll give it a miss and just have a nice day out in London instead," bargained Poppy.

"I don't know," I said. "Joe's in Oxford for a client meeting on Wednesday. I'd have to bring Jack."

"I'm sure that'd be fine," said Poppy breezily.

"But for God's sake don't bring Helen," said Ailsa quickly.

I ignored this and turned instead to the stack of pizza boxes next to me. "Now, Ailsa, let me introduce you to the delights of jalapeño poppers."

Ailsa's horror at my description of jalapeño poppers was matched only by my own on discovering that Helen had somehow eaten the entire tray of poppers. She was now standing in a corner, licking her lips with the slightly alarmed expression of one who is only now registering the spice quotient of what they've just consumed at speed.

The rest of the evening passed in a pleasant blur of pizza, wine, and occasional baby wake-ups, and no further mention was made of my duvet-sofa-throw. Maybe hosting wasn't quite as hideous as I'd always thought? Maybe I was a proper adult now? When I went to feed Helen and rediscovered the basin of dirty dishes in the cupboard under the sink I decided to park this notion for a while.

NEEDLESS TO say, Helen was quite poorly that night. It was nice to have the monotony of night feeds broken up by the dog barfing up jalapeños at regular intervals. I just wished there was even the faintest possibility she might learn something from the experience.

CHAPTER 18

WEDNESDAY MORNING BROUGHT the realization that I should have probably planned slightly ahead for the funeral. The perpetually dire laundry situation meant my options for outfits were limited. I turned to Maya in dismay.

What should I wear to the funeral?

Nothing hemp, nothing tie-dye

It's a funeral, Maya

I know what you hippy lot are like

So long as you're actually wearing clothes I suppose that's a win

I'm not a hippy

And I'm definitely not a nudist!!

If you say so

Just—nothing weird and you should be fine

I can manage that

* * *

"IS JACK wearing Halloween pajamas?" asked Poppy as soon as I arrived at the station.

"They were the only black clothes he owns," I protested.

"He's a baby," said Ailsa bluntly. "No one cares if he's wearing black."

"Now you tell me," I grumbled. Jack did look a little odd in his black pajamas with little ghosts all over them. In fact, now that I thought about it, maybe that was quite poor taste to wear to a funeral. Oh well, it was too late now. Maybe I'd just try and keep him in his pram where no one could see him.

As soon as we settled in our train seats, Ailsa clamped her headphones over her ears, flicked on an audiobook, and sat back, closing her eyes.

After a minute she said, without opening her eyes, "I can feel you staring at me, Alice."

How did she do it?

"Well, I'm sorry if we're boring you," I said, slightly miffed.

"Alice, I have eleven-month-old twins. I get approximately ten seconds of peace per day and it usually turns out that's only because they're occupied doing something awful. So be a love and shut up."

Fair point. Anyway, Jack was optimistically waving his much-loved copy of *Each Peach Pear Plum* at me. I hoped the rest of the train carriage were ready for an hour and a half of back-to-back readings; I reckoned we could get through it at least a hundred times before Paddington. The commuters were going to love us.

IT IS disconcerting being back in a place that thoroughly belongs to your pre-parenting life, but now with a child in tow. London seemed changed. I was adamant that, of course, it wasn't me who had changed. Everything seemed bigger and louder and faster than I remembered. Paddington Station alone seemed to hold twice the population of Penton. The Tube, which I had for so long navigated with ease even through the most befuddling of wine hazes, was now fraught with perils and inconveniences.

I watched with furious envy as a thoroughly London mum hopped her agile city-slicker pram through the Tube doors and steered it deftly down the carriage. Her cosmopolitan baby watched with a bored expression. Jack, meanwhile, was staring wide-eyed at the posters on the Tube, the blinking lights, the multitude of passengers—pretty much everything in fact. Occasionally, he would give a small amazed chuckle. Oh God, I was raising a provincial baby.

I'd expected Ailsa to be a little out of her depth in London. This was definitely extremely judgmental and reflects poorly on me. As does the fact that I found myself quickly getting irritated by the fact that she appeared to have a perfect map of the London Underground in her head. I had lived in London for nearly a decade and was still unsure whether the Circle and District were two separate lines or one weird hybrid.

"How come you know your way around so well?" I couldn't help asking.

Ailsa looked amused. "I used to come up to London all the time."

"For protests?" I asked.

Ailsa actually laughed. She seemed more relaxed than I'd seen her all year. It was probably something to do with not having to watch two tiny humans who were bent on the destruction of themselves and their immediate surroundings. That was Nana Maud's problem for today.

"Sometimes," she admitted. "But mainly just to visit friends. What, did you think I'd never been to the 'big city'?"

I was saved from having to answer by Jack doing a small sick, probably from the sheer overstimulation of the "big city."

Then it was our stop, and (three perilous escalators and the pram getting stuck in the barriers later) we were here. St. Augustine's the Magnificent. And it was magnificent. I don't know anything about architecture so I don't have the right words to describe it, but it was high-end, with turrets and pointy bits and fiddly bits. A host of somberly dressed people were milling around the entrance, all looking extremely smart; one young woman was wearing a black hat with a small net across her face, like a grieving widow from the twenties. Suddenly my extremely old black Zara dress, shading more to gray these days, didn't seem quite so suitable.

Also flanking the entrance were some extremely serious-looking men, two either side of the door, all in black, as might be expected, but not so much funeral black as Kevlar black.

"Well, it certainly doesn't look like a small affair," said Poppy quietly.

As we went to enter the church, one of the men stepped forward, blocking the way.

"Purpose?" he barked.

"Excuse me?"

"Are you family or friends of the deceased?"

"Yes," I said awkwardly, wondering why else he thought we would be here. Although, my conscience niggled, we didn't have so much an ulterior motive as a primary motive thinly veiled with a very tenuous connection to the deceased. "Friends." I cleared my throat, which had stuck on the lie slightly.

On the other side of the door a young man was being turned away with a dismissive "No journalists."

"Bag," barked Kevlar. I held out my bag and he rummaged through it professionally, finding nothing more interesting than enough diapers and snack bars to ride out the apocalypse.

"What about that?" He nodded at the pram.

"That's . . . my son?" I replied, quite baffled.

Kevlar glared at Jack as if he might be concealing a whole arsenal in his admittedly quite capacious diaper. Jack sneezed, spraying Kevlar with biological weaponry. Appalled, Kevlar waved us through. It felt more like entering a high-end nightclub (although I have zero experience of this) than a funeral.

We filed in and took our seats in a pew as near the back as we could go without looking rude.

"Well, that was intense," Poppy breathed. "What's with all the mad security? What on earth are they expecting at a funeral?"

"Trouble, by the looks of it," I said distractedly, lifting Jack out of his pram and attempting to swaddle him in a muslin to hide the ghost pajamas, which I had by now decided were definitely poor taste at a funeral, especially one as fancy as this. Unfortunately, it was sweltering in the church and he kept yanking the cloth off and hooting with laughter at this brilliant new game.

"Oh look, there's Raven and Sam," hissed Ailsa, nodding to a few pews ahead of us. "And I think that's Norah and Enderby next to them, and Sian."

"No Maryam," I whispered back.

"Well, Raven did say they didn't see eye to eye."

"Yeah, but to not come to her funeral . . ."

I gazed around at the congregation. It was a pretty mixed crowd. Toward the front of the church everyone seemed very formal, and extremely smart. All the women were wearing hats and the sorts of dresses that conjure up the word "chic." As my eyes roamed farther back there began to be a more eclectic assortment of guests, ranging from the eccentric (Raven) to the shabby (me) and everything in between.

The organ wheezed into life and there was a general shuffling and rustling as the congregation rose to their feet. The coffin was brought in, carried on the shoulders of four men I didn't recognize, and I wondered briefly why Raven hadn't been included. As it processed down the aisle I felt a tightening in my chest. Leila had been younger than me. I'd barely known her, but from what I'd seen of her, she had been bold and outspoken and sure of what she believed in. And now—perhaps even because of that—she was dead.

The coffin reached the front of the church and was laid to rest in front of a large photo of Leila. I gave a start. She looked completely different in the photo—her hair was long and blond and delicately waved, her makeup subtle but flawless, and she was giving the camera a shy smile that I had never seen on her face in real life. OK so I hardly knew her, but it felt as if I was looking at a completely different Leila. I flipped over the order of service leaflet; the same photo stared up at me from the front page. She didn't look much younger in it, it could only have been taken in the last few years, but in that time Leila had had quite the transformation. And above the photo: LEILA CÉLINE ARNAULT, 1995–2022.

I turned to point out the name to Poppy and Ailsa, but at that moment, Jack burped loudly, and the service began.

Have you ever taken a baby to a funeral? Because with the benefit of experience, I can tell you: don't. Oh, he didn't scream or cry during the service. It was much worse. He laughed. Several times. Each time causing a flurry of turning heads and scandalized glances.

"And now Leila's sister, the Honorable Genevieve Arnault will give the eulogy."

I raised an eyebrow at Poppy. Honorable, eh? I wondered whether Genevieve had married into some swank family, or whether it was hereditary, in which case would Leila have been an Honorable too? We'd wondered whether her family might be well off, but Honorable was a whole other level.

The Honorable Genevieve turned out to be the grieving widow from the twenties with the face net. She mounted the podium with poise, and paused for a moment before touching a delicate hand to her throat and beginning. The whole performance had the air of a golden era film star. Grace Kelly perhaps.

"In losing Leila, I have lost not just my sister, but my best friend," she began.

Jack positively shrieked with laughter. It was awful. I shushed him as best as I could, while Poppy and Ailsa stared at us in horror. The Honorable Grace Kelly faltered.

"Leila was that rare thing, a free spirit," she began again. "She didn't care for the opinions or approvals of others. I have never met someone more free from the restraints of this world."

Cue more peals of laughter from Jack. In desperation, I whacked out a boob and plugged him in. No doubt some of the congregation would be appalled by breastfeeding at a funeral, but it had to be better than Jack's canned laughter echoing through the church. Surreptitiously, I sent Maya a pocket-text to alert her to the situation, which was probably also bad form at a funeral, but I was desperate.

Funeral bad. Jack laughing.
Meet at nearest pub.

By the time we filed back out into the sunlight, blinking moleishly, I was a nervous wreck.

"Can we go?" I hissed urgently to Poppy and Ailsa.

"We should at least say hello to Raven and the others," objected Ailsa. "Look, they're just coming."

I squinted into the darkness of the church interior. A series of pale faces were bobbing toward the exit. Was that . . . ? A middle-aged, middle-classed, generally middling sort of man stepped out into the sunlight. Was that . . . Anonymous Richard? It was hard to tell . . . The man was, by definition, pretty anonymous. Before I could be sure he was moving off down the street, and Raven, Sam, Norah, Sian, and Enderby were joining us on the pavement outside the church. Raven's eyes were very red.

"Thanks for coming," he said quietly.

"Of course," said Poppy. "It was a beautiful service."

"It was a weird service," broke in Enderby. "Why was everything so posh? Leila would have hated that, wouldn't she? She was practically commie. Is her family really swank, Raven? Why didn't you tell us?"

We all awkwardly avoided each other's eyes. Trust Enderby to say exactly what everyone was thinking but absolutely no one else would have said. The guy had zero filter.

Raven shrugged miserably. "I don't know. I never met her family."

"Well, I don't think they're short of a bob or two," said Enderby with a disapproving frown, continuing to showcase his ability to say the most obvious and awkward thing possible.

"Does it matter?" asked Norah a touch nervously. "I mean, there's nothing wrong with being rich."

"For a start, there is," snapped Enderby. "No one got rich without exploiting others. Look at your precious Owen."

My gaze snapped to Norah, who had flushed red. So it *had* been Enderby I'd seen cycling away from Aether yesterday. But why had he been following Norah? Unless, of course, he'd been watching Aether, and had just chanced upon Norah's visit. But even so, the question remained—why?

"And anyway, my point is," steamed on Enderby, "that it's weird to lie about it."

"She didn't lie about anything," snapped Raven. "Her family are her business. It's nothing to do with us."

Enderby opened his mouth, no doubt to continue his crusade of tact and diplomacy. I thought I'd better jump in (being famed for my own tact, of course).

"Pub?" I asked with a forced smile. It was the best I could come up with.

Enderby closed his mouth and redirected his glare at me, which felt unfair—the pub wasn't a *bad* suggestion.

Sam shook his head ruefully. "I have to go start setting up my exhibition. It opens at seven."

"What's the exhibition?" I asked curiously.

"It's called Tipping Point," he said enthusiastically. "It's about the contribution of waste to climate change, a visual protest against the horrors wrought on our planet by humans. It's being put on by my collective, I've contributed some work from the various climate protests I've photographed over the years."

I noticed he avoided Raven's gaze as he said this. Raven, on the other hand, was staring at him, hard, pointedly.

"That sounds really interesting," said Ailsa, and I think she meant it.

"Why don't you come along? It's over in Wapping, doors at seven, five quid entry. Come and support us." Sam gave Ailsa a megawatt smile and fished in his pocket for a flyer, which he pressed into her hands.

"We could do." Ailsa looked round at Poppy, who nodded encouragingly. I looked down at Jack. The thought of taking him to an art exhibition filled me with dread. This was a kid who could get overstimulated at Lidl. But Poppy and Ailsa were giving me unsubtle wide-eyed looks. I knew what they were thinking, it was a good opportunity to try and get a bit more background on Sam. Plus Ailsa probably genuinely wanted to go.

I sighed. "Maybe. But pub first."

Poppy and Ailsa beamed.

"I wouldn't mind a pint," said Norah tentatively. "Just the one, mind."

Enderby grudgingly admitted that a pint wasn't a terrible idea.

"I'm always up for a pint or three," said Sian cheerfully.

"I'll give it a miss," said Raven. "Sam, a quick word?"

As the others moved off down the street, I paused to fiddle with Jack's pram—and, incidentally, eavesdrop on the two brothers.

"You better have taken those photos out," hissed Raven angrily.

"Yeah, yeah, of course I did," replied Sam breezily. Too breezily.

"I mean it, Sam," Raven continued. "Leila didn't want them included. You pissed her off enough last time."

"She's dead, Ray."

"So show some respect!" spluttered Raven.

"What, just like she did?" replied Sam, rather coldly. "Wake up, little bro. You saw them all in there. Haven't you worked out what world she was from yet? She was using you, Raven. It was all some big game to her, and you were just another plaything."

Raven looked like his brother had punched him. He stood staring at Sam, appalled.

Sam seemed to relent. "I'm sorry, Ray, that came out wrong. I didn't mean it like that. I just mean—"

"I know exactly what you mean." Raven's voice was icy.

"No, I just don't want to see you get hurt. Yam agrees with me, Leila was trouble. She—"

"I have just attended the funeral of my girlfriend," snapped Raven. "How much more hurt do you expect me to get."

And with that, he spun on his heel and left, the raven feather in his hair glinting as he strode off down the street.

Sam closed his eyes briefly. Then he opened them, squared his shoulders, and strode off in the opposite direction from his brother.

CHAPTER 19

WE FOUND AN upmarket pub just ten doors down from the church. This was one of the things I missed most about London—they might say that you were never more than six feet from a rat here, but you were also never more than sixty feet from a pub. It was a trade-off I was willing to take.

Enderby was less impressed.

"Do you know how much this round cost me?" he stormed, slamming the tray down on the table and spilling at least a tenner's worth of beer in the process. Ah. Yes, I had been rather surprised when he'd offered to get a round in.

"Thieving capitalist fat cats," he seethed. I wasn't sure if he was talking about the pub landlord, London in general, or Leila's family in particular. The latter would seem a tad unfair as we didn't actually know anything about them, and they almost certainly didn't run this pub.

"Eight pounds for a pint??" he continued. "And as for these . . ." He threw a packet of Pipers crisps onto the table.

"Did you only get one bag?" asked Sian disapprovingly.

"Two pounds fifty!" howled Enderby. I guess that was our answer then.

We huddled round our pints (only a shandy for me as I'm a responsible parent) and partook of a single crisp each. Jack began chewing a beer mat. I handed him a pacifier, which he took solemnly, dropped into my pint, and continued with his beer mat.

"Well," said Norah brightly. "It's nice to get up to the big city for a change."

Her use of "big city" was entirely unironic and made me want to cry.

Enderby, unsurprisingly, disagreed.

"Cities are both the product and cause of capitalism," he began rather pompously. "Marx said that—"

We were spared the promised Marxist lecture as the door banged open and Maya breezed in, swathed head to toe in the products of capitalism and bringing with her zero fucks about Marx or what he'd said about cities.

My heart swelled slightly as I saw her—short black hair stylishly disheveled, sporting a cropped Nike tee and zebra-print culottes (a bold combo), and not wearing a single item made from hemp. However long I lived in Penton, however embedded I became in its organic, mildly pagan culture, a part of me would always belong to the Mayas of this world.

"How was the funeral?" she asked, plonking down in a chair next to me, reaching over and grabbing the remaining pound's worth of crisps. I saw Enderby wince.

"Don't ask." I pinched a crisp back off her.

"Jack loved it," said Ailsa grinning.

"Of course you did, you big weirdo." Maya beamed at Jack, lifting him out of his pram to bounce him on her knee. "Alice, what the hell is he wearing?"

I scowled and threw Jack's blanket over Maya's head, effectively concealing both of them.

"This is Maya," I said to the rather stunned-looking Earth Force crew. "Ignore everything she says."

"Have you worked out who killed Leila yet?" asked Maya from under the blanket, proving my point.

"Er, I think the police are dealing with that," said Sian, looking confused.

"Oh, this lot love to play detective," said Maya, emerging looking slightly tousled. "Last year they caught that guy who murdered those two people in Penton. They found the bodies and everything. Didn't Helen eat, like, the crucial piece of evidence and nearly ruin the whole case?"

Sian, Norah, and Enderby were staring from Maya to us with horror. I tried for a weak smile and Norah looked positively terrified.

"Didn't they tell you about it?" asked Maya, helping herself to my shandy. "Alice, why is there a pacifier in your drink?"

"It never came up," I said, reaching across to whisk the pacifier out of Maya's hand just as she was about to put it, dripping with beer, into Jack's mouth.

"So is that what you're doing now?" asked Norah in a small voice. "Investigating?"

"No," Poppy, Ailsa, and I chorused, just as Maya said, "Yep."

"No, we're not," clarified Poppy. "We came to the protest because we wanted to help save the meadow, and we came to Leila's funeral because it seemed right. She was the one who invited us to the protest in the first place and we wanted to say goodbye properly."

I tried to look like this was definitely the case. None of it was a lie. It just wasn't the whole truth.

"It is interesting though," said Enderby, narrowing his eyes at us suspiciously. "You lot turn up, and a few days later Leila's dead. We had no problems before you arrived."

"Yeah right," said Ailsa, not exactly under her breath.

"What's that supposed to mean?" fired up Enderby.

"I'm just saying, we're not blind," retorted Ailsa. "At that meeting before the protest, you weren't exactly happy with Raven and Leila."

"He threw a firebomb into Owen Myers's house! Of course I wasn't happy!"

"It wasn't a firebomb," put in Norah nervously. "And Owen wasn't hurt."

Sian put her head in her hands. "We don't know that it was Raven—and also do we have to do this? *Again?*"

"It was a bloody terrorist act!" insisted Enderby. "Raven is always taking things too far. And Leila egged him on. He's been ten times worse since she showed up. He won't listen to anyone now, not anyone but her."

"How long were they dating?" asked Poppy interestedly.

"About six months," said Norah quickly. "I think she'd been in the area a little longer, though. I'd seen her around Bishop's Ruin from time to time. Then she joined the group and started dating Raven."

"She made a beeline for him," interjected Enderby.

"They made a lovely couple," said Norah. "I thought they were very well matched."

Enderby scoffed. "She had him wrapped round her little finger. Didn't you notice, as soon as she came on the scene Raven was suddenly pushing at everything. Wanted us to be more forceful, wanted us to get more visibility, more recognition. If you ask me, Leila wanted Raven to replace Maryam as the head of the group."

"Raven would never do that," said Norah firmly. "He loves his aunt—more than he loved Leila, even."

Enderby shrugged, managing to convey his incredulity at Norah's naivety.

"Can we just keep the focus on what we're supposed to be about?" said Sian frustratedly. "Which is fighting against climate change, not each other. Honestly!"

Norah and Enderby looked slightly chastened.

Sian checked her phone. "There's a train back to Penton in half an hour. I think I'm going to try and get it."

Norah and Enderby muttered their agreement, and the three of them drained their glasses, Enderby making sure he got his last fifty pence worth of beer.

Maya pulled a face at their departing backs. "Do this lot have any sense of humor?"

"Come on, Maya, we've just been at the funeral of one of their friends."

"Don't give me that," said Maya, brushing this excuse aside. "They clearly couldn't stand the girl."

I had to admit she had a point there. Beyond Raven, there seemed to be precious little love for Leila in the Earth Force ranks.

"So what is the deal with this Leila character?" continued Maya. "People seem to get pretty worked up over her."

I puffed out my cheeks. "I wish we knew."

"There's definitely something a bit odd about her," said Poppy. "I can't get a handle on her."

"Talk about contradictory," agreed Ailsa. "Earth Force have got a pretty anti-capitalist vibe going on, then she's from this swank family and, based on the fancy apartment and the designer clothes and the hundred-pound-plus cosmetics, it's not like she'd left that lifestyle behind."

"So she liked nice stuff," said Maya. "That doesn't mean she didn't care about the planet. I like nice stuff but I also think we can achieve it in a more sustainable way."

I could see Ailsa eyeing up Maya's Adidas hi-tops, probably about to tell her that they were made from the souls of dead pangolins or similar.

"Yeah, but Enderby said she was 'practically commie,'" I remembered. "And her lifestyle—at least the one she was living on the side—definitely didn't qualify as commie. It sounds like she was living two pretty separate lives."

"I'm not so sure," said Maya robustly. "I think a lot of people are quite contradictory when you really boil it down. I mean look at you, Al, with your reusable diapers and your local veg box—not to mention joining some nude activist group. But I'd bet Jack's inheritance you've had McDonald's within the last week."

Dammit. How did she know these things?

"Thanks for making it personal," I muttered. "And have I mentioned that it's not a nudist group?"

"I agree with you, Maya," said Poppy reasonably. "I mean in general, not about Alice."

"But a bit about Alice," chipped in Ailsa.

"I think you're right, everyone has contradictions in their life," continued Poppy. "Probably especially people who are trying to make a positive change, because at least they're trying! But Leila, I don't know . . . It seems more extreme. That's some pretty intense double standards."

"Plus the fact that she was murdered," I added. "Which strongly suggests there's something at least a bit dodgy going on."

There were murmurs of assent from the others.

"Also"—I had been wanting to tell them about this since we got to the pub, but hadn't wanted to bring it up in front of the Earth Force guys—"I overheard Sam and Raven talking just now, as we were all leaving the funeral."

I filled them in on the conversation I'd ever so slightly eavesdropped on.

"It keeps coming back to these photos," said Ailsa, once I'd finished talking.

"And it sounds like Sam is most likely including them, whatever they are, in his exhibition," said Poppy.

"All the more reason to go," said Ailsa. "Let's go see what these incriminating photos can tell us!"

CHAPTER 20

BY THE TIME we got to the warehouse in Wapping where Sam's exhibition was being held, I was feeling more awake than I had in months. The pint of shandy had given me a slight buzz (I know, pathetic) and I was enjoying the sense of vibrancy that London exudes. I loved Penton and had wholeheartedly embraced my new country lifestyle (well, maybe not *wholeheartedly*, more of a slightly awkward embrace where a handshake might've been more appropriate), but a part of me would always miss the energy of London. Having heavily partaken of the London energy, Jack was now fast asleep.

Brightly colored festoon lighting hung across the alleyway down the side of the warehouse, illuminating in red, blue, and green the faces of the smokers that clustered here and there. Posters for the exhibition, shouting TIPPING POINT in toxic green, were pasted all over the walls. I was, needless to say, the only person with a pram.

One of the smokers by the door raised a hand in greeting. It was Sam.

"You came!" He sounded pleasantly surprised. "And you brought your baby. How nice."

I wasn't sure what to say to that; short of popping Jack in a station locker I had very few options.

"Is, er, my brother with you?" Sam sounded slightly nervous.

"No, I don't know where he went. He didn't come to the pub with us," I replied.

"I'm sure he'll come though," said Poppy. "I'm sure he wouldn't miss your exhibition."

Sam shot Poppy an unreadable look. "I doubt that very much."

"Oh?" I couldn't help asking. "Not a fan of your artwork?"

"When it suits him." Sam shrugged.

A tall man wearing painters overalls sauntered over and slipped an arm around Sam's waist. He had beautifully high cheekbones, with a splash of white paint across one, glowing in the twilight against his dark skin.

"Guests of yours?" He grinned at us.

"Friends of my brother," said Sam. The two of them exchanged a glance.

"I'm Marcus." He held out a hand to shake—also paint splattered. "I'm part of the collective here."

"Oh nice," said Poppy. "What sort of stuff do you do?"

"Can't you tell?" asked Sam grinning, gesturing at Marcus's general paint-covered demeanor. "He's a painter. Best I've ever met."

"Don't let Vi hear you say that." Marcus tightened his arm around Sam affectionately.

"Keep an eye out for his oil painting of the whale's eye," said Sam. "First room. It's magic."

Sam's attention was rapidly turning to Marcus, who was now idly stroking the back of Sam's neck.

"The exhibition's on the fifth floor." Sam nodded to the door behind him in a rather obvious bid to be rid of us. "Head on up. I'll be up once I've finished this." He gestured with his cigarette.

I peered inside at the steps ascending into an uninviting gloom, despite the fairy lights that had been twisted round the bannister.

"Where's the lift?" I asked.

"Oh, there's no lift." Sam laughed.

I stared helplessly at my unwieldy pram.

"Just leave it here," Poppy suggested.

"What if someone nicks it," I protested.

"Come off it, Alice," said Ailsa. "No one's gonna nick that."

I tried to look haughty as I parked the pram in the darkest corner I could locate. I had been very proud of my find—the pram had been £15 on Facebook Marketplace. So it was a bit . . . weathered. But it had plenty of mileage left in it.

When we stepped into the first room I gave a sharp intake of breath. It was like slipping underwater. Empty milk cartons had been turned into deep-sea fish, with lanterns glowing inside. Jellyfish made from shredded carrier bags hung from the ceiling, wafting gently as the movement of people in the room sent eddies of air across them. All around us, rubbish had been transformed into undersea creatures—crabs made from takeaway coffee cups, corals from tampons, giant clams from Styrofoam takeout boxes, barnacles from chewing gum. In the center of the room an enormous red papier-mâché squid loomed menacingly. On the walls, various prints and paintings hung, some clearly depicting scenes of devastation, bleak, empty landscapes, others more abstract (by which I mean I had no idea what they were). All of it lit with a shifting, shimmering blue-green light.

"This is amazing!" said Maya, spinning to take it all in. It was.

Jack reached up to grab at a cereal-box turtle dangling from the ceiling. I couldn't blame him—this room was like being inside the largest most interactive mobile ever. Hastily, I shoved some crackers in his hands in the hope this would distract him from dismantling the entire exhibition.

Maya was already drifting away toward the largest painting in the room, pushing aside hanging Pepsi bottles and manta rays made from coat hangers. There was something magnetic about the image at the far end of the room. It showed an enormous dark eye, surrounded by thick, gnarled gray skin. Something glittered in the depths of the eye, drawing us toward it.

"Marcus's whale eye," breathed Poppy, appearing beside us.

I will be the first to admit I know very little about art. Over the eight years I lived in London I visited the Tate Modern once, when I was extremely hungover and Maya said it would make us feel better. Unfortunately, the exhibition had been of paintings entirely made of gazillions of tiny dots which had felt like the very embodiment of my hangover. Anyway, I don't know art. But this? This was incredible. It was the most alive eye I had ever seen—and I include all actual living eyes in that. As we drew closer we saw there were shadowy shapes that seemed to shift in the depths of the eye, figures reaching, contorting, toward the viewer.

"OK he is seriously good," said Maya, who is almost as good an art critic as me.

The rest of the exhibition was equally mind-blowing—well, maybe not *equally*, but it was pretty damn good. As we wandered through, we went from under the sea to a burned-out forest, where whole charred trunks had been lugged inside (fifth floor! No lift!) and artfully scattered. Then the horrors of the landfill room, where brilliant blue flames flared from amid the heaps of rubbish. I did have safety concerns about this particular room.

"We should've dropped some acid before coming here," whispered Maya in my ear, who apparently didn't share my regard for health and safety.

I lifted Jack and raised an eyebrow.

"Oh yeah, I keep forgetting you're boring now," she sighed.

"I'm sorry you find investigating a murder so dull," I sniped back.

"I don't think we're going to find the murderer in an art collective," said Maya.

"I wouldn't be so sure, you've got to keep an open mind about these things," I disagreed. "Anyway, it could definitely have been Sam, so . . ."

As I said it, I felt a funny lurch in my stomach. This was the bit of detecting I hated, having to suspect people of doing the most heinous of things. Generally speaking, I'm predisposed to quite like most people. I find it extremely socially awkward then suspecting them of murder.

FINALLY, WE came to the last room, the protest room, filled with a forest of placards, with mannequins glued to the walls in various poses of outrage. Interspersed around this room were huge photos, mainly portraits showing the intense, often fanatical, faces of various protestors.

"These must be Sam's photos," said Ailsa quietly. "So somewhere in here . . ."

We began circling the room, looking intently at each photo. I set Jack down on the floor as there seemed to be little here he could eat or destroy.

"Over here," called Poppy. She was standing before a triptych of photos. In the middle photo, center stage, was Leila, bare chested, with COAL IS DEATH painted across her torso, her mouth wide open in a howl of rage, eyes alight. Slightly behind her was Raven, an almost animalistic look on his face as he screamed his defiance. It was an incredibly arresting photo;

the otherworldly beauty of both Leila and Raven transformed into something primal, and almost disconcerting.

"People may argue over whether or not art is truth, but photographs never lie." Sam had materialized just behind me.

I looked at him in confusion. Was this the kind of thing arty people said at exhibitions? I had zero response. Should I come out with some other aphorism? If life gives you lemons, make lemonade? You can't judge a book by its cover? Impossible is nothing? Actually that last one might have been an Adidas slogan . . .

Sam was looking at the photo with a wistfulness.

"That was where they first met, her and Raven," he said. "At that protest. He was drawn to her like a moth to a flame—if you'll excuse the cliché."

But that was exactly what they looked like in the photo, Raven dark but with a fragility to his features, and Leila practically aflame with rage and beauty.

"I thought this photo would be all that she left in our lives. One of my finest pieces. She seemed . . . ephemeral, you know? There was nothing real about her. But two months later, she turned up at an Earth Force meeting, still full of the same fire—only now it was directed at Aether." He smiled sadly. "And a little bit reserved for me."

"She didn't want you to include this photo in the exhibition?" I asked. "Why?"

"I don't think she minded about the exhibition so much," he said evasively, a slight emphasis on "exhibition." I was confused.

"She wasn't a fan of you displaying a topless photo of her?" I asked. It seemed a pretty fair objection to me. If Sam was using topless photos of Leila against her will then that was basically a crime, wasn't it? If not, it definitely should be. And either way, he lost any respect I'd had for him.

Sam laughed, however. "Leila? Object to a topless photo? She couldn't have cared less about that. Have you seen her Instagram?" I hadn't, but was aware that roughly 50 percent of the times I'd met her Leila had been naked.

"Look, I overheard you and Raven after the funeral earlier," I said, deciding that blunt was probably the way to go—I've never had much truck with subtlety. "What's the deal with this photo? What did Raven mean when he said you pissed her off last time? What happened 'last time'?"

Sam didn't appear to be listening, he was gazing over my shoulder.

"Is your son planning on buying that artwork or just defacing it?" he asked, gesturing to where Jack had managed to pull the foot off one of the mannequins, which he was now sucking with apparent enjoyment.

I hurried over to separate Jack and the foot, which Jack objected to—loudly. By the time I turned back to the photos, Sam had disappeared.

WE LOITERED around the exhibition for another half hour, hoping to catch sight of Sam again, but he appeared to have disappeared into the warren-like depths of the warehouse. The atmosphere in the exhibition was heating up. Conversations were becoming louder, gestures more expansive, eyes shining brighter and brighter in the somber lighting.

"I think we'd better head off," I said to Ailsa and Poppy eventually, as Jack lolled back in my arms, sound asleep. While babies can sleep anywhere (although apparently not in their own cots), it felt like it would be good parenting to take him home at this stage.

Maya was deep in conversation with an arty-looking couple, something about whether or not recycling was actually a con invented by Big Plastic in the nineties, and waved vaguely at me.

"See you Saturday," I reminded her.

She looked blank.

"Jack's birthday party?"

"Absolutely. Wouldn't miss it." She turned back to her animated conversation. With a small pang, I left to gather up my various possessions—more luggage than I would have once packed for a hen weekend.

I couldn't blame her for forgetting about Saturday's party. After all, it was a little behind the times. Jack was nearly fourteen months old, but his and Noah's proposed joint birthday had coincided with a bout of chicken pox, followed by a major work project for Joe, followed by me taking a while to get myself organized. Normally, this wouldn't have been a problem, because Poppy would have taken charge of, well, everything. But it had been around this time that I'd started to notice Poppy was not her usual proactive self. I'd tried to step up to the plate, I really had, but the net result was that here we were, celebrating the boys' birthdays a mere two months late.

Five flights of stairs later, I wrestled the pram out of its dark corner in the ground floor lobby—and screamed. Something, some*one*, was staring up at me from the depths of the pram.

Poppy and Ailsa came rushing over.

"Are you OK? Is Jack OK? What's happened?"

My heartbeat slowed to roughly that of a hummingbird as I realized what the creature in the pram was. I reached in and pulled out a puffer fish made from an old beach ball, complete with staring googly eyes.

"It's not funny," I grumbled, as Poppy and Ailsa cracked up.

Jack, who had woken abruptly at my scream, was already drifting back off, his eyes starting to roll back in his head. He reached sleepily for the puffer fish and hugged it tight.

"Er, that might be quite dirty," said Poppy, as I tucked him into the pram alongside his new chunk of detritus.

"I'll remove it once he's properly asleep," I conceded. "Ailsa, what are you doing?"

Ailsa had moved away from us and was peering furtively through a half-open door that led into the ground floor of the warehouse.

"Shhh," she hushed. "I can't hear what they're saying."

Poppy and I joined her, peering around the door. Inside was a vast warehouse space, filled with ominous looming shapes draped in dust-sheets. Half-hidden behind one, Sam and Marcus were talking—well, arguing. Definitely arguing. I watched Sam lay a hand on Marcus's arm but he shook it off roughly.

"I don't think we should be listening in on some lovers' tiff," I objected.

"I think I heard Leila's name."

Ah, well, that was different. I leaned in.

"I don't know why you're denying it, Sam," Marcus was saying. "Vi heard you speaking to Quirke on the phone. He wanted to meet with *me*, not you. So what the hell were you doing?"

"OK fine, yes, I did meet him last Wednesday, but it's not what you think, I was—"

"It's not what I think? Let me tell you what I think. I think you were jealous that an agent was interested in my work and you saw an opportunity to make something out of it for yourself. That's what I think."

"I wasn't doing it for myself!" argued Sam. "I met with him on behalf of the collective, it wasn't just about me, it was about all of us."

"If that really was the case, why the hell didn't you tell us!" exploded Marcus. "Then we could have discussed it as a group. Decided who was best placed to take the meeting. You don't run this collective you know, Sam!"

"It's not—I don't think I—"

"It was selfish and it was petty, Sam. And it was a betrayal, that's the worst thing of all."

"Marcus, I'm *sorry*. I didn't mean to—"

"Look, just forget about it." Marcus turned and began storming toward the door we were lurking behind.

We scurried backward at top speed. I wrestled with the pram brake, which often jammed (curse you, £15 Marketplace bargain!), until Ailsa lifted up the front of the pram and we half fell, half ran outside carrying Jack like a sedan chair.

"You never heard Leila's name," I said accusingly as we slowed to a sedate walk in the alleyway.

Ailsa shrugged. "No, but I wanted to listen in. So sue me."

As an inveterate eavesdropper, I couldn't really argue with that.

"So it sounds like Sam really *did* meet with an agent on Wednesday night," mused Poppy as we headed stationward. "But it sounds like he may have done so under, let's say, false pretenses."

"Yeah," I said. "If this Quirke guy actually wanted to meet with Marcus . . . Well, stealing an agent off your boyfriend? That's pretty low."

"Sam's an interesting character," said Ailsa. "Seems nice enough on the surface, but it appears you can't trust him as far as you could throw him."

"No," I agreed. "That's at least two people he's managed to piss off—Leila and Marcus. And it doesn't sound like his brother's too happy with him, either."

"But what was it about that photo that Leila objected to?" mused Poppy.

"If it wasn't the fact that she was topless. It didn't seem any different from any of the other ones in that room. If anything, it was one of the best!"

We fell silent as we made our way back to Paddington through the gathering dark, each of us dwelling on the haunting photograph of Leila. Leila Arnault turned Leila Smith. Leila, who charmed, dissembled, lied . . .

CHAPTER 21

THE TRAIN BACK to Penton rumbled gently through the darkness. London had been great, it had felt like waking up after dream-drifting through the last few months. It had also been exhausting. And, to my surprise, it hadn't felt like home. Home felt like the nearly falling down cottage, waiting, with Joe inside, back in Penton. But that was still over an hour away.

I rummaged in my bag. Unbelievably, I had forgotten to pack snacks for myself—something I'm not normally remiss about. What I had instead was a selection of sugar-free and taste-free baby snacks all emblazoned with flashes declaring them "organic" and "one of your baby's five a day." This was not what I was in the mood for. I opened a super-oaty fruit-plus apple bar and bit into it joylessly. It tasted like sadness.

I was bored. Ailsa was listening to her audiobook, Poppy was reading her book, Jack was asleep. I'd even have settled for Helen for some company. Without really noticing I was doing it, which happens alarmingly often these days, I found myself staring at Instagram. I didn't even remember opening the app.

A memory struck me. I dug about in my backpack and pulled out the order of service from Leila's funeral. I removed a bit of satsuma peel that was stuck to it and flattened it out on the table in front of me. There on the front was her full name: Leila Céline Arnault. And what had Sam said? "Have you seen her Instagram?" I felt a rush of anticipation as I typed Leila Arnault into the profile search. But there was nothing.

I tried Leila Smith and—bingo. Fifth Leila Smith down was our girl, @greengirl95. It was broadly what I would have expected—until today, that is. It showed Leila in full-on activist mode. Leila in a plain T-shirt, makeup free, raising a placard saying PLANET OVER PROFIT at a protest. Leila bundled in an oversized cardigan that looked like a Goodwill reject, glued to the gates of some mega-corp. Slogan posts declaring that the climate can't wait, the truth about private jets, and five things Big Oil don't want you to know. A couple of photos of Leila and Raven looking cute but deeply earnest at a climate march. One obligatory photo of the two of them nude and besloganned, protesting up at the meadow—presumably taken by Sam.

It was a far cry from Leila Arnault, the glossy blonde on the front of the order of service in my lap.

I flipped through the pages to the eulogy. "By the Honorable Genevieve Arnault."

I found Leila's sister straightaway. Blue tick to her name and all. A *verified* Honorable. The couple of lines in her profile head gave little away: "Socialite, girl about town, sometimes model," and a *lot* of emojis. I tried not to instantly judge. But seriously—who actively describes themselves as a "girl about town"; what does it even mean?

I might not know what it meant, but after just a few seconds I was pretty sure Genevieve was it. Her profile was the Instagram dream: heavily filtered, glossy content, sometimes featuring D-list celebrities who I, of course, instantly recognized—contestants off *Love Island*, members of the *Made in Chelsea* cast, a woman I remembered from *Married at First Sight*—not the bride, but maybe like a bridesmaid? Many of the photos were in exotic places: Saint Lucia, the Maldives, the Cayman Islands, often at resorts with names like Sunset Glory or Ocean Dreams, and frequently featuring flamboyantly garish cocktails, dreamy beachscapes, and infinity pools. In all of them Genevieve was stunningly dressed (although sometimes barely), with flawless makeup; that girl knew how to contour.

Just over a year into Genevieve's back catalog I was brought up short by a photo of Genevieve and another girl, arms around each other, raising their wine glasses to the camera as they leaned against a terrace balcony, a vineyard stretching out behind them. It was Leila. But not the Leila we had known. Gone was the raven pixie crop and the charity shop dresses. No, this was Leila as she had appeared in the photo at her funeral—glossy blond hair, delicate bronzed makeup, and a slinky white dress with cut-out sides.

I read the caption: "With my sis and bestie @ladylei at @goldenvine-yards. Best wine, best times. Love you Lei Lei x."

@ladylei . . . That wasn't the Instagram account I'd found for Leila Smith. I clicked through onto the profile. It was Leila all right. But this account was the twin of Genevieve's, featuring the same rotating cast of manicured women and chiseled, bronzed men, the same exotic locations, fine dining and premium experiences. Leila in a bikini on a yacht. Leila popping the cork on a bottle of Moët. Leila on the steps up to what looked like a private jet. I almost laughed, it was so clichéd. Her account practically *was* Rich Kids of Instagram.

The last post, however, was just over a year ago, just before Leila had moved to Bishop's Ruin. It showed her on some sort of spiritual eco retreat in Thailand. One of those deeply paradoxical ones where a lot of rich, Botoxed people wearing very expensive yoga gear drink kombucha and "commune with the planet." That was the last post. Since then, nothing. I flicked back to the account I'd previously found for Leila, @greengirl95, and scrolled down to her first post. June 2021. She had started this account when she'd left off the previous, just weeks after her final post from the eco retreat.

I showed what I'd found to Ailsa and Poppy.

"That's pretty Jekyll and Hyde," said Poppy, pulling up Leila "Smith's" account and laying her phone next to mine, which showed RKOI Leila Arnault.

"Are there any more?" asked Ailsa.

"What do you mean?"

"Has she got any more accounts? If you go right back to Genevieve's earliest posts, is Leila in any of them? And what's she tagged as?"

I looked at Genevieve's profile and groaned. "She's got nearly 10,000 posts. I can't go through all that!"

"Of course you can," said Ailsa briskly. "Instagram stalking is your key skill."

I sighed. She had a point. And there was still a long train journey ahead.

I sighed, and prepared to do my duty as the least skilled member of our unskilled amateur detective band.

Genevieve had clearly been an early adopter of Instagram. I decided to start back at her earliest posts, in 2011. These showed a teenage Genevieve, maybe eighteen years old. Already poised and glamorous but lacking the instinctive ease in front of the camera that she had developed in later years. And there, in every fifth or sixth post, was Leila. At least, I was pretty sure it was her. She looked younger than Genevieve, maybe fifteen or sixteen. And she looked different again—as, admittedly, most people will do a decade earlier, particularly if it's the teen years. But there was no account tagged—perhaps she hadn't had Instagram back then.

As the years progressed, Leila came and went, sometimes not appearing in her sister's posts for months, then popping up in a spate—on holiday together, skiing, sunning themselves on a beach or, failing that, a yacht. The family clearly went beyond "a bit of cash" and into the stratosphere of the insanely rich.

"Someone google Genevieve Arnault," I said absently, scrolling past a series of stunning Caribbean sunsets.

"On it," said Poppy. A few seconds and then, "Here we go. Ooh. 'Genevieve Arnault is a British-French socialite—'"

"Girl about town," I muttered.

"—what? Shh listen. 'She is the oldest child of petrochemical billionaire Simon Arnault and his wife Marguerite Arnault.'" Poppy looked up at us, eyes wide. "A petrochemical billionaire?"

"Petrochemicals as in, like, petrol?" I asked, just wanting to be clear.

"Yeah, as in, fossil fuels. As in, everything Leila was protesting against . . ." clarified Ailsa, who had actually pulled both earphones out now. "And billionaire as in disgustingly rich off the smoking remains of our planet."

Poppy gave a low whistle, which I didn't know she could do, but felt appropriate. "No wonder she was pretty cagey about her family around the Earth Force lot."

"She didn't have to be, surely," I said. "It seems like she had a pretty major change of heart. I mean, it looks like she made a clean break with her family, moving to Bishop's Ruin, working for Aether, joining Earth Force. Everyone has the right to change their minds, to choose what they believe in rather than what their family believe in."

"Somehow I don't think Enderby and co. would be quite so understanding," said Ailsa dryly. "Besides, do we really think she had a change of heart? All the stuff at the apartment—the apartment itself!—would suggest she hadn't exactly cut all ties with her family. Not with her family's bank account, at least."

This was a fair point. And a slightly troubling one.

"Do you think Raven knew?" I asked.

Poppy shrugged. "We'd have to ask him. But, at a guess, I'm gonna say no. He seemed kinda clueless about all those things in her apartment."

"Yeah, but he must have realized something was a bit . . . odd," I countered. "I mean, we realized after like less than a week."

"That week did involve her murder," pointed out Poppy. "Which was a pretty major red flag. And I suspect Raven might have only seen what he wanted to see . . ."

"But, he must have googled her," I said weakly.

"Who googles their girlfriend?" said Ailsa, as if this was utterly unthinkable. I didn't say anything. I had very much googled Joe when we first met, and had found nothing other than an extremely out-of-date LinkedIn page and an equally untouched Facebook page where his profile picture was still him doing pub golf during the first week of university (we were twenty-nine at the time).

"He might not have known her real surname," said Poppy. "Or her sister's name, if she was keeping her family background under wraps. He wouldn't find anything from googling Leila Smith."

This was true—I had tried.

"We need to ask him," said Ailsa. "We need to establish how much he knew about Leila's background."

"We could swing by Fox Hollow Farm tomorrow," suggested Poppy. "You know, check how he is after the funeral?"

"Subtle," I said dryly. Poppy just grinned.

"Good plan," said Ailsa. "And who knows, the conversation might just come round to how moving Leila's sister's eulogy was—"

"Not at all," I interrupted. Because, well, it hadn't been. All the right words, zero genuine emotion.

"—and whether or not Raven knew her sister," continued Ailsa.

At this point Jack stirred in his pram. I hefted him onto my lap and settled him on the boob, enjoying his comforting, warm weight in my lap. I was glad my family was—well actually, not particularly normal, but certainly not as mysterious or cold as Leila's, nor as wealthy, though, come to that.

"OK so Leila came from a petrochemical billionaire family," I said, trying to get my thoughts straight. "This explains quite a lot about her, but not really why anyone would want to kill her."

"I dunno, it's got to be a pretty murky world in fossil fuels," said Ailsa darkly. "And with money like that involved . . ."

"I think it all swings on what exactly Leila was up to," mused Poppy.

"What do you mean?" I asked. "Like, she could've been . . . a spy? For her family?"

Ailsa snorted. "Come on, I'm sure major disruptors like Greenpeace and XR have . . . infiltrators. I don't think anyone is sending undercover agents into local protest groups like Earth Force."

"I think a spy is a little far-fetched," said Poppy delicately, "but anyway, I wasn't thinking so much about Earth Force, I was thinking of her time working at Aether. I wonder if Owen knew about her family connections?"

"Ohhh, she could've been spying on *Aether*?" I gasped.

Ailsa looked marginally less skeptical.

"I'm not saying that," said Poppy hastily. "I'm just saying it's an interesting move on her part. And there are still quite a few unanswered questions about her time at Aether. Like, whether she was having a relationship with Owen."

"Or blackmailing him," chipped in Ailsa.

"That doesn't seem so likely now," I pointed out. "Her family are so wealthy, she had literally zero need to blackmail anyone."

"I'm erring more toward some kind of affair," said Poppy. "But either way, I think we need to find out more about Leila—her work background and her family background."

"Let me see what else I can dig up." I turned back to scrolling the ancient history of Instagram.

"And you can put your boob away now," added Ailsa, nodding to where Jack had drifted off again in my lap. This often happened to me—Jack would fall asleep mid-feed, but I wouldn't notice, and would happily sit chatting for the next half an hour with one boob needlessly bared to the world.

Jack's face was slightly tilted up toward me, as if making sure I was still there while he slept. I found this very distracting. I still stand by my pre-parenthood statement that watching your children sleep is creepy. However this absolutely does not mean I don't do it. I'm a serial offender. I love watching Jack sleep, can't get enough of it. Of course this is in part because when he's asleep he's not demanding anything of me. (But if I'm honest, it's also because secretly I'm completely obsessed with him.)

I dragged my eyes away from Jack's sleeping face and back to the endless cocktail hours and sunsets of the Honorable Genevieve's Instagram feed, so far removed from my own reality of miscellaneous bodily fluids and mystery stains. The images were starting to blur together when, finally, something made me scroll back to a photo I had initially dashed past. It was unsurprising that I hadn't recognized her at first, but I was pretty sure it was Leila in some sort of historical garb—Tudor? Edwardian? What was the difference? It had been posted on 27 November 2013 and the caption read: "So proud of my baby sister @leilei, playing Vittoria in #thewhitedevil One of the best student productions I've ever seen. Go Leila!"

@Leilei . . .

And there it was, another account. This one seemed to be from Leila's student days. The profile head read "'All the world's a stage.' Chemistry student @ManchesterUni, you'll find me in the theater." This confused me slightly, but then I'd dropped out of uni in my first term—in part because people had said stuff like this. Scrolling through the photos, it mainly seemed to be Leila in various costumes, performing in a dizzying array of student productions. Leila the street urchin. Leila the circus master. Bonneted Leila as Abigail in *The Crucible*. Beglittered Leila as Titania, queen of the fairies. Leila the . . . dog?

And then, three years later, 2016, it stopped. There was a graduation picture from July, indicating that she had, somehow, between all these productions, managed to gain a degree in chemistry. There was an arty headshot from August, captioned "RADA audition day! #wishmeluck." Then, nothing. I flicked back to @LadyLei. First post, December 2016, a newly blonded Leila in a hot tub in Cancun, captioned "All I want for Christmas is champagne in the hot tub #livingmybestlife."

"Hmm."

I borrowed Ailsa and Poppy's phones and opened a different Leila account on each one. I looked down at the three phones on the slightly sticky train table in front of me.

Three Instagram accounts. Three Leilas. Each picking up where the previous one had left off. One of them, at least, had pissed off the wrong person.

CHAPTER 22

I IMAGINE THERE are families who all sit down around the breakfast table together, with glasses of orange juice and cereals in those glass decanters you get in posh hotels. Our family is not like that. Not least because in our shoebox-size kitchen there's only realistically space to squeeze one person plus a highchair around the tiny table. There is definitely *not* space for Helen to squeeze under the table and yet somehow she managed it without fail. She was currently fielding any Wheaties that Jack sent flying—which is to say, most of it. Joe was sitting on the kitchen counter eating peanut butter and Marmite on toast, a combination I do not approve of. I took the spoon off Jack and tried to get some Wheaties into his actual mouth.

"How was London then?" asked Joe.

"Weird," I said, truthfully.

I filled Jack in on the overall weirdness of Leila's funeral, the weirdness of Sam and Raven, and the weirdness of the exhibition. By the end, Joe was looking almost wistful.

"I dunno, sounds kinda fun," he said. "Do you remember that warehouse party we ended up at in Hackney once, when Maya found the fuse box and thought it would be funny to plunge everyone into darkness?"

"And everyone just carried on partying like nothing had happened."

"And then she made friends with that fiddle player and decided she was going to learn the tin whistle and join a folk band."

We both sighed nostalgically and gazed two whole years into the past. Yep, a lot had changed in two years.

"I think she had a pretty similar night last night to be honest," I said. "She stayed at Sam's exhibition long after we left."

I had received a text from Maya at 3 A.M. which simply read:

We all need to start wearing and eating bamboo, and recycling our pee

I showed it to Joe. He snorted. "She'll be joining my dad's commune next."

I laughed, although I did also wonder at what point Joe had started referring to Camran as his dad, as opposed to his usual pedantic "my biological father."

"And did any of your high-level detectoring pay off?" asked Joe, slightly mockingly I felt. "Worked out who did it yet—Watch where you're putting that spoon."

I turned back to Jack and realized I was posting Wheaties into his hair.

"We are following up on various leads," I said with dignity. "Chuck us a cloth."

"What are you doing today?" Joe asked, flinging a cloth my way. With my customary dexterity it hit me in the face.

"Gonna head over to Fox Hollow Farm," I said, sponging half-heartedly at Jack's hair. It would have to do.

Joe looked blank.

"Where Maryam lives? And Raven? And sometimes Sam?" I clarified.

"Oh yes, this year's hobby," said Joe dryly.

"It is not a hobby!" I retorted. "It's taking an important stand for the environment and"—what was it Ailsa had said?—"preserving the integrity of our delicately balanced local ecosystem."

Joe didn't dignify this with a response. "Well at least take Helen."

I looked down to where Helen was picking Wheaties out of her tail, and eating quite a lot of her own fur as she did so.

"Do I have to?"

"Yes."

MY TRIP to Fox Hollow Farm was somewhat delayed by that delightful pastime, a police interrogation. Something I was altogether too familiar with these days. We had evidently finally reached the top of Harris's list and I was treated to a rather cursory visit from the great detective herself.

Joe ushered her in with a rather resigned look on his face.

"I'll be upstairs, working, if you need me," he said, rather noticeably not offering to take Jack up with him. Oh well, I supposed the kid might as well get an early introduction to the workings of the Penton police force. The way things seemed to be going around here, it was only a matter of time.

Inspector Harris declined a cup of tea, which was a relief because I was pretty sure we didn't have any clean mugs.

"Let's keep this brief," she said brusquely, which suited me just fine. "I just need a statement from you detailing the events of last Wednesday night and Thursday morning."

I dutifully plowed through my memory of the event, already beginning to fuzz at the edges—as most things do when you're operating on minimal sleep. Occasionally, Harris would interject with a question. She seemed particularly interested in Raven's movements, very few of which I'd seen, having been on the far side of a tree facing the opposite way, and she was not impressed by my regaling of the adult diaper incident. But she asked twice if I was sure Raven had been chained to the same tree as Leila—which I wasn't. I felt her heavy focus on Raven showed a distinct lack of imagination, but then—classic Harris.

Halfway through, Helen slunk under the kitchen table we were sitting at and laid her head fondly on Harris's feet. Harris pulled them out from under her and tucked them under her chair, but Helen gently shuffled herself across and resumed the position.

When I had finished my not-particularly-helpful statement, I tried to ease in a few questions of my own.

"Did the post-mortem tell you what was used to strangle Leila?"

Harris fixed me with a beady eye. I could see her weighing up whether it would simply be less hassle to tell me now, rather than wait until Ailsa inevitably went through her home office.

"There were traces of nylon found in the wound on her neck," she said eventually.

"So like, a rope? Or a belt, or a . . . a . . . dress tie?" I hazarded. Now I came to think about it, nylon was probably in . . . pretty much everything?

"Could be," said Harris noncommittally. She closed her notebook, indicating the interview was at an end.

"I presume you've spoken to the Arnault family?" I asked quickly and, I hoped, casually.

Harris stiffened, then sighed.

"Of course we have. Mainly through their lawyers, unfortunately. The family have . . . closed ranks. And I'm not even going to ask how you know about Leila's family because I'm quite sure I don't want to know."

I decided not to mention that we'd attended the funeral the previous day. I was pretty sure this didn't count as withholding information from the police. Right?

Harris stood to leave, then looked down at her shoes in dismay.

"Ugh, look what your animal has done."

I bristled at what I felt to be an unnecessarily derogatory slur on Helen. However, it transpired Helen had not only drooled all over Harris's shoes but also had a stealthy chew on one of her shoelaces, reducing it to a mangled pulp.

"Er, sorry," I said weakly. I peered at the soggy mess. "Do you know if it had one of those plastic bits on the end? Only that could lodge in her throat or stomach and cause real issues."

Harris clearly had fewer concerns about my dog's digestive tract. Her only response was an impressive harrumph as she made speedily for the door, before Helen could eat any more of her footwear.

"I'm well aware I'm wasting my breath here," she said, turning back to face me in the doorway, "but, Alice, stay well out of this. And don't get my sister involved—she's got enough on her plate as it is right now, thank you very much."

This was so deeply unfair. I personally felt I had been nothing short of press-ganged into this investigation by Poppy and Ailsa, but once again Harris seemed to have pegged me as some sort of ringleader. I have never been a ringleader in my life. I'm barely even in the ring. I very much see myself as an innocent bystander led astray by my more impulsive and charismatic friends.

I hoped she spent all day tripping over that mangled shoelace.

I headed back inside and gave Helen a whole handful of dog biscuits to wash down the lace.

CHAPTER 23

I FOUND MY way to Maryam's house with relative ease this time. Admittedly because I was following Ailsa's car the whole way there. With the whole troop in tow we now required a minimum of two cars, and mine was feeling pretty crowded with Poppy and co. wedged in, particularly as Helen and Ronnie insisted on hanging over the back seats, trying to cadge snacks out of Jack and Noah's hands.

We drew up in Maryam's yard and decamped. It felt like unloading a circus. I opened the trunk and Helen and Ronnie exploded out like canine cannonballs. Then from the back seats I unloaded Jack and Noah, who took a few tentative steps after the dogs and were immediately knocked flat by the flying hounds on their return run. Not that either of them appeared to mind. Apparently deciding the ground was safer, they began crawling toward a bounty of hazardous-looking farm equipment.

Ailsa somehow managed to make handling twins look positively easy in comparison. She had agreed to take one dog in her car, provided it was Sultan. He loped down from her trunk gracefully and went to lie in a patch of sun by Maryam's front door, pointedly ignoring Helen and Ronnie. He immediately raised the tone of the building to look like a quaint Cotswoldian postcard.

Unsurprisingly, the general commotion had alerted Maryam to our presence, and she appeared in the doorway, waving to us.

"We just popped by to see Raven," said Ailsa. "We wanted to see how he is after yesterday."

"Oh my dears," said Maryam, "I'm afraid you've had a wasted journey. Raven is out this morning."

Ah, that put paid to our subtle interrogation plans.

"And it looks like you're just heading out," remarked Ailsa, nodding at the empty basket slung over Maryam's arm. At this rate it really was going to have been a wasted journey.

"I was just about to go mushroom harvesting," Maryam said brightly. "There's a wonderful crop of chicken of the woods in the dell above the house."

I was slightly confused—was she hunting chickens or fungi? Or possibly both?

"I don't suppose you'd like some company?" asked Ailsa, visibly brightening. "I haven't managed to get out foraging at all this summer. It's almost impossible with these two in tow."

"Of course!" Maryam sounded delighted. "Here, let me help you with one of those babes." And without further ado she popped Ivy into her mushroom basket. Ailsa looked a little taken aback, but Ivy seemed delighted.

Jack gave me a look that seemed to ask where his luxury basket carrier was. I hefted him under one arm.

Maryam bustled around gathering extra baskets for the rest of us. Experimentally, I plopped Jack into my basket, which appeared to be woven from sticks. He squirmed delightedly, and immediately slithered out the other side. Meanwhile I'd already given myself a splinter. I decided I'd stick to the baby carrier.

Calling to our errant dogs, now peeing on various items of rusted machinery, our strange procession set off.

We followed Maryam up a narrow, steep path that skirted her property, running between the crumbling stone walls and wild hedgerows that overflowed with nature (I'm afraid I can't be more specific), a lot of which attempted to tangle itself in my hair or trip me up.

After a few hundred yards, the path entered a dense woodland. It felt old. I couldn't say why, it was just giving off a vibe of ancientness and, possibly, just a hint of witchiness. I looked around hopefully for the red-and-white-spotted mushrooms of my childhood fairy-tale books.

"I can't see any mushrooms," I said plaintively.

"Just wait," said Maryam. "They're here, we just need to let them show themselves."

This seemed a bit much for me. Were we hunting mushrooms or fairies here? I glanced at Poppy, who pulled a face. But Ailsa obediently lowered her gaze and seemed to relax into the woodland. After a few moments, she pointed at a tree.

"There."

And she was right. Clustered around the roots were a handful of elegant golden yellow flutes, which I could've sworn hadn't been there a moment earlier.

"Chanterelles," said Maryam happily. "Well done. You clearly have a knack." She gave Ailsa an approving nod.

Maryam produced a wooden-handled switchblade from her pocket and swiftly nipped off a handful of chanterelles.

We made our way slowly through the woods and honestly it was bizarre how many mushrooms there were. I swear they were popping out of the ground at our feet.

"Once you call them, they're everywhere," said Maryam happily, as she decapitated mushrooms left, right, and center.

Not only were they everywhere, but they were WEIRD. We found a cluster of lion's mane mushrooms growing straight out of a tree trunk (when I say "we" found, I mean Ailsa), which had definitely come from space. Or possibly deep under the sea; the two are very similar in my book. They were big white fluffy aliens, a cross between sea anemones and shag furniture (never a good look). We also found Maryam's chicken of the woods—which, it turns out, is simply a very confusing name for a mushroom. These were huge tawny frills that erupted from tree trunks like an Oscars-worthy ballgown. Soon, our baskets were all overflowing.

"I didn't think mushrooms grew in summer," I admitted. They'd always seemed more of a cold weather phenomenon to me—although I admit I had never previously given it much thought.

"Common misconception," said Maryam briskly. "Autumn is the best time of year, but mushrooms can be found year-round. A wet summer yields a better harvest, but as you can see there are plenty to be found even in a dry spell like this."

As we worked, we tried to steer the conversation toward Leila, which I was considerably more interested in than Maryam's ongoing fungi lecture. Conversation was frequently interrupted by the need to field wayward babies, who were reveling in the coolness of the dell after the stifling heat of the day. Noah was blissing out in the shade of some ferns, Jack sitting next to him alternating between eating soil and rubbing it experimentally in his (and occasionally Noah's) hair. The twins, however, were all but climbing trees—something I suspected they'd have mastered by the age of one.

"How is Raven coping?" asked Poppy. "I mean, with losing Leila and everything."

Maryam's back stiffened slightly, as she bent over a particularly promising crop of chanterelles.

"Oh. He'll be OK," she said, not turning round. "I don't think it was a particularly serious relationship."

This wasn't the impression I'd got. On the one hand, Maryam knew them both far better. On the other, I couldn't help wondering if this was what she *hoped* to have been the case.

"No, I don't think so," agreed Ailsa, bending down to help load the chanterelles into a basket. "Leila wasn't really a one-man kind of girl, was she?"

This seemed uncomfortably close to slandering the dead, but I could see what Ailsa was driving at.

"Meaning?" said Maryam. She sounded guarded, but also slightly eager. Was she as big a gossip as the rest of them? If there was one thing I'd learned about village life in my year living here, it was that gossip is the social engine the community runs on. I tried not to think what my fellow Pentonites said about me and Joe. And Helen—although they often said that to my face.

"I heard she still had a thing going on with her old boss, Owen Myers," said Ailsa candidly, reaching out to grab Robin before he poked his sister's eye out with a twig.

Maryam looked genuinely taken aback at this.

"Well, I hadn't heard that," she said—and I believed her. "Not that I'd have put it past her, mind you."

I nodded awkwardly, feeling like a terrible person.

"I hope it's not true," said Maryam. "It would break Raven's heart." This seemed to directly contradict what she'd just said about it "not having been particularly serious." But then, a lot of what Maryam said about Leila seemed a little contradictory.

"Did you know her family at all?" I asked.

Maryam shook her head. "Didn't know she had any. She never mentioned them. But Raven said they made quite the showing at the funeral yesterday."

"You could say that," I muttered.

"Fancy lot, are they?" Maryam asked disinterestedly.

"They're the Arnault family," said Ailsa. "As in Arnault Petrochemicals. Leila was pretty much royalty. If money equals status, that is, which it sadly does."

Maryam paused in the act of harvesting a fresh crop. Her hand holding the knife trembled slightly. "Is that right then?"

"Er, didn't Raven know?" I asked, trying to sound innocent. "He must have known who his girlfriend's family were."

"No," said Maryam shortly. "No, he didn't. He did say something when he came back from the funeral yesterday—something about 'Smith' not being her real surname. But he didn't elaborate and I didn't want to push him. Poor boy, he must feel so betrayed. You're sure she's from the Arnault family?"

"Pretty sure," said Ailsa.

Maryam was silent for a moment, then began cutting at the mushrooms mechanically. I watched her out of the corner of my eye. In the space of about ten minutes, she had directly contradicted herself about Leila and Raven's relationship several times—why?

"Makes you wonder what Leila was doing working as a PA for a green energy company, hidden away down here," said Poppy lightly. "And, well, her family can't have thought much of her involvement with Earth Force."

"No, I'm sure they'd love to pin her death on Earth Force," said Ailsa.

Maryam's hand slipped, the knife nicking her other hand.

"Damn," she swore, sucking the wound. "Well, they'll have a job accusing any of us, what with everyone being tied to trees at the time. No, it was Aether behind it, mark my words."

We remained silent. Honestly, I had no idea what I thought anymore. Perhaps it had been Aether, perhaps it had been Earth Force. Perhaps it had been Maryam—there was clearly no love lost there! Could it have even been Leila's family? We knew now that money—serious money—was involved. Who would inherit? Her sister? Surely not Raven, not after six months together? Owen, Raven, Sam, Genevieve . . . Could any of them have had a motive to kill Leila? Could all of them? It seemed incomprehensible that there could have been that many people with a motive to kill her.

"Leila was a dangerous person," said Maryam finally, as if reading my thoughts. "I didn't want her near my boys."

Boys plural, I noticed with interest. What exactly had Leila's relationship with Sam been? I couldn't get a handle on it. The two had clearly antagonized each other—but was that the old double bluff, trying to hide an illicit attraction? Or was I reading too much into it? Goddammit, I'd forgotten how hard this detecting lark was!

"I'm not sure Helen should be eating so many of those," said Poppy concernedly, breaking my train of thought. I looked over to where Helen was scarfing down a bright orange mushroom with every apparent sign of enjoyment.

I threw a pinecone at Helen, which bounced off her nose. She gave me a mildly affronted look and moved on to investigate some brown mushrooms.

"Or those," added Poppy, as yet more mushrooms disappeared down Helen's throat.

I sighed and headed toward Helen, pausing to upend Jack, who had turtled himself and was utterly failing to flip himself right way up.

"What do you mean 'dangerous'?" I asked Maryam, as I tried to corner Helen, who danced backward out of my reach with every step.

Maryam shrugged. "I just think there was more to her than met the eye. And, well, hearing who her family are . . . I think that just confirms it really. She was a snake in the grass."

"I'm not sure about that," said Ailsa. "I mean, I know she kept a lot of secrets, but she did seem pretty committed to the cause. She was dead against Aether building that wind farm."

I felt the phrase "dead against" was a little insensitive in the circumstances but was distracted from pointing this out by Helen flipping onto her back and writhing like she had itching powder in her fur. Then she went completely rigid, all four paws in the air, before abruptly pinging back onto her feet like one of those pop toys you used to get in Kinder Eggs. She stood frozen for a second, then tore off, zigzagging through the trees with such speed I was sure she would crash into one.

"Do you think she's tripping out?" asked Ailsa with interest.

I shrugged. "It's hard to say. This is quite standard Helen behavior to be honest."

Helen slowed to a standstill and began snuffling around again, no doubt looking for more fungal snacks.

"Could she have been against Aether specifically?" I said. "The company, rather than the wind farm itself. Leila I mean, not Helen."

Ailsa gave me a withering look at this clarification. But Poppy was looking thoughtful.

"It's a point," she said carefully. "I mean, it's interesting that immediately after she left Aether she took up with a group that directly oppose them."

"We do have other projects," interrupted Maryam slightly reproachfully. "You've just joined us at a time when our point of focus has been this wind farm."

"And when did you start focusing on that?" Poppy asked.

"Well, now you come to mention it," said Maryam slowly, "it was Leila who brought the wind farm to our attention, when she joined, oh, must have been about six months ago. They'd been very sneaky about the plans you see—advertised them in Bridgeport, not in Bishop's Ruin. Like any of us would have been popping into the council offices all that way away."

Bridgeport was probably about seven miles from Bishop's Ruin, but after living here for over a year I had come to appreciate that this was essentially "foreign parts" in some residents' minds. But the timing of all this was very interesting. Poppy and I exchanged a glance.

"So Leila joined with a bit of an axe to grind against Aether?" said Poppy.

"Oh yes," said Maryam, a little too eagerly. "There was definitely some bad feeling there."

"What do you think, Ailsa?" I asked.

"I still think she's tripping," said Ailsa, who wasn't paying attention but was watching Helen meander aimlessly among the trees.

"She's fine," I said dismissively. "She's always like this."

Helen walked into a tree.

"Point proven," I said.

BACK AT the farmhouse Maryam began dividing the spoils into four equal piles.

"Oh, you must take some with you!" she declared when we protested. "This is far too much for me on my own." Poppy and Ailsa gratefully accepted. I did, with rather more qualms.

As we were loading the babies and dogs into the cars, Penton's only taxi turned in to the farmyard and dispensed a slightly disheveled figure.

"Is that . . . ?" said Poppy.

"I think so," I replied.

Marcus turned round and looked rather taken aback to find a full-on welcome committee awaiting him.

"Er, hi," he said awkwardly.

"Marcus!" said Maryam warmly. "How lovely to see you!" The unspoken "but what are you doing here" hung in the air.

"Hi, Maryam," said Marcus. "And hi, didn't we meet at the exhibition last night? Are you Maya's friends?"

How did it happen, I wondered, that even down here I ended up being "Maya's friend"?

"I'm afraid so," I replied. "I hope she didn't cause any damage last night." It was the kind of apology I was used to making for Helen.

"Not at all," said Marcus with a trace of a smile. "She was the life and soul, you could say."

"I'll bet . . ."

The taxi driver leaned out of the window to hand Marcus some change, then started the engine.

"Is Sam with you?" asked Maryam, rather eagerly, looking round Marcus as if hoping Sam was suddenly going to spring from the trunk of the slowly reversing taxi.

Marcus's face fell. "No. I came here looking for him."

Maryam looked confused. "He's not due here till Saturday. I thought he was in London with you?"

Marcus shifted awkwardly. "We had a . . . row last night. He said he was going to come down here for some headspace."

I carefully didn't meet Poppy and Ailsa's eyes.

Maryam looked concerned. "Come inside and I'll put the kettle on," she said, picking up Marcus's backpack for him. "I'm sure it's just a misunderstanding. We'll find Sam and sort the whole thing out. I'll call him now." She began ushering Marcus into the house, pausing to wave to us over her shoulder and catching me in the act of accidentally-on-purpose abandoning my mushroom heap.

"Don't forget your mushrooms!"

AS SOON as we were in the car, I emptied my fungal bounty into Poppy's lap. "You have these. Absolutely no way am I risking poisoning myself."

"I'm pretty sure Maryam knows what she's doing," said Poppy mildly.

"She might, but I don't. If you cook these things wrong you probably see dancing pixies and decide you can fly. I'm not risking it."

Not these days, I thought with a sigh. Many years ago that would have sounded like a great adventure. Maybe I should palm the shrooms off on Maya instead? Still, it sounded like she was having plenty of fun without me.

"Fancy Marcus turning up here," I said, as I performed a six-thousand-point turn to get out of the farmyard.

"Sounds like that argument really took off," agreed Poppy. "I wonder where Sam is?"

"Hiding in shame somewhere," I said unsympathetically. I took a pretty low view of Sam's behavior toward Marcus.

"Well, if anyone's going to find him, it'll be Maryam," said Poppy. "She's pretty protective of those boys."

"Yes . . ."

There was a tense silence for a moment.

"I think she suspects Raven had something to do with Leila's death," Poppy said bluntly.

"I wondered about that," I agreed. "She's very keen to distance him from Leila. But at the same time let us know that he's heartbroken about her death."

"And very keen to point the finger at Aether. And away from Raven."

"I mean, statistically, it's almost always the boyfriend."

"Although, as Maryam pointed out, he was tied to a tree like the rest of us," mused Poppy. "And Norah had the only key."

"Could she have been in on it, and unlocked him in the night?" I wondered aloud.

"Norah?" scoffed Poppy. "I can't see it! She's such a mouse."

I didn't say anything; I wasn't quite sure I agreed with Poppy's character assessment there. I suspected Norah had hidden depths. Didn't we all? And generally they were hidden for a reason.

CHAPTER 24

I STOOD LOOKING out of the kitchen window the next morning, across the tangle of our garden to where Penton Vale rolled away from our cottage in a series of interlocking green spurs that faded into misty blue. I'm not a morning person, but even I had come to appreciate the beauty of early morning in the countryside. It has a clarity and a freshness to it that genuinely feels as though the world was remade overnight.

I spooned more oatmeal into my mouth and frowned slightly.

"What's wrong?" Joe had wandered sleepily into the kitchen.

"Can oats go off?" I asked, inspecting the Oat-so-Simple packet. "These expired in 2019."

"Dunno." He rummaged in a cupboard for alternative carbs. "Do they taste off?"

"They taste like dust."

"I think that's just what oatmeal tastes like."

I nodded, and added a healthy spoonful of golden syrup, which improved matters slightly.

"Don't forget Mum's arriving this afternoon, ahead of the party tomorrow," Joe reminded me, putting four slices of bread in the toaster. *Four?*

I had absolutely forgotten this.

"Of course not," I said, looking around in dismay at the whirlwind of chaos that was not mother-in-law friendly, even for one as laid-back as mine.

"Maybe I should tidy," I mumbled half-heartedly.

"Aren't you going to forest school today?" asked Joe.

"Nah. Ailsa texted at five this morning to say the twins had been up all night and she can't face it, and Poppy has to take Ronnie to the vet. Plus I need to do some party prep."

"What's wrong with Ronnie?"

"What isn't. Specifically, this time I think it's his . . . ear? Or possibly his toe?"

Joe nodded, slathered the peanut butter on a piece of toast and wandered out again. Thirty seconds later I heard the shower start. I'm a big advocate for the freedom of snacks—they should not be restricted to any particular times or places—but I found Joe's habit of eating toast in the shower odd and slightly disconcerting. The texture combinations were all wrong. Damp and crispy? No thanks.

I currently had bigger problems though. Tomorrow was Jack and Noah's somewhat delayed first birthday party. I was . . . kinda looking forward to it? It felt like a very parenty thing to do. And so I felt about it as I felt about much of parenting, a nervous excitement tinged with dread. I wanted it to be a spectacular party, and it felt like it should be, given we'd had an extra two months to plan it—but I also wanted to put in as little effort as possible. Not because I'm lazy (although sometimes I am) but because I had spent a year full-time parenting on extremely little sleep and I was knackered through and through. I spent so much time dealing with meltdowns over wrongly textured food (a big no with Jack), I had extremely little bandwidth to deal with color-coordinated cupcakes or children's entertainers or even "themes," which seemed to be a staple of every toddler's party according to Instagram.

Just to underline this point, Jack chose that moment to throw an almost full bowl of tomato soup in my face. Yes, he was eating tomato soup for breakfast, it was currently one of three items of food he deigned to eat. Luckily his food is only ever lukewarm at best, so I wasn't horribly burned, but it still left me looking like Dracula's bride.

Right on cue, Hen knocked on the door, then pushed it open without waiting for a reply.

"Only me! Oh my God, are you OK?"

"Fine! Fine! It's just tomato soup."

Hen began bustling round the kitchen wetting cloths for me and Jack and the floor.

"What should I do about the dog?"

Helen had caught a light spattering and merely looked like she had mild chicken pox.

"Her name's Helen," I said pointedly. "But just leave her, she'll lick it off."

Hen nodded and deposited the gory wipes in the sink.

"And thanks," I added belatedly. "I promise it won't be like this all day."

"Maybe," said Hen noncommittally. "But it's fine—Arora always comes back from yours in a good mood."

This made me feel disproportionately proud. A one-year-old enjoyed my company!

"Anyway I have to run," said Hen. "Owen's got a press conference this morning about the wind farm development." We both ignored the enormous elephant in the statement.

"Hen," I said quickly as she kissed Arora goodbye, unable to stop myself. "Owen's old business partner—the one who actually invented the wind turbine . . ."

"What? Who?" She barely looked up from rifling in her handbag for her car key.

"The guy who invented the Aether turbine. He wasn't called Richard, was he?"

"What? No, I think it was a woman? Typical isn't it—the woman does all the brainwork and the man reaps the profits. Ah, found it!" She held up her key with a flourish.

Damn. That put paid to my neat little theory I'd been compiling.

Hen paused at the doorway. "Can I do anything to help? For the party tomorrow?"

"It's all under control," I said with a slightly manic cheeriness.

Hen glanced around at the post-soup chaos. "I doubt that," she said frankly. "Look, just call me if you need anything."

I smiled and nodded. I knew I'd be calling her at least a dozen times in the next twenty-four hours.

* * *

ONE HOUR later and I had not achieved any party prep. Jack had knocked Arora over and she had poked him in the eye, giving him the beginnings of a black eye. Helen had, for some reason, not licked any of the tomato soup off her fur, so she looked like a plague victim.

My phone pinged. It was Poppy.

What you up to?

Going slowly mad with two toddlers and a dog. You?

Sewing six thousand feet of bunting for tomorrow

Why are we doing this again?

How was the vet?

Fine. Ronnie tried to hump a chihuahua in the waiting room but the owner took it quite well

Is his toe ok?

Ear

Yeah turns out Noah had put a Wheatie in it

The vet took it out and Ronnie ate it

Gross

Helen ate a teething monkey this morning and Joe says it's cabin fever so I have to take her for a walk in a bit. Want to come?

We walked her yesterday, how has she got cabin fever?

With Helen I think it's more a cabin fever of the mind

Oh. That's a pretty small cabin.

We went to the woods, because it was too hot to walk anywhere else, and managed about two hundred meters of dog walk. It was one of those days. For a start, I had Jack in the sling and Arora in the buggy which meant my top speed was about one mile per hour. How Ailsa ever got anything done with two was a mystery to me. Then Jack wanted to feed, and I've never mastered feeding in the sling—I think women who can do this must have some kind of superpowers. So we pulled up about a hundred meters from the car so I could sit on a stump and feed him.

"I wonder if Maryam and Marcus found Sam," said Poppy, fanning Noah to keep him cool.

"I expect he'll show up," I said rather disinterestedly. The oppressive heat was making my brain sluggish—more so than usual—and for once I thought I'd rather talk about tomorrow's toddler party than the murder.

"Do you think we've ordered enough food?" I asked.

"What?"

"For the party tomorrow?"

"Oh, probably. Listen, I was thinking—we need to find out more about Leila's family history."

"Really?"

"Yes," said Poppy firmly. "We need to know what her relationship with them was. What was a petrochemical heiress doing shacked up with an eco-warrior, and what did her family think of it all?"

"Harris said the family are only communicating through their lawyers," I said vaguely.

"To the police, sure," said Poppy. "But we can take a different approach."

I didn't like the sound of this.

"Meaning?" I asked cautiously.

"So, from her Instagram, one of her accounts anyway, it looks like she was pretty close to her sister—or at least used to be."

"Yeah, I guess so," I said noncommittally, trying to get Jack to switch boobs. His preference for left made me feel distinctly lopsided and I was starting to worry it might be permanent.

"Exactly," said Poppy, jumping on my lackluster agreement. "So I was thinking, you should DM her sister on Instagram, see if she wants to meet up, talk about Leila."

"Whoa, wait, no!"

"Hear me out. If we've any chance of finding out what happened to Leila, we need to speak to her family, that's the bottom line. I know it feels uncomfortable, but there's no way round it. And talking to us will be far less stressful for Genevieve than talking to the police—think about Harris's interpersonal skills! No wonder they're doing everything through the lawyers. But Genevieve probably wants to talk about Leila. People do, after they've lost someone. And if she doesn't"—she plowed on over my objections—"she can just say no, or not reply to you. It's a no-lose situation."

"Why does it have to come from me?" I grumbled.

"Because you're our social media whizz," said Poppy winningly.

I snorted. I spent a lot of time browsing social media, without in any way contributing to its bottomless depths.

"Pleeease?" wheedled Poppy. I marveled again at how a murder investigation seemed to have been the tonic Poppy needed. She was back on form—but at what price?

"Ugh. Fine. But you owe me."

"A babysit and a bottle of wine?"

"Two bottles."

"Deal."

Under Poppy's dictation, I began to tap out a message.

> Hi Genevieve, you don't know me but I was a friend of Leila's

"I can't say that," I objected. "I barely knew her."

"Of course you knew her, you'd seen her naked, you'd spent a night chained to a tree with her, that's more than most friendships achieve in a lifetime."

"I'd love to have one of those friendships," I said wistfully. "A nice, boring friendship. But look, this feels like lying to the deceased's sister, which definitely feels like a bad thing to do."

"It's a moral gray area," said Poppy.

"I don't like moral gray areas."

"Alice, you *are* a moral gray area."

This stung but was undeniably true. It appeared Poppy had gotten to know me pretty well over the last year of our distinctly not boring friendship.

"Fine, now what?"

> I'm so sorry for your loss. Leila was a wonderful person and you must miss her very much. I was wondering, if it's not too much to ask, would you like to meet up at some point? There's so much I never got to ask Leila—it feels as though there's a whole side to her I never knew. Of course, you might not feel up to it, which I totally understand. In fact, don't even feel you need to reply to this message. My thoughts are with you and your family.
> Alice

I'd insisted on adding the last three sentences. I still felt a bit icky about the whole thing. I hadn't made my peace with the many, many aspects of detecting that made me uncomfortable. However, there was no denying the rush that came with following a trail of thought through to conclusion, to uncovering a detail (I liked to call them clues) that unlocked a whole new aspect to the mystery. It spoke to the part of me that would trawl back through five years of Instagram posts of a person I had chatted to for five minutes at the pub, to find out if they had in fact cheated on their partner. Or peruse the details of an old school acquaintance's LinkedIn to see if there was any clue as to why they'd suddenly left their prestigious and well-paid job to go backpacking at thirty-three. I am inherently nosy and love an ITV crime drama; detecting, or whatever the hell we were doing, gave me an absolute rush.

Not today however. We walked another hundred meters, but then Noah did an explosive shit and we decided to call it a day. Some days you just have to know when to give in.

* * *

WHEN I got home it was to find my mother-in-law safely ensconced in our house. She had already tidied the sitting room—which I really *had* meant to do before I went out—and was now wiping the inside of the microwave—something I had zero intention of doing, ever. I realize some women would find this deeply irritating. I was delighted.

"It looks great, thanks, Laura!" I received a perfunctory hug before Laura swooped down on her grandson.

"Jacky boy! Come to Granny!"

Jack chirruped happily as he was swept up by his granny and spun round the room. I slumped down next to Joe on the freshly hoovered sofa.

"I forgot to get anything for dinner," I confessed.

"That's OK. Mum bought a fish pie down, said she figured we'd have enough to do with the party tomorrow."

God bless mothers-in-law.

"Also"—Joe sat forward eagerly and gestured to a bulky parcel on the table—"something came from Spain."

"Spain? Are you sure?" This could only be from my parents, which felt extremely unlikely. I mean, sure, after they'd missed his actual birthday I'd dropped a fair few hints to Mum over the last few weeks, from the subtle references to party planning to the less subtle "remember it's your only grandson's first birthday party next Saturday." But I hadn't expected them to actually remember. This was disconcerting.

Tentatively, Joe and I cut open the packaging to reveal what was unmistakably a wrapped birthday present and card with "Jack" written on it. They'd even got his name right! The wrapping paper said "Olé" and had martini glasses all over it, but I was willing to overlook this.

"Can we get him to open it now?" I begged Joe.

"Yeah, go on then," he agreed easily, clearly as eager as I was to see what my parents had bought Jack.

Jack, however, was less interested. He poked the box a few times, licked it once, then crawled off. I shrugged and tore off the wrapping paper to reveal—a "my first cocktail bar" playset, for ages 7+. Well, at least they had tried.

CHAPTER 25

THE DAY OF the party dawned early and stressful. Jack was awake at 5:30, not out of any kind of excitement—he's one, his understanding of the concept of "birthday" is nil—but just because he's a baby, and babies are knobs like that.

Maya arrived, fresh faced and perky, around midday.

"Look what fun Auntie Maya has brought you." She waved a packet of chocolate buttons in Jack's face. Jack beamed.

"Oh good, because he's not going to have enough sugar today," grumbled Joe, as he pulled Maya into a hug.

"Yes but *I* won't have to deal with that," replied Maya grinning. "That's why godmother is a superior position to mother."

She had a point there.

"Did you bring any for me?" I asked, elbowing Joe out the way to get my own hug.

"Nope, you're not my godson and it's not your birthday."

"I will teach him an important lesson in sharing," I declared, opening the packet. "One for Jack, three for me." I popped three chocolate buttons in my mouth. Jack gave me an accusatory stare. I stared back.

"What? I'm like ten times the size of you, really I should have ten to your one."

He continued staring.

"Anyway it's not like you can even count."

Stare.

"OK fine, have two more."

I really resented getting stared down by a baby.

I settled Maya in the "guest room"—the sofa in the sitting room, which she would likely have to share with Helen—and turned my attention to some serious party prep.

We had agreed to hold the party in our garden because it was bigger than Poppy and Lin's and because this meant that Lin, who was a gardener, had come round every weekend for the last month and tidied, pruned, and spruced our garden so that it now looked passably acceptable, a huge improvement on the feral wilderness it had been before.

We'd hung some bunting haphazardly across the bushes and Joe and his mum had wrestled up a large gazebo that would house the food table. I had been in charge of refreshments and had done a pretty damn good job, if I said so myself. I knew what Penton was like. I knew the other mums would bring organic falafels, sugar-free beetroot muffins, and salads from their allotments. I also knew what a toddler party table *should* look like. So there were crisps, candy, and various other snacks. There was an enormous Jell-O mold. There were bowls of Smarties and Jelly Babies and Rolos. And olives, because Jack inexplicably loves them, proving that my one-year-old toddler has a more developed palate that I do. In the middle of the table was an enormous birthday cake—shop bought, because I have things to do and hate baking. I had, however, taken the time last night to liberally cover it with sweets and stick a big "1" candle in the top. I considered it a masterpiece.

BY THE time Poppy, Lin, and Noah arrived at one I was ready for bed.

"Party day!" cried Poppy, bustling down the path in a wobble of balloons, presents, and dogs. *More* bunting was erected until it looked like we were hosting a festival.

Parents and toddlers began trickling through the gate just after two. I didn't really have any friends in Penton beyond Poppy, Ailsa, and Hen. Meeting and befriending them through NCT—involving two murders, a hippy commune, and some highly embarrassing social interactions—had been traumatic enough; I wasn't ready to go through that again. So our contribution to the guest list mainly consisted of Joe's mum (briefly of said hippy commune), Joe's half brother (also of hippy commune), and

Maya (firmly non-hippy non-commune). We'd invited Joe's dad, Camran (leader of the hippy commune—it's a long and tangled story), but he had declined. This seemed fair enough, as his relationship with Joe's mum had been short and, let's say, problematic.

The party was soon in full swing. By which I mean the babies were rolling around happily on the floor while the adults made small talk over juice and pretzels. We hadn't organized any party games—because the babies were one; most of them could barely walk. We'd hired a ball pit and scattered some random and well-chewed toys around the garden and they could make do with that. Rowan and Maya mostly kept to the sides of the garden; I imagine it is a strange thing to be a free-range adult at a baby party. Fortunately, Joe had purchased a keg of local beer, through which Rowan and Maya were making steady progress.

I, unfortunately, was sticking to juice, and had barely managed to finish a cup of that as it was, as there seemed to be incessant demands on my time, often from Hen, who I knew felt she could have organized this party better. Arora's first birthday party, needless to say, had been textbook.

"Alice!" Right on cue I heard Hen's voice calling, and pretended to be busy stacking paper cups.

"Alice!" She was persistent, I'd give her that.

"Alice! Your dog just peed in the ball pit!"

Ah shit.

Of course I'd known it was a bad idea to let Helen loose at a toddlers' party. But the only other option had been to try and secure her in the house somehow and Helen could break out of Alcatraz if she put her tiny mind to it, and I didn't really fancy horror-film-esque claw marks on the inside of all our doors.

Once the ball pit had been cordoned off as a biohazard area, I decided to try and rescue matters with the cake. Joe and Lin held Jack and Noah as Poppy and I paraded the cake across the lawn, navigating such trip hazards as babies, dogs, and piss-covered plastic balls. Noah promptly burst into tears, and Jack stuck a fat and sticky hand into the cake, pretty much designating that a biohazard zone too. It was a magical moment.

* * *

THE AFTERNOON ground on. I don't care what anyone says. I don't care how it looks on Instagram. Toddler parties are not quite hell on earth, but they are pretty damn close. My garden, house, sanity, and dog would never be the same again. At one point I found the twins patiently caking icing into Helen's fur. Helen was alternating between licking herself and the twins, who were pretty well iced themselves.

Halfway through the afternoon a precious little girl took a swipe at Jack and left talon marks across his cheek. OK fine, I might be exaggerating *a bit*. But it did leave a mark. I tried not to take umbrage with the little hooligan (but did unaccountably miss her out when passing round the cake).

Someone had put a party hat on Sultan. He looked appalled.

I was just contemplating escape tactics—fake a panic attack? Have a real panic attack?—when my phone buzzed. I glanced briefly at the Instagram notification on the screen, then did a double take.

"Poppy!" I grabbed her as she hurried past, holding Ronnie, who was covered in Jell-O, at arm's length.

"Can it wait, Alice? I've got a bit of a situation here."

"Stick him in the shower, come on."

I hustled Poppy and Ronnie through to the bathroom and flicked the shower on Ronnie, who squawked as a jet of icy water hit him.

"Oops, sorry, Ronnie!" Once the water was at an acceptable temperature, I turned to Poppy.

"Leila's sister just replied."

"Oh my God, the Honorable Genevieve?"

"The very same."

We huddled over my phone, even Ronnie poking his snoot in to see what all the fuss was about.

> Hi Alice. Thanks for being in touch, I really appreciate that. I'd not heard my sister mention you—but then we hadn't been in touch so much over the last year, so maybe that's not surprising. She had . . . changed. It would be lovely to meet up and talk about Leila. Why don't you come over for tea? To be honest, I'd love to hear more about what Leila was up to the last few

> months, it feels weird not knowing what she was doing. We used to be so close . . . Anyway, I'm rambling now—sorry! How about Tuesday?

Poppy and I stared at each other.

"Oh my God, it worked!" said Poppy eventually. "She's invited you to tea!"

"Us!" I said hurriedly. "Invited *us* to tea, no way am I going on my own."

"She doesn't know I exist," pointed out Poppy. "Or Ailsa."

I realized, horrified, that this was true. "Well I'll just have to tell her." No way was I facing the Honorable Genevieve without backup.

We hurried back to the party to fill Ailsa in on the news—Poppy doubling back when we realized we'd left Ronnie in the shower.

CHAPTER 26

I CAME DOWNSTAIRS the next morning to find Joe asleep on the sofa and Jack watching *Baywatch*. This was a disconcertingly regular occurrence. He had learned to operate the TV remote with alarming efficiency, achieving a level of technological competency it took me nearly three decades to master. Having plumbed the more bizarre depths of our limitless TV—a channel showing bootleg Serbian movies, *Hillbilly Handfishin'*, *Toddlers & Tiaras* (which he seemed quite taken with—note for Christmas)—he appeared to have settled on a channel that exclusively showed *Baywatch* reruns.

"Morning," I said to him sleepily. He ignored me—Pamela and the Hoff were being airlifted to safety by a helicopter and to be fair it seemed like a pretty dramatic scene.

Then I noticed that Maya wasn't on the sofa/guest bed. I wondered if, in some unlikely turn of events, she'd decided to take Helen out for an early morning walk. Then I saw Helen reclining upside down on the sofa, legs spatchcocked, icing still crusting her fur.

Where you?

Don't tell me you've gone for a run

You could at least have taken Helen

Al, don't be mad

Oh god, I'm mad already

What have you done?

I'm at the commune

This gave me pause. What the hell was she doing there?

Are you . . . joining?

Not exactly. I'm with Rowan

I paused while I tried to consider all the possible innocent reasons behind this statement.

Tell me you took a midnight gong bath or something

Astral surfing?

Foraging?

Ooh I've never called it astral surfing before

But I quite like that

At this point Joe yawned and stretched.

"Good to see you're on the ball with the whole childcare thing," I observed dryly.

Joe glanced at Jack, riveted to the TV as the Hoff smoldered into the camera.

"Oh bloody hell, *Baywatch* again? It was on Teletubbies when I fell asleep, I swear." He grabbed the remote and switched to the eternal hell that is children's TV, then stretched again and looked around the room.

"Where's Maya? She wasn't here when I came down with Jack."

"Shagging your half brother up at the commune." I was too tired to dissemble. I had a toddler in a *Baywatch* meltdown, six thousand crushed pretzels to pick out of the carpet, a gazebo to take down and a dog to de-ice.

Joe nodded. "Yeah, saw that coming."

I froze in the act of removing a half-sucked Jelly Baby from Helen's fur. "You did?"

"Yeah, didn't you see them yesterday? They were getting pretty cozy. Ailsa was looking less than impressed."

Oh good, an angry Ailsa. That was one thing I didn't need to deal with on top of all this.

"Why didn't you say something!"

Joe shrugged. "What's there to say? They're both grown-ups, they can do what they want, Al."

"I know . . . but . . . I mean . . . they can't *sleep* with each other!"

"Sounds like they just did."

THIS WAS very much the attitude Maya took when she returned around midday, looking slightly sheepish but with an edge of smugness.

I was preoccupied dealing with a stand-off between Helen and Jack, who were both claiming ownership of a rubber giraffe that honestly could have belonged to either of them, and Maya took advantage of the situation to make her escape to the bathroom.

"You can't wash away the guilt!" I shouted to her retreating back as she disappeared down the hall.

"That's OK, I don't have any," she called over her shoulder with a grin.

I gave her five minutes—long enough for me to adjudicate in Helen's favor based on the tooth marks on the giraffe—before heading for the bathroom to pester Maya through the locked door.

"Maya, I'm trying to talk to you!"

"And I'm trying to shower, Al."

There was a brief silence then Maya's echoey voice. "Why do you have ketchup in your shower?"

"It's for Helen."

Another brief pause. "Oh. In case she fancies a mid-shower snack?"

"No, it's for when she's rolled in something gross. It—I don't know—neutralizes the smell or something."

"So . . . I'm showering in the shower where you clean shit off Helen?"

"Yes. And Jell-O off Ronnie. Look, can we stick to the subject?"

"What do you want to know? You want to know if it was good sex? You want the details? Who did what to whom?"

"No! Gross! That's my brother-in-law you're talking about!"

"Great, so we've established you *don't* want to hear about it. In which case can you leave me to ketchup myself in peace please."

"Ailsa's gonna be mad!" was my parting shot as I headed back to the sitting room and giraffe-gate.

"Ailsa's always mad," I heard echoing from the bathroom.

WE'D ARRANGED to meet the others at The Crossed Keys pub for a party debrief over lunch. I'd expected it to be a very different debrief from the type I recalled from my twenties, which had mainly consisted of who'd drunk too much and embarrassed themselves (me) and who'd slept with whom (seldom me). Unfortunately, there was more similarity than I'd hoped.

"You slept with Rowan??" asked Lin, wide-eyed, when we joined them in the sun-soaked beer garden.

"Yes," said Maya, sounding exasperated. "It's not a big deal."

"Ailsa's going to be pissed," said Poppy, sounding slightly awestruck.

"So I've been told," said Maya dryly. "Can we talk about something else now please? Jacky, did you enjoy your birthday party?"

In response Jack did a small vomit that was alarmingly multicolored. Most likely yesterday's Jelly Babies were the culprit, although I did quickly google whether rainbow vomit was a symptom for anything dire.

At this point, Hen arrived.

"Maya slept with Rowan," announced Poppy, before Hen had even parked the pram.

"What is it with you country people?" exploded Maya. "You want to put a notice in the local paper? Call the town crier? You do know people have sex all the time, right? And sometimes, it doesn't even have to be other people's business?"

"Does Ailsa know?" asked Hen, raising an eyebrow.

Maya slumped forward, head on the table.

I would have put a stop to the teasing, but I knew Maya was secretly enjoying it. She loved playing the cosmopolitan city dweller to our country bumpkins. I suspected she might enjoy it slightly less after Ailsa arrived.

It was ten years since Rowan and Ailsa had briefly and catastrophically dated, and yet the tension between them was still next level. I contemplated briefly whether Rowan had any idea who the twins' father was, before summarily dismissing this idea—Ailsa barely gave Rowan the time of day, let alone personal information she guarded more closely than the Official Secrets Act. It was possible she'd confided in Hen, but I wondered when, if ever, I'd be taken into the inner circle of this knowledge.

Five minutes later, when Ailsa had arrived and been informed of the latest updates in Penton's version of *The Archers*, it became clear I would never make the inner circle.

"I expected better of you, Alice." Ailsa sniffed, passing Robin to Lin and settling herself on the bench at the opposite end to Maya, while Ivy rolled at her feet.

"How is any of this my fault?" I asked, outraged. "I haven't slept with anyone! Not for years!"

"How old is Jack?" I heard Joe muse to no one in particular. "I'd say about one year nine months since Alice slept with anyone."

"She's your best friend, and he's your brother-in-law," said Ailsa curtly.

"Which makes me responsible for precisely neither of them," I pointed out.

"I'm very happy for Alice to take the blame, however," Maya chipped in.

I was about to object when a woman from a neighboring table leaned over and tapped me on the shoulder. "One of your babies is escaping."

I followed her pointing finger. Ivy was making a determined beeline for the pub gate. I gave chase, scooped her up, and contemplated following her example and just . . . quietly exiting.

When I returned to the table, it seemed things had escalated a notch.

"As far as I'm aware, he's not spoken for," Maya was saying, a touch more icily.

"No, he doesn't really go in for that sort of thing," said Ailsa cuttingly; apparently Rowan's cheating tendencies still stung.

There was very little that could make the situation more tense, but Fate has always had a wicked sense of humor. So at that point Rowan turned up.

"You're kidding me," I groaned. "What's *he* doing here?"

"So I invited my brother to the pub!" Joe raised his hands in mock surrender. "No one warned me it was going to be worse than an episode of *Oprah*!"

As Rowan approached the table he took in our shocked faces.

"You've heard then," he said, in an uncharacteristically grave voice. I saw Maya look a little stung at his tone.

"I think everyone has," said Hen dryly.

"Awful, isn't it," said Rowan.

"Excuse me??" Maya looked justifiably offended.

Rowan gave her a startled glance as he squeezed onto the bench next to her, then kissed her on the cheek. Maya looked confused, and flushed slightly. Talk about mixed messages.

"Did Raven tell you?" Rowan asked, glancing down the table to where Ailsa, Poppy, and I sat.

"Did Raven—? What? No! Maya did," I spluttered.

Rowan looked at Maya in surprise. "How did you know?"

There was a moment's confused silence as we all replayed the last two minutes of conversation in our heads.

"Can you clarify exactly what you're talking about?" said Hen carefully.

"Sam, of course," said Rowan.

"Sam?!"

All heads turned to Maya, who shook her head. "No, pretty sure I didn't sleep with anyone called Sam last night."

"What about him?" I asked, turning back to Rowan.

"He's dead."

CHAPTER 27

THERE WAS A long silence. Eventually, it was broken by Maya.

"Like, *dead* dead?"

Then the questions came thick and fast and from every direction.

"How?"

"Are you sure?"

"What happened?"

"How do you know?"

Rowan held up his hands to stem the tide.

"First off, I'm getting a pint. Anyone need a top-up?"

It really didn't feel like the right moment, but once Joe tentatively put forward that he could take another pint, it turned out everyone needed a drink, until Rowan ended up having to make a list on his phone and taking Joe into the bar to help him carry everything. It was a frustrating but possibly necessary interlude.

"Don't talk about it until you get back outside," I called after their retreating backs. "We want to hear too!"

Then we sat and stared at each other for a few moments.

"Well, I feel like that puts my shagging antics into perspective," said Maya.

We all nodded silently. I don't want to sound as if we were being insensitive or crude. But, really, is there an "appropriate" way to respond to news like that? Other than to order a drink. Because you're probably gonna need it.

Pints in hand, we all turned to Rowan as soon as he was seated.

"I really don't know much," he said immediately. "I was on the Sunday shift at work this morning and was called into the editor's office straightaway. There aren't many details yet, the police aren't saying much, but Sam was found dead in his darkroom this morning."

I gave a sharp intake of breath. "In his darkroom? Up at Maryam's?"

Rowan flicked open his little notebook. "Maryam White? Lives at Fox Hollow Farm? Yes, she's his aunt apparently. He usually stayed with her when he was down from London."

"We know," I said in a small voice. "We've been there. We've seen his darkroom . . ." I remembered the strange room of floating images, pervaded by that dim red light that now seemed even more sinister.

"What did he die of?" asked Hen. "I mean, was it . . . an accident?"

Oh please have been an accident, I thought.

"Police aren't saying," said Rowan somberly. "But given his brother's girlfriend was murdered just over a week ago, I expect they're taking a pretty dim view of this."

"Is it Jane, taking the case?" asked Ailsa.

"Of course."

Who else? Jane Harris was Penton's only homicide detective, and in my limited experience of country life, Penton and its surrounds kept her pretty busy.

"I'll see if I can get anything out of her this evening," said Ailsa. "What exactly have the police said, Rowan?"

"But before that," I broke in. "Food?"

Ailsa rolled her eyes but waited impatiently while Lin took food orders and went back in to place them at the bar—leaving us under a strict injunction to stop discussing it until she was back.

"OK, can we ask about the murder now?" Ailsa asked before Lin had even sat down.

"You can ask, but that's literally all I know." Rowan raised his hands in mock surrender. "They're not saying anything—not cause of death, not even confirming it's murder."

"It's murder," said Poppy confidently.

"The question is, is it linked to Leila's murder?" Ailsa asked.

"Got to be, surely," I said. "Even in Penton two unrelated murders within a fortnight would be a bit much."

"We can't be sure of that," said Hen more cautiously. "I mean, it most likely is, but I'm just pointing out that we know literally nothing about how Sam died." Trust Hen to be the voice of reason. Although it would be distinctly in her interests for the two to be linked, as it would surely point the finger away from Aether whom, as far as we were aware, had no link to Sam.

"What was Sam and Leila's relationship?" asked Maya, through mouthfuls of bacon sandwich. I watched her enviously. I still enjoyed a good bacon sandwich, but felt myself annoyingly driven to impress Ailsa—an impossible task—so I made token attempts occasionally to appear vegetarian-ish in her presence. And after my meat-fest of a pizza the other night, I felt I had ground to make up. My Caesar salad *without chicken* was disappointing. Basically iceberg lettuce.

"Definitely a bit tricky," said Poppy thoughtfully. "It sounds like there was some sort of beef between them. Something about these photos that Sam had taken and Leila objected to. From everything we've heard, there was no love lost there."

"Could that have been a front?" asked Maya. "Like, they pretended not to like each other in order to hide the fact that they were having an affair?"

"And you think Raven might have found out about it and killed them both?" I finished for her.

"Exactly." She jabbed her sandwich at me. I exercised an impressive amount of self-control not to chomp it straight out of her hand.

"I had wondered about that . . ." I mused. "It's not out of the question, I just . . . I don't know. That's not the vibe I'm getting."

Maya snorted. "I don't think solving a murder is supposed to be vibe based."

On this, I disagreed. While we'd been presented with some pretty incontrovertible facts in our first (and only) case, a lot of the work to get there had come down to following hunches, feeling our way blind, and a fair bit of guesswork.

"Or . . ." Maya did one of her trademark swift about-turns. "What if Sam really *didn't* like Leila? What if he hated her enough to kill her?"

"And then he dropped dead from, what, bad karma?" asked Ailsa skeptically.

"No, listen, then Raven killed Sam in revenge for him killing Leila." Maya sat back triumphantly.

But I shook my head. "Seems a bit of a stretch. We don't know of any motive Sam had to kill Leila—if anything it was the other way round. He was the one who had those photos she didn't want surfacing. And I definitely can't see Raven killing his own brother out of revenge over a girl he'd only known six months."

Maya shrugged. "People do weird things when they're in love."

"Speaking of which, Marcus was down on Thursday . . ." I said. "Just after he'd had a huge row with Sam."

"Did you say Sam was found this morning?" Poppy turned back to Rowan, who checked his notebook.

"Yes, found first thing this morning by his aunt. Nothing to say how long he might have been dead for."

"And we don't know if Marcus was still around or whether he went back to London," I added. "Or whether they made up over their row."

"Or broke up," interjected Poppy.

"Or worse," said Ailsa darkly.

"But if Marcus killed Sam—just hypothetically—then is it nothing to do with Leila?" I asked. "And we assume it's just a coincidence they both drop dead within two weeks of each other? Because that's one hell of a coincidence."

"But did Marcus even *know* Leila?" wondered Poppy.

"Sorry, who is Marcus?" broke in Lin, looking confused and a bit annoyed. She and Joe had been noticeably, and probably disapprovingly, silent on the subject of Penton's most recent murder case. The conversation broke down into confused recollections of Marcus, from mushroom foraging to Maya's midnight antics in a warehouse in London.

And that was about as far as we got on any sensible theories as to how Leila and Sam might have died and why, and whether the two were in fact linked. Beyond agreeing that it was too much of a coincidence for them *not* to be, no one could agree on anything, and the conversation was frequently derailed by Maya and Ailsa sniping at each other incessantly. Rowan studiously took notes in his little notebook—ostensibly for his report on Sam's death but I suspected also so that he could avoid engaging with either Maya or Ailsa.

CHAPTER 28

I FELT THE usual wrench dropping Maya off at the train station that evening. A part of my old life walking away. She was still everything she always had been—my lynchpin, my truth-teller, dare I say it, my soul mate—but it also felt as though with every passing month our lives diverged further.

"Come back soon," I said with feeling, lugging her excessively large bag (one night, she'd stayed one night) out of the trunk while Maya and Jack said their fond farewells.

"I expect I will," said Maya with a guilty grin, jerking her head at a familiar curly-haired figure lounging by the station entrance.

"Oh no, what's he doing here?" I liked Rowan, I really did. But Maya was my best friend and I resented this intrusion on our last few minutes together. Plus Rowan had *such* a habit of popping up when I wasn't in the mood.

"He wanted to say bye before I got my train," said Maya, a touch self-consciously.

"Couldn't he have done that at the pub?"

"With Ailsa watching? We'd be the next murder case for her sister."

"Hey, Alice, how you doing?" Rowan had strolled over, and casually hefted Maya's bag from me—which immediately annoyed me, I'd been doing just fine with it, apart from a mild hernia.

"Er, yeah, fine."

"You'll miss Maya I expect." He nudged her playfully. I didn't like it.

"I suppose so," I said loftily.

"Of course you will," said Maya with a grin. "What are you doing this evening? Weeping over Domino's?"

"No, ah . . ." I was actually heading on to Ailsa's after this, but mentioning that right now would have felt about as tactful as dropping a grenade into—whatever this was.

"You don't mind me gate-crashing your fond farewell?" Rowan gave me a grin which, to me, looked sleazy—but probably wasn't. I'd always liked Rowan, I couldn't start disliking him just because he was . . . interested in my best mate.

Hang on—he'd put his hand on her bum. On her actual bum. I tried not to stare. Was this appropriate behavior in our thirties?

"No, no, don't mind me," I said, backing away. "I'll just . . . we'll just . . . I'll just stand over here." I moved away a few steps, then realized I was making this even more awkward. "Actually, I'll just go, that'd be better. I'll go. See you soon, Mai, bye. Yep, and Rowan, see you soon too."

I gave Maya a weird half wave, half salute which she responded to with an appropriately horrified look then pulled me into a hug.

"Don't be a freak, yeah," she whispered in my ear, giving me an extra tight squeeze. "I'll be back before you know it."

"OK," I agreed weakly, climbing back into my car. As I reversed, the two of them were positioned center stage in my rearview mirror, full-on making out in front of the station like a pair of teenagers.

"DOOR'S UNLOCKED," shouted Ailsa when I knocked at the door of the cottage she shared with her sister. "A little help in here!"

I walked in to pandemonium. Robin was safely secured in one of those bouncy chair things that hung in the doorway to the sitting room, but Ivy had climbed up the back of the sofa and was balanced precariously on the top, and meanwhile Ailsa was on her knees next to the fan in the corner.

"Grab her, can you grab her!" called Ailsa frantically, weirdly making no attempt to move. I leaned over and scooped up Ivy, just as she prepared to swan-dive off the back of the sofa.

"What's going on? Why didn't you—"

"OK, now come and free me," interrupted Ailsa. It was only now that I noticed that a handful of Ailsa's dreads were tangled in the spokes of the fan.

"Oh my God!" I rushed to try and help. This involved quite a lot of swearing—from both her and me. And I admit I did make things momentarily worse when I trod on the floor switch and turned the fan briefly on again. But eventually Ailsa was free, and I'd only had to resort to hacking one dread off with a pair of scissors.

"We're never talking about this again," said Ailsa firmly.

I wondered if I could use this as leverage to get her to tell me who Ivy and Robin's dad was—then realized that I was contemplating blackmailing a friend, so scratched that thought and resolved to be a better person.

"What happened?" I asked.

"I bought a secondhand fan off Marketplace," said Ailsa grumpily. "Turns out it was a bad idea."

I bit my tongue to stop myself saying I avoided secondhand electrical goods. Ailsa's commitment to reducing consumerism one fan at a time was going to be her downfall. Or at least leave her bald.

"Maya headed off OK?" asked Ailsa, looking in the mirror over the fireplace and trying to tuck in the stumpy dread we'd had to sacrifice for her freedom.

"Er, yeah."

There was an awkward silence.

"So," I said. "Sam's dead." It seemed the best way to move the conversation on.

"Yeah," said Ailsa. "Didn't see that one coming."

"Should we have?" I was a little concerned over this. I was aware that our actions in the last case had potentially prevented another murder from taking place—if we'd been a bit quicker off the mark this time, could we have saved Sam?

"I don't think so," said Ailsa thoughtfully. "I mean, we thought he might be the murderer, sure. But I can't think of anything that would have hinted that he'd be next."

"You think it was the same person as killed Leila?" I asked.

Ailsa shrugged. "Probably, right? I mean, how many murderers can there be running around Bishop's Ruin?"

"After living here for a year, I'm not even going to answer that."

"All right, who do *you* think it was?"

I thought for a moment. "The obvious suspects are Marcus or Raven. My money's probably on Marcus? When it was just Leila who'd been killed I even thought it might've been Maryam, but no way would she harm a hair on Sam's head. Anyway, to be honest, with so few details it's just guesswork. It's not even a hunch."

"You're right," said Ailsa thoughtfully. "We need more information."

We shared a look.

"Is your sister in?"

"Nope." Ailsa grinned. "Shall we have a poke about?"

We grabbed armfuls of babies and hurried upstairs to Jane Harris's office. Ailsa wrenched at the doorknob—and nothing happened.

"I don't believe it, she's locked it."

"Doesn't she normally?"

"No. She must've done it because I told her you were coming over."

I wasn't sure if Ailsa was joking or not.

"I guess that's that then," I said.

"You're such a quitter," scolded Ailsa. "We pick the lock, obviously."

"Do you know how to pick a lock?"

"No, do you?"

I sighed, and took out my phone. "How to pick a lock" brought up an alarming number of search results.

Three YouTube videos and several mangled paperclips later, unbelievably, there was a click, and the door handle suddenly dropped.

"We're in," hissed Ailsa.

We crept into Harris's office—which was, unsurprisingly, regimentally neat. It looked like she'd airlifted the office set from an Ikea showroom and dropped it in wholesale.

"OK, so what are we looking for?" I whispered, hovering near the desk, not wanting to touch anything. After all, Harris had my fingerprints on file.

"First off, you don't need to whisper. There's literally only me and the babies in the house. Also please stop Jack from doing that."

I looked over: Jack was sucking Robin's thumb. Robin didn't look too bothered by it.

"And, secondly, you know what we're looking for. Details on Sam's case. You start at the desk, I'll check her filing cabinet."

Who actually owns a filing cabinet in their own home? Well, the Harrises of this world, clearly. And probably anyone with a proper job. Or proper grasp on their home finances.

There was a neat stack of papers in the center of the desk. I picked up the topmost file.

"Preliminary crime scene report: Case 00452," I read aloud. I flipped the file open and a picture of Sam stared up at me.

"Er, think I've got something."

I felt a small bubble of fizzy optimism well up inside me. Sometimes, detectoring was easy.

Ailsa and I settled cross-legged on the floor behind the desk to read the report, while the babies trundled around looking for things to chew, eat, or poke each other with. It turned out Ailsa was a very fast reader. I kept having to stop her turning the pages at lightning speed. Although it turned out there were only five pages to get through.

"Well," I said, as we eventually sat back. "Not a huge amount, but it fills in some of the gaps. He was found by Maryam at 8 A.M., at which point he'd been dead between ten and twelve hours—so he was killed some time between eight and ten on Saturday night."

"If he even was killed," put in Ailsa. "Look—no sign of a struggle, no obvious injuries, nothing obviously taken."

"You sound like Hen," I said distractedly.

"You say that like it's a bad thing," said Ailsa, sounding a bit offended on Hen's behalf.

"He was developing photos at the time of death," I mused, choosing to ignore this comment and running my finger along a line in the report. "Oh, weird. The film had come up blank."

"Let's see." Ailsa tugged the report toward her. "The film was still in the tank . . . So he hadn't finished developing the film when he died . . ."

"Meaning . . . ?"

"You have to develop the film into negatives before you can turn it into prints," said Ailsa, still scanning the report. "You put it in a tank with, oh, various chemicals—developer, fixer, stuff like that—which turns the light-sensitive film into something more stable that you can develop into prints."

"Oh." It amazed me how she knew things like this.

"But Sam's film was still in the tank, and the report says it was blank. So either he hadn't finished developing it or it was corrupted in some way."

"Is that important?"

Ailsa shrugged. "It could be. If he was killed because of what was in the photos, the murderer would have wanted to destroy the film. Or deliberately corrupt it."

"But in that case, why not just take the film," I pointed out.

"True . . ." Ailsa tapped the report with her fingers. "I want to know what stage of development the film was at."

"Will that tell us anything?" I asked.

"Maybe."

This was the stage of detectoring that I found particularly baffling. When bits of information start swimming around, but you have no idea what's coincidental and what's important—and there seems to be no way of telling them apart. So you follow up every detail you can. Maybe the film was important, maybe it wasn't. Either way, we'd dig deeper.

I had another rifle through the papers on Harris's desk.

"There's nothing here on the film. But there's a preliminary fingerprint report on prints found at the scene." I pulled a loose leaf of paper that we'd missed from the back of the file and scanned it. "Oh shit."

"What?" Ailsa leaned over my shoulder.

Fingerprints on record:
Sam White (deceased)
Raven White
Maryam White
Leila Smith nee Arnault (deceased)
Ailsa Harris
Alice Nutall

Three sets unidentified: 2 likely female; 1 likely male

"Shit," echoed Ailsa.

I looked down at my hands. They felt stained.

"Jane is not going to like this. Jane is not going to like this at all," muttered Ailsa.

"Didn't she say anything about it?"

"I haven't seen her today, she must've popped back and dropped these off while we were at the pub."

"Well, that's a fun conversation to look forward to . . ." I had been so pleased to think that for once it hadn't been me finding the body. For once I wasn't linked to the crime. For once there was no reason for Harris to roll her eyes at me and make snide comments about me contaminating her precious case in some way.

Oh well. I should've probably known better.

I looked down at the list again. "The male fingerprints could well be Marcus. How can you tell if a fingerprint is male or female?" I examined my whorled fingertips—what about them screamed "female"?

"Dunno," said Ailsa. "But Marcus is a pretty safe bet for those. What about the women?"

"Well, one of them is probably Poppy," I admitted. "Seeing as both our prints are there. She must've touched some stuff."

"Oh yeah," said Ailsa. "Oops."

"Oops," I agreed. "As for the other—who knows."

At this point, Ivy caused a small diversion by falling off Harris's office chair—although how she'd got up there in the first place I had no idea. Ailsa caught the falling baby with superhuman reflexes.

"I think we should go," I said, feeling slightly nauseous as I glanced down at the list in my hand again.

"Yeah," agreed Ailsa.

I neatly squared off the papers in the center of the desk again, while Ailsa herded the babies out into the hall. Then I closed the door behind us—but the lock didn't click.

"How do we lock it again?"

Ailsa looked at me blankly.

"I mean, can we unpick it or something? Is that a thing?"

The reverse operation was considerably more time consuming, and the babies were getting thoroughly fed up of our antics by this point. Eventually, Ailsa banished me and the babies to the sitting room to leave her in peace with her growing pile of paper clips.

"Do you think your sister will fingerprint her office?" I asked nervously when she reappeared, looking unusually flustered.

"Knowing Jane, probably yes."

THAT EVENING, when Jack was finally settled, Joe and I settled in for a much-needed TV marathon.

"Should we debrief on the party and the weekend and, y'know, everything?" I said, a little half-heartedly as Joe brought up Netflix. My brain felt like a crusted egg pan; you know, when you've left it for a day without washing it and it starts peeling away from the sides.

Joe gave a weary sigh. "Probably, yes."

"Or we could tomorrow," I countered.

"Tomorrow is good."

"Yeah, let's talk tomorrow. Is the new series of *Queer Eye* up yet?"

But my dreams of a conversationless evening were shattered by the ringing of my phone. What was worse—it was Harris.

"I'm sure I don't need to explain what I'm calling about," was her abrupt opening. This immediately threw me, because as it turned out there were a few reasons she could be calling—my guilty brain immediately jumped to our small-scale break-in to her office earlier that day.

"Er . . ."

"Your fingerprints, Alice. All over the room where a man was found dead yesterday. Care to explain?"

All over? She made it sound like I'd been finger-painting the guy's darkroom. I was pretty sure I'd touched like three items including, of course, the note to Leila.

"You mean Sam's darkroom?"

"Unless there's been another mysterious death in the last twenty-four hours that you've somehow got yourself mixed up in, then yes. Sam's darkroom."

Wow, Harris was learning sarcasm.

"We had a look round there the other day," I said, in what I hoped was a casual tone. "We were over at Fox Hollow for an Earth Force meeting and Poppy wanted to see the darkroom, so Raven showed us round."

"And that's it?" Disbelief sat heavy in her voice.

"Well . . . yeah." I didn't know what else to say. That was literally it.

"I suppose it at least tallies with Ailsa's version of events," grumbled Harris begrudgingly.

"Of course it does," I said, slightly stung. "It's the truth."

Harris made an odd huffing sound. "I'll be in touch—*officially*—in the next few days. In the meantime, Alice, please just try and keep your hands to yourself."

I disliked the way she made me sound like a pervy old man, but had to admit she may have a point. Having needlessly involved ourselves in this case, we were getting more tightly enmeshed by the day. Part of me was still pretty keen to drop the whole thing. The other part of me was pointing out that quite clearly this was no longer an option.

"WHO WAS that?" asked Joe as I re-entered the room.

"Ugh, Inspector Harris," I said, flomping down on the sofa and raising a small dust storm of dog hair. "Wanting to know why my fingerprints were all over the crime scene where Sam was found."

"What?" Joe looked horrified.

"I know." I suspected I should be more alarmed than I currently was, but honestly, I was dog-tired and I just wanted to watch Netflix.

"Alice, what are your fingerprints doing at a crime scene?" persisted Joe, taking the remote away from me before I could restart *Queer Eye*.

"We just had a look around, like a week ago, when we were at the farm," I said wearily, trying to grab the remote back. "I'm sure it will all be fine."

"Alice, will you look at me."

I looked at Joe. Would he suspect me of being involved? I liked to assume not, but there was a nagging voice that irritatingly reminded me that I had suspected him, well, semi-suspected him, of being mixed up in something pretty unsavory the previous year. Although I hadn't been *entirely* wrong. You can be as comfortable as you like with another person, but you never truly know what they're capable of.

"Alice, please don't get mixed up in all this again," said Joe seriously. "It was bad enough last time—now you've got Jack to think about. I don't want him dragged into all this. He's one, for God's sake. He should be hanging out at soft play, not being carted round crime scenes."

I was about to snap a reply that I'd taken Jack to soft play the previous weekend, then bit it back. Because Joe had a hell of a point. And he hadn't said anything that I hadn't thought myself over the last week and a half. So I caught myself and paused. Parenthood had made me snappy in a way I didn't like—it was the sleep deprivation, the unremitting burden of responsibility (something I had never excelled at), and the constant nagging feeling of fear and uncertainty, all combining to create a sort of itch behind my breastbone that I could never quite scratch.

So yeah, I wasn't in the most receptive frame of mind. And I couldn't deny that I was enjoying having something to focus on beyond sleep routines and feeding schedules. Plus, there was no doubt that Poppy was flourishing since we'd thrown ourselves into this ill-advised investigation, and it was a joy to have my friend back. Not that I could, in all honesty, say that I was doing this entirely for Poppy. I might be conflicted, but I retained enough self-awareness to recognize that I was also doing this for myself.

But I didn't want to make things hard with Joe—not again. It had been a tough year for us; show me the new parents for whom it isn't! We hadn't been prepared for the total reorientation of our relationship with each other in order to accommodate Jack—and our pretty fledgling relationship had already been on fragile grounds after the revelations of last year's murder case. When you co-parent you become colleagues as well as (or in some instances instead of) friends, lovers, companions. And so your home is suddenly invaded by office politics. It's avoidable, sure, but that takes effort. Sometimes we were successful, sometimes not so much.

"I know," I sighed. "Let's do something as a family next weekend. Something suitable for a one-year-old."

"There's the children's farm park over at Little Prinkton. Wholesome and child appropriate?"

I wrinkled my nose. "Will I have to touch the animals?"

"For Jack's sake, yes," replied Joe firmly, with a hint of a smile.

I tried not to look too horrified. In my opinion, nature is supposed to be beautiful and smell nice, and for this reason I do not think farm animals qualify.

"Sounds . . . delightful."

"It's a date. And, Al, no more investigating?"

I hesitated; I couldn't in all honesty make that promise.

Joe reached out and took my hand. "Please, Alice, is it worth it?"

Gah, what to do, what to say? I was saved from having to answer this unanswerable question by a wail from upstairs. Jack. Weighed down with guilt, I dragged myself off the sofa to attend to his needs—almost certainly involving my boobs.

CHAPTER 29

I AWOKE THE next morning filled with a new resolve to a) be a better parent and b) be a better person. Unfortunately, before my conversation with Joe I had already messaged Poppy, mainly to warn her about a potential incoming from Harris, but also to fill her in on the relatively meager new details we'd gleaned about Sam's death. She was also intrigued by the blank film and wondered, as Ailsa and I had, if this could somehow be linked to the photos that had caused such strife between Sam and Leila. We had agreed that the most productive route forward was to try and establish a link between Sam and Leila's deaths. Could I backtrack on her now? It seemed cruel. And my friendship with Poppy meant a lot to me—she had made Penton feel like home to me at a time when I was hopelessly out of my depth and floundering. Admittedly, I was still out of my depth and floundering, but now I had several lifelines, and Poppy was one of the strongest.

That said, there were times when I wondered about my friendship with Poppy, and this morning was one of those times. She was so relentlessly *pro*active, whereas I'd always found inactivity saw me through very nicely. It was 10 A.M., I hadn't showered and was wearing my ancient leopard-print pajamas that were a disgrace to leopards everywhere, Jack was wearing a diaper and a lot of oatmeal—I'd found the most efficient way to feed him was naked; it minimized the laundry casualty. Helen was despairing of ever being walked and had pointedly lain down across the front doormat. Then my phone pinged.

Wanna go for a run?

I'd rather eat my own feet thanks

The dogs need exercise

And so do we!

You're welcome to have Helen

Temporarily or permanently, I'm easy

Come onnnnn, Alice

You said you'd come running with me

That was very much an empty promise

How do you not recognize that by now?

I'll pick you up in fifteen

I sighed and walked through to where Joe was "working" in the kitchen.

"Can you watch Jack for half an hour while I go for a run?"

"Nah, I'm working."

"I can see that. What are you watching?"

"YouTube of Viennetta production. It's incredible."

"Like, those ice cream cakes from the nineties?"

"Yeah—look how many nozzles this machine has . . ."

"Are you working on a campaign for Viennetta?"

"No."

I went and put on my running gear. When Poppy arrived ten minutes later (being early was one of her greatest character flaws) both Joe and Jack were watching Viennetta production lines, entranced. Even Helen seemed reluctant to be dragged away.

* * *

"WHERE ARE we running?" I asked in the car, struggling with the laces of my running shoes, which appeared to have fossilized in place.

"I thought we could go up to Hawkbit Meadow," said Poppy innocently.

From the trunk Helen started up her weird ululating howl that she makes when she hears mention of her favorite places. Her vocabulary is limited and extremely selective—she recognizes "walk," "woods," "meadow," and "cheese," but inexplicably not "stop," "stay," "fuck off," or even "Helen."

I echoed it with a groan-howl of my own.

"Really? Of all the many, many places there are to run in the entire countryside, we're going back to the scene of the first crime?"

"It's a lovely spot for a run," she said defensively.

"We live in the Cotswolds. Everywhere is a lovely spot for a run. You want to look for clues," I countered accusingly.

"Nonsense. There won't be anything there," said Poppy briskly. "The police will have done a job on the place."

"Maybe," I cut in darkly. I had opinions on the efficiency of Harris's team.

"Fair point. But it's still pretty unlikely there's anything there after all this time. I was just thinking we could remind ourselves of the set-up—who was where, what the visibility is like from tree to tree. That kind of thing."

"It was dark and we were all asleep," I interrupted. "Visibility was pretty much nil."

"You're not being very helpful," commented Poppy.

"Sorry," I said. "I guess I'm just finding this whole thing a bit . . . itchy."

"Itchy?"

"Yeah. Like, Hen doesn't want us doing this, Joe doesn't want us doing this, I'm guessing Lin doesn't want us doing this. And really, there's no reason for us to be involved. We've got *responsibilities* now. I guess I'm just wondering if we shouldn't just let the whole thing drop."

Poppy was silent for a while. Then she said, "Actually, Lin doesn't seem to mind. She even said yesterday that it was good to see me back to my old self."

This was the closest we'd come to discussing the fact that Poppy had *not* been herself of late.

"Are you . . . y'know, all right?" I asked.

Poppy kept her eyes fixed on the road. Eventually, she said, "I don't know. This parenting thing. I love it, I love Noah—of course I do. And I do my best."

"You're an incredible mum," I interjected at this point—and I meant it. Poppy was wonderful with Noah—gentle, patient, attentive—you could see how much she loved him in every gesture.

"But that doesn't mean it's not also hard," she continued. "Or that there aren't times when I wish, well, that I wasn't doing it."

And I wholeheartedly agreed. The two were by no means mutually exclusive, and that really was parenting in a nutshell: seemingly impossible contradictions, all the time.

"Forget hard, it's bloody soul-destroying," I muttered.

"Yeah, that too. And then I feel terrible for thinking it," she mumbled. "But most of the time, to be honest, I don't feel anything. Just tired. Really, really tired."

I nodded with feeling. I'd never realized before parenting that tiredness was an emotion. Or at least, that it was capable of overwriting pretty much every single emotion.

"But with the investigation, we're actually doing something," continued Poppy, her voice strengthening. "Something that doesn't involve pee or poop or singing mindless rhymes about five little ducks or frogs or spacemen or whatever. It's like I can feel my brain waking up."

The phrase "agony of indecision" can be applied to a lot of my life. I hate making decisions. And right now I felt absolutely torn. I could see Joe's earnest face, hear his voice, "Is it worth it, Alice?"

"And you're enjoying it, right?" said Poppy with a hint of a grin. "I mean, tell me you're not?"

Damn her—she knew me too well. I thought of the burning curiosity kindled by what we'd found in Leila's apartment, the trip to London, the growing *need* to understand who Leila had been and what had happened to her. And now Sam—all the new questions thrown up by his death, questions that needed answers.

"OK fine. I suppose, yeah, it's the most fun we've had all year. Well not fun—obviously I don't mean that, that was a terrible choice of words.

And obviously parenting is *fun*. Well, actually that's also not the right word—"

I broke off. She'd won. We both knew it.

"So we'll take tea with the Honorable Genevieve tomorrow?" she wheedled.

"I supposed it's too late to cancel now," I grumbled. "Without looking rude."

Poppy grinned. "And she's expecting all three of us?"

"Yep," I confirmed, although I felt a pang of sadness—really it should be all four of us. And Hen, of all of us, would actually know how to behave for tea at the manor.

Poppy parked up at the gate into the meadow and bounded out far too energetically.

"But for now, nothing like a light jog to wake the brain up even more."

I'd assumed, when Poppy told me where we were heading, that this meant we wouldn't actually be running. We'd be poking around, pottering, looking for my all-time favorite: "clues." But apparently Poppy wanted to do it all.

"Let's just run to the trees," she said encouragingly. "That can't be more than three hundred meters."

"Which is nearly half a kilometer," I pointed out.

"Which isn't very far."

Our definitions of "far" clearly differed. But I was gratified to find that my first run since Take That had been in the charts didn't actually finish me off. I made it to the trees at a pace probably slightly slower than your average Londoner walks. In one of the many weird paradoxes of parenting I was probably in better shape than I had been for years. Pregnancy and parenting destroy your body in an unholy number of ways, but they also force you to give up or at least curb the more vicious vices. I hadn't smoked in years, I barely drank, I hadn't had a late-night burger from a dodgy chicken shop in forever (these do not exist in the countryside—a Kentucky Fried Pheasant does not count and yes that was a thing in Penton).

Poppy, who had reached the trees at Olympic-medalist speed, was waiting for me on the cusp of the copse. She was holding herself tensely.

I remembered that it had been Poppy who had found Leila's body—if waking up chained to a tree and opposite a corpse counts as "finding." I reached out and took her hand, and we stepped forward into the trees together.

It was a blindingly bright summer's day in the meadow, and it took my eyes a few moments to adjust to the dim light within the trees. It amazed me how enclosed they made the space feel. Shafts of light pierced down, creating little spotlights that danced across the ground. I couldn't help but be glad that the copse was, at least temporarily, saved—albeit at far too high a price.

"So," said Poppy in a determinedly brisk voice. "We were at . . . this tree?"

"Hmmm, no, I think it was this tree." I wandered along to a tree three down from the one Poppy was standing by.

"Are you sure?" she asked.

No, I absolutely wasn't, all trees look the same to me. I inspected the trunk near ground level.

"I think it was this one," I said cautiously. "I remember this little nub here grinding into my back all night."

"Then that would mean . . ." Poppy paced around the tree, and stopped facing another, very similar, tree. "This was Leila's tree."

We stood and contemplated it for a few moments. It was . . . just a tree. There was nothing sinister or malevolent about it. Due to the nature of Leila's death, there were no bloodstains, no gouge marks in the bark, nothing. If it was the even the right tree, that was.

I scuffed around in the debris at the tree base. It was already pretty disordered—I mean more so than is average in nature—and the police would have been through it with a fine-tooth comb. Probably.

"There's nothing here," I said to Poppy, eventually.

She sighed, and nodded.

"Let's just sit for a moment, see what we can remember from that night," she suggested, clearly unwilling to give up just yet.

I was perfectly happy to take a seat in the shade, if it meant postponing having to do any more running. I circled back round to our tree and found my old friend the back-prodding branchlet. I leaned against the trunk and tilted my head back, then closed my eyes.

I remembered . . . the silence of the trees, the rustle of the other protestors, the crackle of a radio somewhere in the distance . . . the news reporter had been talking about . . . a body washing up, somewhere? More bodies . . . Then there had been those footsteps late at night—could I remember which direction they'd come from? But it had been dark, I'd been disorientated even at the time, and I certainly couldn't trust my memory now.

Frustrated, I opened my eyes and hauled myself to my feet, brushing leafy debris from my leggings. Poppy was doing the same.

"Anything?" I asked. It felt as though I'd brushed against the edges of something, but, like my chronically sleep-deprived brain, it was foggy and indistinct.

Poppy shook her head. "Come on, let's run."

"Let's jog," I corrected her.

We trotted off down the gentle slope of the meadow toward where it petered out into the tangled hollows and shadows of Stricker's Wood. I was starting to get concerned—the gentle but inexorable downward tilt to the land meant that Poppy's car was now, inevitably, *up*hill. When we reached the tree line I paused for a breather and was about to suggest we head back to the car—possibly at a walk—when I spotted movement through the trees.

I squinted through the tangle of trunks. A man was doing something to a tree—not an unusual sight in Penton and its surrounds, I'd gotten used to that. But something about the way this man was standing—cautious, poised—made me think he was doing something at least a little illicit (vibe-based, I'm telling you). I nudged Poppy and pointed.

We lurked behind a tree in a way that would make anyone watching *us* highly suspicious. The man was reaching up to flip open the lid of what looked like a bird box, lodged halfway up the trunk. There was a crack from the woods, a branch breaking, the man turned sharply, and I saw his face. Oh FFS. Anonymous Richard? Here? What was this guy's deal?

Unfortunately, the crack we'd heard had apparently been Helen and Ronnie, who erupted out of the trees with the force of a natural disaster. Helen threw herself at Anonymous Richard as if he were her long-lost owner, while Ronnie danced around barking happily and occasionally trying to sneak-hump Helen if she stayed still for longer than two seconds.

It was, understandably, too much for Richard. Glancing left and right, but apparently not noticing us, he abandoned his birding pursuit and hurried away into the woods, the dogs dancing merrily around him and ignoring our attempts to call them back.

I plunged after the dogs—reflecting that this "run" had already involved far too much exercise. When I got back, now extremely sweaty and out of breath, delighted dogs in tow, Poppy was still standing at the base of Richard's tree, looking up.

"Thanks for the help," I said sarcastically.

"What do you think he was doing with the bird box?" she asked, ignoring me.

"Birdwatching, at a guess."

Poppy shook her head. "Unlikely. It's June, I shouldn't think there'll be any birds nesting in there now."

"I dunno. Maybe he was checking for stragglers."

"I reckon if you sort of kneel then I could stand on your thighs and probably reach it."

Which is how I found myself squatting at the base of a tree, hands braced against the trunk, while Poppy wobbled unsteadily on my lap, trying to open a bird box. Helen and Ronnie took advantage of my helplessness to poke their snoots in my ears, eyes, and hair, and Ronnie did a wee perilously close to my foot.

"There's something in here . . ." Poppy wobbled again, then jumped down in a move that nearly broke my leg.

"Ow," I began, but was swiftly distracted by what was in her hands. It was a standard Jiffy bag—beige, uninteresting in the extreme—except that you don't normally find Jiffy bags in bird boxes in the woods.

Excitedly, we peered into it.

"Cash," I breathed.

"Lots of it," agreed Poppy. She went to put her hand in but I grabbed her wrist.

"What?"

"Prints," I said. Then, slightly smugly because I couldn't help it, "And yours are already all over the bird box and the bag."

WE CALLED Inspector Harris, like the good and responsible citizens we are. She was predictably delighted at our contribution to the case.

"Let me guess, Alice, you've already copiously handled the evidence and your prints, and possibly your dog's, are all over it."

"Actually no," I said delightedly. "But Poppy's are."

Harris's sigh almost blew me away down the phone.

"YOU SAID you'd be back in half an hour," said Joe pointedly, when I returned two hours later. "Did you run a marathon or something?"

"Just think how many Viennetta videos you must have fitted in," I retorted. "Poppy and I ran into a bit of a situation."

"You amaze me," said Joe dryly. "How many bodies? I really don't want to know, but I suppose we'd better get the worst of it over. Oh, and I saved this for you."

He handed over Jack, who was sporting a suspiciously full diaper.

As I scraped and wiped and tried to breathe through my mouth, I filled Joe in on the events up at the meadow.

"So then Harris and her lot turned up and started doing their thing—dusting for fingerprints, taking statements from me and Poppy. Honestly, you'd think Harris would be more grateful when we literally hand her evidence on a plate. But no, she just seemed annoyed that we could only give her the name 'Richard,' no surname, and when she asked how we knew that was his name, and I said well that's what he said it was, she muttered 'unbelievable,' I heard her. I mean, what does she want from us? She tells us to back off from the investigation and then complains that we're not giving her enough information!"

"Alice, Alice," groaned Joe, holding up both hands. "Stop! What did we discuss literally last night? You promised—no more investigating."

"Actually, I didn't promise," I pointed out. Joe's face darkened.

"No wait, hear me out," I continued. I'd been practicing this in my head on the drive back. "I know—it's not super responsible parenting to get mixed up in all this. I'm well aware of that. But at the same time, I *am* mixed up in it. I knew Leila, I was there when she was killed. I knew Sam. I know the people involved. And you know how much this investigation is helping Poppy, she needs something like this. And if I'm honest, so do I. I'm not saying I'm depressed or anything, because I'm not, I'm just saying it feels good to use my brain like this. And Joe," I added, looking at him, "I'm *good* at this. Well, at bits of it, anyway."

I slid a clean diaper expertly under Jack.

"So please, I'm asking you to trust me on this. I won't take unnecessary risks, and I *definitely* won't take any risks with Jack. You know me better than that."

Joe looked deeply troubled, but he was listening to me. That wasn't guaranteed these days—oh, I was just as guilty as him; half our conversations were spent with me wondering if there were any Fritos left, or if I'd remembered to put laundry on, or whether Heather and Tarek from *Selling Sunset* were on the rocks. Eventually, I saw resignation settle over his face, and felt a teeny bit guilty but also a tiny bit triumphant.

"So—who is this Richard guy?" asked Joe, clearly making a huge effort. I loved him for it. He *did* trust me, and I wouldn't let him down.

"Well," I said slowly, "as Harris pointed out, hard to say from what we know at this point. So far he's popped up at the Earth Force meeting, at the Aether offices, at Leila's funeral—and now in the woods. None of the Earth Force lot know him—I asked Sian. And he claims he doesn't work at Aether, but then he looked pretty at home in their office, so I had thought that maybe he was Owen's ex-business partner, the one who actually designed the wind turbine. But I asked Hen and she said she was pretty sure it had been a woman—so that scuppered that idea . . . So now I'm wondering if he isn't someone from Leila's past . . . When I first saw him at the Earth Force meeting I got the impression she recognized him."

"But if that were the case, what was he doing at the Aether offices?" asked Joe.

"That," I said, poppering Jack's diaper shut with aplomb, "is a very good question."

CHAPTER 30

"HOW COME YOU always manage to be there at the opportune moment," grumbled Ailsa when we filled her in on our eventful run the next day. We'd met for a pre-tea tea. In just over an hour we would be taking tea at the manor with the Honorable Genevieve. For now, we were having a quick cuppa in the Gloucester rest stop en route—which, believe me, is a lot posher than it sounds. Even the rest stops around here were organic and free range, with a deli and a farm stand and bread for five pounds a loaf. It even had a grass roof. *On a rest stop.*

"Part of my overwhelming talent and skill as a detective, I suppose," I said airily, cracking the top of my millionaire's shortbread.

"Luck," said Ailsa grumpily. "Sheer bloody luck."

I had never thought of myself as lucky. Particularly not when it came to stumbling across dead bodies or associated events. But I had to admit I did seem to be building up quite a track record.

"What did Harris say about it?" Poppy asked.

Ailsa pulled a face. "You really think she's gonna tell me? Especially now that the three of us have managed to turn up or leave remnants at two crime scenes?"

I didn't like to think of my fingerprints as "remnants" and opened my mouth to tell Ailsa so, but she was barreling on.

"She's super pissed at all three of us. She's refused to do any babysitting until she's convinced I'm keeping my nose well out of all this."

This silenced us—the loss of babysitting was a heavy blow. While Joe and Lin were on childcare duty today, Ailsa had had to bring the twins with us. They were currently slumbering peacefully in their enormous double pushchair, which I knew from bitter experience meant they would be awake and raising seven kinds of hell at the Arnault mansion later.

"I'm not poking the bear anymore," said Ailsa definitively. "Much as it pains me to admit it, I need dear sister Jane right now. To keep a roof over our heads if nothing else. So if you want any more favors from her, you're gonna have to get them yourselves."

"Not a problem, your sister loves me," I said brightly, raising a half smile from Ailsa.

"So the main question now is, who is this guy?" said Poppy. "Anonymous Richard. And what was he doing faffing about with money in a bird box in the woods?"

"Was he putting the money in, or taking it out?" asked Ailsa.

"Couldn't tell," I admitted.

"If only Helen hadn't scared him off," said Poppy in frustration.

"Ronnie was there too!" I corrected her indignantly. "She's as good as gold without Ronnie egging her on."

"Well, it's obviously got to be something dodgy," mused Poppy, ignoring my blatant lie. "Drugs? Hush money?"

"Are we back to our old friend blackmail?" I contributed.

"Could be," admitted Poppy.

"You mean Leila again?" asked Ailsa. "But she's dead, she can't be blackmailing anyone anymore. Besides, we thought she was blackmailing Myers, where does Anonymous Richard fit into that?"

"I don't know," I said honestly. "I just think money seems to run through this whole case. Between Leila's family and Aether and now this . . ."

"What about Sam? He didn't seem to have any money."

"No, but he wanted it," I pointed out. "Enough to screw over his boyfriend and steal his agent."

"We only have Marcus's word for that," said Poppy.

"Not exactly," I remembered. "Sam's whole alibi for missing the protest was that he was out with an agent—he said so himself."

"We need to check this alibi out," said Poppy firmly. "What was the agent's name again?"

"Quirke," I said, because I wasn't going to forget a name like that.

A few seconds later, Poppy laid her phone on the table facing us.

"Quirke Talent: representing the finest forward-thinking artistic talents of today," I read from the website banner. I scrolled down to a photo of a man in a suit who looked more like an accountant, albeit one with a florid taste in ties, than the face of the "finest forward-thinking artistic talents of today."

"Robert Quirke," I read. "He looks like a Robert. Less like a Quirke."

"There's a contact number," said Poppy, pointing. "Let's give him a call."

"And say what?" asked Ailsa.

"Well . . . we could pretend we're from Sam's collective, and we want to talk about the representation of his work following his tragic demise."

"His 'tragic demise'?" said Ailsa, raising an eyebrow.

"I'm sure you'll word it much better than me." Poppy smiled encouragingly at her.

"Me?" said Ailsa, startled. "And why will it be me phoning?"

"Because, well, it's not going to be Alice."

"Rude."

"And it's not going to be me, because I know naff all about art. You're the arty one."

"And the activisty one," I interjected. "She's right, it should be you."

Ailsa sighed. "Maybe. I'll think about it."

"Well, there's no time like the present." Poppy slid her phone across the table to Ailsa, who looked mildly panicked.

"What, now? Here?"

"Why not?"

"Because we're in a rest-stop café?"

"It's as good a place as any."

Which is how Ailsa found herself impersonating an artist from a collective we'd briefly visited once, inquiring after the work of a dead "friend."

Poppy and I leaned in close, trying to overhear the tinny voice on the far end of the phone—Ailsa having, probably correctly, refused to put it on speakerphone in a crowded rest-stop forecourt.

"Hello, Quirke Talent."

"Hi, my name's . . . Alice," said Ailsa after a panicky pause. We hadn't discussed the basics—like her name. But *Alice*? Seriously? I gave her a furious look and she shrugged at me. "I was wondering if I could speak to Mr. Quirke?"

"And are you an existing client?" chirped the distant voice.

"Not exactly," said Ailsa. "I'm calling on behalf of Sam White, who is, was, a client."

There was a slight pause, perhaps as the person on the far end of the phone took in Ailsa's sudden change of tense.

"One moment please, I'll put you through."

Some sort of terrifying electronica played down the line.

"Alice?" I hissed at Ailsa. "What the hell? What's the point of giving a fake name if you give *my* name?"

"Sorry, I panicked," she admitted guiltily. "It's fine, there are loads of Alices in the world."

"Thanks, I'm sure that'll stand up in court."

But a new voice was now booming down the line.

"Robert Quirke speaking."

"Oh hi. My name's Alice, I'm phoning about your recent interest in Sam White's work," said Ailsa, avoiding my eye. "I'm part of his collective."

"Sam! How is he?"

Ah. We exchanged looks.

"Haven't you heard?" asked Ailsa awkwardly. "He, um, I'm afraid he passed away."

There was a shocked silence. Then: "Are we talking about the same person? Sam White? Photographer? Hangs around with the talented painter chap, what's his name, Mark?"

"Marcus? Yes, I'm pretty sure it's the same person . . ."

"But that's not possible," said Quirke, sounding genuinely shocked. "I met with him just a couple of weeks ago. He was fine!"

"It was a . . . sudden death," said Ailsa delicately. "On Saturday."

"Good God . . ." There was a pause then. "Thank goodness he signed in time."

"I beg your pardon?"

"Well, from a business perspective this is going to put a premium on his work, to be frank."

Robert Quirke appeared to have gotten over his shock pretty quickly.

"He'd already signed with you?" asked Ailsa.

"Didn't he say? Yes, we signed all the paperwork, must've been nearly two weeks ago."

"Would that have been on the Wednesday night he met with you?" asked Ailsa carefully.

"Yes, I think it was, now you mention it. Yes it was a Wednesday, because we went to Alchemy Seven and they have a jazz band in on Wednesdays."

"He said it was . . . quite the night. You were out late?"

There was a chuckle down the line. "A real all-nighter," Quirke confirmed, followed by a somber silence. "Shocking news. Absolutely shocking. So young. Such talent. Such promise." I could almost hear him shaking his head at the other end of the line. The unspoken rider: *Such earning potential*. "And Mark, I don't suppose you happen to know if he's still looking for representation?"

"I think you'd best speak to Marcus himself."

"Of course, very sensible, yes. What's the best number to reach him on?"

"Er . . ." Ailsa looked at us wide-eyed. How to say that, as a member of the tight-knit artists' collective, she didn't have his phone number.

"Actually Mark, sorry Marcus, is grieving right now. You know he and Sam were very close. Perhaps it would be best to leave it a couple of days."

I gestured wildly with my hands, hoping Ailsa could interpret my semaphore.

"But I'm sure he would love to hear from you, in time," said Ailsa, correctly decoding my whirling hands.

"I will, absolutely. Thank you for informing me of this sad development," said Robert Quirke, rather pompously. "And you're from Sam and Mark's collective? What did you say your name was again?"

"Alice," squeaked Ailsa. "Well, thought you should know. Thanks so much for your time, bye."

She hung up looking unusually flustered.

"That went well," said Poppy encouragingly.

"Never make me do that again," glared Ailsa.

"But we achieved what we needed," I said, offering Ailsa the last bite of my millionaire's shortbread, which was pretty big of me considering her betrayal. "That's Sam's alibi confirmed for the night Leila died."

"Which leaves us with Owen Myers from the Aether perspective," said Ailsa, "or Raven from the Earth Force side."

"Plus Anonymous Richard, who seems to have a foot in both camps," I added. "Not to mention Norah, who seems to have had a bit more than a foot in when it comes to Myers, and was the only one not tied to a tree when Leila was killed. And Enderby is a bit weird and was hanging around outside Aether that time. And then there's Maryam, who was less than fond of Leila."

"But would never hurt Sam," put in Poppy.

I stabbed at the remaining crumbs on my plate with my finger. How come our suspect list seemed to be getting longer rather than shorter?

Ailsa drained her coffee. "Then of course there's one final option . . ."

"A murderous family member," I completed. "Right, let's go and take tea with the Honorable Genevieve Arnault."

CHAPTER 31

OH MY GOD. It was an honest to goodness stately home. Like the ones you need National Trust membership to look round or however it works. It had columns. It had an obscene number of windows. It probably had a West Wing. And an East Wing, come to that. A wide gravel drive (more of a private road) swept up to the front of the house where it circled round a large stone fountain. It was like a miniature Buckingham Palace.

"You can't drive this old banger up to the door," hissed Poppy.

"Of course we can," Ailsa said tartly from the back seat, where she was wedged between two baby car seats. "These people live in fantasy worlds, it will do them some good to see how normal people live."

"This isn't how normal people live, it's how Alice lives."

"You can walk home if you like," I replied. So my car had a few nicks and dents. And quite a lot of bird shit on it. And the inside, well, it transported Helen and Jack who were both biological hazards—and me come to that, and I consumed a lot of my daily snack allowance in my car and often forgot to clean it out—so what? I wasn't walking up to the house.

There was a Bentley parked outside. I parked aggressively close to it.

A side door to our right flung open (the front doors probably required a winch and two carthorses to open) and a young woman came out. I was a little disappointed to see how normal she looked. After my extensive Instagram stalking, combined with a little light googling, I'd come to expect a supermodel dripping in diamonds. But the Honorable Genevieve wore no makeup (or it was just so cleverly done it looked like that), jeans, and a plain, although admittedly expensive-looking, jumper. Not a diamond in sight.

"Come in, come in!" she cried. "Sorry, we don't really use the front door. The front of the house is rather an embarrassment isn't it!"

I'd never understood this—rich people who flamboyantly displayed their wealth by, for example, owning a stately home and parking a Bentley in front of it, and yet purported to be embarrassed by the results. I had year-old tubs of McDonald's BBQ sauce in my car—*that* was embarrassing.

Ailsa unloaded the twins, and shoved one of them (Robin?) into my arms.

"I hope you don't mind, I had to bring my kids," she said to Genevieve. She glanced up at the house. "The nanny's off sick," she added dryly. Genevieve didn't seem to notice the barb.

"Of course! How adorable! Bring them on in."

She led us through a disappointingly dingy set of dark corridors—almost certainly "below stairs"—until we emerged in a beautiful light-filled orangery. And when I say orangery, I mean it literally. The room was lined with orange trees which filled the air with a delicate citrus tang, twenty or thirty of them. Huge windows and skylights meant the summer sun poured in; it would have been stifling but the quietly expensive air conditioning kept it cool and fresh. Genevieve led us over to a cluster of chintzy armchairs where a light tea was already laid out. This was looking more promising.

I was immediately distracted by the array of delicious treats before me—scones (sweet and savory), mini quiches, tiny pastries, macarons, little bowls of fruit. Was this the sort of tea where you were mainly meant to look at it, and possibly photograph it for social media purposes, or could I actually tuck in? Because Helen had stolen half my breakfast that morning and I was starving. I had regretted giving Ailsa my last mouthful of shortbread at the rest stop.

Poppy nudged me, and I realized Genevieve had been addressing me.

"Sorry, I was thinking about cake," I said without thinking. I really needed to develop a better filter.

Genevieve laughed and handed me a plate. "Please, help yourself."

Well now I was too embarrassed to. Ugh.

"I was just asking how you knew my sister," Genevieve repeated herself.

"To be honest we didn't know Leila all that well," said Poppy, charitably rescuing me from my cake-based embarrassment. "We got to know her through Earth Force recently."

"You're with Earth Force?" A wariness immediately darkened Genevieve's beautiful face, and she froze in the act of handing a plate to Poppy. "You didn't say." Her eyes flicked nervously from side to side. "I really can't—You shouldn't be here. Why did you come? What do you want?"

"No no," I said hastily. "We're not *with* Earth Force, we're just sort of . . ." I trailed off. How exactly to explain our involvement with Earth Force when I didn't understand it myself?

"We met Leila when we were out on a picnic and she invited us along to an Earth Force meeting," Poppy stepped in smoothly once more. "We're not members of Earth Force, but that is where we really got to know Leila."

Not that we got to know her at all, I silently added.

"You're not members?"

We all shook our heads vehemently.

Genevieve unfroze and, rather reluctantly, handed Poppy a plate. Sensing that we were no longer about to be turfed out, and possibly have the hounds set on us, Ailsa released Ivy on the floor, and I followed suit with Robin. They immediately zoomed off in opposite directions at a high-speed crawl. The old divide and conquer tactic.

"I'm sorry," said Genevieve, recovering her gracious hostess posture with a visible effort. "It's just that if it weren't for that group"—a bitterness laced those last words—"my sister would still be alive and with us."

"You think Earth Force had something to do with her death?" I couldn't help asking.

Genevieve gave me an incredulous look. "She was murdered at one of their protests!" she spoke slowly as though I might be hard of thinking. "Quite clearly, it was Earth Force's fault."

She placed four grapes on her plate and sat back, as if that were plenty.

"Earth Force. Leila's latest fad. Her most extreme one though, I'm afraid." She sounded very deliberately cool, almost offhand, but there was an edge of pain beneath her words.

"Latest fad?" I echoed.

"Oh yes," said Genevieve. "She was like that, you know. She'd get caught up in something, swept away by it all. It would consume her life for months, sometimes more, and then, well, she'd move on."

"You don't think she really believed in what Earth Force stand for, then?" I asked hesitantly. My first impression of Leila had been that this was someone driven by her passion, by deeply held belief. But perhaps I'd been mistaken. Perhaps she had been driven by . . . something else.

Genevieve shrugged. "Perhaps she did. Or wanted to believe that she did. How would I know? It's not like she talked to me about any of it, not anymore."

"You'd fallen out of touch?" I asked.

"Leila had ceased contact with the family," she corrected me, careful to apportion the blame. "But we . . . kept an eye on her activities."

Wow, because that didn't sound sinister at all.

"She enjoyed reinventing herself, playing a part," Genevieve continued, pausing briefly to sip her tea. There was an edge of bitterness to her voice, suggesting it was something that had hurt her in the past. I couldn't quite get a handle on Genevieve; there was a sadness there, a grief, but it was tempered by another emotion I couldn't quite put my finger on. She talked about Leila as if she had been dead far longer than a fortnight.

"There was usually a boy involved," continued Genevieve, inspecting one of her grapes. "I understand she was seeing someone in the group?"

"Yes, Raven," said Ailsa.

"Raven . . ." repeated Genevieve. "You know, he didn't even come and speak to me, or any of the family, at the funeral."

We all remained tactfully silent, unwilling to point out to Genevieve that her family stood for everything Raven and his group were opposed to, while she quite clearly blamed them for her sister's death. I couldn't see that conversation going well, least of all at the funeral. We all watched Ivy and Robin wrestle on the floor together and tried to think of something suitable to say.

"Raven and Leila seemed very happy together," I said tentatively. Based on their naked stroll together through the meadow they had seemed pretty compatible, after all. "Do you think she was doing it to impress Raven?"

"Oh, Leila didn't care about impressing anyone." Genevieve gave a rather brittle laugh. "She did enjoy annoying people though. I used to find it so funny when we were children. Brave, bold Leila, always speaking out where she shouldn't. It grew less amusing, as we got older. She had to push things further and further. Taking up with a climate protest group was a calculated attack on our father. She misjudged it this time, though."

"Oh, how so?" asked Poppy.

Genevieve gave her a direct look. "You must know what our family business is," she said, as if daring Poppy to dissemble.

"You're in petrochemicals," said Ailsa, equally bluntly. "Yes, I can imagine Leila taking up with an environmental group didn't sit so well."

"We care about the environment at Arnault International," said Genevieve, looking slightly offended. "We have extensive carbon offsetting programs. But the world needs fuel. It needs the products our company produce. Do you have any idea how many goods require petrochemical derivatives? They're fundamental to how we function as a modern, developed society."

I saw Poppy lay a warning hand on Ailsa's leg. Behind Genevieve, I could see Ivy shredding the lower leaves off an orange tree. I suspected that Ailsa had also seen and was silently cheering her daughter on.

"I'm not sure that's how Earth Force sees it," said Poppy delicately.

"Well, there's no pleasing some people," said Genevieve dismissively. "The protest Leila died at was against green energy. So what's it to be? They don't want traditional energy sources, they don't want green energy? Do they want us all to go back to living in caves?"

"It's a matter of standards," said Ailsa. "Yes we need green energy, but we need to hold the emerging green energy industry to higher standards if we're to avoid falling into the same old pitfalls we saw with the fossil fuel industry. The company Earth Force were protesting against, Aether, aren't a *bad* company. I'm sure Owen Myers isn't a bad man, and he certainly talks a good game. But bulldozing a meadow, a delicate and unique ecosystem, to build his new wind farm? That's so far from responsible energy—"

"There you go," interrupted Genevieve, slightly triumphantly. "People are so keen to demonize the traditional energy industry but really the so-called green energy industry is just as bad. Worse in some ways, as they put such a sanctimonious face on it."

"That's not what I said," retorted Ailsa hotly. "Owen Myers and Aether are infinitely preferable to the fossil fuel industry. It's the first step in the revolution, I just think we need to be clear from the outset where the boundaries lie and—"

"Yes, yes, I've heard it all," said Genevieve breezily. "I know all about Aether. They've come across our radar, of course. Not as competition you understand—they're a very *small* company; interesting, but somewhat limited in scope. But of course we had to do our due diligence when Leila insisted on working there—a studied insult to Daddy."

I tried to suppress a shudder—I am not on board with grown-ups referring to their Mummies and Daddies. And why is this exclusively the preserve of the monied classes? What a weird affectation to hang on to. I would give Jack until he was five, maybe six, and then I would be enforcing Mum and Dad, end of.

"A lot of people think Owen Myers is something of a visionary in the energy world," said Poppy mildly.

"Yes, people really love him, don't they?" mused Genevieve, sounding thoughtful. "Leila did, when she worked for him. Owen this, Owen that. It was really very boring. Seems she rather went off him in the end though." She gave a small, prim smile, rather like a cat. I remembered what she'd said earlier: *There was usually a boy involved.*

"Why did she leave Aether?" I asked rather bluntly. I was feeling less warmly toward Genevieve as the afternoon went on. I reminded myself that she had just lost her sister, in horrific circumstances. And while she didn't seem devastated as such, there was clearly genuine grief there, it was just mixed in with a lot of anger and bitterness all suffocated under a veneer of crushing social etiquette.

"She fell out with Owen," Genevieve replied. "Didn't she tell you about it?"

"No," Poppy said. "She didn't say much about her time at Aether." This was perfectly true—albeit because we'd barely exchanged five sentences with Leila.

"They had some sort of big row," Genevieve said vaguely. "I tried to get her to move home after it, but it was just after her terrible falling out with Daddy. So I guess she decided she could better get revenge on Myers by joining Earth Force—and get another dig in at Daddy at the same time."

I was a little startled by that statement—the idea that Leila might have joined the action group as an act of revenge was unpleasant, and cast a distinct shadow over the picture of her we'd been building up. But then, Leila's character had always been rather slippery to pin down.

"What did she and Myers row about?" I asked curiously.

Genevieve shrugged. "I don't know. Leila was always falling out with someone. She could be utterly charming, but she could turn. And, by all accounts, she turned on Owen."

"You don't think they were . . . you know. Romantically involved?" I asked, sounding bizarrely like a maiden aunt. "And then split up or something?"

Genevieve's immaculate forehead wrinkled briefly. "It's possible," she conceded. "Once upon a time I would have said no, she'd have told me about it. But she'd already begun to pull away by the time she went to Aether."

"Pull away?" prompted Poppy delicately.

Genevieve sighed, and suddenly looked much older. Her face was touched with what seemed to be a genuine sadness, whereas before there had always been a slightly performative aspect to her.

"We were close, as kids," she said, her voice sounding a little less under her control. "Really close. There's only two years between us and, well, we were as different as two sisters could be but it worked, you know? I was the good kid, and Leila was, well, not the *bad* kid, she wasn't *bad*, just naughty and she liked to push people's buttons. Even as a tiny kid." She gave a funny, hoarse laugh. "She seemed to feed off it, getting a rise out of people. And Daddy, well she could never resist seeing how far she could push him. But me, never. She was always on my side. Until a couple of years ago. When I started working for the company it all . . . changed.

Of course, she wanted to work for the company too, but when Daddy offered her a junior position it didn't sit well with her. He said she had to gain some proper experience before she could take on a more senior role and she didn't like that, not at all. So she left. And because I worked for Daddy, suddenly I was the enemy too . . . But she shouldn't have pushed him away so much, shouldn't have pushed all of us away."

"You said she fell out with your"—I coughed slightly—"dad. What was that over?"

"She took it too far," said Genevieve with a sigh. "The fight they had the last time she came home was the worst they'd ever had. And, well, Daddy cut off her allowance. I don't think they'd spoken since, not for eight months. Which seems . . . awful now."

"She received an allowance?" I asked, confused. Leila was a grown woman with a job—well, she'd had a job at the time anyway. I hadn't received an allowance since I was, what, eight?

"Of course," said Genevieve, looking surprised. "She wasn't due to come into any inheritance until her thirtieth birthday, so of course Daddy paid her an allowance—she had to live on something!"

"Most people just get jobs," said Ailsa dryly.

"Well, of course, and she *had* a job," said Genevieve, a little flustered. "But from all accounts it didn't pay very much. Not enough to *live* on."

I bit my tongue. Like, actually bit it.

"Why did your father cut off her allowance?" Poppy asked, more civilly than I would have managed.

Genevieve leaned forward. "Well, Leila had been working for this Aether company for a few months, which was bad enough, and we knew she was messing around in this whole eco activist scene, which was even worse. But I really think Mummy and Daddy would have overlooked it, let her get it out of her system like she always did. But then there was a protest against our company, against Arnault International, about eight months back. We were opening a new coal plant and we had the usual protestors—placards, people supergluing themselves to anything they could, black paint thrown over the head offices—the usual. But when it was covered in the press the next day—there was Leila! In one of the photos. Front and center. Her breasts out and everything. It was absolutely shocking," Genevieve said primly. "Really very degrading. But I mean the worst thing about it was the betrayal. Protesting against the family company, and in such a lewd manner! Well, it was too much for Daddy. He cut her off. Threatened to disinherit her as well, I think. Oh he was furious."

Poppy, Ailsa, and I shared a look. We knew the exact photo Genevieve was talking about—we'd seen it less than a week ago. And we knew who had taken it. No wonder Leila had been mad at Sam, his photo had cost her a comfortable monthly income—and potentially a not-so-small fortune. No doubt he hadn't been aware of it at the time—she'd just been some girl he and his brother met at a protest, that's what he'd told me. It must have been quite a shock when she turned up at Earth Force two months later, that dazzling rage now turned on him. Leila had wanted to have her cake and eat it, it seemed, but Sam had unwittingly put paid to that.

Talking of cake, I reached surreptitiously for a miniature Victoria sponge.

"Still." Genevieve put on a falsely bright smile, clearly pulling herself back into her glossy shell. "That's families for you!"

I paused, tiny sponge halfway to my mouth. Honestly, what to say to that? I wasn't one to claim any sort of ideal family, but jeez.

"Are your delightful babies allowed to eat those?" continued Genevieve brightly.

Ivy and Robin had pulled themselves up against the low table and were cramming brightly colored macarons into their mouths, their eyes wide with joy at the illicit sugar.

"Shit," said Ailsa.

GENEVIEVE TOOK us out through the front entrance. The entrance lobby was larger than my cottage. I wondered if she was trying to impress us, or perhaps, my darker brain suggested, to intimidate us.

"So nice of you to pop round," she said as she waved us off. There was no polite suggestion that we do it again, but then, I think we'd all gotten what we wanted from each other. I wasn't entirely sure what Genevieve had wanted from us, but having met her I was sure she didn't do anything without an agenda.

"Well. What did you make of that?" I asked as we wound our way back down the never-ending driveway.

"She seemed nice enough, on the surface," said Poppy carefully. "Very . . . proper."

"Cold though," said Ailsa. "Underneath it all, she was cold."

I had to agree—for the most part. It was clear there had been a close bond between the sisters, but it was equally clear that it had eroded, possibly beyond repair, in recent years, and Genevieve had pretty efficiently suppressed any remaining affection for her sister.

"Do you think she had anything to do with . . . you know?" I asked, not quite able to articulate the question.

"Killing her sister?" said Ailsa bluntly. "Not really. She seemed pissed off with Leila, which is a bit much when she's dead . . . But I couldn't see her actually having a hand in it. What would she stand to gain?"

"Money?" I pointed out.

"If Leila was being disinherited it probably all came to her anyway," said Ailsa.

"Protecting the family?" Poppy suggested. "It sounds like Leila was bringing in some pretty bad press."

"I think a murder in the family is about as bad press as it comes, don't you? Or I'm sure Jane would have bumped me off a long time ago. She's got the know-how."

This was the kind of Ailsa joke that made me very uncomfortable.

"Talking of bad press . . . At least we found out why Leila and Sam fell out," I said. "He sold that photo of her to the press—ruining her relationship with her family and costing her, well, at least her allowance, possibly much, much more . . ."

Ailsa shook her head. "And then a couple of months later she ends up dating his brother. That's messed up."

At this moment Robin did a small bright pink vomit. Ivy shrieked with delighted laughter.

Ah, the macarons were hitting.

Brace.

CHAPTER 32

I HAD JUST dropped Ailsa and the twins at their cottage in central Penton, the babies shrieking loudly as the unaccustomed sugar burned through their systems. As I passed the train station, I noticed a figure slouched on the bench outside, framed between two pristine hanging flower baskets. His lanky figure looked strangely familiar.

"Hang on, is that . . . ?"

". . . Marcus?" completed Poppy.

Without really thinking, I pulled over and lowered the window.

"Marcus, hi. What are you doing here?"

He looked up, startled. He looked terrible. His face was gaunt and his eyes sunken. He looked like he hadn't slept in a week. He also clearly did not recognize me at all. His brow furrowed.

"Sorry, do I . . . ? I mean, hi. Sorry." It was a lot of apologies in a very short sentence.

"Sorry," I joined in. "I'm Alice. You probably don't remember me, we met at the exhibition up in London, and at Fox Hollow the other day. I'm Maya's friend? We sort of knew Sam . . ." My voice tailed off as his face crumpled at Sam's name.

"I'm so, so sorry for your loss," I mumbled. "Are you . . . OK?" It's a pointless question, I know, but what else can you ask someone who's just lost their boyfriend, even if they're quite clearly not OK.

Marcus stared at me, uncomprehending.

"I came to . . . see Sam." He paused, rewinding those words in his head. "I mean, obviously not see him. His family. You know . . ."

Poppy leaned over. "Is someone picking you up?" she asked, her voice full of concern. "Is someone meeting you?"

Marcus looked up at the clock above the station. "Raven said he or Maryam would pick me up. But I've been here an hour."

I hesitated, but only briefly. He looked so lost. And what was he going to do, no bus was making it down those tiny lanes to Maryam's, and from personal experience I knew he could at best hope for a taxi sometime before the weekend.

"Hop in," I said. "I'll take you over there."

"Are you sure?" The relief on his face convinced me I'd made the right decision.

"Of course." I climbed out and popped the trunk open to stow his bag, then paused. The entire trunk was lined with a sort of felting of Helen's dog hair, a good two years' worth of it. You could have made an entire extra Helen out of it—although why anyone would want that I do not know.

I closed the trunk. "Er, I think we'll put your bag in the back seat."

Marcus looked faintly perplexed, perhaps wondering if I'd forgotten about a body I'd stashed in the trunk, but nodded.

I wedged his backpack in Jack's car seat and turfed Poppy out into the back seat, then surveyed the passenger seat, which was a minor improvement on the trunk. "Sorry about the mess," I mumbled, trying in vain to brush away the crumbs, fluff, and general debris. There was an odd, slightly sticky substance that could have been jam, but then again could have been something much worse. I decided not to mention it. The faint odor of macaron vomit hung in the air, sweet and sour.

I had to drop Poppy home, as she and Lin had Lin's mother coming over for dinner. She gave me a rather uncertain look as she climbed out of the car.

"Text me when you're home, OK?"

Which left Marcus and me in a slightly awkward silence, broken by Marcus's stomach giving an almighty rumble.

"Hungry?" I asked, realizing that actually I was starving. The tiny cakes at Genevieve's had barely touched the sides, and it hadn't really been a load-your-plate-up kind of atmosphere.

"A bit," he admitted. "I'm not sure I've eaten anything today."

I stared at him in horror. I've never understood this in some people—the ability to go hours, a whole *day*, without food. And to not remember when they last ate. At least 50 percent of my brain at any given time is occupied with considering my next meal/snack.

"If we divert via Bridgeport there's a McDonald's drive-thru," I offered.

He didn't reply at first. I didn't get huge McDonald's vibes off him. Given the subject of his exhibition, I expected he hadn't set foot in a McDonald's for many years. I am, of course, fully aware of the climate impacts of the McDonald's of this world—I'm friends with Ailsa, how could I not? But I also accept that while I try my best I am a deeply flawed human being who does love a chicken nugget.

"I know it's not very ethical, and I know it's bad for the planet, but they do a vegan burger and we can recycle the packaging," I added. By recycle I meant leave to fester in the back of my car for two months.

"Is it any good, the vegan burger?"

I stared at him confused. "I have no idea, I always get chicken nuggets. Or a proper burger."

Marcus's shoulders relaxed a little and he even gave a small smile.

"Go on then," he said. "Let's get McDonald's."

I smiled. I'm a terrible influence on people. But sometimes they need it.

WE SAT in the McDonald's car park in a greasy, comfortable silence. I couldn't help contrasting it with the tense aesthetic of the Arnault Manor orangery and Genevieve's Instaperfect spread.

"Are you *sure* you don't want a chicken nugget?" I asked for the tenth time.

"Positive." He grinned. "The vegan burger was . . . acceptable."

My phone buzzed, and I swiped at it, leaving a greasy smear across the screen. It was Poppy.

> Hey, be careful yeah? We don't know anything about Marcus and, well . . . Look just don't ask him any questions about Sam's death. Don't antagonize him.

I felt a chill sweep across my skin. Of course, Marcus was, if not a *suspect* suspect, certainly in the ring for Sam's murder. And now I was about to drive alone with him into the deepest darkest Cotswold countryside, where there would be no phone signal and very little other traffic. The sun was down and the shadows were pooling. I was painfully reminded of my promise to Joe, just days ago, that I wouldn't take any unnecessary risks. I even wished I had Helen in the car with me, but obviously I hadn't taken her to Arnault Manor, although part of me (quite a large part) would have really enjoyed watching that.

"OK let's get going," I said briskly, popping the last nugget in my mouth and chucking the empty bags into the back seat. My hand shook ever so slightly releasing the handbrake.

Apparently unaware of my increasing unease, Marcus seemed to have relaxed a bit after his McDonald's.

"So," he asked as we sped off into the growing dark, "how did you know Sam again? Did he say you know his brother or something?"

"Kind of," I replied. "Although not that well really. I did a protest with Raven up at Hawkbit Meadow. You know, the whole chain-yourself-to-trees kind of thing."

Marcus half turned in his seat to look at me. "Not the one where Leila died?"

"Er, yeah actually, it was."

I felt his eyes on me, and kept mine resolutely fixed on the road. After a minute, he looked away again.

"Sam was really cut up about it," he said abruptly. "Leila dying like that. Horrible."

"Really?" I couldn't keep the questioning tone out of my voice.

"Of course!" said Marcus, sounding a little—what? Surprised? Annoyed? "She was his brother's girlfriend. Of course he was upset—more than upset!"

"Of course, of course," I said quickly, Poppy's warning ringing in my ears. "I just . . . got the impression they didn't get on that well. That's all."

Out of the corner of my eye I saw Marcus rub his face.

"No," he said eventually. "They didn't get on. They were always at each other's throats. He thought she was a phony, but he also, well, he didn't behave brilliantly toward her."

"Selling that photo of her at the Arnault protest to the press?" I said, without thinking.

"She told you about that?" He sounded surprised.

"Er, yeah . . ." I said, feeling a flush of shame at the barefaced lie. "Yeah . . . She wasn't very happy."

"I mean, now we know who her family are it makes sense," said Marcus. "But at the time Sam thought she was overreacting; he was a bit dismissive of it. I mean, as far as he knew, she was just some random girl at the protest. And he did try to apologize. I mean, he shouldn't have sold it without at least trying to get her permission, that was really wrong of him. I know he needed the money but . . ." He breathed in sharply. "I loved him, I think. But Sam could be . . ." There was a pause as he struggled for the right word. "A bit self-serving."

Yuh, I thought to myself. Selling a topless photo of someone to the press without their permission? That didn't sit well with me. Whether they were a phony or not. And screwing over his own boyfriend to nab his agent? Although I didn't think I'd bring that one up . . . That was probably what Poppy would refer to as antagonizing him.

"So, Sam didn't know who Leila's family were?" I asked tentatively.

Marcus shook his head. "No, not until the funeral. Leila was super cagey about her family—I mean, she used a fake surname for God's sake. I think she gave Raven the impression she didn't really have any. Which, given what Raven and Sam went through, losing their mum so young, was pretty shady of her."

"What happened to her? Their mum?" I asked. Raven had given us the barest bones of the story.

"Car accident," said Marcus somberly. "When they were just kids. Hit and run."

"Did they ever catch who did it?"

"No, and it drove their dad to distraction. I never met him, but from what Sam says, he wasn't exactly there for his sons . . ."

"No, Raven said that Maryam pretty much brought them up."

"Yeah. Not officially though. I think there was a bit of nastiness around that, actually. She wanted to take legal guardianship of the boys but their dad refused, and it all got . . . messy."

"So they stayed with their dad?"

"Barely, from the sounds of it. I think they more or less grew up at Fox Hollow. Don't try telling Maryam those boys aren't her sons! She's like a mother bear over them. I think Sam finds it a bit much sometimes." He paused, shifting tense, painfully, in his mind. "Found it a bit much."

"She didn't like Leila much, did she?"

Marcus gave a humorless laugh. "Leila could have been Mother Teresa and she wouldn't have been good enough for one of Maryam's boys. And, let's face it, she was no saint."

"Did *you* like Leila?" I couldn't help asking.

Marcus shrugged. "I didn't really know her." He turned to look out of his window. "I don't think any of us did."

WE TRAVELED in uncomfortable silence for a while; the post-McDonald's glow had worn off, leaving its usual greasy hangover.

I had to ask . . .

"So . . . did you manage to make up with Sam? You know, when you came down last week?"

Marcus turned to look at me. I kept my eyes firmly on the road. In the evening gloom he was just a shadow in my peripheral vision.

"How do you know about that?"

Was I really so very forgettable?

"We bumped into you, up at Maryam's, remember? We'd been out picking mushrooms when you arrived on Thursday."

I sensed him relax ever so slightly.

"Oh. Yes," he said shortly. "We made up. Sort of. Maryam phoned Sam and read him the Riot Act, and he came down Friday morning. We were going to make it work. It was over a stupid thing, an agent. Sam was going to call him and sort it all out."

"That was good of him," I mumbled, not wanting to reveal that we'd overheard the two of them arguing and knew the whole sorry story.

"Sam was Sam," said Marcus distantly. "I knew what I was getting into when I got involved with him. I probably shouldn't have, but sometimes you can't help yourself."

"Had you been together long?"

"Just a few months . . ." Marcus's attention seemed to be floating outside the window, somewhere in the darkness beyond. "I loved him, or was starting to, maybe. Don't know if he felt the same way . . . But I loved him. Could've killed him sometimes though . . . Selfish bastard. And now he's dead . . ."

Those words trickled through my brain like a melting ice cube. Ever since confronting death, head on, in our last case, I'd felt very uneasy about people's ability to say things like "I could've killed him." Because words and actions are two sides of the same coin. If you say something too often, it becomes your truth.

"You, er, you made up though," I squeaked.

"Hmm? Oh, yeah. More or less. If he kept his side of the bargain. I suppose he never will now . . ."

"And did you . . . stick around?" I asked tentatively. "After you made up? Did you stay at Fox Hollow?"

"I went back to London on Saturday morning," said Marcus. "Sam was supposed to join me on Sunday. Only he didn't."

"No." I didn't know what else to say. So according to Marcus, he'd been back in London at the time of the murder. But I only had his word for it—which doesn't count for much. Detectoring, unfortunately, often seems to involve thinking the worst of people, which doesn't come particularly naturally to me. I'm more or less expert at thinking the worst of myself, but tend to give others the benefit of the doubt. But "he said he didn't do it" doesn't cut much ice in a murder case.

"What will you do now?" I asked, hoping to steer the conversation onto safer ground.

"I'll see Sam's family. There's going to be a memorial on Thursday, for Sam and Leila, so I'll stick around for that. Then I'll head back to London."

"Back to the collective?"

"Yep. They're my family, really. And they were Sam's too. It's where we were happy together. Before things got—" He broke off. "There's an agent I might get in touch with, see if I can get representation."

Ah yes, Quirke. I kept quiet on this front.

"And if what Sam told me was true"—there was a slight pause as we both contemplated the likelihood of this—"then he left the rights to all his work to me."

I went cold. Sam had done what? Was Marcus literally handing me a motive? Sam had been an up-and-coming photographer but he'd still had quite a long way to go, from my interpretation of the situation. How much would his work actually be worth? Enough to murder for?

MARCUS DIDN'T murder me. He was very grateful for the lift and tried to give me ten pounds petrol money—which I'd have quite liked to have taken, but even I recognized that was extortionate. I told him to buy me a drink sometime, in the full knowledge that I'd likely never see him again.

I liked Marcus, but murderers could be superficially likeable. That was another uncomfortable truth. And I admit I turned back onto the main road toward home, with street lights and other cars, with a deep sense of relief.

My phone buzzed as I re-entered the land of the living/phone signal. Poppy.

> Can you let me know you're not dead in a ditch??

CHAPTER 33

I STILL FELT jittery the next morning. Tea at the manor with Genevieve and drive-thru McDonald's with Marcus: it had been a day of extremes, and my sleep-deprived brain hadn't really processed any of what had been said.

I decided to take advantage of my slightly devil-may-care mood (only slightly, mind) and phoned my favorite grumpy detective, Inspector Jane Harris.

"Hi, Jane, how's it going?" Since we'd befriended her sister, Inspector Harris had been forced to accept that Poppy, Hen, and I were going to occasionally pop up in her life and inconvenience her. I don't think any of us had expected to be quite so involved in her professional life, however.

"Alice. A pleasure as always."

"I was wondering if you'd got the fingerprint results back from the bird box and the Jiffy bag of cash?" I asked hopefully.

Even down the phone, Inspector Harris's exasperated sigh nearly blew me away. "Alice, do you really expect me to hand over sensitive information about a case in which, might I remind you, you are a potential suspect?"

"Not a proper suspect though," I countered.

"How about you let me decide that?" she snapped back.

"But Poppy and I did find the bird box and the cash," I argued. "So you kind of owe us . . ."

"I do not *owe* anyone anything!" exploded Inspector Harris. "How exactly do you think the law works, Alice?"

"I've no idea," I replied cheerfully. "That's your job. I've already done my bit, handing over crucial evidence."

"You've also managed to *once again* get your own fingerprints all over a crime scene *and* some crucial evidence."

"Ah, that would be Poppy, not me, with the evidence this time," I pointed out.

"Alice you really are . . ." Inspector Harris bit off her comment, which was a shame. I'd have quite liked to know what I really am.

"Please?" I tried.

There was a brief silence, then: "Four sets of prints were found on the bird box, one identified as Owen Myers, another as Leila Arnault's, the third of course from your friend Poppy contaminating the evidence—"

"Discovering the evidence," I corrected.

"—and the fourth as yet unidentified. We're still trying to track down this Richard, only you haven't given us a lot to go on there."

The gratitude of the woman.

"There were two sets of prints on the envelope, belonging to Leila Arnault and Owen Myers, but only one set of identified prints on the cash, belonging to Owen Myers. Now no more questions, Alice, or I swear I will arrest you just to get some peace."

"Interesting," I said. "So that suggests that it was—hello? Jane? Inspector Harris?"

But she'd hung up. Oh well, I'd got what I was after.

"SO THE unidentified prints on the box will be Richard's," said Poppy. It was an hour later and we were debriefing in the garden at Poppy's house which, thanks to Lin, was a glorious riot of bright flowers and shady bushes to shelter the babes under. Jack and Noah were taking it in turns to hug Sultan, who was accepting this adoration with condescending grace. Helen and Ronnie were doing something unspeakable in a bush.

"Almost definitely," I confirmed. "And the fact that both Leila and Owen's prints were on the Jiffy bag, but only Owen's prints were on the cash suggest that it was him leaving the money there for Leila, and that this wasn't the first time—otherwise how would Leila's prints be on the bag and the bird box?"

"But in that case, what was Richard doing there?" said Poppy frustratedly. "Whoever the hell he is."

I still had my suspicions on this last point—although things didn't quite add up . . .

"Maybe he was pinching the money?" I suggested.

"How would he even know it was there?"

I shrugged. "Maybe he was in on the blackmail with Leila, and now that she's gone he went to claim the latest spoils all for himself?"

"So we're back at blackmail . . ."

"It looks that way. I can't think why else you'd dead-drop a bundle of cash in a bird box in the woods . . ."

"And if 'Daddy' had cut off her allowance, she'd be looking for a way to keep herself in little luxuries."

"So that's her motive, but what could she have been blackmailing him over?" I asked.

"Even if they were having an affair, or had had one previously, it's not like he's married," said Poppy thoughtfully. "According to Hen, he doesn't even have a girlfriend, not that she knows about anyway."

"When there was that attack on his house, just before Leila died, I'm pretty sure they said something on the radio about him entertaining a female guest at the time, or something like that," I mused.

"There's Norah," I pointed out. "Judging by what we heard between her and Myers in the grotto the other day, there was definitely something going on there."

"Not anymore, though. It sounded like that was long over. So if Myers was probably a free agent, I can't see him being blackmailed over some affair with Leila—Noah, don't do that—no please—" Poppy lunged for her son who was putting something, possibly a slug, possibly a stone, in his mouth. I didn't want to know. I lay back and stretched full length on the grass.

It was unspeakably hot, that kind of oppressive heat that slows your brain—and given that we were both operating on minimal sleep it wasn't going to be long before our brains ground to a total halt. I draped a wet muslin over Jack to try and keep him cool, and another over my own head.

"Could it have been something to do with the company?" I asked. "Maybe, I don't know, Owen was fiddling the accounts or something?"

"He's like a multi-millionaire, why would he need to fiddle the accounts," said Poppy distractedly, wiping out the inside of Noah's mouth.

"Seems to me that rich people are the keenest ones to get even richer," I said, rather astutely I thought. "They're always committing tax fraud and stuff so they can add a few hundred thousand to their bank balance."

Money, it always came back to money in this case. Oh, there was eco-activism, and climate protest, and green energy and artistic tempers, but there was also always money. Who had it, who didn't, and who wanted it. But was that *really* what this was all about? Or was it just a convenient sideshow?

Despite our best efforts, Jack and Noah were now draping their wet muslins over Sultan. Oh well, at least someone was benefitting from them.

"But even if we're right," I continued slowly, "and Leila was blackmailing Owen—whatever it was about—and just supposing that's why she was killed . . . What's that got to do with Sam?"

"I know! It doesn't fit," groaned Poppy.

"There's so much that doesn't fit," I replied. "Like bloody Anonymous Richard." This was really beginning to bother me. "I mean, where the hell is he going to pop up next?"

At this point Ailsa arrived pushing the twins in their double buggy, looking hot and sweaty.

"This global warming has got to stop," she puffed, pulling off her T-shirt and lying down in the shade in just her bra. "Someone set Robin and Ivy loose please."

Poppy and I unclicked the twins and set them down in the shade. They threw themselves on their mother who groaned and fanned herself. "Too hot, babies, go cuddle a dog." She pushed them toward Sultan, who gave her a deeply aggrieved look.

Eventually, Ailsa rolled over and pulled some suncream out of the bottom of the buggy.

"Poor kids, if only they'd inherited their dad's complexion," she complained. My sluggish brain pinged into life. It might be struggling to process a murder case, but gossip like this and it was on fire.

"Oh?" I asked innocently. "Tanned, was he?"

"Ask me no questions I'll tell you no lies," said Ailsa in a singsong voice. This seemed extremely unfair—*she* was the one who'd brought him up. But I was swiftly distracted as she began stripping the twins' shorts and T-shirts off. To reveal . . .

"Ailsa is that a *disposable diaper*?" I asked, part horrified, part delighted. Ailsa's vendetta against disposable diapers was the sole reason why Joe and I were wading through seas of laundry, dealing with the indignity of scraping poo off bamboo diaper liners, and currently had a bathroom like a medieval peasant's hovel. This might have been an exaggeration, but barely.

"Judge me and I will hex you to oblivion," warned Ailsa.

"Me? Judge?" I held up my hands in a peace gesture.

"Robin started getting diaper rash and in this heat it just didn't seem fair to keep putting him through it. The disposables, deplorable as they are, do seem to clear up the rash."

"Hey, I'm not judging. That sounds totally legit," I countered. "I honestly don't know why you put yourself through it with two at the best of times. Do you ever stop doing laundry?"

"No, my life is an unending cycle of wiping faces and arses and doing laundry," said Ailsa, flopping back onto her back. She opened one eye to look at me. "You're still here then?"

"Was I . . . not meant to be?" I asked.

"Poppy was convinced you'd been murdered and left in a ditch last night," said Ailsa, sounding supremely unbothered.

"So you rushed out to rescue me?"

"Well, if you were already murdered it would've been a bit late so I figured it could wait till morning."

"I'm touched."

"Seriously though, Al," said Poppy. "It wasn't the brightest idea, going off with him like that."

"I know, I know," I said, remembering the creeping sense of unease I'd felt as we'd headed into the darker depths of the Cotswolds. "But I did find out from him when he went back to London—or when he says he went back to London—which was Saturday."

"The day Sam was killed," said Poppy.

"He said he left Saturday morning, and Sam wasn't killed until the evening."

"Can we confirm that, though?" asked Ailsa skeptically.

"I don't see how," I said. "It's not like we know anyone who could corroborate it. We don't even know anyone else at the collective."

"What about Maya!" said Poppy, lifting herself up on one elbow in excitement.

"What about her?" asked Ailsa rather frostily.

"Well she was out all night with them, wasn't she? After the exhibition? See if she's got a number for one of them."

I saw Ailsa open her mouth to make a snarky comment, but she caught my eye and closed it again. I might bad-mouth Maya from time to time, but it was pretty much always to her face, and also I was allowed. Other people were not. Even Ailsa, to whom the usual rules did not apply.

"I'll drop her a text and see."

Hey, Mai, you still in touch with any of that lot from the collective?

Fortunately, Maya could usually be relied upon to reply within seconds. She was worse than Joe for being glued to her phone. Especially when she was at work. Although this didn't necessarily mean she would be helpful.

What are you talking about?

You know, the artist's collective

??

We went to that exhibition

You partied with them all night

Honestly Mai, it was like a week ago

A lot can happen in a week

Why what's going on with you?

Nothing, why?

You're very frustrating, you know

"Well?" prompted Poppy.

"Hold on, hold on," I protested. "We're just establishing the basics."

"You've exchanged like twenty messages in about thirty seconds," said Ailsa.

"Yes but she's not saying very much. I think she's in a bad mood."

"Lovers' tiff?" asked Ailsa, a little sourly.

"I'd rather not ask."

You DO remember

It was in a warehouse with fish made out of tampons and stuff

Oh yeah

The whale eye place

What about it?

Are you in touch with any of them?

Not really

One of them asked me to go for a drink on Thursday

Nice girl

Vi

Purple hair

Great! Could you go?

Why . . . ?

You hate me having other friends

Yeah, I don't want you to be friends with her

Just to ask her if Marcus came back to the collective last Saturday morning like he says

And if he was there Saturday night

Like between say seven and midnight

You want me to check an alibi for you?

Yep

Without befriending the purple-haired girl preferably

You ask a lot, Al

I know

It's lucky you're such a wonderful and understanding friend

She went offline.

"Well? Is she gonna check it out?" asked Poppy eagerly.

I shrugged. "I really have no idea. I'll let you know."

In the meantime I filled them in on Sam's legacy to Marcus—if, of course, he had actually gone through with it. Poppy was skeptical.

"I can't see his work being worth enough to kill for," she said.

"Quirke did say his death would put a premium on it," I pointed out.

"Yeah but even so . . ."

"Combined with their fight over stealing Quirke's representation though . . ." chipped in Ailsa.

I remained unconvinced. Yes, I'd felt apprehensive at times on the drive over to Fox Hollow last night, perhaps even mildly terrified at points, but that had surely been no more than the combination of dark country roads and lingering heartburn from the McDonald's. Did I really think Marcus was capable of murder?

"He's staying down until tomorrow," I said. "There's going to be some kind of memorial."

"Yes, for Sam and Leila, up at Hawkbit Meadow," said Ailsa. "I already said we three were going."

"What? How did you know about that?" I asked, thrown once again by Ailsa's ability to be five steps ahead of me.

"Honestly, Alice, can't you just unmute the Earth Force group chat?"

"Absolutely not."

CHAPTER 34

I MIGHT HAVE been roped into a memorial service I had never signed up for the following evening, but today I was quite looking forward to an afternoon and evening of doing nothing. Well, childcare, obviously, but Jack was currently quite easily entertained by a spoon, so I was planning on introducing him to a ladle and hopefully sitting back and mindlessly reading the internet for quite a large portion of the afternoon. (I knew from past experience that this was deeply unlikely, but I live in hope.)

My carefully laid plans of idleness were scuppered by a text from Ailsa.

I can't make it to the Aether summer party with Hen tonight, can you go instead?

What? Why?!

Ivy just threw up all over Robin who threw up all over me

It's carnage here

I'm thinking of just moving house

You said you weren't doing anything—so you go

Er

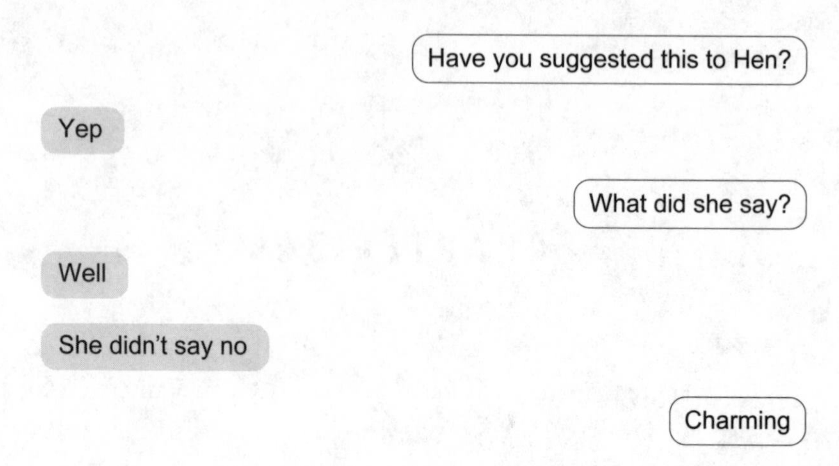

Great, now I had a social event to contend with. Who would I talk to? What would I *wear*?

I opened my wardrobe and gazed, horrified, at the contents. Since moving to the countryside and becoming a parent I had really embraced what Joe referred to as my "color-blind toddler" look—a lot of baggy, brightly colored clothes, which inevitably clashed.

From the very back of the wardrobe I dug out an old oversized floral dress I'd picked up in a vintage shop. It was about three sizes too big and missing a button, but if I belted it like this . . . and actually put on some makeup, maybe even earrings . . .

"How do I look?" I twirled for Joe.

"Actually quite nice," he said, sounding more surprised than I would have hoped.

HEN DIDN'T comment on my actually quite nice outfit. She, of course, looked stunning in a fitted coral dress with a twenties vibe.

"So, what's the deal at the garden party?" I asked, a tad nervously. I felt completely out of touch with social engagements. Too many of my social adventures over the last year had involved either people getting incredibly up close and personal with my cervix, or murder. I very much hoped tonight would involve neither.

Hen looked at me curiously. "It's a party, Alice. You know, people milling around, chatting, having a few drinks."

I clutched the steering wheel. It sounded awful.

"Alice, relax!" said Hen. "You're good at this kind of thing. You know, aimless small talk. Talk to people about *Love Island*, or the weather, or, I don't know, your dog."

It was a typical backhanded compliment from Hen. Still, she'd given me three topics of conversation—it was a good start.

THE AETHER grounds had been transformed from the rather anodyne golf-course-esque landscape into *A Midsummer Night's Dream*. Huge gazebos had been erected, which had somehow been liberally overgrown with twisting vines and fairy lights. Unless Aether had a sideline in growing triffids (entirely possible) I suspected these were fake. A small stage had been set up in the center and a band was playing, only barely audible over the hum of people.

One tent was significantly busier than the others, which I suspected meant it housed the bar. Naturally, we gravitated toward it. I had nobly offered to drive; as a single parent, Hen's opportunities to have a drink or two were even more limited than mine. Still, I couldn't help a twinge of envy as the bartender handed her a jewel-like Aperol spritz. I consoled myself by tugging at a strand of ivy running along the bar—yep, fake, as I suspected. One year in the country and I was pretty much an expert. (As opposed to the year Joe and I had spent assiduously watering what turned out to be a plastic plant that came with our old Peckham apartment. We'd left it when we moved out, with watering instructions for the next occupant.)

"Now what?" I hissed to Hen as we left the bar tent, me clutching my elderflower cordial.

"Now we *enjoy ourselves*. Honestly, what's wrong with you, Alice?"

Ten minutes in and my worst nightmare was realized. Hen was swept away by a colleague—"you simply *must* meet my partner Darren"—and I was left behind like Cinderella's spare shoe. Logically I know it is not the case, but if I ever find myself alone at a social function I immediately assume everyone is glancing at me and wondering who the loner is.

Bathroom trip. When in doubt, make as many bathroom trips as you can get away with. Worst-case scenario, people will think you've got the shits. Which I consider marginally preferable to people thinking I'm incapable of adult conversation. As I wended my way through the crowd, taking the long route round in order to really eke it out, my eye caught on someone who, really, I had been expecting to see here.

Anonymous Richard.

Like me, he was on his own. Unlike me, he looked perfectly at ease in his own company, sipping on a glass of red wine and taking in the scene around him. Oh well, I was going to interrupt all that.

"Hello again," I said.

He smiled, looking genuinely pleased to see me. "Ah, the young activist with the rogue dog," he said. So he *had* seen us up at the woods on Monday. To be fair, as I'd crashed through the trees yelling for Helen and Ronnie I hadn't been exactly inconspicuous.

"Sorry about Helen," I said automatically. I'd once estimated to Joe that over the last two years I've apologized for the dog about two thousand times. When I worked out that this is only three times a day I realized that's a vast underestimate.

"She's an interesting hound," he commented.

Now, normally I love to talk about my dog—not to mention that it was one of the three conversation topics Hen had gifted me in the car—but right now this felt like evasive action on Richard's part.

"Have the police been in touch?" I asked, deciding to cut straight to the heart of the matter. This probably *wasn't* on Hen's approved conversation list. Not to mention that if Richard was who I thought he was, then Hen was going to be less than impressed at me even talking to him, let alone interrogating him.

Richard looked a little startled; it was quite satisfying to ruffle that perfect veneer.

"The police? With me?"

"Yeah, you know, about the cash in the bird box."

I may have mentioned, a few times, that we have a very successful track record in solving crimes (one out of one); it should also probably be mentioned that absolutely none of this is down to my tact.

Richard laid a gentle hand on my elbow and began steering me through the crowd. I hate it when men do this; it has the guise of a gentlemanly gesture, but really they're just controlling you. I tucked my elbow back in to my side.

"Let's just take a wander down to the lake," said Richard. "I don't think this is a conversation for a party."

The mention of a lake immediately rang warning bells. He must have seen it on my face.

"I'm not going to push you into the lake," he said with a wry smile.

"If you were, I doubt you'd tell me," I retorted.

"OK fine, let's take a walk to the Portaloos, how does that sound?"

"Much better."

We took a leisurely stroll loo-wards.

"You're Owen's business partner," I said as my opening gambit.

"Ex–business partner," he corrected. "Owen bought me out years ago. I no longer hold any stake in Aether."

"But the original patent for the Aether wind turbine was yours," I continued.

"Sort of." He shot me a sideways look. "You have done your homework, haven't you?" He was glossily polite at all times, but there was the merest hint of patronizing tone that irritated me.

"So why did Owen buy you out? Why leave?"

Richard shrugged. "I wasn't that interested in it anymore, it's as simple as that. I'm a designer, an engineer. Not a businessman. Owen wanted to turn it into a nationwide business, which he has done, and extremely successfully I might add. But that wasn't my dream. So he offered to buy me out. Must have been ten years ago now."

"You weren't . . . angry?"

He gave a small laugh. "Heavens, no. I did very well out of the deal. Owen's lawyers advised him to offer me far less. But he did right by me." He cleared his throat awkwardly, as if that last sentence had caught slightly.

"You'd be much better off now if you'd kept your share of the business."

He gave me a shrewd look. "How would you know that? You don't know how much he paid to buy me out." He paused. "Do you?"

I enjoyed that I'd slightly rattled him.

"I don't," I admitted. "But if it was ten years ago, Aether was barely on the map at the time. It wouldn't have been worth anything like what it is today."

Richard nodded in assent. "And why are you so interested in my financial affairs, if I might ask?"

"I'm interested in knowing why you were checking inside a bird box that Owen clearly used to drop off money for Leila."

His eyes flicked from side to side. "And why would you say that?"

"The police found Owen and Leila's fingerprints on the bird box and the bag, but only Owen's on the cash. He must have dropped it off for her just before she died. She never had time to pick it up."

"Very smart," said Richard, as we looped past the Portaloos and started walking back toward the party. He'd dropped the patronizing tone now; he clearly hadn't expected me to know quite so much. I was well aware of how people underestimated me, and in all honesty I often enjoyed it, and it could be very useful at times. Not that I manipulated it, that was far too much effort, I simply . . . let it happen.

"And what's all this to you?" he continued. "Why are you asking all these questions?"

"Oh, I'm just nosy," I said cheerfully. "And I'm very intrigued as to where you fit into all this."

"I don't," said Richard shortly.

"And yet you keep popping up."

"I could say the same about you."

Touché.

"I knew Leila," I said—which absolutely was not a lie. I simply did not specify how well or for how long.

Richard made a noise in the back of his throat.

"You didn't like Leila?" I asked.

"On the contrary," he said shortly. "When I first met Leila I liked her a lot. In fact, I introduced her to Owen, helped her get a job as his PA." He paused. "You can't imagine how I regret that now."

I shot him a sharp glance. "Because of what happened to her?" Was he as good as admitting that Aether were responsible for her death?

"No. Because of how it all ended. Because she had the cheek to come running to me when my best friend was forced to fire her. And because what she did next was inexcusable."

"Owen fired her? Why? What did she do afterward?"

So many questions! I could barely get them out before the next one lined up. Briefly, I wondered if it would look too weird if I started taking notes.

"Why did he fire her? Quite simply because she was absolutely terrible at her job!" said Richard exasperatedly. "She'd clearly never worked a day in her life and had no intention of starting now. She was more interested in ferreting around in his private papers than getting anything useful done. It was embarrassing—I'd recommended her to Owen and she quite frankly let me down."

"And the blackmail?" I asked.

"You really are nosy, aren't you?" He smiled but it no longer seemed genuine.

"Personality flaw." I shrugged. I had a lot of them and found them a very useful get-out clause.

"Well, the answer is I don't know and it was none of my business."

He was lying. Definitely.

"In that case what were you doing collecting the money?" I asked.

"I was doing Owen a favor, OK? He couldn't go back to get it so I said I would. Look, can you just explain exactly what your interest in this is?"

Er. I mean I could have explained, but I doubted "I'm an amateur detective / nosy person with too much time on my hands" would have cut much ice. This is probably why in detective dramas the detective always seems to avoid asking the obvious questions, which as a viewer always frustrates me—just ask them where they were / why they did it / what they knew! Perhaps it turned out this was because detectives on TV actually know what they're doing and how far to push people. Plus it creates a nice bit of suspense. I blundered in, killed any suspense, and pissed off the person I was questioning. What can I say—personality flaw.

Fortunately, at this point I was saved from having to respond by Hen.

"Alice!" she called, waving at me. "I've been looking for you all over! Where have you been?"

I turned to make my excuses to Richard but he had left without a word, heading back toward the crowds. Hen appeared at my side.

"Who were you speaking to?"

"Funny you should ask—"

Hen checked her phone then cut me off. "Not now actually. We'd better get back to the party, it's speeches in a minute."

"All the more reason *not* to go back?" I suggested.

"Don't you want to see the mysterious Owen Myers?"

She had me there.

AFTER ALL this time, I was finally seeing the man himself. The real-life Owen Myers was much smaller than I'd imagined, as often seems to be the case. I was a little disappointed.

"Friends," he began, throwing his arms out to the assembled crowd. "*Family*." That seemed a bit much.

"It's so great to see all the spouses and partners here."

I nudged Hen. "That's me."

"You're not my partner."

"In *some* ways I am—"

"Nope."

I wanted to ask her whether she considered Ailsa her partner. Of some sort. Romantic, platonic, somewhere in between. Of course the reality is that a lot of relationships don't simply fall into a neat category, and I suspected the Ailsa–Hen relationship fell into "uncategorizable," by anyone, including them.

". . . we have an opportunity to build something *more than* a business. Aether is more about a way of life. A way of life that supports us, the wonderful civilizations we have built, *and* this beautiful planet of ours."

Ailsa was right—he talked a good game. I felt my usual unease when confronted with Aether—it was everything we needed in this messed-up world, and yet something, somewhere, wasn't right. My unease swiftly gave way to boredom, however. Even Hen was looking pretty glazed.

"So who were you talking to earlier?" she whispered.

"That was Anonymous Richard," I whispered. "Turns out he *is* Owen's ex–business partner. I thought you said they were a woman?"

Hen looked confused, and slightly appalled. "What? No I didn't. Anyway, you can't go around talking to people like that, Alice! What did you *say* to him?"

"Nothing bad," I whispered defensively. "He was the one blabbing, couldn't get him to stop!" OK this might have been stretching the truth. "Anyway, he said that Owen *fired* Leila and then she started blackmailing him, but he wouldn't tell me what about."

I could see the conflict on Hen's face. She so badly wanted to tell me off for talking to someone as influential as Owen's ex–business partner, but what I had said had also clearly resonated with her somehow.

"Everything OK?" I asked.

"I think I need to show you something," she whispered.

"OK . . ."

"After the speeches."

Which went on forever. Owen droned on and on about respect for this beautiful planet of ours, harnessing the natural energy of this beautiful planet of ours, working in synergy with this beautiful planet of ours (he repeated that phrase so many times, the guy was clearly gunning for a catchphrase). Meanwhile, I was squirming like a toddler who's been promised sweets after church. What did Hen want to show me?

Once the head of publicity had had her moment in the spotlight—mainly spent praising Owen, his vision, his commitment to, yep, this beautiful planet of ours—there was the final round of applause and people began heading determinedly bar-wards again.

"Come on," muttered Hen, leading me up the lawn toward the main office building.

A couple of colleagues called out to Hen as we passed.

"Left my phone in my office, just popping in to collect it," Hen called back casually. "Oh this is Alice, she's a friend."

"Ooh, I've been promoted to friend?" I asked.

"What did you consider yourself before?"

"Not sure? Acquaintance? Colleague? Pain in the arse?"

"You're still those things too."

I smiled to myself. Of course Hen was a friend—and a very good one, despite her protestations—but I still enjoyed making her say it. A few months (and a murder or two) after moving to Penton I'd been surprised to realize that I had made friends here. Genuine friends. The sort who would drive over to your house at 3 A.M. with a baby thermometer because yours was broken (edit: you'd never bought one but didn't want to admit it). Or babysit your child despite having two of their own to look after as a single parent. Or kindly but honestly tell you that pink cord dungarees are never going to work for you.

"So what are we doing in your office, friend?" I asked.

"If you call me that again I won't show you."

I kept my mouth shut.

The office was eerily dark and quiet after the lights and bustle of the party. Only the security lights were on, casting a half-hearted glow that merely highlighted the shadows.

"This is creepy," I muttered as we made our way down a long corridor to the stairs—I refused to take the paternoster.

"It's an office at night. They're always creepy," said Hen dismissively. "So, what did you make of Owen Myers, in the flesh?"

"Meh," I replied. "To be honest I'm not sure what all the fuss is about. Why all the secrecy? He's a very good public speaker, why does he never do public appearances?"

"He likes his privacy," said Hen.

"Why, what's he hiding?"

"Don't push it, Alice. That's my boss you're talking about. Plus you're currently enjoying his hospitality."

I looked at my admittedly very nice and clearly quite fancy elderflower cordial (with a sprig of mint, very classy) and tried again. "He clearly has a very good speechwriter."

"He writes his own. What did you make of the speech?"

"That he's very much in love with this beautiful planet of ours," I said wryly.

"Mhmm," said Hen, flicking on the lamp above her desk and sitting in her office chair (I wondered if she'd refused to spend all day sitting on a beanbag). She seemed distracted, unsure now that we were here.

"What did you want to show me?" I prompted gently.

She paused with one hand on her desk drawer, and blew out a huff of air. "I didn't know whether to share this with you guys," she said slowly. "But, well, I think Leila *was* blackmailing Owen."

I didn't want to tell her that we had pretty much come to that conclusion anyway, so I just nodded encouragingly.

"I was cleaning the filter on Owen's paper shredder—honestly, he clearly hadn't done it for *months*—and this was jammed inside it . . ."

She opened the drawer, pulled out a piece of crumpled paper, and thrust it at me. It was a handwritten note.

> I might be leaving, but before you think you've won—our deal still stands. I'm sure the shareholders—and the public—would be very interested to know about your little arrangement with G.S.
>
> L x

Silently, I praised the god of malfunctioning office hardware. This sounded pretty incriminating. No one refers to "little arrangements" and means something legally or morally sound.

"So Myers was up to something and Leila found out what it was," I breathed. "The question is—what?"

"We don't *know* that for sure," said Hen nervously. I saw how taut her expression was and decided not to point out that there was really no other interpretation of this note.

"G.S., G.S. . . ." I mumbled instead. "So who the hell is G.S.? A company? A person?"

I ran through the various people we'd come across over the course of the case. No one had the initials G.S. Great, I'd just solved one mystery identity in Anonymous Richard only for another one to pop up. This case was like a game of Whac-A-Mole. I looked up and saw Hen still looking dithery and generally very unlike her usual decisive self.

"Do you know what G.S. means?" I asked.

"No," she said reluctantly. "Not exactly. But . . ." She flicked open her laptop and clicked a few times, then beckoned me over. The screen showed Owen Myers's private Outlook calendar.

"Look at this, on Friday at ten, a private appointment, even I can't see it."

Sure enough an hour had been blocked out, simply marked "private" with a little padlock next to it, to reinforce the point.

"But if I do this . . ." Hen's fingers danced across the keyboard, she clicked again, and the appointment miraculously opened.

"How did you do that?" I asked, amazed.

"I used to hack Antoni's work diary all the time," said Hen, not looking at me. "You know, when I thought he was having an affair. I guess I fell into checking Owen's just out of habit."

There was a brief pause as we both contemplated how much simpler life would have been if Antoni had only been having an affair. Then we turned our attention back to the screen. There were very few details in the private appointment. "G.S.—Nightingales."

"He's meeting G.S. this Friday?" I breathed.

"It could be nothing," said Hen miserably. "Just another business meeting, or something. But along with the note . . . I didn't know what to do. I wanted to tell you, of course I did. If Owen is doing something that might be . . . slightly outside the bounds of usual business practice . . . Oh God, I hope he's not. I *need* this job, Alice!"

My heart wrenched for her. What a hideous position she was in—her boss, to my mind, was quite clearly doing at least *something* "outside the bounds of usual business practice." The safest option for her would be to turn a blind eye and continue with her comfortable job and steady salary. But she was Hen, she would always do the right thing.

"Thank you," I said, hoping she could hear in my voice that I understood, as I wasn't quite sure how to put it into words. I reached out and squeezed her hands.

"OK, well, now you have it. I'm out." She closed and locked her desk drawer with a finality.

"Want another Aperol spritz?" I asked.

"Try and stop me."

CHAPTER 35

THE NEXT MORNING I trawled the internet for "Nightingales." All I could find locally was a garden center of that name in Little Wallop, a village about ten miles from Bishop's Ruin. It seemed unlikely that Owen Myers would be conducting a clandestine meeting with a mysterious associate in a rural garden center. Of course, there were about six million establishments with that name in London, and a good few in Bristol, any of which could have been where the meeting was taking place. The more I thought about it, the more likely this seemed. Which meant my options were hanging around pointlessly at the local garden center on Friday morning or giving up on pretty much the only live lead we had.

I sighed with frustration and with a great effort refrained from throwing my laptop across the room. Something else had been nagging at the back of my brain like a mental hangnail, so I decide to distract myself with that instead, and messaged Hen.

> You definitely said that Owen's ex business partner was a woman you know

Unlike Maya, Hen had a strict no-personal-messaging-while-working policy, so it was quite some time before I heard back from her. In the interim I achieved extremely little; I entertained Jack with some spoons and fed Helen, who threw her food bowl across the kitchen in disgust. When Hen's reply came it wasn't particularly illuminating.

What?

The other day, when I asked if they were called Richard

Oh that

No you asked me if the inventor of the turbine was called Richard

. . . they're the same person

Richard was Owen's business partner, and he invented the turbine

Pretty sure the inventor was a woman

But suit yourself

Also please stop messaging me at work

Especially about stuff like this

I would definitely leave her alone. In just a minute. It was just that her words had triggered a memory of something Richard had said, which had sat oddly with me at the time.

Richard said he "sort of" owned the patent to the Aether wind turbine

What do you think he meant?

I don't know, I'm at work Alice.

Did Richard co-own the patent? With someone else, a woman? I tried googling the patent for the wind turbine, but as I had neither the patent publication number nor even Richard's full name, there wasn't much I could unearth. I tried Hen again.

Is there an Aether archive or something I could take a look at?

I must've caught her on her lunch break as the reply was swift this time, albeit rather abrupt.

Yes there is and no you can't.

I threw my phone across the room in frustration. I understood Hen's predicament, I really did. But that didn't stop it from being wildly frustrating.

My phone pinged reproachfully. It would no doubt be Hen again with further admonitions. I left my phone in the corner and went to fetch more spoons for Jack to play with.

It is not in my nature to go more than an hour without checking my phone, so while it felt like an age later that I retrieved it from its corner, it was probably about twenty minutes. I glanced at the screen and silently apologized to Hen, before scrabbling together my own approximation of a diaper bag (snacks for Jack, snacks for me, some diapers, more snacks, spare T-shirt for Jack, spare T-shirt for me, snacks, more snacks, sunscreen).

Why don't you try the little museum in Bishop's Ruin, they have a whole exhibition on Aether.

I LOVE local museums. This may sound a little out of character as I will readily admit that my main cultural intake is the trashier end of reality TV. But there's something about the combination of weirdness and banality in a local museum that really speaks to me. The things some local curator has felt will be of interest to the visiting public, or should be recorded for posterity. Particularly hot summers. Record rain falls. Droughts, floods. They often seem to be quite weather oriented.

The Bishop's Ruin museum lived up to all my expectations. It was in what appeared to have been the old village school, a Victorian redbrick building with a rusted school bell in its own tiny tower on the roof. The door was closed, but swung open at a gentle push. After the heat of outside, the museum had that special musty chill to the air, reserved for museums, libraries, and crypts (none of which I spend a particularly large amount of time in). It was also, as expected, completely empty. My footsteps echoed as I tiptoed in, rather self-consciously. In terms of staffing, there was an old margarine tub on a stool by the door with a cardboard sign saying DONATIONS WELCOME. There was twenty pence and a Snickers wrapper in it. I added a further fifty pence, possibly tripling the museum's income for the month.

The faded display boards featured mismatched labels in spidery handwriting or apparently done on an ancient typewriter. I spent a while lingering over a cabinet that displayed such curiosities as a set of dentures, a faded green dog collar, and a fly in a matchbox. The captions were not forthcoming on why any of this was worthy of display. Jack had found a cabinet featuring Matey bubble bath bottles through the ages and had his little face pressed against the glass, entranced. Eventually, however, he got bored and began pounding the glass with his tiny fist, so I hurried him off before he got a criminal record for beating up a museum.

I found the Aether exhibition in a side room at the back of the museum. This room was a little more up to date. The display labels had been printed off a computer, for a start. Jack made a beeline for a model wind farm in the corner and began spinning the windmills in a frenzy. I began browsing the crowded display boards. It was, essentially, a major love-in to Bishop's Ruin's most successful and famous resident. Which, possibly, wasn't a particularly high bar. But Owen Myers had smashed it. There was a photo of him receiving a science prize at the local secondary school; another from his graduation; newspaper clippings of every time he'd ever appeared in print, initially in the *Penton Bugle* but building up to the larger nationals, until there was even a double-page spread on him in *Time* magazine. There was no doubt about it, the guy was making waves in the energy world.

I found a board dedicated to the Aether Hybrid Charge Rotator 2000—the new wind turbine that had revolutionized wind energy and really put

Aether on the map. There were schematics, and photos of prototypes, and a map of the original wind farm site up on Rushey Hill, and . . . Jackpot! A slightly grainy photocopy of the original patent. I glanced around, but there was no one else in the museum (what a surprise), so I unpinned the document and sat down cross-legged on the dusty floor to peruse.

The patent was filed under the ownership of a Richard Whitehouse. Just Richard Whitehouse. So what had he been talking about when he said he "sort of" owned the original patent? I tried to force myself to read the whole document, in detail, but honestly it was so dull. It was full of technical language and schematics which I could make neither head nor tail of. It talked about wind speeds and kilowatt hours and kilovolt-amperes and all those things I had tuned out of in GCSE physics.

Then I got to the "Named inventor(s)" section; there was Richard's name, but this time it wasn't alone. And the other name was most definitely not Owen Myers.

I pinned the paper back to the board in a thoughtful state of mind. I rescued the model wind farm from Jack's enthusiastic attentions. And I left.

"Well now, Jacky boy," I murmured, dropping a whole pound in the margarine tub as we exited. "That *is* food for thought."

CHAPTER 36

I WAS STILL deep in thought when Joe dropped me off at Hawkbit Meadow for the memorial that evening, before taking Helen and Jack far, far away for a walk. The thought of Helen gate-crashing a memorial was too painful to contemplate.

The light over the meadow was golden. It couldn't have been a more perfect evening. As Poppy, Ailsa, and I walked across the meadow to the distant gathering I recalled the first time we'd met Leila, in this very spot, walking naked through the thigh-high grass—perfectly poised, so assured, so full of fire for her cause. And yet everything we'd learned about her since then suggested we had seen nothing more than one of the many masks Leila liked to wear. And now, she had been killed for one of these masks. But which one?

We were slightly late—which was my fault, Jack had been sick on my top just as I'd been about to leave, so I suppose technically it was actually Jack's fault—and most of Earth Force were already gathered at the far end of the meadow. Marcus stood slightly apart from them all, his tall frame huddled in on itself. Two small pyres had been built, stacked side by side; far too small for actual funeral pyres, these were merely ceremonial. Atop one sat a photo of Leila, looking intense and brooding. I wondered whether the photo had been taken by Sam. Atop the other was a photo of two boys—presumably Sam and Raven. The lower half of a woman's body was just visible behind them—I wondered if this was Maryam, or whether the photo had been taken before their mother died.

Raven led the memorial. For someone mourning his girlfriend and brother, he held it together well. His voice broke a few times, particularly when he talked, briefly but movingly, about his childhood with Sam, losing their mother so young, but finding a new protector in Maryam.

At this Maryam utterly broke down. Her howls echoed across the meadow. I barely knew Raven, and had known Sam even less, but tears were flowing down my face. I couldn't imagine facing so much loss in one life, and at such a young age. I felt a hand grasp mine. I looked down and was surprised to see that it was Ailsa's. But then, there was a lot that Ailsa kept tucked away behind those defenses of hers. I gripped her hand back.

When Raven stepped forward to light Leila's pyre, Maryam turned away, an unreadable expression on her face. Norah, too, looked down, as if unable to watch. Marcus was dry-eyed, but there was a hollowness to his face and movements. When Marcus lit Sam's, Maryam sank to the ground.

The flames danced up and quickly devoured the two photos. I could feel the heat from the flames, reaching as far back as us. But then, equally swiftly, they died down, until there were just two smoldering heaps, side by side.

AFTERWARD, VARIOUS bottles began appearing and being passed around. Norah had, of course, brought a Tupperware of homemade cookies. The mood was somber, as you would expect, but there was also an edge of tension. Two deaths in the group, in as many weeks. People were on edge. The usual cliques had formed; the largest surrounding Raven. Maryam stayed propped against Raven, shaking with sobs. She seemed incapable of speech. In fact, she seemed barely aware of where she was. I remembered what Marcus had said—she's like a mother bear over those boys. Only someone had slipped past her guard.

I looked around. Sian was with her small coterie of what I thought of as the normcore protestors. A bunch of twentysomethings who all, like Sian, seemed to have their heads screwed on and their hearts in the right place. They sat in a circle on the grass, sharing a flask of something and talking somberly. We hadn't seen Sian since Leila's funeral over a week ago, and she was the one person there seemed no need to actively investigate, which was a disappointingly rare occurrence these days. A group of older individuals reclined on folding camp chairs they'd brought with them. Then there was Raven's posse and, keeping a considerable distance, the group I had come to think of as Enderby's dissenters, although currently minus Enderby himself. Norah was flitting from group to group with a Thermos. I wanted to talk to her, but it wasn't the right time. I wondered where Enderby was, he was usually somewhere within Norah's orbit.

Just as the thought passed through my head, "Funny to have them side by side like that," said Enderby's voice quietly, right behind my left shoulder. I spun round in shock. He was stood just behind me, looking at the ashy piles that had represented Sam and Leila, next to each other.

"Isn't it," agreed Poppy. "They really didn't get along, huh?"

Enderby snorted. "That's putting it mildly. Leila threatened to kill Sam once."

We all froze. That's quite a comment to make when you're attending the memorial of the threatener and the threatenee.

"Like, seriously?" asked Ailsa.

Enderby shrugged. "She sounded pretty mad at the time."

"What happened?" I asked curiously.

"Oh, it was ages ago now, not long after Leila had joined Earth Force. I was over at Fox Hollow helping Maryam shift some old machinery from the barn when Leila came storming in shouting for Sam. Sam wasn't there at the time—he came and went on his own schedule—but Raven came out and tried to calm her down."

"What was she saying?" I pressed.

"I honestly could barely make it out, she was so angry. Plus I was with Maryam and we were both trying to pretend we weren't listening in." He gave an awkward half smile. "No one wants to overhear a row."

"But you heard her threaten to kill Sam?" persisted Poppy.

"Yeah, she said something about him being a selfish bastard, that he'd ruined her life and if she ever saw him again she'd kill him."

"Ouch," said Ailsa. We all stood silently.

"But, I mean, she didn't," said Enderby awkwardly. "By the time a couple of weeks had passed they were back on speaking terms. A bit frosty, I suppose, but whatever he'd done it can't have been that bad after all."

I caught Poppy's eye. We knew exactly what Sam had done to piss Leila off—he'd cost her probably tens of thousands in allowance—and potentially millions if her father had done as he threatened and disinherited her. People had killed for far less. But then, as Enderby said, Leila *hadn't* killed Sam. Someone had got to her first—and then to Sam barely a fortnight later.

"What did Raven say?" I asked curiously. "When she was shouting about all this?"

"Oh, you know Raven," said Enderby vaguely—but of course we didn't, not really. "He got her to calm down and that was an end to it."

But I wasn't so sure it had been an end to it. By all accounts, Leila had never quite let Sam's actions go. She had, after all, been living with the consequences all that time.

"Anyway, we shouldn't speak ill of the dead," said Enderby piously. "And I should probably go and help Norah with the clear-up."

"He seems a very sad man," said Poppy thoughtfully, as he wandered off.

"Yeah, well, unrequited love and all that," I muttered.

Poppy and Ailsa stared at me.

"What do you mean?" asked Poppy.

"You must have noticed!" I was genuinely surprised. I wasn't exactly known as the perceptive one in the group, but maybe watching all that *Love Island* had finally paid off. "He's mad about Norah! But she's not really into it. She's giving off recently divorced vibes, or something like that. All those Tupperwares of home-baking . . ."

"Still mooning over Owen," said Poppy.

"Hmmm," I said noncommittally. I hadn't told the others about my little museum trip this afternoon yet and didn't fancy doing it right now, under the very nose of the person involved. I would text them later.

"How'd you figure all that out?" asked Ailsa skeptically.

I shrugged. "Observation?"

Ailsa gave me a disbelieving look. But it didn't really matter, Norah and Enderby's tangled love lives weren't relevant to the investigation. And potentially neither was what we'd just heard—but it seemed a strange coincidence. Leila threatened to kill Sam, and now both of them were dead.

* * *

MARCUS sat on his own, looking out over the valley. I sat down next to him, and we gazed out silently for a while.

"How are you doing?" I asked him eventually.

He shrugged. "Been better."

I nodded. There was nothing comforting to say, really.

"Are you staying at Fox Hollow, with Maryam and Raven?" I asked.

Marcus shook his head. "No, it got weird."

"How so?"

He pulled a face. "They're both so edgy," he said, feeling his way through the words. "Which is not surprising with everything that's gone on. But they don't trust me—I can tell. Sometimes I'm not sure they even trust each other."

It was a curious thing to say. I opened my mouth to press him on this, but at that moment, on the grass between us, my phone screen lit up. We both glanced down automatically.

> **Maya:** Just saw Vi. Marcus's alibi checks out.

I looked up and met Marcus's eyes.

"My alibi checks out, does it?" Hurt and anger warred across his face.

"Er," I said eloquently.

"You've been checking up on me?"

OK, now anger definitely seemed to be winning.

"It's not like that . . ." I tailed off, because it quite patently *was* like that.

"What is wrong with you people?" he said tightly. "You, Maryam, Raven, poking around, asking weird questions, suspicious of everyone you come across—probably because you've all got horrible secrets you're keeping from each other. Well, you can leave me out of it."

He got up and stormed away, leaving me feeling wretched.

I SLUNK miserably back to where Poppy and Ailsa were sitting on the grass at the edge of the meadow, just where it suddenly sloped steeply away, down toward the woods below. We could see out over Penton Vale. Most of Earth Force had gone home now. The pyres had died down and the ashes been kicked out and scattered across the meadow. I knew they weren't human ashes, merely symbolic, but the sight of the floating ash clouds from the two pyres mingling and dissipating had made me feel melancholic.

Ailsa pulled a bottle from her bag.

"Wine?"

"Wine."

We passed the bottle between us for a while, unspeaking. The sun was sinking toward the horizon, bathing the meadow in liquid gold. Despite the sadness and horror of what we'd come up here to commemorate, it was unaccountably peaceful.

The bottle slowly meandered back and forth, from hand to hand.

"Should've bought cups," said Ailsa eventually.

"Nah." I took a swig. "We've all got the same toddler germs."

We watched two figures detach from the small remaining group and make their way back through the long grass toward the car park, one figure propping up the other, who was stooped and stumbled at every other step.

"Poor Raven," said Poppy. "His brother and his girlfriend . . ."

"Poor Maryam," I added. "By all accounts Sam was basically her son."

"No parent should have to go through this," said Ailsa feelingly.

I glanced at Ailsa. She never mentioned her own parents, and in over a year of friendship I'd never met them. I'd met Poppy's parents, Lin's mother (frequently), even Hen's parents a handful of times. But Ailsa's were just quietly out of the picture, much like the father of the twins. Mind you, my parents had made just one fleeting trip over from Spain to meet their new grandson, and that had been cut short when there was a last-minute cancellation at my mum's favorite salon and she'd shot off explaining that "appointments at Les Bouffes are like gold dust!" i.e., more valuable than your only grandson.

"Do you . . . see your parents much?"

Ailsa shrugged and took another swig from the bottle. "Yeah, from time to time."

"What are they like?"

"Like parents."

Which of course told me absolutely nothing. Parents, in my experience, ranged from the ones who helped their kids with homework, took them to play football, or to the aquarium, and knew the names of their friends, to the ones who forgot birthdays, forgot to pick their kids up, and occasionally appeared to entirely forget they had kids (mine).

"Did you fall out or something?" I asked tentatively.

Ailsa looked surprised. "No, why'd you ask that?"

"Well, you just never really mention them," I said lamely. "And you've said before that you didn't live with them as a teenager, so I figured . . ."

"Oh, that was more about Jane," said Ailsa. "Now we *did* fall out."

"Funny how two siblings can be so different," I mused.

Ailsa gave a dry laugh. "What, like me and Inspector Perfect?"

"Yeah, but also Sam and Raven."

I thought of my own brother. He was probably in a hammock somewhere, almost certainly smoking a joint. We were different, but possibly more the same than we sometimes liked to think. Sometimes I thought the same of Ailsa and Jane—although I would never in a million years say this out loud.

Raven and Maryam had reached the edge of the meadow, two small stick figures on the horizon. The evening heat haze made the figures dance and split, so sometimes it almost looked as though there were three figures. Two brothers and their almost-mother.

CHAPTER 37

I COULDN'T SLEEP that night. I was haunted by memories of the flickering pyres—plus Jack decided to cluster-feed like an absolute leech. It was six thousand degrees in our attic bedroom and Jack kept sliding off the boob because we were both slick with sweat. What no one tells you (one of the many things no one tells you) is that breastfeeding is an extremely sweaty business, and that's without a heatwave thrown in. It made both Jack and me very hot and then very angry. He pounded my boob with his tiny fist which didn't help matters. I could only imagine that the milk he was getting was upsettingly warm, like when you've accidentally mixed juice using the hot tap.

"Ow! Jack, chill out," I muttered.

"Can you keep it down," muttered Joe, ever supportive.

Eventually I gave up, hauled myself out of bed and wandered outside with Jack, and collapsed into the one moldering deck chair that served as our garden furniture. It gave a groan and I held my breath, but somehow the ancient webbing held.

Helen slunk out the back door after us, glowing faintly in the moonlight, moving like liquid mercury. She really was a magnificent hound. Then she spoiled this by rolling onto her back at my feet, displaying her belly and genitals to the world. The three of us sat in semi-nude, contented silence in the silvered garden, which rustled and exhaled around us.

Occasionally, a breath of air would stir and it felt like bliss on my sweat-soaked skin. Jack settled into a feed and soon his eyes were half-closed, a strip of blue iris just visible beneath his shell-like eyelid. I felt the regular pulling sensation in my chest and tried to relax.

I have mixed feelings about breastfeeding. Oh, I know people talk about it as an almost mystical connection with their child, but I found it . . . disconcerting at times. On the one hand, there was something beautiful about the rejoining of two bodies who had, until so recently, been one; it was, perhaps, when I felt closest to Jack, most like a mother. On the other, it gave me a strange feeling deep inside, in my very core, an almost melancholy. If Jack fed for too long, like he was this evening, the feeling swelled and grew and threatened to overwhelm me.

As was usual, my phone was in my hand. I wondered what mothers had done during midnight feeds before the invention of the phone. The thought of being alone with my own thoughts was hideous. I felt the need for some outside connection, beyond the bubble of me and Jack, Jack and me.

Maybe I could lure Maya down for a visit? After all, she had an added incentive now . . .

I often wondered about Maya's long-suffering neighbors, who tomorrow morning would awake to some sweaty, disheveled nightclothes in their shared back garden. Naturally, they'd make assumptions about how they'd ended up there . . . Speaking of which . . .

Spoken to Rowan much?

A bit . . .

. . . and?

He's all right

Omg it's like getting blood out of a stone

What happened to Maya the oversharer?

🤷‍♀️

OK, Mai, what's going on

Oh shit

You like him??

You actually like him??

Curse you, Alice

I'm right then

Fine

Yes

I like him

Damn you

Ah shit

What am I doing, Al??

I'm too young for a boyfriend??

I'm a year younger than you

I have a boyfriend a baby and a vegetable patch

And a Helen

You have a vegetable patch?

Untended

Ailsa planted it for me

But this is beside the point

I'm definitely too young for a vegetable patch

You don't have to get a vegetable patch

You can just, like, date him

Come down for the weekend

He already invited me

Oh!

Are you coming?

I think so, yeah

See you Saturday?

You can show me your veg patch

Haha

I couldn't quite get my head around the idea of Maya coming down to Penton not just to see me. Would she stay at the commune with Rowan? That was a weird thought. I tended not to visit the commune too much. It held a lot of memories for me, good and bad, and these days I didn't feel I had a tight enough handle on my emotions to confront that. You could call it repression; right now I was calling it survival.

I listened to the heavy breathing of both dog and child as they slept soundly, unencumbered by troubling thoughts of murders past or present. Then I checked the time. Shit, it was gone one, and I had to be up and about the next day for my big trip to Nightingales, the garden center.

I indulged in a few minutes of watching Jack sleep, because there was no one there to watch me and accuse me of being a creep/doting parent. I know there's nothing wrong with the latter, but it just didn't fit with my mental image of myself. Eventually, I hefted him onto my shoulder and returned to the stifling heat of the cottage and an uneasy sleep.

CHAPTER 38

IT WAS NOT a calm morning. The heat overnight had left the world feeling slightly overcooked. The air had a soupy quality to it that made it unpleasant to breathe. Jack was tetchy, which was unusual for him, and I was underslept and overmilked.

Ailsa, who was supposed to accompany me to the garden center, given that she actually gardened, had texted at 5 A.M. to bail on me, which, given that she'd been up all night with *two* crotchety babies, seemed fair enough. Poppy, fortunately, had been happy to ditch lunch with her mother-in-law and accompany me. Both had been shocked, baffled, by my discovery at the museum the other day, but ultimately we couldn't work out how it could be connected to the murders of either Leila or Sam.

We pulled up at Nightingales feeling slightly frazzled. Owen was due to meet the mysterious G.S. in two minutes time and we had two babies and a dog to unload. We bundled the kids haphazardly into the wrong prams and hauled a confused-looking Helen along behind us.

"What do you reckon, try the café?" I suggested. But when we strolled oh-so-casually into the café there was only an elderly couple sitting in malevolent silence and glaring at each other over fruit scones. We awkwardly backtracked, to the confusion of the woman behind the counter.

"They're almost definitely not meeting here anyway," I panted. "Who meets in a garden center?"

"People who are having meetings that need to not look like business meetings?" pointed out Poppy.

And as if to prove her right, at that very moment I spotted the slight figure of Owen Myers ambling unconcernedly toward the outdoor section.

"There!"

We gave chase—slowly and cumbersomely, with Helen's lead getting caught in the pram wheels and nearly throttling her. By the time we emerged into the bright sunlight, Owen was disappearing behind the trellises on the far side of the bedding plants. We trundled resolutely trellisward.

As we emerged from a rather fancy trellis archway, we were brought up short. Owen was in the next aisle. A man in a cream shirt with pale brown checks (truly horrible) was greeting him, leaning casually on his flatbed trolley full of border plants. They seemed to be exchanging vague pleasantries. The man in the horrible shirt lifted a few begonias out of his trolley, which Owen inspected with due diligence. Was this the mysterious G.S.? Or just a friendly fellow shopper with poor fashion sense? Then the two men began gently strolling toward the ornamental features section together—it looked like we had our man. Poppy and I strolled after them.

"How will we get close enough to hear anything?" hissed Poppy.

"I don't know—we'll just have to wing it."

Fortunately, at this point G.S. raised his voice, and it carried clearly back to us.

"You're asking too much, Owen!"

"I'm not asking anything I haven't asked before, Gordon—and keep your voice down," hissed Owen. "Besides it's only hypothetical. What with this whole murder there's been a delay, naturally, and the project manager has been making noises about a need to re-evaluate the site."

Gordon, eh. He looked like a Gordon. Or at least his shirt did. We wheeled closer and began minutely inspecting a grotesquely ornate sundial just meters away from the two men, shielded by some elegant topiary—bay trees, according to the label. And—bloody hell—£149 a tree. The woods were full of the things! The coverage wasn't great, but fortunately Owen had never met either Poppy or myself (unless he had an incredible memory for faces in the crowd at the Aether garden party), so the risk of being noticed was minimal. And, to be honest, what with the toddlers and the dog and the general (genuine) air of frazzled motherhood, we didn't exactly look like crack detectives.

"Look, if the council insist on another inspection it can't be me," Gordon was saying. Owen opened his mouth to speak but Gordon held up a hand to stop him. "No, this isn't some ploy to get you to up your offer, Owen. I'm not after more money, I'm just saying—it won't be me. I'm sorry, my hands are tied."

Owen muttered something I couldn't catch.

"To be quite frank," Gordon continued. "I don't think we should be pursuing this anymore. Didn't you say someone was pestering you about our . . . arrangement?"

"That's gone away now," said Owen dismissively. With a start, I realized he was referring to Leila. Who had indeed "gone away," in the most terminal way.

"Even so," countered Gordon. "That's not good. We should exercise a little caution. So I'm sorry, but I'm out—for now."

Owen didn't look best impressed by this. "Look, Gordon, I can't have the site re-inspected—unless it's by you. There's some rare flower or something growing there and there's a high risk it would be designated a triple-S-I, which means no development, which means a lot, and I mean *a lot*, of money down the drain. You need to put a halt to any sort of re-inspection, or you need to do it yourself."

"And I told you—I can't."

"Just remember, your signature is on that report approving the site for development," Owen was saying—not in a particularly threatening tone, but the implication was clear.

"I'm well aware of that." Gordon's tone had a new chill to it. "And if need be I'll stand by my—ah—decisions on the matter. But it won't come to that. I would recommend you get the developers in without delay. My current report is still valid despite all the recent . . . unpleasantness. Just get the damn thing up and running before the council make the most of this hold-up and call in another inspection from Natural England."

Owen ran a hand down his face. "I'm on it, I'm on it. Developers are rescheduled for tomorrow, as it happens—but keep that quiet. I just—Good God! Is that a dog in the fountain?"

I looked down—at the trailing empty lead in my hand. Shit. I should never have switched to a slip-lead; a straitjacket would be more Helen's style.

Helen was indeed frolicking joyously in a beautiful decorative stone fountain, snapping at the spray she was kicking up and liberally soaking any shoppers foolish enough to come near. Noah gave an excited shriek and strained at his pram straps.

"Oh no you don't!" said Poppy. She laid a hand on my arm. "I'll watch Jack, you fetch Helen."

With a sigh, I went in.

Obviously, it involved me having to climb into the fountain.

Obviously, Helen pushed me over once I was in.

I really don't want to talk about it.

Poppy, to her credit, almost hid her laughter. Unlike the other shoppers. When I hauled myself and Helen out of the fountain, she handed me a baby muslin to pat myself dry with.

"Café," I said flatly.

"You're soaking wet."

"Cake."

"Yeah OK."

SOMETIMES THERE just isn't enough cake in the world to overcome the sheer embarrassment that is life. But I was giving it a good try.

"Are you seriously going to have a third slice?" asked Poppy. "That's like, nearly half a cake."

"Watch me."

Given the heat of the day, I was already beginning to dry out, the damp patches on my shorts shrinking and fading under the sun's onslaught. The memory would take longer to fade. I rubbed more suncream onto Jack's face as displacement activity.

"Well, now we know what Leila was blackmailing Owen about," said Poppy in a low voice, glancing around slightly nervously. Owen Myers was still hanging around the garden center, apparently now actually purchasing garden supplies. I suppose he was the kind of person to maximize the efficiency of every trip.

"Yep, she must've stumbled over his arrangement with Gordon," I agreed. "Which seems to be something to do with fiddling reports about—what was that weird word he used?"

"A triple-S-I, I think?"

I googled it.

"Site of Special Scientific Interest," I read aloud. "A conservation designation denoting a protected area in the UK." I skimmed the rest of the Wikipedia article and tried to sum it up. "Basically, an area that has like rare plants or animals or some other biological or geological feature . . . and pretty much means that even the owner of the land isn't allowed to mess about with it."

"Ah," said Poppy. "So probably no wind farm development."

"Nope. So Owen has been paying this Gordon guy to head off site assessments before they get designated as triple-S-Is."

"Which is pretty dodgy," said Poppy.

"Oh, absolutely. And not exactly in keeping with his deeply professed love for our beautiful planet. And it looks like Leila found out and decided to cash in on it."

"The question is: did he kill Leila to make the blackmail stop?"

"It's a big step from a spot of corruption to murder . . ." I said slowly. "Unless something had changed."

"Like what?"

"Like if she decided she was going to go public on him to stop the development."

Poppy looked thoughtful. "But that would be stopping her cash cow . . ."

"So what do we think she cared about more? Stopping the development, or keeping the money coming in?"

We were both silent for a moment. It had been hard to form a clear picture of Leila. From what we'd heard from her sister, and seen in her apartment and her old Instagram account, money was an important part of her life. She'd been willing to turn to blackmail in order to maintain a certain income. But had her time with Raven and Earth Force changed her? Had she perhaps started to really care? Or, if we wanted to be even more cynical about her, had revenge trumped everything? Had she been willing to give up her cash cow if it meant publicly shaming Owen and scotching his company's multimillion-pound wind farm development? Would she have gone that far, simply to get revenge on him for firing her?

"He's joining the queue at the till, come on!" hissed Poppy suddenly, stuffing muslins and suncream back into her capacious diaper bag. "Quick!"

"What? Why?" I started panic-shoveling the last of the cake into my mouth before she'd even answered. I knew Poppy.

"We need to follow him!"

"Again, why?"

"Because that's what detectives do!"

I didn't argue, but resignedly crammed the final bite of cake into my overstuffed mouth and hauled dog and babe after Poppy, choking slightly on an errant crumb.

CHAPTER 39

HAVE YOU EVER tailed someone with two babies and a dog in the car? *It's not easy*.

For some reason, both Jack and Helen are allergic to the car being stationary. So every time we stopped at a red traffic light they set up an outcry.

"It's not like Owen can hear us from three cars away," reasoned Poppy, as I sweated nervously.

"Wanna bet," I replied darkly, as Helen and Jack broke into a renewed chorus.

Twenty-five painful minutes later, we entered Bishop's Ruin.

"I told you, he's just going home," I said, disgruntled. "We've literally followed a man driving from a garden center back to his house."

And sure enough, Owen pulled up outside some fancy-looking electric gates which opened soundlessly, and his Range Rover disappeared inside, swiftly hidden behind high walls. A prominent security camera scowled down at us from above the gate.

"That looks new," commented Poppy.

"Wouldn't you up your security after some loon threw a firebomb at your house?" I pointed out. "Well, this was a waste of time." I slapped the steering wheel in frustration. From the back seat and trunk Jack and Helen were howling discordantly and my top was still damp from my jaunt into the fountain, unless that was just sweat, seeing as it was about six thousand degrees in the car.

Poppy laid a soothing hand on my arm.

"There's a park literally right there," she said, pointing across the road. "Let's take five, let the boys have a play, let Helen have a run . . ."

IT WAS basic, as parks go. A large field of crispy grass with a huddle of play equipment in one corner which had seen better days. But glory be—there was a sandpit. Jack and Noah immediately began posting sand in their ears, mouths, and diapers, while Poppy and I pretended not to notice. I loosed Helen who, despite the heat, began tearing around like a Tasmanian devil.

"So we have a pretty credible motive for Owen to have murdered Leila," said Poppy, digging her toes into the sand.

But I wasn't so sure.

"If Owen had killed Leila, why would he have delivered the money to the bird box?" I pointed out, heaping sand into rudimentary ramparts. "He'd know there was no need."

Poppy huffed in frustration. "Maybe he wasn't intending to, so he dropped off the money before the protest, but then in a fit of rage he killed her?"

This still didn't sit right with me. The method of Leila's murder did feel like an act of desperation—why else would you strangle someone in a wood surrounded by potential witnesses, any of whom could have woken up? But if it had been Owen, he would have had to come to the protest deliberately, presumably with the intention of killing Leila. In which case—why drop the money first? None of it fitted.

I idly poked twigs into the top of my row of sandcastles.

"I do agree that it was probably an unplanned act," I said slowly. "But I think that points toward someone in Earth Force. Someone who was already there that night. And something that night sparked . . . well, whatever makes someone kill another person."

This was something I still couldn't quite get my head around—the moment at which one human was able to deliberately take the life of another. And then continue in their daily life without having a complete and utter breakdown. A shiver ran over my sweat-soaked skin.

At this point, Helen interrupted my philosophical musings, as was so often the case. She came careening through the sandpit, flattening my carefully constructed battlements, on her way to accost a woman who sat reading on a park bench.

I groaned and dragged myself to my feet.

"Keep an eye on Jack will you?" I called over my shoulder as I headed Helen-wards. The woman was trying to ignore Helen, which was difficult as Helen frenziedly licked her hands, knees, ankles and, occasionally and possibly accidentally, book.

"I'm so sorry," I called, breaking into a reluctant jog.

The woman looked up, startled, at the sound of my voice.

"Oh!" I stumbled slightly. "Norah!"

"Er, hi, Alice," she said, sounding slightly nervous. "What are you doing in Bishop's Ruin?"

"Oh, we heard there was a pretty good park here," I said. I saw Norah's eyes travel to the cracked slide, the solitary swing hanging by one chain, the patch of tarmac where a roundabout had presumably once stood.

"It has a sandpit," I added lamely.

There was a slightly awkward silence. There was so much I wanted to ask Norah, but she was giving off the vibe of a deer that would startle at any sudden movement—or indelicate question.

"What are you reading?" I asked. Norah glanced down at the book in her hands as if she wasn't quite sure what it was doing there.

"Just some romance," she said.

"Any good?"

"Not really."

Poppy arrived with both boys in tow.

"Norah!" she said, sounding delighted. "What a coincidence bumping into you here!"

"Well, I live just down the road," mumbled Norah. I knew categorically that this wasn't true; Sian had told me that Norah actually lived in Little Singer, several miles outside Bishop's Ruin.

Poppy glanced at me, her expression full of the questions we needed to ask. The tension felt, to me, unbearable. I've always wondered about this—is there literally something in the air that every party involved can feel? I don't know, a pheromone or something (I've never been quite sure what those are)? Or is it just me being oversensitive? Norah folded and unfolded the corner of her page nervously.

"Shall we get an ice cream?" I suggested, gesturing to the lonely ice cream van in the corner of the park.

Poppy and Norah both looked at me as though I was mad.

Five minutes later, however, as Norah delicately licked her Calippo, Poppy cracked the chocolate off her Magnum, and I licked all the pineapple ice cream from around my Twister, I was feeling pretty smug. There's nothing like ice cream to break the tension. You can't be stand-offish when you're racing against the clock, or more accurately the sun, to consume a Calippo before it melts into orange soup.

The boys had Mini Milks, which felt the least like bad parenting. They were basically frozen milk right? Definitely no added sugar or anything.

"Owen's house is quite something," I said conversationally, nodding to the fortress across the road, with its high walls and swiveling security cameras.

"Oh, is that Owen's house?" replied Norah in a slightly high-pitched voice.

Poppy laid a hand gently on Norah's (mine were far too sticky for such a gesture—plus I would be too awkward to pull this off).

"I think you know that it is," she said softly.

Norah's shoulders sank.

"It must make you angry," I said, trying to imitate Poppy's gentle tone. "Seeing Owen in his swank mansion, in *Time* magazine and everything, getting all the credit for your work."

Norah gave a half laugh, half sob. "Oh you know about that, do you?"

"I saw your name on the patent for the wind turbine," I said. "You and Richard, you were the ones who invented it."

"Many years ago, yes," said Norah, sniffing. "Richard and I were the engineers. We were all at school together. We stayed friends when we went off to uni and when we graduated, Richard and me in engineering, Owen in business and economics, we thought we'd team up. Give it a go, see what we came up with. It was just a bit of fun, really." She shook herself slightly. "He's right really, it's all in the past. No sense dragging it up now. But . . ." She gestured helplessly to the imposing building in front of us.

"So why now?" I asked, genuinely curious. This, I had not been able to work out.

Norah looked at her hands. "I got divorced last year and, well, it's not exactly been easy since then. Financially, I mean. I never really minded before, I was doing fine, I didn't need money. But now, when I'm at risk of losing my house, my family home, and he's living in that . . . It just didn't seem fair."

"How come you don't own the patent?" I asked.

Norah shrugged. "Richard was the one who said we should patent it. And he did most of the work so I was happy for him to own the patent—I was credited as the co-inventor. And when Owen and Richard set up Aether a few years later, I didn't really want to be involved. I had two small children, I had my hands full! I didn't want to be involved in setting up a business—not to mention the huge financial risk."

"You must have regretted that, once Aether started getting so successful," I said, perhaps not that tactfully. Surely it must have been galling, I thought, but Norah shook her head.

"I honestly didn't," she said. "Yes they were doing well for themselves, but it all worked out—at first, anyway. As long as the patent was in Richard's name, as long as he was involved in running Aether, I was credited, and I received regular payouts as they began rolling out my wind turbine."

"They paid you?" I asked, surprised.

"Richard did," said Norah.

"But then Richard left . . ."

"And Owen cut me out, simple as that," said Norah, bitterly. "As the inventor, I don't technically hold any rights other than those that the patent-holder chooses to bestow upon me. And Owen doesn't bestow his favors lightly."

"Didn't Richard say anything?" asked Poppy.

"What could he do? He's not a stakeholder in the company anymore, and he doesn't own the patent anymore. He sold the whole lot to Owen."

"But . . ."

"Richard is fiercely loyal to Owen," said Norah abruptly. "Owen was always the charismatic one, the ringleader. Richard worshipped the ground

Owen walked on—still does by all accounts. I think he felt bad for me, but I'm sure he found a way to justify it to himself. Or Owen did, anyway."

I breathed out. It was a brutal tale, but it didn't appear to link to the deaths of either Leila or Sam. Now if it had been Owen or Richard who had been murdered—Another penny dropped into place.

"You threw the firebomb," I blurted out.

Norah flushed bright red.

"It wasn't a firebomb," she said defensively. "It was just a jumping jack—a firework. Basically harmless. I just wanted to give him a shock. The newspapers blew it entirely out of proportion."

Poppy was staring at mild-mannered Norah in shock. On the surface she didn't seem the type to chuck a firework through someone's window, but I thought there had always been a quiet desperation to her that hinted at darker extremes.

"She was there that night, you know," Norah said abruptly.

"What? Who?" I asked, confused.

"Leila."

Poppy and I exchanged glances.

"At Owen's house?" clarified Poppy. "The night you threw the firework at it?"

Norah nodded. "I could see them in the kitchen together. She was betraying us all. Pretending to be one of us, pretending to care about the meadow. But the whole time she was involved with *him*. Sleeping with the enemy."

Norah practically spat the words in disgust. I thought it best not to mention that for quite a long time we'd suspected that it was actually *her* who was having the affair with Owen.

"I'm not sure that was quite what it seemed," said Poppy cautiously, but Norah wasn't listening. Having decided to vent, she was going for it.

"And again on the Wednesday—right before the protest! I saw her go into Owen's house, probably telling him all our plans, the double-crossing little . . . And Raven, poor Raven," she continued. "He was besotted, couldn't see her for what she was. He was heartbroken when I told him, but it was the right thing to do," she added piously.

I looked up sharply. "When you told him what?"

"Told him about Leila and Owen's affair, of course," said Norah. "He had a right to know!"

"And this would have been when?" asked Poppy.

"When I got to the protest! I told him as soon as I got there."

The night Leila was murdered.

CHAPTER 40

"IT'S GOT TO be Raven," said Poppy in the car on the way home. "He'd just been told that his girlfriend was not only cheating on him, but with the man who was running the very development they were protesting against. Imagine the betrayal he must have felt! And Raven is pretty hotheaded."

"It's a strong motive," I agreed cautiously. "But where does Sam fit in?"

"Maybe he found out? And confronted Raven?"

I pulled a face. I couldn't imagine Sam siding with Leila, whom he had clearly disliked, against Raven. Or, for that matter, Raven killing his own brother to silence him. It just didn't work.

I shook my head.

"It's not right," I muttered.

"It's a classic motive," argued Poppy—and she was right of course. But throughout this case it was the motive that had snagged for me. It felt like a crime of fury, but also of desperation. And I struggled to make this fit with any of the motives we'd discussed so far.

"We're missing something," I mumbled. "Or, no, we're not looking at what we know the right way round."

Poppy sighed in frustration. "Well, this is our best lead so far. We need to speak to Raven again."

"Mhmm." My mind was wandering. Maybe it was the heat. Or the sleep deprivation. Or the fact that my mind has always been prone to the occasional detour.

Maya was arriving that night. But she was, with many apologies and disclaimers, spending the night at the commune with Rowan. It was an auspicious moon or something. I didn't ask any further questions in case it was a sex thing. I looked at our last few messages.

I'll see you tomorrow though yeah?

Yeah, sure

Don't know if the moon will still be auspicious but Joe wants to take Jack to the children's farm

Sounds . . . fun?

Have your fun tonight

Tomorrow it's chickens

I suspected this exchange had something to do with my strangely disconsolate mood. Either that or it was the auspicious moon.

"Alice?" Poppy's voice broke back through.

"Huh? What?"

"I said, do you think he could have slipped out of the chains without anyone noticing? On the night Leila was murdered?"

"Oh. Oh, no. Probably not. Why?"

Poppy banged her head on the steering wheel.

BACK AT home, I slumped on the sofa and stared blankly at Jack, who stared equally blankly back—and no one can rival a baby for a blank stare.

I broke first, and glanced at the time. Maya's train got in half an hour ago. I wondered what she and Rowan were doing—actually no, that wasn't a line of thought I wanted to follow. The case. What about the case. Everything felt subtly wrong about this case. We were looking at it back to front somehow but I couldn't quite work out which way to flip things round.

Jack crawled into my lap with the TV remote and looked pleadingly at me. He'd learned this look from Helen—it was disconcerting.

I caved, and turned on the TV—but I drew the line at *Baywatch*. I stuck on *In the Night Garden*, a feast of horrors that entranced Jack almost as much as Pamela and the Hoff. Of course, I'm aware that all kids' programs appear to have been conceived of, written, and produced by people who are, quite frankly, tripping balls. Historically, we had *CatDog*—anyone remember that? The poor tormented double-ended freak with a cat head one end and a dog head the other. In one episode Cat tried to stealth-brush Dog's teeth while he's asleep (the kind of thing you genuinely fear your parents might do when you're a child) by *climbing inside his own mouth and sneaking up his own body to the dog end.* I think he turned himself inside out in the process. It was horrendous.

In the Night Garden was following in this time-honored tradition. It was a nightmare world of weird monsters with even weirder names that, in my highly strung state, seemed a hideous parody of the equally terrifying real world.

The Pontipine Russian dolls bobbled around their immaculate, tiny doll's house. *Leila's apartment, the swank juicer, the range of expensive cosmetics.*

The Tombliboos snuggled into their gloomy tree-trunk cave. *Sam's darkroom, the dim red light, the chemical tang to the air.*

Makka Pakka aggressively sponged the face of every hapless character he came across. *Raven, his eyes burning with fervor, as he thrust a placard skyward.*

The Ninky Nonk trundled along the forest floor, twigs snapping and moss flattening underfoot. *Owen, relentlessly building his business empire for the betterment of "this beautiful planet of ours."*

The Pinky Ponk glided through the sky, its propellers whirling. *Norah, throwing a firework through a window.*

Upsy Daisy danced in a circle, faster and faster, her skirt swirling around her. *Maryam, in her sensible linen overall and sturdy Doc Martens, sinking to the ground at the memorial service.*

The Tittifers squawked and shrieked in their tree. *Marcus, shouting at Sam across the empty warehouse, loving him and hating him.*

The carousel folding up as night falls in the garden, the trees fading to darkness. *The tinny crackle of a radio through shadowy trees.*

Iggle Piggle lay down in his boat and set sail across a dark sea under an even darker sky. *Leila, dead. Sam, dead.*

I hugged Jack closer to me, my anchor, and drifted into an uneasy sleep.

CHAPTER 41

THE HEAT THE next day had reached almost unbearable levels. It felt as though the air was closing in around me, pressing on my eyeballs, constricting my skull. With only a minor twinge of guilt, Joe and I unanimously agreed that it was far too hot to traipse around petting goats and feeding chickens. The children's farm would have to wait until tomorrow. Instead, we had spent the morning fending off the encroaching heat as it overwhelmed our tiny cottage.

"Gonna be a thunderstorm soon," said Joe as we went round the house flinging open all the windows and doors in a vain attempt to get the slightest breath of air through the stifling rooms. Jack made a petulant noise from his seat in front of our only working fan, where he and Helen were jostling for position. Even Jack's normally unassailable cheerfulness had deserted him and he was only placated by a steady stream of spoons from the freezer to entertain him.

"Forget the weather, everything's going to blow up," I mumbled, half to myself.

"What?" asked Joe, who rarely heard me first time round.

I shrugged and flapped a curtain hopelessly, trying to create a breeze in the dead air. I had nothing concrete except a feeling that it might be the kind of day to take cover, and these days I didn't trust my feelings so much, in any sense. It was probably just the weather, I told myself.

The four of us lay down in a semicircle around the fan. I wondered if Jack and Helen would let us stay here all day.

"How many ice lollies have we got in the freezer?" asked Joe.

Ah. I had severely depleted our stash over the last few days.

"Can you order ice lollies on Deliveroo?" I picked up my phone to check, and it immediately pinged with an incoming text. And again and again and again.

Ailsa: How did it go at Nightingales yesterday?

Poppy: Owen's been paying off some guy called Gordon to sign off sites for development before they get SSSI status

Ailsa: I knew it!

Did you? You could've said something

Ailsa: Someone got out of bed on the wrong side today

Poppy: Also Norah DID design the wind turbine and she's pretty pissed off with Owen and she's the one who firebombed his house

Ailsa: Holy shit. You've got to watch the quiet ones

Poppy: Sounds like he might have deserved it tbh

Hen: Can you talk about this on a different group? I don't think this is a conversation I should be involved in

Seconds later, Ailsa popped up in the Aether Sucks group chat.

Ailsa: Any other firebombs from yesterday?

Poppy: Oh shit. Yes! @Alice, didn't Owen say to Gordon that the developers are moving in on the meadow today?

I groaned. This sounded like something that would require action.

Er, yeah, I think so?

Ailsa: Wtf?? And you're mentioning this NOW?

It's been very hot . . .

Poppy: What should we do?

Ailsa: @Alice, you need to go tell Maryam

What? Why me?!

Ailsa: I can't put the twins in the car in this heat

@Poppy??

Poppy: Noah's got a rash

So have I?

Ailsa: Get over it

Can't you just message the Earth Force group chat @Ailsa?

Ailsa: I will, but Maryam doesn't check the group chat, nor does Raven

Ailsa: You'll have to go over there and tell them

What if I say no . . . ?

Ailsa: Get a move on

I rolled over and lay face down for a moment, but the carpet was a horrific miasma of Helen hair and toddler crumbs and it was not something you wanted in close contact with your face.

"What's wrong?" asked Joe from under a wet muslin.

"I have to go to Fox Hollow."

"Why?"

"The developers are moving in on the meadow today. Ailsa says I have to let Maryam know."

"So it's too hot to go to the children's farm, but not too hot to drive to a different farm to run around delivering messages for Ailsa?"

"I'll get more ice lollies on the way home?"

"Fine. Don't be long."

I heaved myself to my feet and looked down at my prostrate family, who didn't look like they intended to ever move again. Bastards.

"Alice," called Joe as I reluctantly picked up my car keys. "Don't get caught up in anything yeah? Just come straight home?"

"Absolutely," I confirmed.

"Via ice lollies," amended Joe.

THE CAR was unbearably hot.

Even with all the windows down and the air con on full blast (very bad for the environment, I know), I was sticking to the car seat within minutes. I stewed, figuratively and literally, all the way to Fox Hollow Farm. Wretched Poppy and Ailsa dropping me in it like this. Couldn't they feel it? The way everything was accelerating? The tension rising faster than the air pressure was dropping? I couldn't have said why or how but things were moving. Which made me want to stay at home with a damp towel over my head and a ten-pack of rocket ice pops for the next twenty-four hours thank you very much.

When I got to Fox Hollow, however, things were very much not moving. The courtyard was baked and silent, the abandoned farm machinery pinging and clinking in the heat. The ancient thatch looked dry enough to self-combust.

"Hello?" I called pointlessly. It was patently obvious there was no one around. I half expected a tumbleweed to roll past.

I pushed open the farmhouse door and stepped into the shaded cool of the large kitchen.

"Maryam?"

There was only the creak and groan of the ancient house in response. I was absolutely parched, and the drip of the tap seemed to fill the room. I stepped over to the chipped ceramic sink, took a glass from the sideboard and filled it with slightly rust-scented water, which I drank feeling as if I were doing something illicit.

Although seeing as I was here, alone, perhaps I *should* have just a little poke around . . . It couldn't hurt.

I followed the narrow hallway down to the stable block where Raven lived, and tapped lightly on the joining door. There was no response—but more than that I could feel that the room beyond was empty, in the way that you just can. So I went in.

I almost gave up and left again immediately. If anything, the chaos was worse than the last time I'd seen it. I supposed what with the deaths in the family of late, tidying up had been pretty low on Raven's agenda. Where to begin? I sifted through the contents of his bedside table: a couple of crusty mugs, a chipped glass, an ashtray and the stub of a joint, some herbal lozenges that smelled more potent than the joint, and some tissues that I definitely wasn't going to touch. Nothing suspicious there. I kicked idly through the jumble on the floor—old clothes, a photography magazine—and headed for the table beneath the window, which was piled high with books and sketch pads and jars of pencils and feathers and twigs.

My foot kicked something beneath the table that clanged. I knelt down and pulled out a battered old olive oil can that appeared to serve as a waste-paper basket—although it was quite hard to tell in this room, it could simply be part of Raven's collection. I took one of the longer sticks off the table and used it to stir through the contents. A vaguely familiar bottle surfaced in the general detritus: Green & Free. Leila's moisturizer—or at least the one she used in her eco warrior role. I remembered Poppy's cynical comment, "She probably filled the bottle with one of her swank lotions." I gave the bottle a sniff. It actually smelled quite pleasant, lightly fragrant—nothing like the acrid scent I remembered from the same bottle in her apartment. Had Poppy been onto something?

I stood up slowly, the bottle still in my hand. When we see a bottle, we instinctively read the label. It says shampoo, it must be shampoo. It says beans, it must be beans. It says poison, it must be poison. When we see a person, we read the labels they present to us: activist, rich kid, "mum."

Thoughts were swirling, forming. I daren't prod at them lest they break apart into meaningless dots, like the marbling we used to do at primary school. Oil on water.

In a bit of a daze, I walked over to the door on the far side of the room and opened it. I stared into the dim red gloom of Sam's darkroom, now stripped of most of its equipment, the walls bare of photos. The chemical tang had faded with disuse but a certain taste lingered in the air. What I needed wasn't there—although I wouldn't have known what to do with it if it had been. Harris would have it. But she might not know what she had.

My brain was speeding up, fighting against the lethargy of the stifling day. It felt like pushing through thick banks of storm clouds, with the occasional flash of lightning, a streak of gold in my mind. A streak of gold in a memory . . . I left the darkroom pretty certain that I knew who had killed Sam and how. Which threw up some very interesting ideas about who might have killed Leila and why. But I needed evidence. I needed *proof*.

I wandered back into the cool cave of the kitchen and stared around hopelessly. The main farmhouse was a scaled-up version of Raven's room; full of nooks and crannies and corners and hiding places. You could hide something—a murder weapon, say—in full sight here and no one would think anything of it. The place was deserted today, but I'd seen it bustling with people, coming and going, picking things up, putting them down.

I wandered over to the fireplace—people burned evidence, right? That was a thing. But the fireplace was empty and well swept.

I should go.

I scribbled a note and left it on the kitchen table for Maryam or Raven to find, then turned and walked back out into the blazing white heat of the day. My eyes stung in the sunlight. I blinked around the courtyard, one hand already on the car door handle. A soot-stained old chiminea caught my eye. I'd just take one last look, then that was it. I would go home.

Unlike the fireplace, the chiminea had not been swept out. There was a tangle of charred wood in its belly, some scrunched-up newspaper, and assorted twisted and burned debris. I swept it all out onto the ground. A cloud of ash and cinders blossomed in my face, half choking me. I could taste bitterness in my mouth. I pawed through the scraps. They were mostly unidentifiable. But, was this . . . ? Inspector Harris's admonitions ringing in my ears, I took a dog poo bag out of my pocket (clean, I hasten to add) and used it to pick up a small, twisted item. It could be nothing. It could be everything.

CHAPTER 42

AS SOON AS I re-entered civilization and its hallmarks like phone signal, my phone began pinging madly. I glanced down as the latest message flashed up on the screen.

> **Ailsa:** Alice WHERE ARE YOU?

This seemed a bit rich, seeing as she was the one who had sent me haring off to Fox Hollow. I pulled over by a five-bar gate and killed the engine. There was a slew of messages from Ailsa and Poppy. Plus a couple from Joe. And—shit—several messages and missed calls from Maya.

> Al, you still want to do something today?

> I'm free when you are

> Shall I come to you?

> Alllllll? Can I come over now?

> They keep giving me biscuits made out of leaves and shit

> Al seriously, I'm communed out, I need to come round and eat Pringles

I'm gonna put some voodoo curse on you, bitch

The messages from Ailsa and Poppy were equally urgent.

Ailsa: Where are you? Everyone's gathering at the meadow at 3 to stop the construction vehicles

Poppy: Sorry we sent you off to Fox Hollow! Turns out they already knew about the developers—Enderby got a tip-off from someone at Aether . . .

Ailsa: 4 p.m. Meadow.

Ailsa: No dogs, no babies.

I looked at the time: 2:30. Shit. I fired off a message to Maya telling her to meet me at Hawkbit Meadow, and another to Joe, apologizing while being somewhat vague about what I was apologizing for, then turned the car around and headed back through the maze of twisty lanes that surround Penton and Bishop's Ruin.

As I raced (at a sensible 25 mph) through the countryside, clouds were piling up in the sky, great massing banks of them, heavy with the threat of thunder. The sunlight had turned from a hard white to a sickly yellow.

I knew what had happened. At least, I thought I did. I was pretty certain. Say, 80 percent. Certain enough to call Harris. Who didn't even waste time telling me I was an idiot for once, but promised to ring the lab that very minute and meet me at the meadow.

The first dry heave of thunder rolled across the valley.

THE SKY was almost black as I pulled in at Hawkbit Meadow. The cluster of construction vehicles shone neon bright in the gloom as if spotlit. They hadn't got very far, in large part due to the human barricade of protestors, strung out across the entrance to the meadow. From a distance, they looked like a chain of paper dolls that would blow away in the rising wind.

I half fell out of my car into the small huddle waiting for me at the car park gate. Ailsa and Poppy were there, as was, surprisingly, Hen. Maya had obviously got my message and was there with Rowan. All five looked on edge, any tensions over who was sleeping with whom set aside while the real storm took center stage.

"Alice, what's going on?" asked Ailsa. "Jane called and said she's on her way. She said to tell you the lab confirmed your theory. What's your theory?"

"I know who killed Leila and Sam," I said.

I told them.

There was silence.

Then.

"That's impossible," said Ailsa bluntly.

But of course, it wasn't.

"SO... what happens now?" asked Maya, always the first to break the silence. "Are we in like a Poirot situation, where you get them all together in the library and unveil the killer?"

"Bit short on libraries here," I said. With an impeccable sense of narrative build-up a barrage of thunder rolled around the valley, like a cascade of rocks hurtling toward us. The line of protestors seemed to waver under its force.

"Someone's calling us over," said Poppy. It was Sian, gesturing to us to come join the ragged line of protestors. They looked like they needed the reinforcements.

"We can't just join them like nothing's happened," hissed Hen. "Also I'm not one of them. I'm not one of *you*! That's my boss over there!"

I looked over and, sure enough, there stood Owen Myers himself, flanked by the ever-faithful Anonymous Richard and a man in a hi-vis and white helmet, holding a clipboard—presumably the foreman of the construction company—the three of them facing the strung-out Earth Force.

Owen looked furious at the stand-off. Richard looked as placid and inscrutable as ever.

"I can't go over there, I'll be fired," said Hen. "We should wait here, wait for Harris."

"I don't know. It's a bit awkward, hanging about by the gate," I said.

"Seriously?" said Maya. "You're about to accuse someone of murder, and you're worried about being socially awkward?"

"Thanks, now I feel sick as well."

"What are you doing?" shouted Sian over the rising storm. "Get over here!"

As if following her orders, we all stepped forward.

"Is this gonna be like last time?" asked Rowan, sounding a touch nervous. This was unsurprising as his own dad had been in the firing line last time.

"I hope not," I said fervently.

The chain broke as we approached, opening a gap between Sian and Enderby for us to join. But we didn't. We stopped, just meters in front of the line.

And then came the rain, in a crashing wall of water. An assault on the land from the sky. The protestors flinched under the onslaught, but the line didn't break. The foreman swore and ran for the vehicles, holding his clipboard over his head as if that would protect him. Owen and Richard remained, Owen now frowning at the sky as if that, too, was doing this just to annoy him.

Blinking rainwater out of my eyes, I locked gaze with Maryam.

"You got new laces," I said, nodding to Maryam's boots, with their shiny gold laces. Understanding flickered across her face like lightning. I saw her hand jerk in Raven's, as if she was thinking of breaking free, but she didn't. Instead she just stared at me, unblinking, rainwater coursing down her face like tears.

I hadn't anticipated doing this with quite such an audience. To be honest, I hadn't really anticipated doing it at all. But Harris still wasn't here and it felt like the stage was set, the curtain ready to be lifted. The protestors in front of us—Maryam, Raven, Sian, Enderby, Norah—were glancing back and forth—mostly looking confused, sensing that something was going on, but unsure what.

"It was the radio, wasn't it?" I asked, trying to speak quietly, but of course everyone was straining to hear over the pounding rain. Several people looked at me perplexed, probably wondering what I was talking about, but Maryam's eyes remained fixed on mine—afraid, hunted, defiant. She nodded curtly.

"Someone brought a radio with them to the protest," I continued, raising my voice slightly. "Who was it by the way?"

One of Sian's posse timidly raised a hand, looking slightly nervous. "Did I . . . do something wrong?"

"No," I said heavily. "No. It was just . . . a horrible, horrible misunderstanding."

I took a deep breath. "There was a news broadcast—oh, I don't know, some time just before midnight? A young man's body had been found in the Thames near Wapping. Where Sam lived. Sam, who was supposed to be at the protest, but hadn't turned up. Who wasn't answering his phone. You thought it was him, didn't you?" I addressed this last to Maryam. She nodded wordlessly once more.

"You thought Leila had killed him."

A pause, and then the smallest of nods, barely a twitch.

"But why?" asked Enderby, looking confused.

"You told us why," I answered him. "You were there that day at Fox Hollow when Leila came storming in, looking for Sam, ranting that she was going to kill him for what he'd done. And Maryam was with you, too, wasn't she? You might have dismissed Leila's ravings as a passing temper tantrum, but in many ways Maryam saw Leila far more clearly than the rest of us. She saw in Leila an unstable young woman with a very, very dangerous streak. She saw what Leila was capable of, and from that moment on, she was afraid of what Leila might do to Sam—to either of her boys. She watched as Raven and Leila grew closer, and as Sam and Leila grew more and more . . . antagonistic."

It felt as though the wind was pulling the words from my mouth and throwing them away. I didn't see how anyone could hear what I was saying, but every face seemed turned toward me. I continued to speak directly to Maryam, trying to understand her as I laid it all out.

"So when you heard the radio broadcast . . . I expect you remembered Leila arriving late to the protest, refusing to say where she'd been. Combined with what you'd just heard on the radio, thinking Sam was dead, you put two and two together and got five. Maybe you wanted to punish

Leila, I don't know, but I suspect you were also afraid of what Leila might do to Raven. Maybe Norah or Raven had even told you about Leila's supposed affair with Owen Myers. So you did what, I suppose, you thought was necessary . . . You had to stop her. You had to protect your boys."

"But we were all chained to trees," broke in Enderby again. "Norah had the keys."

Norah nodded dumbly, her eyes wide.

"Yes, we were tied up—with chains that Maryam had sourced. That was no big deal. Almost all those chains come with a spare key. I imagine Maryam kept one on her, in case of emergencies. So that didn't present much of a problem. And then . . ." I swallowed. "And then you strangled Leila with your bootlace, didn't you?"

Everyone looked at Maryam's feet. At the battered old familiar Doc Martens, with their shiny new laces.

I took a gamble—I wasn't so certain on this point—and pulled my "evidence bag" from my pocket. "And you burned the old ones in the chiminea at Fox Hollow. But most laces have a high plastic content. They don't burn that well."

"Is that . . . a dog poo?" asked Sian uncertainly.

It wasn't quite the dramatic gesture I'd been going for, but I had to admit that I was just brandishing a non-transparent dog poo bag. Not that the half-consumed lace inside it was much more impressive.

"No, it's the bootlace." I sighed.

"But any of us could have seen her," protested Enderby. "What a stupid move, no offense meant."

I think, in the circumstances, he probably didn't need the apology. Although it is true that offending a murderer is probably not the wisest of moves.

I shrugged. "I don't think you cared, did you?" I asked Maryam. There was no response. "I think you were, what's the expression, blinded with grief and rage." Still nothing.

"Did you?" asked Enderby, addressing Maryam for the first time. "Did you kill her?"

A blink. A slow nod.

"But . . . you didn't kill Sam," piped up Norah, horrified, her voice barely more than a whisper carried on the wind. "You wouldn't!"

"Oh no," I said. "No. Maryam was right about that. It was Leila who killed Sam."

There was silence as this sank in, broken only by the pounding of the rain and the occasional crash of thunder.

"From . . . beyond the grave?" asked Sian, sounding skeptical.

"Not exactly."

To my relief, I saw blue lights flashing through the rain. Harris was here. My role was essentially over. I just had one last thing to explain.

"Did any of you know that Leila had a degree in chemistry?" I asked. "Probably not—she wasn't one for oversharing about her previous life—or lives, I should probably say. But Leila was a highly skilled chemist. And photography, of course, is part artistry, part chemistry. Sam had a darkroom full of some pretty potent chemicals. Not particularly dangerous, unless you drink them—and Sam wasn't stupid enough to do that. But Leila knew that a few simple changes could turn Sam's basic chemistry set into a chemical weapon. I think, I'm pretty sure, she switched out one of the chemicals he used to develop his photos so it reacted with the other chemicals to create something pretty toxic."

"Hydrogen cyanide," came Harris's voice from behind me. "A highly toxic gas. Ingenious really."

She gave me a cursory nod as she came to stand beside me, facing the crumbling ranks of Earth Force. "I ran the checks on Sam's equipment that you, ah, suggested when you called earlier. The lab did them immediately. It looks as though Leila had switched the developer solution for hydrochloric acid. Her prints are all over the bottle. It turns out Sam was something of a traditionalist, practicing a development process called the collodian process, which uses potassium ferricyanide as a fixer. Old-fashioned, but not particularly unusual. When Sam poured the fixer into the film tank and it mixed with the doctored developer solution, the resultant hydrogen cyanide gas would have overwhelmed Sam within minutes. We'll have confirmation as soon as I can get the pathologist to run the necessary checks on Sam's body."

"I think she took the hydrochloric acid over to Fox Hollow in a moisturizer bottle, not long before she died," I supplied. "We saw the bottle at her apartment and I noticed it smelled . . . strange. Chemical. I expect she intended to get rid of it. Only, of course, Maryam got rid of her first . . ."

For the first time, I allowed myself to look at Maryam. She had sunk to the rain-sodden ground. She wasn't weeping, or shouting. She'd said nothing when I'd declared that Leila had been behind Sam's death after all, although it must, surely, have felt like something of a vindication. But she simply huddled there, defeated, as if hoping to dissolve into the ground itself.

Raven stood next to her, staring down at her as if he had no idea who she was. Or possibly who he was. There was no expression on his face. Nothing in his eyes.

I handed Harris the dog poo bag. She gave me a questioning look.

"Bootlace," I said shortly. "I reckon it might match those fibers you found on . . . on Leila's neck."

Harris gave a curt nod and pocketed it, then jerked her head and a couple of officers stepped forward and handcuffed Maryam. They lifted her to her feet with surprising gentleness and tried to walk her forward, but it was as if she had no life left in her body. Her feet simply slid on the wet grass and her body slumped forward again. Eventually, after several false starts, the officers managed to get their shoulders beneath hers so she slumped on them like a legless drunk.

They took her. Half carried, half dragged away through the mud. Throughout it all, she hadn't spoken a word.

I TURNED away from the blank, staring faces in front of me. I couldn't bear to look at them. My eyes found Maya's and suddenly she was there beside me, arm through mine, shoulder pressed against mine.

"I'm sorry I said I'd put a voodoo on you," she said in a small voice. "It sounds like you've been pretty busy today."

I nodded. I wasn't sure I had any words left. There was no thrill of a successful deduction. There was no adrenaline, no rush. There was just tiredness and resignation and still the storm, raging all around us, violent and uncaring.

The Earth Force line had collapsed into sodden huddles, frantically discussing what had just happened. Except for the group just in front of us. The group I couldn't bring myself to look at.

Once again, it was bittersweet. In uncovering who had killed Leila and Sam, we had pulled the last stable ground from beneath Raven's feet. He had lost his parents, he had lost his girlfriend, he had lost his brother, and now he would lose his last protector. All to needless violence. People who kill don't just destroy the lives they take, they destroy the lives of so many around them. Once again, I wondered what ever made it seem like the solution—to anything.

I forced myself to look at Raven. Surprisingly, it was Enderby who was comforting him. He didn't seem to be saying anything, but just sat, arm around Raven's shoulders, just being there. I hoped he would continue to be there for as long as Raven needed.

As for what I needed: I needed Jack. And I needed Joe. God help me, I even needed Helen.

I needed to go home—to my family.

EPILOGUE

"PASS THE CRISPS will you?"

I lobbed the bag toward Poppy—missing by a stretch and hitting Ailsa instead.

I was back at Hawkbit Meadow with Poppy, Ailsa, Hen, and associated dogs and babies. Two weeks had passed since the dramatic thunderstorm showdown. The summer heat had broken, leaving a pleasant freshness in the air.

It was the first time we'd been back to the meadow. We'd filled the intervening two weeks with soft play, coffee dates, even mum and baby yoga—the things you're supposed to do with mat leave. Of course, the recent murders and their consequences had never been far from our minds. And we'd made a point of visiting Raven a couple of times. He was still living at Fox Hollow while preparations were made for Maryam's trial. Enderby had moved in with him for the time being, and the two of them were keeping themselves occupied with ensuring that the development plans for Hawkbit Meadow, currently indefinitely delayed, remained that way.

Owen was being investigated by the Crown Prosecution Service, Harris having happily handed over this rather more boring investigation. What this would mean for Hen's job, we weren't yet sure.

And me? I had watched a lot of *Baywatch* with Jack. I had walked the dog. I had continued to obsess over Jack's incoming teeth. I had pretended everything was normal. We have to continue as if the world is normal, because most of the time it is. Because if we realized that normal people can do horrific things, that anyone can break the boundaries, that a single act can tip you from regular person to killer . . . that the skin of normality, of order, that stretches over everything is terrifyingly thin . . . well, I suspect we would all go mad.

And a new normality loomed. Poppy and I were both returning to work the following week—yet another great shift lurking on my horizon. It hadn't been quite the end to maternity leave that I'd expected. But then, it hadn't been quite the start to maternity leave that I'd expected. Perhaps, in Penton, I just had to learn to expect the unexpected—and roll with it. I felt I was doing a pretty good job of this. In fact . . .

I looked around—there was no one else about. Did I even care if there was? I sat up and pulled my T-shirt over my head, then unclipped my bra and tossed it aside, where it landed on Helen, who gave it a cursory chew. I stretched out in the sun, feeling it warm on my skin.

Ailsa gave an approving nod. Even Hen looked faintly amused.

"Do you want me to write something on your boobs?" offered Poppy.

I closed my eyes against the sun.

"How about 'The End'?"

(Obviously it wasn't.)

ACKNOWLEDGMENTS

Dearest reader, if you have read this *second* book in the series, I thank you from the bottom of my heart for sticking with me and my funny old cast of characters (I know you're only here for Helen, and that's fine by me). I do hope we'll see you back for the third installment!

I love the Acknowledgments because it's such a lovely moment to thank everyone who made this book, and there are so many! First of all, my wonderful agent, Jemima Forrester, who really got this whole thing kick-started—there would be no book one, let alone book two, without you! To my UK publishing team at Zaffre, thank you for everything you have done to create these beautiful books! In particular Kelly Smith and Izzy Smith, for their work shaping the book and getting the word out there. I also want to thank Sandra Ferguson for copyediting and Jenny Page for proofreading—their eagle eyes saved me from many a gaffe. And, of course, huge thanks to Kitty Kelly for providing the absolute perfect voice for Alice on the audiobook, which has been getting so much love.

And to the US publication team at Minotaur Books—Catherine Richards, Kelly Stone, Kayla Janas, Allison Ziegler—I honestly don't have the words to thank you. You've all been so wonderfully enthusiastic about these books, and worked so very hard on them! You are all absolute legends. Likewise to Drew Kilman and Emma West for their amazing work on the audio. And to Ken Diamond and Jennifer Rohrbach for Americanizing my very English book with such sensitivity—I love discovering which words and phrases cross the ocean and which cause absolute bafflement. Turns out they don't cut chalk horses into hills in the US. When asked why we do that over here, I really had no answer.

An especially heartfelt thanks to Jemima, Kelly, and Catherine for their support and understanding, as I wrote this book during a rather difficult time for me and my family and when it was particularly hard to be writing about pregnancy, birth, and parenthood. Your patience, empathy, and care were so deeply appreciated and allowed me to pause and breathe and come back to these books when I was ready. Publishing a book relies on so many people, with all our human dramas and messy, complicated lives, and I'm lucky to work with some of the very best humans there are.

On which note—this book is dedicated to my family—my first family as it were (it would be handy to have a way of distinguishing between the family you grow up with, the family you build, and the family you choose). Mum, Dad, Colin, absolute marvels the lot of you. My brother and I were lucky to grow up in a house full of books and stories. Dad, thank you in particular for your patient and endlessly inventive responses to my demands to "tell me a story." My son now makes this request of me approx. a thousand times a day and I only now understand how exhausting it can be (I also love it, obvs, but I do only have so many PAW Patrol dinosaur stories in me).

To Liz, Fran, and Indira, my chosen family, the godparents of my children, and just my very best people, as well as my earliest readers who have stopped me from making many a blunder. Liz, always my first reader, and there to point out that no one eats a bacon sandwich with a fork, that my *Love Island* dates were off, and how very dated my reference to *MTV Cribs* was (but what a show that was!). Fran, I put the papier-mâché squid in for you. Indira, I do sometimes steal your turns of phrase for Maya—I can't help it, you say such excellent things.

To all my friends, who have been absolute lifesavers this last difficult year, you are wonderful people one and all. The support you showed for my first book was so incredible and I just feel so lucky to have you all. For putting bums on seats at book events, turning up at signings so I don't feel like a lemon, buying my books, saying lovely things, and generally making me feel like less of a fraud. To the Stroud collective, the Reading originals, and the Lakes crew—you all have jobs and partners and pets and babies and important and interesting skills and hobbies and really have far more interesting things to be doing than listening to me wittering on about my books and yet here you are, every time. I love you all. To my friends with twins, Fran B., Fran J., and Steph, I salute you (and thank you for providing twin material).

Many thanks to my in-law family: my sister-in-law, who is single-handedly supplying the Romanian market for *The Expectant Detectives* (and yes you *would* be the perfect Ailsa in the movie); and my parents-in-law, who are endlessly supportive and enthusiastic and beyond generous with their time, especially when it comes to babysitting.

I have to thank my dog . . . I know it's weird and I promise I'm not one of those people who signs Christmas cards from the dog, but I do have to acknowledge here that she is the absolute light of my life (as well as the bane of my existence) and I love her terribly and am thankful to her for getting me out of the house when I'm in a writing hole.

Almost finally, a particular thanks to my secondary-school chemistry teacher, Dr. Perry, for providing science knowledge where I had none. She went above and beyond researching the chemicals involved in photo developing and I should note here that she did urge me to do further reading on the subject, not all of which I got through, and so it goes without saying that any incorrect science is 100 percent my own.

And finally, finally, to my glorious little family, Jamie, Caleb, and our latest arrival, Cleo. You guys are perfection. Everything becomes an adventure with the three of you; you're all weird af, the most hilarious people I know, and also the most loving, kindest, and brilliant. I know I work with words, it's meant to be my job, but really there *are* no words. I love you all.

ABOUT THE AUTHOR

Indira Birnie

KAT AILES (she/her) works in publishing as an editor and freelanced for several years to take a couple of belated gap years, including hiking the Pacific Crest Trail from Mexico to Canada. She now lives in the Cotswolds with her husband, their son and daughter, and her beautiful but foolish dog. *The Expectant Detectives* was her debut novel, the first draft of which was written largely in three weeks after she submitted the first few chapters to the Comedy Women in Print Prize and was unexpectedly shortlisted.